The Fractured Few

Brimstone Chorus

Elizabeth J. Brown

Kobold Books

Contents

Kobold Books Limited
71-75 Shelton Street, Covent Garden
London, WC2H 9JQ
koboldbooks.com

Paperback ISBN: 978-1-7398170-7-7
Hardcover ISBN: 978-1-7398170-8-4
E-book ISBN: 978-1-7398170-6-0

Cover design by Ben Baldwin: www.benbaldwin.co.uk
Editing by Kate Gallagher: nerdgirledits.com

To my friends, who never fail in their unwavering belief and support. Thank you for all the encouragement, kind words, hot drinks, cake, confectionery and, on occasion, cheese. Without you I wouldn't be half the person I am today (my jeans can attest to that).

Prologue

England, 1984

ARCHIBALD MORGAN SWALLOWED THE last bitter dregs of the Blue Lotus tea and took a breath. He could already feel the infusion working its way into his bloodstream; potent enough to overcome the natural defences of his magic, but not so much as to render him a drooling simpleton. The blend had taken years to master, and it had been worth every one.

He placed the mug on the desk. Thin curls of smoke spiralled up from the smouldering bundles of white sage and cedar in the soapstone dish next to it. Exhaling, he turned and shrugged out of his robe. He barely felt the chill; perpetual youth had its advantages. And he should know. It had been a long time since age had ravaged his body; magic kept him forever suspended in his late thirties. Standing naked, he picked up the dagger.

The effects of the tea would not last more than a few minutes. He needed to remain in a higher state of consciousness for as long as possible. Just one moment of distraction, just one slip could spell death. And he had not worked so hard, not given the best part of his life to fail now.

After all those years of searching, after everything he'd been through, he'd only found Kar'roc's Maw in a pawnbroker's shop.

Ludicrous.

Blood magic had hidden the dagger's location but he'd known that if he bided his time, the Boswells would one day make a mistake. And if the one thing walking this Earth for two-hundred-and-thirty-four years had taught him, it was how to wait.

He heard only the soft padding sound of his bare feet and his steady breathing as he walked over to the ritualistic circle, drawn in chalk on the floor of the basement. Stopping inches from the circle's perimeter, Archibald cast one final look at the complex arrangement of sigils and symbolic objects. Then he accessed the energy pulsating within him.

'Abernon, he who resides in the realm of flame and shadow, I call unto thee. Abernon, master of ruin and decay, hear my plea. Abernon, submit unto this mortal plane until my will be done.'

One by one, the sigils blazed with blue light. An invisible wall of energy rushed up to enclose the circle. The air shuddered with a pressure so intense, it prickled his naked flesh. He held his ground, unflinching; it would be a mistake to show weakness.

A writhing mass of dark tendrils like choking smog coalesced inside the barrier, slowly dissipating until a solitary form remained.

The demon regarded Archibald through several white, beady eyes. As its gaping maw stretched into a wide grin, rivulets of drool dribbled from rows of jagged teeth.

'You have finally dispensed with the Latin, I see.' Its low, rasping voice resonated in the space between them.

Archibald smirked, looking up to meet its gaze. 'Ratio in omnibus, Abernon.'

'Droll.' The demon blinked; thin, translucent membranes slid over its eyes and disappeared into its thick, bark-like flesh. It shifted position without touching the circle of energy enclosing it, and considered the glowing sigils at its feet—no doubt searching for a weakness. Its grin gone, Abernon faced Archibald and the dagger he held. 'Am I to assume that is Kar'roc's Maw?'

'Your assumption would be correct.' Archibald tightened his grip on the dagger's handle, the mottled-black marble smooth and sure against his skin.

'You seek counsel?' Abernon's words were thick with greedy enthusiasm.

'I seek answers.'

'And in return for my knowledge?'

Archibald felt his stomach lurch, despite the calming properties of the tea. 'Nourishment. In exchange for your knowledge, I permit you to feed.'

A breath rattled in the creature's throat as it contemplated the offer. Abernon cocked its head, darting its long, black tongue over its teeth, releasing a spray of saliva that sparked then fizzled against the walls of the barrier. 'I see the rot in you has spread since last we spoke.'

Archibald's fingers twitched by his sides; he resisted the urge to touch the webbing of black veins covering his chest and collar bone. 'If the exchange is not satisfactory, I shall conclude the summoning.' He would not succumb to Abernon's attempts at distraction.

Abernon hesitated then nodded. 'The exchange is satisfactory.'

'Excellent. Then we may proceed.'

Archibald held the dagger out to the demon, hilt first, so that Abernon could inspect the red gemstone set into the pommel.

The creature recoiled. A low hiss escaped its oozing mouth.

'So, it *is* Solomon's stone?' Archibald mused aloud.

The demon wrenched energy from Archibald—his payment. Archibald grunted and with it, his satisfied smile slid from his face. He gritted his teeth until the sensation passed.

Abernon shuddered, breathing deeply. Residues of Archibald's syphoned life force flickered like sparks of electricity across the fissures of its coarse skin before dissipating into its body. The slits of the demon's nostrils flared.

After a moment it opened its eyes, staring at Archibald with renewed hunger. 'It is only a fragment. The stone is fractured.'

Archibald cursed his own eagerness. Even rhetorical questions came at a cost. 'Yes, but does it still function?' He needed to exercise caution. Another mistake would only offer the demon an opportunity to prolong its feeding.

Abernon's hollow-sounding laugh echoed around the basement.

The demon gorged on more of Archibald's power, drawing it from him so violently that to stand was a chore. Eyes squeezed shut, Archibald clenched his jaw. Beads of sweat rolled down his skin, dripped from his forehead. The muscles in his stomach cramped. He forced his eyes open, his breath coming in stilted gasps.

'Its potency is diminished,' the demon answered. It edged forward as much as the barrier would allow, its knotted claws gouging out divots from the concrete.

Archibald steadied his breathing, replaying words in his mind before he said them aloud.

Abernon waited, ravenous anticipation gleaming in each of its unblinking white eyes.

Archibald spoke slowly. 'Is the power enough to free my master from the archdemon that claims dominion over him?'

Abernon fed again. Each fibre of Archibald's body tore as the energy was ripped out of him. Payment had never been this bad. Never. But with the veil between realms diminishing day by day, Abernon's strength had intensified.

Archibald was truly exposed. Weak. Vulnerable.

The dagger slipped from his grasp, clattering against the cold, hard floor. With a grunt, he staggered forward. It took every ounce of strength in his trembling muscles to stop a hair's breadth from the circle's perimeter.

Chest heaving, he looked up. The demon was staring down at him.

It grinned, showing him its teeth.

'No,' Abernon replied. 'You will need to unearth the rest of the stone. Make it whole once more. Even then, it is likely that you will fail and that your master, Barrow, will perish.'

Archibald glanced at the dagger on the floor, where he'd let it drop.

Foolish. If it had fallen just a few inches to the left... if it had broken the circle... he would be a dead man. Worse, Abernon would have been unleashed into the mortal realm.

'I can tell you where to find the other fragments,' Abernon said. 'All you need do is ask.'

Over two centuries of searching. Over two centuries of seeking out every last shred of information, chasing down every lead, travelling to every corner of the Earth, and all he had to do was ask one more question. Just one more and he would finally have everything he needed. Everything he wanted. He was so close.

Archibald sucked in a breath, battling against the throbbing pressure mounting in his skull. The influence of the Blue Lotus tea was waning.

He straightened up and looked down at his hands. The skin was slack, no longer that of a young man, as it had been mere minutes ago, but so thinned and fragile that it revealed blue veins and protruding tendons. If he'd needed any more proof of the demon's gluttony, his quivering, wasting muscles gave it in spades. It was time to bring this to an end.

'That will be all, Abernon.' The rasping sound of his suddenly aged voice took him by surprise. 'You have been most accommodating. As always.'

The demon narrowed its eyes and growled. It was not a threat but a promise of sadistic intent.

Archibald shook his head. If nothing else the creature was predictable.

He bent to retrieve Kar'roc's Maw, weakened muscles straining to support the weight of his frail body, sweat dripping from his brow. Blood rushed to his head. His vision dimmed. Catching himself, he stepped back from the perimeter, dagger in hand.

Abernon cackled.

The sound forced Archibald to whip his head up. His jaw dropped in shock.

The circle of energy containing the demon had collapsed.

Just one moment of distraction, just one slip...

He cursed his stupidity, eyeing the droplet of perspiration that had broken the circle's edge, and reeled back. Abernon hammered its fist into the ground, sending out a spray of shattered concrete from where he'd just stood.

The demon roared, releasing an ear-splitting mix of bloodlust and frustration.

It charged and Archibald launched out of the way. The demon missed him by a hair's breath. He hit the ground hard, the force driving the air from his lungs. Pushing to his knees, Archibald held the dagger aloft.

'With Solomon's Seal I—' The creature darted its slick tongue out and constricted it around Archibald's wrist. Needle-like barbs pierced into his flesh, injecting him with venom that scorched like fire. Archibald cried out.

Digging into the remaining energy that had not been taken, he unleashed a blast of magic at Abernon. The hit sent the demon hurtling across the room to collide with the wall, in an explosion of brick and dust. The now severed tongue detached from Archibald's wrist and dropped to the floor. It flopped around in a pool of gelatinous black liquid.

Archibald sucked air through his teeth and tightened his grip on Kar'roc's Maw.

'With Solomon's Seal I banish thee. With Solomon's Seal thou art banished. With Solomon's Seal I compel thee. Return to the realm of flame and shadow.'

The demon lifted its head, shaking off the debris with a snarl, and attempted to stand.

'Return to the realm of flame and shadow,' Archibald continued.

The snarl became a bellow.

'Return to the realm of flame and shadow!'

The gemstone in the dagger glimmered. Specks of red light refracted across the room, twisting and spinning faster and faster until they enclosed Abernon in a glaring circle. The demon shrieked, thrashing and clawing as the floor morphed into an intricate pattern of glowing red symbols. As Abernon sunk back into the hellish depths from whence it came, it stared at him. The unadulterated loathing would have sent a chill down Archibald's spine were his skin not on fire from the poison coursing through his veins.

Silence descended on the room.

Archibald let the dagger drop and crawled towards the desk, body shaking. Each movement sent a jarring pain through his throbbing arm that made him want to vomit. With every shallow gasp, he smelt the putrid stench of venom seeping from his punctured flesh.

He hauled himself up to his knees, reached a trembling hand towards the wooden cabinet and jerked open the doors. Glass bottles and vials clinked beneath his quivering fingers as he searched. His vision swam, making it hard to see. He plucked out a vial, tore out the stopper, and smelt the contents. With a grunt, he discarded the wrong vial and grabbed another.

His muscles spasmed. The glass shattered in his firm grip.

Jaw clenched, he forced his fist open and sniffed the bloodied contents.

Yes, the right one.

Flicking away as many shards as he could, he tipped the mix of dried husks and ground powder into his mouth. Fragments of glass crunched between his teeth as he chewed. He swallowed and collapsed to the floor in a heap.

The fire surging through his body gradually reduced to a dull ache as the remedy took effect.

Dried foxglove, poppy husk and a few other specially selected ingredients. A fraction of what he'd consumed would kill a healthy adult within minutes. But magic had given him the ability to render most toxins inert. And what his magic lacked, his master—Black Barrow—had compensated for. He had trained Archibald to ingest every poison, hallucinogen, narcotic and venom known to man, until his body had formed a natural immunity or, at the very least, tolerance.

Minutes felt like hours, passing in nauseating bursts as the concoction neutralised the demon's toxin. When the last of the excruciating stomach cramps had turned into uncomfortable twinges, Archibald stood and retrieved his robe. Now that the fire had been replaced by a cold sweat, he was grateful for what little warmth it provided. With a shuddering sigh, he shuffled across the room to recover Kar'roc's Maw.

He picked it up and straightened with a groan of effort, his spine cracking in objection. He surveyed the basement with a frown.

All that remained of the summoning was the severed hunk of Abernon's tongue and extensive cosmetic and structural damage to the room. He would deal with it in the morning. Now, he needed rest. A good night's sleep would help regenerate the energy the demon had taken from him.

Eyeing the dagger in his hand, Archibald smiled and headed for the stairs leading out of the basement. Ninety-six years it had taken to find it again, after his last efforts had been frustrated by that Boswell slattern and her degenerate descendants. But here it was, a beacon of hope. Hope for his master. Hope for himself. With Solomon's stone, he could finally rectify his past mistakes and liberate Barrow from the demon realm. All he had to do was keep it in his possession this time. Even in his weakened state, how hard could that be?

Out of the basement, he caught sight of his haggard reflection in the glass door of one of his liquor cabinets. The sight stole the breath from his lungs. Sharp brown eyes—he recognised those at least—stared back at him beneath the sagging creases of a pallid face. It was a face that belonged to a decrepit old man. Still, he should be grateful. What would he look like if his body bore its true years?

Gingerly, he touched the slack skin at his throat and tutted.

'Vanity, thy name is Archibald... No matter. All will be well come daybreak.'

With a shake of his head he shuffled down the hallway, the chill of the oak flooring seeping into his bare feet.

Glass detonated to his right in an eruption of glimmering shards. Archibald flung up both arms, shielding himself from the shower of fragments. He staggered back in shock. His paper-thin flesh stung where the shards had cut him.

'Well, would you look here, Dermot, the old prick's only got it in his bleedin' hand.' The man who accompanied the thick brogue heaved himself through the window, closely followed by a second man.

'Mammy will be pleased, Niall. That she will.'

Drained of energy, Archibald could only brace himself as Niall Boswell drove his fist into his face.

Chapter 1

Thirty-Four Years Later

A SCREAM TORE FROM Banning Lawrence's lungs and bloodied his throat. His young body spasmed where he stood, the agony too intense to move. The unbearable heat consumed him. Liquid green flame lapped at his flesh, tearing it open with each greedy lick. He opened his mouth to beg, to plea, but the words were enveloped by another panicked screech...

Banning woke with a start, his breath coming out in sharp, rapid pants. Louder than the sound of his thrashing heart pumping blood through his veins. *No.* He wasn't that boy anymore. But the memory didn't care. It continued to flare across his vision, threatening to swallow him completely.

WEAK.

The voice rose from the deepest recesses of his mind like an eruption of oil. Smothering his reasoning. Poisoning his thoughts. If he couldn't calm himself, if he couldn't regain control, he would sink into its toxic spread until there was nothing left to save.

Ten, nine, eight...

The puckered scars across his upper chest and his arms started to itch.

Seven...

YOU'RE WEAK.

No. No, not again.

He twisted sharply, his body tangling in the sweat-dampened folds of the duvet. Yanking the fabric back, he lunged for the bedside table. His fingers, slick with sweat, fumbled in the dark. Grasping. Desperate.

There.

The autoinjector. He plunged the needle into his thigh. The tip punctured his skin with a soft click. Muscles trembling, he released the lindwurm venom to the count of three, then pulled the needle out and collapsed back.

Slowly, the venom worked its way into his system, silencing the voice inside his head until it became little more than a whisper, then nothing at all. Banning's heart rate slowed. His breathing became deep and even. Exhausted, he could close his eyes right now and sink into a dreamless sleep. But it was a luxury he couldn't afford. The dosage before bed should have seen him through the night. He was going to have to recalculate it. *Again.*

Discarding the autoinjector, Banning sat up. Goose bumps pricked his clammy skin. Judging by the chill in the air, it was late, but there was still enough residual heat for him to draw from it what he needed to raise his body temperature.

He rubbed at his eyes and yawned. Warmth flooded his body and weariness courted him once more. It would be so easy to drink from the currents of energy flowing around him, permeating from the realm of fire and shadow. Will them into something he could use to keep the exhaustion at bay. He could feel them keenly. That was his gift. His curse. Of all his kind. But if that fateful night had taught him anything, it was that to quench his thirst would be to drown.

He reached for his mobile, unlocking it with his thumb, and winced against the glare from the screen. 3.30am. The phone vibrated in his palm; a new message from Mundy Wilcoxson. He read it aloud, finding comfort in the sound of his own voice: 'Sure. I'll meet you there, kid.'

His mouth quirked into a smile.

It was only when he moved to stand that he noticed an unread text. He thumbed the screen again. His stomach dropped.

It read: *Can we talk?*

Naomie. He thought he'd done enough to scare her off. But those three little words threatened to undo everything. They twisted in his gut like tiny black knives. Should he reply? No. *You knew the risks.*

He took a breath and read them again: *Can we talk?*

For all he'd endured—the scars that riddled his body, the voice that plagued his thoughts, the fear that could be his undoing—for all his pain and suffering, he was still just as weak as he'd been all those years ago. He was still that scared little boy.

The autoinjector was barely visible in the dark, but its presence was a black hole, absorbing everything in the room until nothing else remained.

Banning tossed the phone away. No. A life with Naomi belonged to the young man he should have been. Not the monster he'd become.

Banning watched in silence as Archibald Morgan leant forward. He placed his elbows on the rustic oak desk and steepled his fingers. He was disappointed. Nothing good ever came of those who disappointed Archibald Morgan. And he should know; he'd been on the receiving end of his mentor's displeasure too often.

Archibald Morgan. The man in the suit. That's what he'd worn when eleven-year-old Banning had first met him at the funeral for his parents and sister. But then, all the men had been wearing suits. He hadn't known that this particular man was more than another mourner. And when Archibald had passed his condolences on to Banning's grandmother, pressed a small white business card into her hand, and told her that should she ever need anything to contact him, well, why would he give it a second thought? In fact, as soon as the brief interaction was over, Banning had already forgotten about him.

Just another face. Just another stranger offering hollow comfort and pity.

It had taken another two years before Archibald Morgan made a reappearance, six months after Banning had been expelled from secondary school for nearly hospitalising a much older boy. His grandmother had conceded that she had neither the patience nor the skill to home-school him. That little business card had been her last resort, and the phone call that followed had changed the course of Banning's life.

Banning schooled his expression and pushed the memory away. He focused on the man stood in front of him and Archibald. The man Banning had been instructed to escort to and from the property—a job for an errand boy. The muscles beneath Banning's eye twitched with irritation.

The stranger—Heimerich something or other—shifted uncomfortably on the spot, avoiding Banning's gaze. He was twice Banning's age at least, clearly in his early forties, and taller than him by a good couple of inches—pushing six feet two at a guess. He had a fair amount of muscle—no bodybuilder but clearly no stranger to the gym either. Similar to Banning in that way. The way he avoided eye contact, the way he held himself so rigidly... it sparked something predatory in Banning. Something dark that lingered just beneath the surface of his calm exterior. Something he'd carried with him ever since the night of the fire, the night he'd received his scars.

Heimerich shifted his gaze to the two men standing sentry either side of the solid panelled-wood door. Their suits—tailored three-piece ensembles in the deepest blue—matched Banning's own in style. Banning's suit, however, was black, its buttons gold rather than silver, marking him as more than just a lackey. He'd earned every stitch of that suit. Every last thread was testament to the blood, sweat and tears it had taken to win his mentor's respect. To make Archibald Morgan see him as more than just the wilful and disobedient boy he'd first taken on.

Nevertheless, he'd noticed the shift in his mentor's attitude towards him in recent months. The menial tasks were becoming more and more frequent. Sure, Archibald had been preoccupied with his current endeavour, but was it more? Had Banning's most recent slip in control been the final straw?

'You are certain?' Archibald Morgan asked Heimerich. His tone was even, yet the stranger flinched.

'Yes, sir.' Heimerich flicked his dark eyes to his feet. He cleared his throat and looked up. 'Kar'roc's Maw has a new master. Charlie Haynes. He's currently under the surveillance of O.O.T.I.S. They're keeping a close eye on him. Monitoring his every move. He's staying with his daughter and granddaughter, while his house is being repaired. The demon that attacked him caused quite a lot of damage.'

Banning lifted his eyebrows. The Order of the Iron Seal? Now *that* made things interesting. From what he understood, the organisation had been a thorn in his mentor's side ever since its inception, over two hundred years ago. Not that he'd have believed it to look at him; Archibald Morgan didn't look a day over thirty-eight.

Archibald contemplated the news, lowering his hands to stroke the mottled brown-and-black cat lounging on the desk. It opened one large, yellow eye to consider him. The soft rumble of its purr sounded before it promptly shut its eye once more.

'Mundane?' Archibald asked.

Heimerich's forehead wrinkled in confusion, until the question sunk in. 'Yes. Just a normal human. In his mid-sixties, I think.'

Archibald levelled his gaze on Heimerich. 'Your source is reliable?'

'Yes.' He winced, like the answer pained him. 'Very. The true memories were concealed. Buried under layers of spellwork. But I managed to extract them.'

Memory extraction? Banning frowned. The magic he and his mentor shared did not, as a rule, involve the manipulation of the mind, like it did for witches. But Heimerich couldn't be a witch. Banning would have detected his magic by now...

A cryptid of some kind then.

Clearing his mind, Banning gave Heimerich his full attention. Everything else fell away, until it was just him and his heartbeat pulsing in time to the power coursing through his body. Effortlessly, he drew energy up from his core and extended his senses out towards the cryptid.

Yes, there.

That he'd not detected it before was proof of his distraction... The creature's link to the realm of fire and shadow was obvious now. He practically throbbed with it.

He pulled his gaze from Heimerich to find Archibald watching him. His mentor's lips twitched with the hint of approval.

'He is an incubus,' Archibald said. 'As you well know, Banning, the mind is a fragile thing. It has a natural inclination to suppress the traumatic and unexplainable. Something that O.O.T.I.S takes full advantage of when manipulating the recollections of ordinary mortals to conceal the existence of the supernatural. When an incubus feeds on a sleeping individual's vitality, it gains direct access to their subconscious. Their dreams. Their nightmares. Their secrets.'

Banning regarded the creature. An incubus. A parasite. A *demon*. He swallowed his disgust. Their species was few and far between. He'd never seen one in the flesh.

Not alive anyway.

Archibald tugged absently at his collar, momentarily exposing the black web of veins that marred the flesh beneath, and turned to the incubus. 'Thank you, Heimerich. That will be all.'

But Heimerich remained where he was, his eyes fixed on Archibald's neck.

Of course a loathsome creature such as Heimerich would recognise demon rot.

Archibald arched an eyebrow. 'If you would be so kind as to wait outside, I want to have a quick word with Mr Lawrence before he sees you safely back home.'

He gave a nod to the two men stationed at the door. They escorted Heimerich from the room.

Banning watched them leave.

Mr Lawrence. Not Banning. He turned the address over in his mind, trying to decipher its hidden meaning.

'Sir?' He nodded respectfully to his mentor.

'I have business to which I must attend for the next day or so.' Archibald looked up at the large, wall-mounted antique clock and pressed his lips into a thin line before returning his attention to Banning. 'I trust that I will not have to contend with another unfortunate incident upon my return.'

Banning's cheeks flushed. He averted his gaze and flexed his fingers. The waxy scar tissue that covered the backs of his hands tugged lightly. 'No, sir.'

'Excellent. Then I shall bid you good evening. Oh, and should the need arise, both myself and Mr Evans will be contactable.'

'*Evans?*' That bumbling idiot didn't know his arse from his elbow.

'You are affronted by this?'

Of course he was. First he'd been demoted to escort duties and now he was being replaced. And by Evans no less. Had he really fallen so far from grace for his mentor to sideline him? There *had* to be something he could do. Some way to prove he was more than just a burden.

'No, sir.'

'Banning, I know when you are lying to me. We each must play to our strengths, and Mr Evans is more suited to aid me in my upcoming undertaking than you. That is all there is to it. Now, I really must prepare.'

Keeping his expression neutral, Banning nodded. 'Good evening, sir.' He walked across the room. It took every ounce of restraint not to slam the door shut behind him.

'You can go back in now,' he snarled at the sentries.

A look of unease passed between them before they gave him a nod and returned to their posts. He'd developed a reputation. *Good.* He might not have their respect, but he had their fear, and that would serve for now.

He turned to glare at Heimerich. 'Let's go.'

Focusing on his breathing, Banning led the incubus through the hallway. The undercurrents of his insecurities were fast becoming waves of unbridled resentment. His mentor was abandoning him... Just as his episodes were getting worse, he was being cast aside.

A lost cause. An embarrassment perhaps?

But Archibald had to have seen the signs that Banning was struggling? Not that Banning would admit it aloud; the last thing he needed was to appear helpless. Maybe if Archibald hadn't been so distracted lately, maybe if he spent a little less time chasing down the fragments of that wretched stone...

Banning stopped mere feet from the front door, his shoes scuffing against the oak floorboards.

The stone. Kar'roc's Maw.

He smiled. Finally, an opportunity to prove his worth, to win back his mentor's favour.

Banning turned to Heimerich. 'I assume you have the address?'

'Sorry?' Heimerich stared back at him, his confusion plain.

'The address of Mr Haynes' daughter and granddaughter?'

'Oh, erm, yes. I can write it down.'

Banning waved his hand. 'No need. We're going to pay them a little visit.'

'I don't follow?'

'With O.O.T.I.S on his back, Mr Haynes may be reluctant to part with the dagger. But if we gave Haynes an incentive...'

The incubus blinked, his breath hitching. His eyes met Banning's, perhaps seeking some indication that this was a sick joke. Finding none, he licked his lips. 'You want to *abduct* Charlie Haynes' family?'

'Abduct is such a strong word.'

Heimerich shook his head. 'No.'

'No?'

'I provide information. That's all I do. That's all I've ever done. I don't kidnap people.'

'Then consider this a promotion. Of sorts.'

Heimerich looked unsure. 'And these are Archibald Morgan's instructions?'

'Let's go back and ask him, shall we?' Banning held the demon's gaze, daring him to call the bluff.

The incubus glanced back up the hallway. After a moment's hesitation his shoulders dropped in defeat.

Banning smiled. 'Good. I'm glad that's settled. I'll pick you up in the morning. We can thrash out the finer details on the drive over there. After all, we wouldn't want poor planning to impede our efforts, would we?'

He met the incubus' gaze. The creature flinched at the intensity of his stare. Banning's smile widened into a grin and he gestured at the door.

A road trip. This was going to be fun.

Chapter 2

THREE MONTHS. THAT'S HOW long had passed since Charlie Haynes had watched his friend, Stephen, die. For the second time. He didn't think his life could get any stranger.

He'd been wrong.

In fact, everything he thought to be true had turned out to be wrong.

It had been so much simpler before when monsters had just been people. Granted, they might have been the oozing dross of humanity's rotten underbelly, but still *just* people. Now he had demons, witches and God knew what else to contend with.

Yes, things had definitely gotten weird.

'This way please, Mr Haynes.'

Charlie suppressed a sigh and stepped through the metal detector.

He'd lost count of how many times he'd been inside the headquarters of the Order of the Iron Seal in the last few weeks—not that he'd been given much of a choice.

The sheer scale of the place still amazed him. As Charlie looked around, he thumbed the spot on his left hand where his wedding band had been. It was Romanesque-style architecture at its finest. The interior was dominated by a cavernous, cathedral-like hall at its main entrance, filled with high arches of terracotta, sweeping staircases, and decorative, stained-glass windows. Bodies bustled everywhere, voices melding in a flurry of activity. But it was the juxtaposition of technology that really made Charlie's head swim.

Immense screens were set into the smooth brickwork, displaying streams of rolling text that reminded him of the departure boards at Heathrow. And in neat little intervals were circular marble desks, each with a computer, each manned by someone with a headset and a tough demeanour that wouldn't see them mistaken for the receptionist.

Intricate details revealed themselves, from the decorative panels depicting now extinct species and mythological creatures, to the flora and fauna winding up the length of the immense, hand-carved columns. And incorporated into everything as far as the eye could see were symbols. They ran like the letters of some ancient script, worked into the stone, weaving in and out of the architecture so seamlessly, they could easily be mistaken for mason marks.

But mason marks they were not. On the one occasion Charlie had allowed his curiosity to get the better of him, he'd touched one. The thrum of energy that had skipped across his skin had been enough to deter him from trying it again.

He pulled his attention back to the plastic tray containing his keys, mobile and wallet. After a nod from the man behind the monitor, Charlie scooped them up and placed them back in the pocket of his slate-grey, wool trench coat. He wasn't sure why he'd even brought his phone. Pointless really. He'd learnt from his first few visits that while he was inside the building's perimeter he got absolutely no signal. It was little more than a brick.

His escort gestured for him to follow.

Charlie took a breath and obliged. No doubt they would be taking a different route to the room in which he would spend the next few hours. Whether it was by design or coincidence, both the path he took and the chaperones were never the same.

He wasn't big on coincidence.

He eyed the man ahead of him. Black suit. Clean shaven. Cropped hair. No concealed weapon. That was something at least. Although... maybe he didn't need a weapon.

Charlie's forehead wrinkled. He was still coming to terms with the fact that there was magic in the world. *Real* magic. Gut-wrenching, terrifying magic. It existed. And he had the scars to prove it.

He flexed his left hand as he walked, resisting the urge to look at the raised markings between his thumb and forefinger—the sigil. Three dots to the left of a convex line. Barely noticeable unless you knew they were there. But boy, did he know they were there. They were a permanent reminder of the night he'd bound

Chekonost, a demon, back inside the dagger. A relic that had plagued him throughout his career as a detective and of which he had inadvertently become master.

In an attempt to distract himself, Charlie focused on one of the many sizeable gilt-framed paintings hanging on the walls. A portrait of a man in his late thirties stared back, sitting in a well-upholstered armchair beside a writing desk, one hand resting casually on the pages of an open book, the other clutching a feathered quill. According to the engraved brass plate beneath, he was the late Theodore Inman, 1750-1792. A simple wooden walking cane, more functional than ornamental, was propped beside him. Clearly Theodore suffered from a limp. *Like Stephen.* Charlie winced at the reminder and averted his gaze.

The black suit slowed, cocked his head, and pressed a finger against his earpiece. He dropped his arm and resumed his pace.

Charlie matched the man's stride.

They turned a corner and headed for a hallway flanked by two more elaborately carved columns. There was no attempt at conversation. Not that Charlie minded; he'd always been comfortable in his own company. At any rate, any questions he had would only be met with silence. That's how it had been with the other chaperones.

After several minutes of walking, and more than one inquisitive glance from the people they passed, they arrived at a heavy-duty louvred steel door. The black suit opened it and waved him inside.

Charlie entered, not bothering to look back, as the door clicked shut behind him and the automatic lock slid into place. Experience had taught him well. The next time he saw the black suit would be when it was time to leave.

A quick scan of the room confirmed that nothing had changed since his last visit. Everything was still precisely organised. Still methodically clinical. Equipment—monitors, beakers, bottles and some serious-looking microscopes, all meticulously clean, all strategically positioned—still sat atop the burnished silver surfaces set against the whitewashed walls. At least he could appreciate the orderliness of it.

Part of him wondered if the room choice was deliberate, given his OCD; a psychological tactic to put him at ease. Mess triggered unwanted thoughts, setting off his anxiety, his compulsions. The remains of his childhood, of the physical and mental abuse he'd suffered at the hands of his deadbeat drunk of a dad. Order gave him control, and he didn't doubt for one moment that O.O.T.I.S knew it.

Mind games.

He breathed in the familiar faint chemical smell, and let his eyes travel the length of the square ceiling panels with recessed LED downlights to the nearest surveillance camera. The lens swivelled in its domed casing, fixing him with its unblinking stare.

Subtle.

He dropped his gaze, knowing that all eight would be tracking his every movement from this point onwards. It had taken him no time to spot them during his first visit, but then again that had been the point. The concealed ones, however, now *they* had taken him a while to ferret out.

'Charles, good to see you,' someone with a lilting voice and the trace of a Japanese accent said.

Charlie turned towards its owner, expression neutral, as he removed his coat and hung it on the stand. 'Doctor.'

Ignoring the treadmill stationed next to the examination table for the moment, he made his way over to the padded, grey swivel chair.

He knew the drill.

The doctor's mouth lifted into a smile. It almost looked like she was pleased to see him. She was convincing, he'd give her that.

The doctor made an amused clucking noise and placed the tablet she carried down on the desk, next to something electronic that Charlie couldn't even begin to identify. 'Always so formal. Please, for the last time, call me Sachiko.'

Making a noncommittal noise, Charlie took a seat.

Sachiko smoothed out a few of the wrinkles in her white laboratory coat and came to stand beside him. 'Any changes to report since last time?'

'No. Everything's pretty much the same.'

'Still having the nightmares?'

He looked at her. The pressure of the silence built between them.

'Yes,' he said finally. He flicked his gaze to the box of reinforced glass in the centre of the room. The symbols etched into its surface caught the light. He hardly noticed them, focused on what lay within. Sat atop a white plinth and suspended in mid-air by some unseen force was the dagger.

Kar'roc's Maw.

Its Damascus steel blade rippled beneath the artificial glare of the lighting. The red gemstone set into the pommel of the marbled black handle winked at him, as though feeling his attention.

Charlie looked away.

'The offer of medication is still there if you want it.'

'No. Thank you.'

It was bad enough that he was being forced to attend these appointments. If they thought he was about to let them drug him, they had another think coming. O.O.T.I.S hadn't threatened him, not directly, but the insinuation was there. Either he voluntarily underwent routine testing to monitor the biological and psychological implications of his link to the dagger, or *other measures* would be put into action. For his own safety, of course. His initial reaction had been to tell them to go to hell, consequences be damned, but knowing what had happened to Stephen...

He couldn't risk the chance of becoming a monster.

Undeterred by his abrupt response, Sachiko continued. 'The nightmares must be getting more manageable. We haven't had any incidents for a while.'

'Incidents?' Charlie scoffed. 'That's not what I would call them.'

When he had hobbled out of his house, bloody and broken, after the demon possessing Stephen had nearly killed him, there had been barely enough room in his mind to string together a coherent thought, much less contemplate what that cursed dagger meant for him and his future. He'd been more than happy for it to be dealt with by someone else and had assumed, naively, that once the dagger was gone, it would be the last he saw of it.

But then the nightmares had started. Vivid and horrifying. And when he'd woken, gasping for air and drenched in sweat, the blade had been there—clutched in his trembling fist. The first time it had happened, it'd damn near given him a heart attack. O.O.T.I.S had come knocking, asking him in no uncertain terms to surrender it into their custody.

As they had every time since.

Charlie knew they'd been watching him. It hadn't taken his detective—or more accurately *ex*-detective—skills to figure out that much. He'd clocked them the second he'd been discharged from hospital and went to stay with his daughter, Meghan. Their initial attempts to be covert soon fell by the wayside. And Charlie had seen it for what it was: a power move. They'd wanted him to know that if he stepped out of line, if he screwed up just once, they'd be *right* there. Ready and waiting.

It was as insulting as it was absurd. What was he going to do, use Kar'roc's Maw to unleash the apocalypse?

Tear open the fabric between realms and let loose a hoard of demons?

Sod that for a lark.

He didn't want anything to do with that wretched dagger, the supernatural, or O.O.T.I.S. *Especially* O.O.T.I.S.

Sachiko said, 'It's been almost a month since you unintentionally summoned Kar'roc's Maw. That's progress. You've obviously been practicing those relaxation techniques I gave you.'

'Yeah. Sure.'

She tutted, but her lips held the traces of a smile. 'Right. I'm going to need another blood sample today.'

'Great.' Charlie unbuttoned his cuff and rolled up his sleeve.

Sachiko's brow furrowed as she tightened the tourniquet around his upper arm. She prodded the veins in the crook of his elbow for a few seconds, and then said, 'Make a fist.'

As the needle punctured his skin, the symbols marking the glass casing for the dagger glowed white. Sachiko paused briefly. Charlie kept his eyes fixed on the small plastic vial as it filled with his blood, ignoring the sigil on his left hand that was beginning to itch.

'Still not a fan of needles, I see,' Sachiko said.

He wasn't. Charlie changed the subject, 'I don't see why you don't just destroy that thing.'

Sachiko hummed and swapped out the filled vial for one with a different coloured lid. 'Demon-forged artifacts are virtually indestructible. The best we can do is keep it secured here. Study it. And hope that, given enough time, we can unlock its secrets and render it inert.'

'Virtually indestructible. So it *can* be destroyed?'

'I suppose if you asked Kar'roc *really* nicely...' She smiled to herself then, seeing his shocked expression, rolled her eyes. 'Nothing this side of the veil stands a chance. To destroy something like Kar'roc's Maw you're talking hellfire, hellhounds, ifrits, pit infernals—'

'*What?*' He shook his head in disbelief. 'Hellhounds? Ifrits?'

'And pit infernals. Nasty, nasty creatures. Don't worry, it's unlikely you'll ever see one in the flesh.' She shuddered. 'Thank goodness.'

Unlikely? Christ. What he wouldn't give to go back to the good old days when the most inexplicable thing to ever happen was the occasional disappearance of a sock from the wash.

'Relax your arm.' Sachiko removed the tourniquet, slipped the needle from his vein and placed a cotton ball against the puncture site. 'Put pressure here.'

Samples secured and bagged, she hurried over to the case containing the dagger. She tapped buttons on the display built into the side of the plinth.

'It would appear that your bond with the dagger has strengthened.' She pushed a few more buttons.

'Strengthened?' Charlie cringed. 'You can tell that from my blood?'

'Obviously, I need to get these latest samples tested, but to an extent yes. In the last three months, your red blood cell volume has increased. Typically, absolute levels of total blood volume decrease with age, even in healthy, active adults such as you.'

'What does that mean?'

'It means that you have the blood, and therefore the immunity, of a much younger man.'

'And that's all you're testing for is it, blood volume?'

'We're testing for everything. Hormone levels, cholesterol, anything and everything you can think of. But that's not what I was referring to.' Sachiko pointed to one of the symbols that had flared white when the needle had bit into his flesh. 'If what I theorise is correct, the dagger is responding to you at an emotional level.'

'Emotional level?'

'We need to keep running tests, monitor cortisol levels and such, but I'd wager it reacts to acute stress. It would, given your aversion to needles, explain why every time I've gone near you with a syringe in recent weeks, the wards on the casing for the dagger have activated.'

Charlie drummed out a steady rhythm on the side of the seat. Control.

Tap, tap, tap. Pause. *Tap, tap, tap.* Pause.

Thoughts of Stephen raced through his mind. 'Is it going to get worse?'

Sachiko rubbed a smudge from the glass casing with the cuff of her sleeve, considering her answer. 'Information about Kar'roc's Maw is limited.' Charlie went to interrupt. She held up a hand. 'Yes, there are documented texts, which you of course are familiar with. But historically, they've focused on the practical applications of the dagger's rituals. Summoning, binding, controlling, that sort of thing. Nothing that really details the connection between the dagger and its master. Other than the equivocal "untold power" for releasing Kar'roc into the human realm.'

'So, in other words, you don't know?'

She tsked. 'What I *do* know is that you're certainly reaping the physical benefits of your bond with the dagger. If I didn't know you, based on your blood pressure alone, I would've said you were an athlete. Your hearing has improved. Your eyesight too. Must be nice not to need glasses for anything anymore.' She touched the frame of her own glasses with an almost wistful expression.

'I don't care about any of that. Is it going to change the way I think? The way I act?' If the demon had been capable of corrupting someone as morally stable as Stephen, what would it do to him? The idea that he could become a risk to his daughter or granddaughter filled him with a dread so visceral, he felt physically sick.

'As I said, the information is limited,' Sachiko said. 'You have to understand that before your first encounter with the dagger, in the eighties, it had been lost since the Victorian era. When Jack the Ripper was roaming the streets of Whitechapel.'

The look of incredulity on Charlie's face must have been obvious because Sachiko sighed and shook her head. 'A story for another day. What I'm trying to say is that the dagger is very hard to keep tabs on let alone study. You are aware of its ability to vanish without a trace. If it hadn't been for the unpleasantness involving your former colleague, Stephen Anderson, we'd probably still be none the wiser as to its whereabouts.'

'*Unpleasantness?*' He hadn't meant for the word to sound so hard.

Sachiko held up her hands, and gave the dagger a cautious glance. 'I didn't mean any offence. Those murders brought the dagger back into play. It had likely been with the Boswells for generations. Shielded by magic. Blood magic. Old magic. It differs between cultures, but fundamentally, it's the same.'

'Blood magic?'

Sachiko nodded. 'I'd put money on it. To conceal something as powerful as Kar'roc's Maw would take more than just spellwork. If I were to speculate, I'd say that whoever performed the rite bound the dagger directly to their bloodline, keeping it hidden from the world. As long as it remained in the possession of a direct descendant, that is.'

'And now?'

'And now we keep it here. Your little incidents aside.'

It was clear that Sachiko had no intention of elaborating further. Charlie had learnt early on that his appointments with the Order would be one-sided affairs, and knowing that had done nothing to alleviate him of his misgivings.

He decided to drop it. 'So, are you... you know...' He wriggled his fingers in the air.

'A pianist?'

'What? No. I meant...'

A knowing smile spread across her face. 'You mean, am I a witch? No, just your everyday vanilla mortal. Not everyone in here is a witch or otherwise. Most of us are just regular human beings.'

Unsure whether he had caused offense, Charlie cleared his throat and gestured at the dagger. 'Why does it float like that?'

'It's enclosed within a magical field.'

'For protection?'

'Yes. Among other things.'

'Among other things?' A knot tightened in his stomach.

Christ. No, they wouldn't... would they? That would be madness.

Charlie did all he could to keep his voice level. 'You're keeping the demon alive?'

Chapter 3

'WELL, YES.' SACHIKO'S EYEBROWS drew together, like the answer was obvious. 'The demon's essence is an integral part of the dagger's purpose. In order to study the full—'

'You can't be serious?' Charlie didn't remember standing, but suddenly he was taking a step forward, jabbing a finger at the encased blade. 'I almost died trapping that thing back inside the dagger. It murdered dozens of people. Women. Children. Mutilated them. Ripped them apart. And you're what…*feeding* it? Can't you see how dangerous that is? What if it gets out? What if the same thing happens again?'

'It won't.'

'How do you know?' The symbols on the glass enclosing the dagger flickered again. Charlie blew out a breath, clenching and unclenching his fists by his sides in an effort to regain his composure.

Sachiko waited. Once he relaxed his hands she said, 'Charles, as long as Kar'roc's Maw is here it's safe.'

'What if it happens to me?' His voice became a near whisper. 'What if I become like Stephen? The demon changed him. Turned him into a monster. What if it does the same thing to me? It's already changed my blood, you said so yourself.'

And then it clicked. Deep down, some part of him already knew. O.O.T.I.S wasn't watching him in case he stepped out of line; they were there to put him down if he became a threat.

The gentle pressure of Sachiko squeezing his shoulder took him by surprise. 'You won't, Charles. You're the dagger's master, not a host for the demonic essence inside. If we thought for a second that you'd enact the ritual required to become a vessel...' She trailed off, like she hadn't meant to speak the words out loud. 'The dagger is safe here. I promise you.'

He sat back down heavily in the chair. 'I—'

The door swung inwards, cutting him off.

'Sachiko, I have that—' The words died on the lips of the petite blonde—just a hair over five feet—when she saw Charlie. The staccato click of her heels came to an abrupt stop. She nudged her black-rimmed glasses up the bridge of her nose, her jaw snapping shut.

Charlie said nothing, mouth dry. He'd have recognised her from her perfume alone. An aromatic blend of plum and saffron.

Diane... Dee. She was everything he wanted in a woman. Smart. Ballsy. Gorgeous. But she'd used him. Manipulated him.

He shifted in his seat.

Well, this was awkward.

Sachiko brightened. 'Ah, Diane. Excellent. You don't mind keeping Charles company while I nip these blood samples over to pathology, do you?'

Recovering her composure, Diane tore her gaze from Charlie.

She faced Sachiko, her forehead wrinkling. 'Company?' Her amber eyes widened. 'Wait, Sachiko, I don't think—'

But the doctor was already gone, the steel door auto locking behind her, leaving silence in her wake.

After several excruciating seconds, Diane broke it. 'Charlie, it's good to see you again.'

'Is it?'

'Yes, of course it is. You're looking good.' A flush spread across her cheeks. 'I mean well. You're looking well. Not wearing glasses suits you.'

He didn't need her fake platitudes right now. Between the sleepless nights, the early morning escorts to O.O.T.I.S headquarters, and the revelation that Chekonost's essence was still taking up residence inside the dagger, his temper was frayed.

'Spare me.'

She visibly tensed. 'Excuse me?'

'I don't want to hear it. You used me.'

'Used you?'

'Used your powers to get inside my head. To make me feel something. To make me attracted to you. So you could get closer to *that*.' He jabbed a finger at Kar'roc's Maw.

Diane smiled. 'Do you hear yourself right now? I can't make anyone attracted to me. That's not how it works, and even if it was, it's against everything O.O.T.I.S stands for. We don't force people to act against free will. The attraction was already there, Charlie. I just encouraged it. A little. If it wasn't for me, you'd probably be dead.'

'*What?*'

'If I hadn't let you take those pages from *Ritualistic Sacrifice in Ancient Magical Practices*, if I hadn't been there the night you were attacked, the demon would have torn you to pieces. I need those pages back by the way. They're dangerous.'

Charlie stared at her in stunned silence. Was she serious? '*Let* me?'

'Yes. *Let* you. Do you really think I'd have left you completely unattended with a book that old and rare? It's a priceless artifact. Admittedly, I didn't think you'd actually damage it, but I trusted you. Trusted you to do your job and put all the pieces together.'

'Trusted me? You didn't even know me.'

'Wake up, Charlie. As soon as you searched for that book online, O.O.T.I.S knew. All I had to do was pull up your file and I could see everything about you. I put my neck on the line for you. Because I trusted your abilities. We couldn't get anywhere near Stephen; he could sniff out an agent a mile away. I knew you were the best chance we had of getting close to him and you proved me right.'

Charlie blinked. 'My file?'

'Oh don't be so naive. Every public sector worker, every employee of any large company, every school child is monitored, assessed, evaluated. If they're deemed a suitable candidate, nine times out of ten they end up here. How do you think we keep the world safe? Or did you think Kar'roc's Maw was the only threat out there?'

He opened his mouth then shut it.

'I didn't anticipate that you were going to claim dominion over the athame. I assumed you would just banish the demon's essence.' She gestured vaguely at his left hand, where the sigil marked him. Her voice softened. 'I had no idea *this* would be the outcome.'

He closed his hand into a fist, drawing it down beside his leg.

'You're bleeding,' she said.

Charlie glanced down. The cotton ball had fallen free from his arm. Blood welled on his skin, leaving red trails on the silver scars left by countless cigarette burns and well-aimed belt buckles. Feeling exposed, he pulled his sleeve down sharply.

O.O.T.I.S knew everything about him. Diane knew everything about him. And apparently he'd been found lacking.

If they'd been monitoring him as a child, had they known about his father? Known about the abuse, and done nothing to stop it? What else could they have prevented? What else had they ignored? The implications were sobering.

Tap, tap, tap. Pause. *Tap, tap, tap.* Pause.

Charlie scowled at his hand and forced himself to stop.

Diane watched him over the top of her glasses. The tightness around her eyes eased. 'For what it's worth, Charlie, I *am* sorry. You're a good man.'

He swallowed, cursing the flicker of happiness that her words sparked. *God man, what's wrong with you? She was just using you to get close to the dagger.*

'So, you were a plant?' he said.

'A plant?'

'That morning in the library, when I came in to check out the book.'

Diane shook her head. 'No, I *am* the library manager. Those books are my passion, I've dedicated years of my life to the history contained within those walls, connecting people with knowledge, building lasting bonds.' A genuine smile lit up her face only to slip at her next words. 'But I'm also an O.O.T.I.S agent, and as one, it's my job to provide an initial assessment on anyone who shows interest in a restricted title. It's why certain volumes are only available in branch.'

'And it's why you insisted on tagging along when I went to pick up Ciara and Addison?'

Her posture stiffened slightly. 'No. That was an error on my part. I'm not a field agent. I overstepped the mark by accompanying you.'

'Overstepped the mark...'

He was an idiot. He thought there'd been a spark between them. When she'd asked him to grab a coffee with her. When they'd kissed. But it had all been part of a wider agenda. Just another mind game. And he'd fallen for it hook, line, and sinker.

'Charlie, I wanted to explain...'

'Then why didn't you?'

'Because you wouldn't take my calls. Wouldn't answer my texts. You didn't give me the chance.'

'You're a witch.' She flinched at the hostility in his tone. 'You tried to cover up the truth. Tried to convince me that it wasn't Stephen who'd slaughtered all those people. That there was no demon. That it was all just some headcase in the... what was it you said? That's right, in the *throes of psychosis.*'

Diane lifted her chin, meeting his eyes. 'You're right. I *am* a witch, and I *did* try to alter your memories. It's standard protocol. But answer me this, Charlie, given the choice, wouldn't you rather remember Stephen as he was, your colleague, your friend, instead of what he became?'

'I don't like being lied to,' he said, avoiding the question. They both knew she had his number.

'I'm sorry, Charlie. I'm sorry I ruined things between us.'

Diane took a step forward. Was it just him or did she seem nervous?

She exhaled slowly. 'You know, we never did—'

The steel door swung inwards.

'Sorry.' Sachiko was out of breath, like she'd ran to get back. 'I didn't mean for that to take so long.' She looked from Charlie to Diane and smiled, clearly oblivious to the lingering tension. 'What did I miss?'

Diane clamped her mouth shut and moved to leave.

'He's not ready just yet,' Sachiko said. 'I've still got several more tests to run.'

Stopping, Diane arched an eyebrow. 'Sorry?'

'Before the two of you go.' Sachiko eyed them both again, forehead wrinkling in confusion. 'I just thought that as his handler, you—'

'*What?*' Diane's voice was tight. Her shocked expression mirrored Charlie's as she gawped at Sachiko. '*Handler?*'

'I thought that's why you were here... They didn't tell you?'

'There must be some mistake. I'm going to get this straightened out. Right now.' Diane marched across the room, heels striking the floor in sharp, clipped snaps, and hauled open the steel door. No doubt it would have slammed shut behind her if it wasn't for the mechanism preventing it.

Handler? Charlie clenched and unclenched his fists.

Sachiko blinked. 'I don't think they told her.'

Chapter 4

DETECTIVE CONSTABLE NICK STACEY rubbed the back of his neck and sighed. He felt like shit. No matter how much sleep he got—which lately had been next to nothing—he always woke up exhausted. Maybe Henry was right. Maybe he *should* go to the doctors. Get a blood test. Take some vitamins. Anything to stop him feeling so dead on his feet. Not that he was about to admit that to his husband. It would only vindicate Henry's constant nagging.

Nick checked his watch and swore. 7.20am. He'd have to hustle if he didn't want to be late for his shift. The last thing he needed was for Sergeant Lovett to pull him aside and give him another bollocking. She'd been on the warpath recently.

Fumbling with his tie, Nick raced down the stairs. He'd have to skip breakfast. *Again.*

Pain throbbed behind his eyes. Ignoring it, he stuffed his feet into his shoes, grabbed his coat off the rack, shrugged it on, and patted himself down searching for his wallet.

'Henry?' he called, checking the pockets of the other coats hanging in front of him. 'Henry, have you seen my wallet?'

Muttering to himself, Nick eyed his watch again and entered the kitchen. The smell of burnt food hit him. He screwed up his nose, blinking against the smoke, as the fire alarm began its penetrating morning chorus behind him.

Henry bustled past, tea towel in hand. After several seconds of vigorous flapping, the shrill beeping stopped. He closed the door quickly, gave Nick a peck on the cheek and asked, 'Breakfast?'

Nick frowned dubiously at the blackened remains of what he assumed was a vegan pancake, still smoking in the pan. 'Is it?'

Henry tutted. 'The important thing is that I try. Anyway, charcoal is good for your teeth.' He treated Nick to a dazzling smile, crossed the kitchen, and switched off the hob. 'You don't want any?'

'As appetising as that looks... I'm running late. Have you seen my wallet?'

'Did you check Lily's bed?'

Nick groaned, turned, and opened the kitchen door. Stepping back into the hallway, he lowered his gaze to the large, pink-tartan dog bed and the black-and-tan Rottweiler sprawled across it.

Lily gave a lazy thump of her tail.

'Lily, up.'

In a contortion of scrambling limbs, Lily jumped up and cocked her head to one side, tongue lolling from her muzzle.

Nick gave her a quick scratch behind the ear, then rooted through the assortment of stuffed animals. Behind Mr Quackers—a particularly well-loved plush duck, that had long since lost its squeak—he found his wallet, complete with drool and puncture marks.

With a grimace, he wiped the wallet on his coat sleeve.

Lily huffed out a half-bark, her tail beating the air into submission.

'Naughty girl,' Henry chided from behind him. 'What have I told you about taking Daddy's things? You've spoilt her. That's why she behaves like this.'

'*Me?*' Nick crammed the wallet into his pocket. 'You're the one that keeps buying her toys. Anyway—' Henry opened his mouth to argue and he held up a hand, '—it doesn't matter. Wallet found. I need to go. I'm going to be late.'

'You look terrible. I really think you should go to the doctor.'

'Cheers. You sound just like Charlie.' He winced as soon as the words left his mouth.

Henry stiffened. 'Don't you dare compare me to him. I'm nothing like that old grouch.'

He still didn't understand why Henry hated the man so much. 'Please, I don't have time for this again.'

'I've never liked him. Ever since he roped you into that case with the murdered teenagers, you've been different. It's like I've lost a part of you because of *him*.

You don't sleep. You don't eat. Whatever happened that day changed you. I don't like it.'

Nick clenched his fists. 'It was *my* case, Henry. Charlie didn't rope me into anything. I don't know why you've got such a problem with him, he's a good guy and he's my friend. I asked him for help. If I hadn't, maybe he wouldn't have ended up in hospital. Wouldn't have had his house smashed up.' Nick unclenched his fists and took a breath. Just thinking about it made him lightheaded. It was like the memories of that day were disjointed. Distorted. The twisted details were forcing him to second-guess what was fact and what was the embellishment of his sleep-deprived brain.

A wave of vertigo crashed over him.

He staggered, thrusting out an arm to steady himself against the wall.

Henry grabbed him in an instant. 'Nick? Nick, are you okay?'

Blowing out a breath, Nick nodded. He really needed to stop skipping breakfast. 'Just a bit dizzy, that's all.'

'Do you need to sit down? I think you should call in sick. You're ill.'

Nick shook his head, regretting the action immediately. 'No, it's alright. I'm alright.' He rubbed his forehead and suppressed a groan.

Something unreadable touched Henry's expression.

'Really, I'm alright.' Nick straightened.

'You're not. You need to call in sick.'

'I don't—' Nick lowered his voice; he didn't need another blazing row before work. 'I don't need to call in sick. I've got enough paperwork waiting for me as it is. Henry, I promise you I'm okay.' He put on a smile. 'How about I bring us back some Singapore Ho Fun noodles with crispy tofu after my shift? We can open some wine, watch some TV?'

The lines on Henry's forehead smoothed a little. 'I'd love that, but I'm working a double, remember?'

Nick held the smile in place. He didn't remember. Because Henry had forgotten to tell him.

He may as well have said it aloud.

Henry sucked in his cheeks and exhaled loudly through his nose. 'I did tell you. Last night. I'm car sharing so that I don't have to get an Uber.' He hunkered down beside Lily, nuzzled her fur and wrapped her in a hug. She gave him a big doggie grin, tail thrashing from side to side. 'I'm getting picked up in about half an hour.'

'Maybe tomorrow night then?' Nick grabbed his keys off the hook, walked towards the front door and unlocked it. He turned, waiting for Henry's response, hand over the door handle.

'I really think you should call in sick today,' he replied. 'Henry...'

'It's not as if I'm even going to be here, I'll be at work. You won't need to worry about me being under your feet all day.' His mouth twisted. 'Or need to prolong your shift, just to avoid me.'

And there it was. Right on cue.

Nick wasn't doing this, not today. He didn't have the energy.

'Look, I need to go.' Nick tugged at the sleeve of his coat, glancing at his watch. 7.35am. *Shit.* Lovett was going to tear him a new one. 'I'll see you both later. I love you.'

Before Henry could argue, he'd opened the front door, slipped through, and closed it firmly behind him.

His fingers had barely touched the handle of the silver Hyundai Ioniq when he heard the door open again. He looked back, bracing for the tirade.

'Nick, please be careful. I don't know what I'd do if anything ever happened to you.'

The sudden change of tack and soft pitch of Henry's voice gave Nick pause. What had gotten into him? 'I will. I promise.' Nick lowered himself into the Hyundai and pulled the door closed.

He started the engine and glanced in the rear-view mirror. Henry was still watching him; his anxious expression sent a chill down Nick's spine. Shifting into gear, Nick focused on the road and pulled out of the driveway.

Henry was worrying over nothing. In all his years on the force, the worst that had ever happened to him was getting bitten by a drunk. Why should today be any different?

Chapter 5

Nick gritted his teeth when the light switched from amber to red. He hit the brake. He could have made it if he'd put his foot down, but Henry's parting words still had him on edge. He sighed as their disagreement played through his mind for the hundredth time.

Henry had taken an instant dislike to Charlie the first time they'd met. But recently, that animosity had ramped up a level. Sure, Charlie could be a grouch and his obsessive quirks sometimes got a bit much, but he was a decent guy. And his detective skills were second to none. His seat was barely cold before unsolved crimes had pulled him out of retirement. The man was a legend around the station.

That was the reason Nick had called him in to help after those teenagers had been murdered in Wilcott Road cemetery, three months ago. That and the fact that the killings had shared similarities to the Caravan Cannibal case Charlie had been investigating in the eighties. Nick hadn't been lying when he'd told Charlie that they still used his old case files in training, or that he'd dusted them off when he'd found out Charlie was being brought back in as a civvy.

The Caravan Cannibal. Even as a rookie, the thought of some deranged murderer walking the streets had made the hairs on the back of Nick's neck stand on end. But the man who'd attacked Charlie couldn't have been the original killer; at a push, he'd looked to be in his late thirties...

Nick gripped the steering wheel, knuckles white. A sharp pain stabbed him between the eyes, forcing a breath from his mouth. He squeezed his eyes shut and inhaled deeply, past the pounding in his chest.

What was it about the killer that he couldn't remember? There was a hidden memory there, he knew it. Something about a knife. Something relevant.

No. Not a knife. It was more ornate. Ceremonial. Almost antique looking.

The memory fractured in his mind's eye. He grasped for a fragment, for anything vaguely tangible, only for it to shatter into an insubstantial mist. The more he tried to focus the greater the pressure inside his head became. He was veering towards a migraine, but if he could just hold onto one image, long enough to make out the true detail...

The blast of a horn brought him back into the moment. His eyes snapped open, fixing on the green light. Raising his hand in apology to the driver behind, Nick pulled away and made an effort to steady his breathing once again.

He glanced at the clock on the dash and grimaced. If an RTA didn't finish him off, Sergeant Lovett most definitely would. Maybe he'd get lucky; maybe she wouldn't notice him slip in. As long as he didn't give her any reason to want his head on a plate, he'd be fine.

A nagging feeling tugged at the back of his mind. He glanced down at his chest, where his warrant card should be hanging. His stomach sank.

I can't catch a break.

If there was one thing guaranteed to land him in the shit, it was forgetting that. He could have sworn he'd put the lanyard on. Maybe it had snapped... Had he lost it somewhere?

He rummaged in his left coat pocket. Nothing. Switching hands, he tried the other pocket.

'Fuck.' He slammed his fist down on the steering wheel.

There was nothing for it. He had to drive back home and get it. But first, he needed to phone Lovett and tell her he would be running late.

Nick brought the car to a screeching halt across his driveway, wrenched on the handbrake and clambered out. He slammed the door shut and sprinted towards the house.

Flicking through the assortment of keys on the chain, a low curse escaped his lips. Why were there so many of the damn things? Were they breeding?

After several frustrated seconds, he found the right one, unlocked the front door, hauled it open with a grunt and wrestled the key free. When a quick eyeball of the coat rack revealed no warrant card, he raced up the stairs and into the bedroom.

There, on the nightstand, still attached to its lanyard, was his card.

Exhaling, he snatched it up and slipped it over his neck. He didn't dare look at his watch as he hurried back downstairs.

An ear-splitting screech followed by a metallic *thunk* brought him up short.

His gut clenched.

I left the front door open.

He raced outside, feet pounding the driveway, heart in his throat.

In the middle of the road, slumped across the tarmac a few feet from the dented front of a burnt-orange Mustang was his dog. His Lily.

Nick was beside her in an instant. He dropped to his knees and placed a gentle hand on her back. The soft rise and fall of her fur beneath his fingers sent such a flood of relief through him, he felt moisture in the corners of his eyes.

'Lily, thank God!'

He smoothed his hand over her coat and assessed her for injuries. She lifted her head, pink collar jangling, and whimpered. It was more than he could bear. Warm tears tracked down his cheeks. Maybe if he wasn't so exhausted he'd have been able to keep a handle on his emotions.

'I don't know why you're fucking crying, mate. Look at the state of my car.'

Nick started. His head snapped up towards the voice. He swiped at his eyes. A low growl rumbled through Lily's chest. Hackles raised, she scrambled up—claws skittering on the tarmac—and stood, teeth bared.

'Are you gonna pay for this?' A hulking mass of indignation loomed over him.

Veins bulged at the sides of the man's temples; a flush of anger coloured his cheeks, spreading over the visible tattoos on his neck. His mouth, hidden beneath a thick, wiry black beard streaked with grey, was set in a snarl.

'Are you fucking deaf, you stupid ginger prick? I *said*, are you gonna pay for this?' Flecks of spit flew from the man's mouth as he jabbed his finger in the direction of the Mustang.

Nick rose to his feet, his eyes never leaving the stranger.

Jesus. Only now that he was standing could he truly appreciate the difference between them. Although they were a similar height, five feet eight if an inch, the man was thick with muscle. Hard knots strained the ink on his arms as he continued to point at the dent in his bonnet.

As Lily's owner, Nick was technically the one at fault, even if this guy was being a complete dick. He still hadn't even asked if Lily was okay. But dick or not, he was right. Nick *should* pay for the damage. At the very least offer an apology. Maybe one would defuse the situation.

'You hit my dog, you roided up arsehole.' The astonishment Nick felt as the words left his mouth was mirrored, if only for a moment, in the face of the stranger. He pressed on, adrenaline coursing through his veins. 'By law, this needs to be reported.'

The man's face darkened. His hardened grey eyes flicked to Nick's warrant card. 'Copper, are you? You think I'm impressed? Fuck off. Tell you what I'm gonna do, pretty boy. I'm gonna let you get your wallet out. I'm gonna let you hand it to me. And then I'm gonna leave.'

'You're not serious?'

'Oh, I'm serious alright. Hand over your wallet. Now. Or things are gonna get ugly.'

Nick's lips pressed into a thin line. 'Sir, please get back into your vehicle.'

'Sir? Fucking sir?' The man threw up his arms and made a slow circle in the road. 'Who does this prick think he is?' He dropped his arms and took a menacing step forward. 'Wallet. Now. I won't tell you again.'

Lily edged towards the stranger, head low, ears pinned against her skull. Every movement was precise, deliberate, as she positioned herself between him and Nick.

The man palmed a hand down his beard and scoffed.

Lily barked; the sound was so harsh and sudden that Nick flinched and took an involuntary step back. Loose tarmac shifted under his heel. He tripped and landed on his backside with a jolt. His blood turned to ice. If he didn't get back on his feet, there would be no telling what might happen. Lurching up, Nick readied himself for an attack.

The stranger hadn't moved an inch. His gaze was locked on Lily, his previously flushed face now drained of all colour. His tongue darted across his lower lip, the muscles beneath his left eye twitching.

Maybe, despite the bravado and hostility, he was afraid of dogs?

He raised his hands in a placating gesture. 'Yeah, no... you're right. I'll get back in my car.'

Nick's brow furrowed as he watched the man back away and climb into the Mustang. What in the hell? Had he missed something? He frowned at the damage to the front of the car then looked at Lily.

The throaty growl of the engine tore Nick's attention away from his dog. The vehicle cut around him. Nick quickly made a mental note of the registration before the car roared down the road.

Lily tilted her head and huffed out a breath. Her tail whipped through the air. Looking immensely pleased with herself, she barked again—quieter this time—then trotted towards Nick, nudged his hand with her nose and gave his fingers a lick.

'You don't look hurt. Better call the vet, just in case.'

Fishing his phone out of his pocket, Nick shook his head and led Lily back to the house. This was turning out to be an absolute mare of a morning and he hadn't stepped foot inside the station yet.

Chapter 6

The car jolted over another speed bump. Banning made a disapproving noise, shifting his focus from his window to the driver. He gave the man a sour look.

The driver winced, eyeing him apologetically in the rear-view mirror. 'Sorry, sir.'

'That's okay, Oliver,' Banning said, his smile returning. 'It won't happen again, will it?'

'No, sir.' Oliver's voice tailed off in a whisper. His gloved hands gripped the steering wheel tighter.

Repositioning himself in the leather seats, Banning turned his attention to the incubus sitting opposite him. He narrowed his eyes at the demon. Archibald Morgan had made sure that Banning's ongoing education included the study of creatures that inhabited the realm of fire and shadow. In the eight years he had spent under his mentor's guidance, he'd only just scratched the surface. And the more Banning learnt about the abominations, the more he despised them.

They were vermin. Parasites. Some were little more than mindless beasts, driven by basic needs and bloodlust. And while they posed a threat, it was the intelligent ones you really had to watch. The masters of manipulation and lies. The ones that whispered honeyed words in your ear while plunging a blade into your back. He'd never really understood how so many fell victim to their advances—a demon was still a demon after all. But now, looking at Heimerich, it was easy to see why. Visually, it was impossible to distinguish the incubus from a mortal man. It was like a sick perversion of nature. A sadistic joke at the expense of humankind.

But then, it suddenly made sense. What better way to hunt than to be indistinguishable from one's prey?

'I'm curious,' Banning said, causing Heimerich to startle. 'Does it offend you that your species has become synonymous with sexual deviancy?'

Heimerich frowned. He'd been obstinately quiet since entering the car, speaking only when spoken to and offering nothing in the way of conversation. It had made for a dull journey so far. Maybe Banning *should* have had the creature write down the address. It certainly would've made things easier. But he didn't know the incubus, didn't know his motivations, and that made him a wildcard. If Heimerich exposed their plans, it would ruin the surprise for his mentor. Worse still, someone else might try and muscle in. He couldn't take that risk. It wouldn't be the first time someone had tried to ingratiate themselves with Archibald Morgan at his expense.

Evans.

No. It made more sense to keep the incubus by his side. To control the situation. Even if the creature was as dull as ditchwater. Still, he would never let it be said that Banning Lawrence couldn't make his own fun.

'Preying on unsuspecting women while they sleep?' he said, a smirk tugging at the corner of his mouth. 'I mean, it's got to sting, right? To be considered nothing more than serial rapists? Unless, of course, there's some truth to the folklore?'

Heimerich lifted his chin sharply, a challenge in the set of his jaw. 'There's no truth to it.'

Finally, a little entertainment.

'No? The stories had to originate from somewhere. We're talking thousands of years old, in countries and cultures throughout the world. You can't honestly sit there and tell me there's nothing to it? Wait, wait, don't tell me, I know what you're going to say... Sleep paralysis.'

The incubus met his eyes. 'Humans always turn to fantasy to give meaning to the things they don't understand.'

'Yet you *do* feed on their life force. Without consent. Skulking around in the dead of night, concealed by the shadows. Waiting until your victim is asleep until you quite literally suck the life out of them. Is that really much better?'

'Of course it is,' Heimerich spat. 'Their lost vitality is replenished within hours. What we do doesn't cause any lasting harm.'

'Are you sure about that? Hand on your heart, tell me now that no one has ever died in their sleep because one of your kind couldn't control their urge to feed.

Tell me that not a single person has ever woken to find a demon in their bed draining them dry. The psychological implications alone must be debilitating.' His voice grew cold as the ghosts of his past influenced his next words. 'Everyone thinking you're lying or that you've gone mad. Not a single person believing a word you say, not even those closest to you.'

'I... I can't say for sure.'

'No. I didn't think so.' Banning's lips twitched. This had become distinctly less amusing. 'No wonder your kind is reviled, hunted to the brink of extinction. No wonder why what's left of you usually hides in the veil between realms.'

'*My* kind reviled?' There was a fire in the incubus' eyes now. 'What about *your* kind? Yeah, I know exactly what you are. You're the same as him, the same as Morgan—an energy leech. Jesus, you even sound like him. Nobody your age talks like that.'

'What can I say? Eight years of mentorship has rubbed off on me.'

Heimerich continued as if Banning hadn't spoken, 'It's because of your kind that the witch hunts started. Tens of thousands of innocent people murdered—'

'Tens of thousands?' Banning scoffed. 'More people have died from the flu. And how many people have breathed their last breath at the hands of demons? How many men, women and children have had their lives destroyed by monsters like you?'

'Monsters like me? Archibald Morgan—'

'Choose your next words carefully, *demon*. I think you'd be wise to remember who it is that puts bread on your table.'

Heimerich's teeth clicked together. He turned from Banning and glared out the window.

Banning's blood boiled. How dare this creature pass judgement on him and his kind? Demons had taken everything from him. *Everything.* They were a blight. A disease in need of eradication. The audacity of him...

Perhaps it was time he showed Heimerich his place, established the hierarchy.

'You know, I've never seen an incubus in its true state before.'

The car was quiet, save for the slight creak of the suspension as it crested another speed bump.

Banning added, 'I'd like to see you transform.'

The incubus turned back and spoke in a low voice. 'No.'

'No?'

'No.' Firmer this time.

'It would make me happy.'

Heimerich stared back at him, defiance etched on his face.

Banning continued. 'I really must insist.'

The creature said nothing, merely wrinkled his nose and faced the window again.

'Fair enough...' Banning gave a lazy shrug and nestled into the leather. He leant his head against the headrest. 'It's not like I can *force* you to show me, is it?'

The driver sucked in a breath, his gaze flicking from Banning to Heimerich in the rear-view mirror. He shrank down in his seat.

Banning drew energy from the air around them, pulling it into him without effort. The temperature in the car plummeted and feathers of ice formed in crystalline plumes across the rear windows. Heimerich's eyes widened, his breath fogging.

No harm in a little theatrics now and again.

Banning held out his hand, willing his power forth. 'Did you know magic has its own frequency?' An orb of green blazed bright in his scarred palm, casting an eerie glow that enveloped the back of the car. 'It usually manifests as blue, sometimes white. Mine, as you can see, is green.'

Banning paused, taking great pleasure in seeing the creature's jaw slacken.

'Here's where it gets interesting,' Banning continued. 'What you see before you is pure magic. Being a cryptid, you're well aware of the energy that pervades our world, seeping in from the realms beyond the veil. Certain humans... gifted humans shall we say, like me, have the ability to draw upon it, to shape it to our will. The spells we cast are just a transfer of that energy. But you know that already, don't you?'

The incubus gave a single nod. His eyes darted from the orb to Banning and back again.

'That kind of energy has no perceivable colour. But when converted to pure magic, either through ritual or a conduit—' he pointed to himself with his other hand,

'—it manifests with its own frequency. Now, and this is the *really* interesting part, that frequency is determined by the individual, how their body and mind processes and converts that energy. Like I said, my magic is green. It wasn't always. Care to hazard a guess as to what changed?'

Banning didn't disguise his bitter tone or hide the sharp twist of his mouth. Not that Heimerich would have noticed; his eyes were still fixated on the glowing ball of light. He wasn't sure if the incubus' lack of response made him more or less angry. What was it Banning had wanted? Some kind of acknowledgement from this demon, that he'd been irrevocably changed at the hands of one of its brethren? Whatever the reason for the torment, it was obvious the creature wasn't taking the bait, and Banning wasn't about to reopen old wounds for the sake of an explanation.

'But, I digress,' he continued. 'What you probably don't know is that not all of my kind is capable of creating pure magic. It's a skill. It requires a lot of strength and ability. Of course, the more powerful you become the less effort it takes. What I'm doing here would be a simple illumination for Archibald Morgan. Child's play. So, why am I telling you all of this?'

Banning's misty breath eddied in the space between them. He said nothing more until he had the incubus' full attention. Banning made a slow fist. The sphere of green enclosed his hand, spreading up and out from his ruined knuckles in an ethereal blade. 'I'm telling you this because while being struck by energy hurts, being struck by pure magic is torture.'

He lunged forward, driving the blade into the creature's side, feeling his magic penetrate flesh and muscle.

Heimerich roared. A raw and guttural sound of pure agony.

Heimerich's form detonated into a mass of writhing shadow and shredded clothing. Twisted tendrils, so black they devoured the light around them, fanned out from the incubus like ravaged wings. Its body was carved obsidian. Each chiselled muscle was illuminated by a web of molten veins that pulsed in time with the rise and fall of its chest. Its fingertips were fashioned into lethal claws, marking it for what it truly was: a predator. A monster. But it was the creature's face that really caught Banning's attention. The features had been replaced by hollows where the eyes should be. They smouldered like two pits of magma, wisps of smoke drifting out from their edges.

In the back of the car, the incubus stared at him. The only movement between them was the coiling fronds of shadow. There was no way that Banning could discern the creature's expression, but he could hazard a guess.

He beamed. The spectral light of the dagger winked out when he clapped his hands together. 'Delightful. That wasn't so hard now, was it?'

Banning heard a soft velvet snap as Heimerich transmuted back into his human form. He sat naked and shuddering, hand clamped against his injured side.

A tattered fragment of what had once been his jacket fell from the headrest to join the scraps of fabric around him.

'Don't worry, I haven't caused any lasting damage,' Banning said conversationally, trailing a finger over one of the shimmering streaks on the upholstery, marked by one of the creature's black tendrils. 'But next time...' He left the threat hanging.

Heimerich gritted his teeth. 'He's sick. You know that, don't you?'

The urgency in his words took Banning by surprise. 'Pardon?'

The creature snatched at a breath. 'Archibald Morgan. I saw the demon rot. He's infected.'

'Oh that.' Banning chuckled. 'I'm not blind, Heimerich.'

'Then you know what it's doing to him. What he'll become. It's only a matter of time before he loses control.'

Banning held up a hand. 'Let me just stop you there. If this is the part where you suggest a coup, I have to tell you right off the bat, I'm not interested. I mean, I'm impressed. I really didn't think you had it in you, but I'm not interested.'

'He'll go insane.'

'I'm well aware of the side effects.'

'*Side effects?* The demon rot is poisoning him. His body. His mind.'

Brushing a shred of Heimerich's T-shirt from the seat, Banning kept his voice neutral, 'You would be wise to watch your mouth. If you're trying to appeal to my humanity, let me make this clear, I have none. I know where my loyalties lie. Do you?'

Heimerich bowed his head. 'Yes.'

'Good. Now that that's been cleared up, how about we try for some civil conversation? Heimerich. That's a German name. You don't sound German.'

The creature's jaw stiffened. 'You don't sound like a monster.'

'There's only one monster sitting in this car.'

'Agreed.'

Banning smirked. 'Feisty. I like it.'

The car slowed to a halt.

'I trust you brought spare clothing as instructed, Heimerich?'

The incubus nodded, not looking up, and bent to retrieve a silver ring from the footwell. With a fleeting look of relief, he slipped it back on his finger.

'Excellent, because it looks like we're here.'

Chapter 7

CHARLIE SUCKED IN ANOTHER breath and blew it out. Each pounding footfall on the treadmill sent fire searing through his calves. There was no way it hadn't been twelve minutes yet.

'That's great, Charles. Keep walking as the treadmill slows down.' Sachiko tapped on the console beside him, reducing the speed.

Casting a side-long glance at her, Charlie wiped the back of his hand across his sweat-slicked brow. 'That was *not* a stress test. That was attempted murder.'

Sachiko smiled, unfazed by his tone. He couldn't decide whether her constant sunshine attitude towards everything was endearing or just downright irritating. Right this second, it was the latter.

'For someone in their mid-sixties you're remarkably fit, even without the Maw's influence. I had to push you.'

Charlie pressed his lips together.

Tsking, Sachiko stepped closer and took the blood pressure cuff off his arm. 'Don't be such a baby, it wasn't that bad.' She motioned for him to step off the machine and moved back to the console.

He scowled at the back of her head. 'Really? I don't see you volunteering. Do we seriously have to do this every time I'm here, or is this just some sort of sadist kink?'

Sachiko's shoulders shook; it took him a heartbeat to realise that she was laughing. He huffed out a sigh.

'I'm sorry.' She faced him, eyes crinkling at the corners. 'It's just I've never heard anyone grump quite as much as you do.'

'I do not grump.'

Sachiko's composure crumbled. She covered her mouth to disguise her giggle and ended up snorting. Her eyes widened and it spurred her into a full-blown fit of hoots and titters.

Charlie smiled.

After a minute, Sachiko exhaled and rubbed at the tears that had streaked down her cheeks. 'Come on, let's get those things off of you.' She looked up at his face, eyes dancing, then clamped her mouth shut in what he assumed was another effort to regain control.

Sachiko pulled the electrodes from Charlie's bare chest, they tugged lightly at his skin. Her gaze drifted over the scars that marked his body. It was barely a glance, but it was enough.

He drew in on himself, hunching over in an almost subconscious gesture. No doubt she'd seen worse—who knew what kind of injuries a typical O.O.T.I.S agent might sustain—but it didn't make a difference. Not to him. She'd never asked about them though. And he was grateful for that if nothing else.

'Right, you can change back into your own clothes now.' Sachiko nodded at a door in the far corner leading to one of two wet rooms. 'I've put out fresh towels if you want to grab a quick shower.'

'And then we're done?' Her tight expression gave him the answer and his shoulders rounded.

'We're done with the stress test,' she offered brightly.

Charlie combed his fingers through the curls of his damp hair. Christ, how long was this going to take?

'Just think of it this w—'

The single piercing wail of an alarm cut Sachiko off.

Charlie tensed. He blinked rapidly, seeing the amber light pulsing from the ceiling-mounted beacons.

'What's going on?'

'Containment breach.'

He didn't even want to think about *what* might have breached its containment. 'Do we need to be worried?'

'We're in the middle of the most secure facility this side of London. We'll be fine. It's only an amber alert. If it was red or black, then there'd be some cause for concern.'

'Should I even ask?'

Sachiko offered him a half-smile. 'Probably best not to.'

A dull throb spread from the sigil between his thumb and index finger on his left hand, radiating out until his palm tingled. That couldn't be good.

'Charles?' Sachiko frowned. 'What's wrong?'

The intensity in his hand built until it was no longer a tingle but a sharp, stabbing pain that demanded his immediate attention. Charlie made a slow circle where he stood, scanning the room. Movement in his peripheral vision snapped his head to the right. Sachiko followed his gaze and gasped.

Smoke billowed in from one of the wall vents just above the louvred steel door, bringing with it a vile stench of rotting fish and eggs. Rather than dissipate, the smoke curled in on itself, rolling upward as it solidified into an elongated, eel-like creature. It undulated in place, silver plates gleaming, as it cut repeating S shapes in the air with each serpentine movement of its body. Two penetrating yellow eyes stared at them, set so low on both sides of the creature's head that they were fused with the top row of serrated teeth jutting out from its hissing jaws. Its mouth snapped shut, barbels quivering, as a row of spines connected by a thin membrane shot up from its back with a snap. The creature surged through the air towards them.

Charlie threw out his arm, forcing Sachiko behind him. The creature clamped its teeth on his flesh, where her face had just been a second ago. Pain ripped through his muscle as the eel locked its jaw and jerked his arm violently. Charlie roared as blood flowed from his shredded skin to spatter across the floor. He grabbed at the creature, yanking at it, in a desperate attempt to prise it off. When that didn't work, he forced his hand between its slick, bloodied jaws and pulled. His fingers sliced open on the edges of its razor-sharp teeth. The eel didn't budge. If anything, it bit down harder.

Sachiko was screeching something in Japanese behind him, the words just about audible over his own laboured grunts. A wave of nausea rolled over him. He smelt charred meat. Hot black ooze trickled from his punctured flesh, dribbling down his arm and making a sputtering, sizzling sound against the floor tiles. His exposed skin blistered wherever the ooze touched; the angry red welts burst with sickening wet pops.

Charlie's heart hammered his chest. His lungs were on fire. He fought to gulp down a breath. Spots danced across his vision as vertigo added to the nausea.

The eel was poisoning him.

The sigil flared. Charlie clenched his fist involuntarily. Cool, hard marble pressed into his palm. His eyes bulged as he stared down at Kar'roc's Maw.

The alarm's siren had started again in earnest, yet it seemed oddly distant.

The creature released its hold, teeth slipping out of his arm with a wet sucking noise. It stretched open its dripping jaw and hissed, yellow eyes fixed on the red gemstone in the dagger's hilt.

Charlie staggered; the room spun around him. Beads of sweat dripped off his brow. He blinked the wet away and used every ounce of strength he had to stay upright. With a shaky swipe of his fist, he brandished the Maw at the creature. It hissed again, slinking back through the air in the same strange, rolling motion.

The door exploded inwards. The black suit burst into the room, hands moving in deliberate patterns, as if he were manipulating the threads of some invisible web. He thrust out his palms, sending a glowing-blue disc of intricate shapes and symbols streaking towards the creature. Blinding white light flared bright. Charlie squeezed his eyes shut.

It was a mistake.

The room lurched from the effects of vertigo. If it hadn't been for someone with their arms around his chest, he would have fallen. He sucked in a breath and forced his eyelids open. The creature was little more than a smouldering pile of ash on the floor.

Charlie swayed, the weight of his own limbs threatening to topple him.

'Diane. Quick! Help me get him on the table.' Sachiko's voice strained as she fought to keep him upright. 'We don't have long before the venom shuts down his respiratory system.'

Diane?

He could just about make out the shape of her as she rushed towards him. The rich scent of her perfume wafted around him, spices and fruit. Soft fingers pressed into his bare chest, cold against his burning skin.

'Dee...' His mouth felt clumsy.

'Charlie!'

He pitched forward into the darkness, Diane's voice fading away.

Chapter 8

From inside the car Banning extended his senses out. He detected nothing inherently magical within the vicinity, which meant no Charlie Haynes and, by extension, no O.O.T.I.S. If the Order had any sense, there'd have been someone watching the house at all times, regardless of whether Mr Haynes was there or not. Banning had expected *some* precautions, a latent ward at least. But the organisation had grown arrogant, so sure of its own authority that it had overlooked the little details.

Ignorance was dangerous. But arrogance was lethal.

He faced the incubus. 'I assume your wife is human?'

Heimerich pulled a T-shirt down over his head, flinching as the material grazed his injured side. His scowl gave way to confusion. 'My wife?'

Banning nodded at the silver band on the creature's finger.

'I... oh. Yes. She is.'

'And does she know what you are?'

The incubus stiffened. 'No.'

'A marriage built on lies?' Banning smiled. 'There's no possible way that will end badly.'

Heimerich's scowl returned. His narrowed eyes trailed down Banning's left arm to his hand.

Banning snorted in amusement. He lifted his ruined hand, turning it this way and that, so the incubus could get a good look at the puckered scar tissue. 'Looking for a ring? Or just wondering what happened to me?'

Silence followed.

Banning continued. 'I'm not the settling down type.'

Thoughts of Naomie entered his mind. The sound of her laugh. The smell of her hair. The feel of her cheek beneath his fingertips...

No.

Quashing the ache in his chest, Banning gestured to his face and gave the creature a wide grin. 'Far too pretty to be tamed, and way too young to be tied down.'

When the incubus finished dressing, Banning signalled to the driver. The man exited the car and opened the rear door with a dutiful nod.

'Keep the engine running, Oliver,' Banning said, adjusting his suit jacket as he climbed out. 'We won't be long.'

'Yes, sir.'

The morning air was bitterly cold. Vast swathes of grey pleated the sky, threatening snow. Each breath stung at his nostrils. He pulled instinctively at the threads of natural energy around him—the dormant vegetation, the unseen wildlife, even the men feet from where he stood—to fend off the worst of the chill. Just a little energy. Nothing that would be noticed. Nothing that would be missed.

Banning looked around. The row of terraced houses in yellow brick stretched out as far as the eye could see. Each had its own block-paved driveway and a neat, ankle-high strip of evergreen hedgerow to mark out the property boundary. There were even matching hanging baskets, rendered bare by the season, suspended from the porch canopies above each front door.

Quaint. Worlds apart from the generous stone cottage almost three-hundred miles away, bequeathed to him and his brother by his late grandmother. His jaw clenched at the unbidden thought.

The incubus joined him.

'Isn't this charming?' Banning waved his hand absently. He strode forward.

All that separated him from the occupants was a slab of composite and a strip of glass. He tested the handle.

Locked.

Shaking his head, he willed energy from his core and directed it through his fingers into the keyhole. Metal scraped and clicked as the mechanism yielded to his magic. With a slow smile, he tugged the handle down and opened the door.

Heat hit him, as well as the sounds of a television. Someone was definitely home.

'After you.' Banning moved aside and made a sweeping gesture with his arm. Heimerich crossed the threshold and Banning closed the door gently behind them.

The inside of the house was small, the layout unimaginative. A cookie-cutter new-build if ever there was—staircase to the left, kitchen to the right. It took no time at all to reach the living room, where a raven-haired child sat crossed-legged in the middle of the floor, hypnotised by the screen. Even if she didn't have her back to them, Banning was confident the oblivious girl wouldn't have noticed their arrival anyway.

He pushed past the incubus, leaving the creature to pace in the doorway looking more uncomfortable by the second, and took a seat on the sofa behind the child. The noise of the film drowned out his movements.

Drumming his fingers lightly on his knee with one hand, Banning reached inside his pocket with the other, closing his fingers around an object, and appraised the room. It was neat, excessively so. Surprising, given that the girl in front of him, Charlie Hayne's granddaughter, looked to be eight years old—children were definitely not neat. His eye was drawn to a trio of ornate vases, differently sized, displayed on a copper-framed side table. With the glass facetted at irregular angles, they resembled shards of crystal. Each had a blue, green, pink and gold lustre that reminded him of a petrol spill.

Focusing on the child, Banning flicked his wrist casually at the television. The air shuddered. Momentary static flashed across the screen before it went black. The girl snatched the remote off the carpet beside her and jabbed at the buttons with increasing frustration. She huffed and moved to get up.

Her eyes widened in the reflection of the black screen. She froze in place, a startled gasp stuck in her throat.

Banning offered her a lazy wave.

She turned, almost reluctantly, as though given enough time her mind would stop playing tricks on her. Her mouth made an O shape. She sucked in a breath but before she could release the scream, Banning unfurled his palm and blew a fine white powder into her face. She blinked once then crumpled in a heap.

Simple enough.

Banning stood and brushed the remaining residue from his hand.

'What was that?' Heimerich said, giving the child a concerned glance.

'Just a little sedative.' He stepped towards the vases. 'Pick her up would you?'

'Sedative?'

'Yes, sedative.' He lifted the largest vase, testing its weight. 'You're wondering why I didn't just use my magic?' The look on Heimerich's face confirmed his guess. 'I could have. Perhaps reduced the blood flow to her brain. Same end result. Risky though. And if I didn't maintain that connection, there'd be no telling when she'd regain consciousness. Minutes? Seconds? We wouldn't want her waking up in the back of the car now, would we? All that screaming? Crying? Hard pass.'

'Will she be okay?'

'Heimerich, you cut me to the quick.' Banning shook his head in mock disappointment. 'Of course she'll be okay. I don't hurt children. Now, pick her up.'

The creature made no effort to conceal his disdain, lips thinning into hard lines. He walked across the room and carefully scooped up the child.

'Wait.' Banning heaved out a sigh, staring forlornly at the vase in his hands. His voice was scarcely a whisper. 'I'm not sure I can do this.' He turned to face Heimerich. 'This isn't right, is it?'

Something like hope sparked in the creature's dark eyes, battling with his obvious suspicion.

'I can't carry all three of these vases. I'll have to leave one behind.'

Heimerich muttered something too quiet to make out.

Banning shook his head. 'No, no. You're right. I'll just have to make two trips.'

He grinned as he picked up the second vase, arranging it with the first, so that they were nestled against his chest. He was still marvelling at the fusion of colours on his way to the hallway when he heard a gasp.

His head snapped up.

Stood in the hall was a woman with porcelain skin and chestnut-brown hair. The girl's mother. Her shock quickly morphed to fear, then to anger. Her green eyes narrowed into slits. In one swift motion, she brought her knee up and drove it into Banning's crotch.

Banning doubled over, making a sound somewhere between a grunt and a shriek. As he pitched onto the tiles, the vases slipped from his grip. He curled up into a foetal position, cupping his genitals. He tried to snatch a breath, but it was like an invisible fist was wrenching at his vital organs. Squeezing his eyes shut, he tried not to vomit.

Trying to block out the pain, Banning focused on the power coursing through him. He visualised it until all distractions outside of his body fell away. Mustering his concentration, he willed the power to become a restorative force. It quickly repaired the ruptured tissue.

In seconds he was back on his feet.

The mother must have stepped over him while he was writhing on the floor, because she was now blocking the doorway facing Heimerich, her body rigid.

With a snarl, Banning snatched up what remained of the largest vase and brought it down on the back of her head. Glass shattered, sending out a spray of shimmering shards. The force of the blow jolted up his arms.

The woman dropped to the floor.

Banning's breath came hard and fast. His muscles quivered.

'Bitch.' He clenched his fists as he glared down at the woman, and counted back from ten.

Blood seeped from a gash on her scalp, matting in her hair and pooling on the tiles. A stark crimson contrast to the white porcelain.

Banning waited for the fire in his chest to burn itself out. With it went the urge to drive his foot through her skull. He hunkered down beside her and flipped her easily onto her back. Funny, conscious, she'd come across as a more worthy opponent. Desperation and fury had given her a formidable presence.

A mother's love.

The thought ricocheted like a bullet inside his mind, threatening to obliterate his defences. He felt his face slacken, his muscles tense.

Breathe.

And he did. Deep and slow until the nausea passed.

Banning felt inside his suit jacket pocket for the autoinjector. His fingers came away slick. Biting back a curse, he removed the device, turning it over in his hand. Lindwurm venom was leaking from a hairline crack in the glass cartridge it carried. It must have broken when he'd fallen. He stuck the now useless device back into his pocket and wiped his fingers on the front of his waistcoat.

'Is she alive?'

Heimerich's voice startled him.

Banning studied the woman's face. Her prominent cheekbones. Her long, dark lashes. The Cupid's bow shape of her lips. 'She is. Very much so.' He trailed his fingers down her cheek and fed enough energy into her to stem the bleeding. When the flesh of her scalp had knitted back together he dropped his hand.

Heimerich cleared his throat, unease plain on his face.

Banning stood, his expression neutral. In truth, the silent accusation stung. And that pissed him off. He'd spent years honing his reputation. He was a threat. A weapon. Detached. Deadly. Why should he care about the opinions of this parasite? Why should he care about the opinions of anyone? In the last eight years, the only person who'd ever placed any sort of faith in him, who'd taken the time to really get to know him, was his mentor.

And Naomie.

He smothered the thought before it could spark into life.

Heimerich was watching him beneath knitted eyebrows, the reproach obvious.

'Calm down, Heimerich. There's no fun in *that*. Where's the chase, the sport? I'm not in the habit of taking women against their will.' He caught the *really?* look on the incubus' face and the irony of his words sank in. Banning waved his hand dismissively at the unconscious woman. 'You know what I mean. Give me the girl. You take this one. We may as well give Mr Haynes' more than one reason to hand over the dagger.'

The creature passed him the child and bent to pick up the woman. Banning grinned and poked him in the ribs. A flare of green sparked from one fingertip. The incubus yelped. Tendrils of shadow ripped through the back of his T-shirt, thrashing out in billowing fronds. Fronds that left iridescent scars on the wall.

Banning chuckled and moved the child into a less awkward position. 'Delightful. Seeing you come undone is not going to get old anytime soon.'

Heimerich shuddered.

Casting a final glance around, Banning swept his foot through the shattered remains of the vases. 'Such a waste.' He shifted the girl again, eyes drawn to the stain of lindwurm venom on his jacket, and scowled.

He gripped the door handle and looked at the silent creature. 'Be quick. There's something else I need to take care of.'

Chapter 9

'ARE YOU SURE?' THE vet asked again.

Nick bit back his frustration and nodded. 'Yes. By the time I got outside Lily was on the ground. There was a dog-shaped dent in the bonnet of the car.'

The woman made a sceptical noise and glanced up at him. He got the message loud and clear—she thought he was wasting her time. Lily yawned, pink tongue curling upward as her muzzle stretched open. Nick swore that he'd seen a look of mutual understanding pass between his dog and the vet. *Traitor.*

Stepping behind Lily, the vet prodded the Rottweiler's ribs and stomach, examining the area. 'Everything feels normal. She doesn't seem to be in any pain.' She worked her way back, lifting each leg in turn. Giving Lily a quick fuss, she straightened. 'Other than standing to lose a bit of weight, I can't see any issues. No broken bones. No abnormal masses or change to the size and texture of her organs. Not even a sprain. You say you didn't actually see the car hit her?'

'No.'

'Probably just someone chancing their arm.' She crossed her arms, giving Nick a pointed look. 'Thought they could get you to pay for the existing damage to their car by saying your dog was in the road unsupervised and it caused an accident.'

He felt his cheeks flush. 'But I heard the car hit something.'

'A pothole, maybe? Look, Lily seems absolutely fine. Keep an eye on her and if you notice any change in her behaviour, if she loses her appetite or becomes sluggish, bring her straight back in.'

'Right. Okay, I will. Thank you.'

'Paula at reception will get you all sorted.'

Nick clipped Lily's lead to her collar and walked her back to reception. What the vet said didn't make any sense. He'd heard the screech. The bang. Seen Lily flat on the ground. The car *had* hit her. It was the only logical explanation, wasn't it?

Although, he hadn't actually *seen* the collision. And the driver *had* wanted money... Maybe he'd just imagined the noise. His sleep-deprived brain was just filling in the gaps.

Oh God, what was happening to him?

Nick gave the woman at the reception desk—Paula—a polite smile as he waited to be told the damage. He just wanted to pay and get Lily back home; he'd had about all he could stomach of the morning so far.

His gaze drifted over the mostly empty seats in the waiting area, pausing briefly on an elderly lady with a pet carrier on her lap. The large blue eyes of a Burmese blinked at him. Its owner caught him looking and offered him a wrinkled smile. He returned the gesture and looked up at the clock on the wall.

Shit. Two hours late for his shift already.

Nick stepped into the office. Nodding a quick hello to a few in the Volume Crime unit, he headed through the open-plan space to the bank of desks, where the rest of the Area Crime team were sat.

Sergeant Lovett was frowning at her monitor, the creases in her brow a near-permanent fixture of late. If luck were on his side, he might be able to slip into his seat without drawing her attention. Eyes down, he increased his pace, thankful for the buzz of general activity that dulled his footsteps. One last glance up confirmed that she was still absorbed in her work. Nick touched the headrest of his seat. He wheeled it back, shoulders relaxing.

His empty stomach cramped, rumbling its complaint loud enough to earn him a few glances and one or two amused chuckles. Could this morning get any worse?

'Nick, so nice of you to join us.' Lovett's voice was like iron.

He considered explaining why he was late, but her glare and flared nostrils warned him otherwise. 'Sorry, Vanessa.' He smiled weakly and sat down.

She returned her attention to her monitor, muttering.

'You look like shit.' Sam Bennett swivelled in his chair, one hand on the desk, the other holding a mug of coffee.

'Hello to you, too.'

'Given up on eating all together, have we, vegan boy?' Sam offered him a playful grin. 'Don't tell me you're one of those breatharians? You've already cut out all the best food groups, so it's probably the next logical step.'

'A what?'

'Breatharian. They get all the nutrients they need from air... or it might be light. Maybe both.'

Nick gave him a flat look. 'That's not a thing.'

'It's not a thing for long. Couple of weeks tops, before they keel over, I'd say.' Sam beamed at his own joke, took a sip of his coffee and placed the mug on the desk.

With a shake of his head and a smile on his lips, Nick logged on to his computer and opened up his case files. He scanned the content on screen and grimaced. Another domestic abuse case. Screams had been reported by the victim's neighbours. What was wrong with people? He'd learnt many things over the course of his career. To trust his gut. To recognise when he was being lied to. That good people were capable of bad things and bad people were capable of pure fucking evil. But above all, the one thing that somehow still managed to take him by surprise was that the job never got any easier.

An ache grew behind his eyes. Nick kneaded his brow in an effort to dull it. When it got worse, he exhaled. It was no good; the glare from the monitor was like a knife to his brain. He yanked open one of the desk drawers and rooted inside. After a few fruitless seconds, he pressed it shut. He glanced up to see Sam was watching him, a smile tugging at his lips.

Nick narrowed his eyes. 'What?'

'Didn't find them then?' Before Nick could voice his confusion, Sam leant forward. 'Your balls. I assume that's what you were looking for? I think they're in Lovett's desk.'

'Dick. I was looking for paracetamol.'

'Sure you were.'

Rolling his eyes, Nick shifted back in his chair. He scanned the crime report open on Bennett's desk. 'What've you got?'

'Another aggravated assault at the Green. If they're not throwing bricks through car windows or breaking into neighbours' gardens, they're beating the absolute shit out of one another.'

'Some things never change.'

'Sam?'

The two men turned as one. Sergeant Lovett was standing behind them, report form in hand. Without so much as a glance at Nick, she held the form out to Bennett. 'Duty DS has just allocated us a case. Mother and daughter reported missing from their home by a Mrs Eleanor Bell, a friend who was supposed to be meeting them there. Door ajar, broken glass in the hallway, signs of a struggle. Meghan and Evelyn Bowden-Haynes.'

Nick's heart skipped a beat. '*What?*'

Whether at the interruption or the shock in his voice, Lovett turned to regard him. Her features were tight.

'That's Charlie's daughter and granddaughter.' Nick took a breath. 'Charlie Haynes. He works in unsolved crimes. He's on sick leave.'

Sam let out a low curse.

'I want the case,' Nick said. The sergeant pursed her lips. It sent a jolt of frustration through his chest, but he held her gaze.

Lovett sighed and pinched the bridge of her nose. 'You come in late, *again*, and now you want to choose which cases you're allocated?'

Schooling his expression, Nick said nothing. He wanted this. Needed it. Did that make him a selfish bastard? Probably, but if he could help Charlie in some small way, maybe it would alleviate some of the guilt. Help him work through whatever was still affecting him from that night. Maybe he'd get a decent night's sleep.

She squinted at him. 'You and Charlie are close, are you?'

He knew where this was going.

'Charlie and I are friends. I know Meghan and Evelyn, but not enough that it would cloud my judgement or have an impact on my performance. I'd like to do this.'

Lovett sighed again. 'Nick, you look like sh—'

She broke off, casting a look at the other detectives who were eavesdropping in on their conversation.

She cleared her throat. 'You look like you haven't slept in weeks. I've half a mind to send you home.'

'I'd really like to work on this case. Please, Vanessa.' He ran his tongue over his dry lips. Waiting.

'Fine. Partner up. The two of you can work on it together. Assuming you're alright with that, Sam?' It wasn't a question; apparently Nick needed a babysitter.

The pair exchanged a look before Sam gave her a lazy shrug.

Lovett clucked her tongue. 'Eloquent as always, Detective Bennett.' She turned to leave then paused. 'Eleanor Bell is waiting at the house next door to the crime scene. Number nineteen.'

Nick exhaled. 'Thank you.'

The sergeant gave Sam one last look before returning to her desk.

Downing the last of his coffee, Sam switched off his monitor. 'Come on then, let's see if there are any CID cars left.' He rose from his seat and pointed at Nick's computer. 'Don't forget to log off.'

Obliging, Nick stood and pulled his mobile from his pocket. As an afterthought, he grabbed his A4 notebook from the tray on the desk and tucked it neatly under his arm. He wasn't about to give Lovett any more ammo.

'I'm going to call Charlie.' Nick dialled his number and pressed the phone to his ear. As they walked, his stress levels rose with each ring.

Come on, Charlie, pick up.

When the ring clicked off, he breathed out. But his anxiety lifted again when Charlie's voicemail played.

'Shit.'

'No answer?' Sam asked.

'No. He's staying with them at the moment, Meghan and Evelyn. If they're missing, there's a chance he could be too.'

Sam muttered an incoherent reply.

Nick tried Charlie again. Voicemail. He hissed and pushed open the office door, holding it for Sam.

'I'm sure he's fine,' Sam said. 'Probably just busy. Don't worry.'

Nick wished he shared Sam's confidence.

The detective smiled and clapped him on the shoulder. Nick's mobile slipped from his fingers, landing on the floor with a dull thud just behind him.

Blood rushed to his head as he fumbled for his phone. He straightened in time to see Lovett at her desk give Sam a single nod. When she noticed Nick looking her way, she quickly focused on her monitor.

Nick stood and strode out after Sam. Why did he suddenly feel like he was missing something?

Chapter 10

WITH ANOTHER SCOWL AT the venom stains on his suit, Banning pressed his finger to the biometric scanner. The deadbolt retracted with a low *whir*. Yanking down the handle, he pushed the door open and gestured for Heimerich to enter.

The safe house was never intended as permanent accommodation, but over time it had become a second home. Banning's magic, and the fact that he didn't always play well with others, meant that he'd needed his own space. Something secure. Something isolated. Away from nosey neighbours.

It's not that he was a liability. It was just better this way. Safer for everyone. At least that's what he'd told himself when Archibald Morgan had first broached the subject with him.

It made sense, Banning supposed. He did enjoy his independence, even if it didn't afford him the same perks as living under his mentor's roof. Having the freedom to prepare his own meals and launder his own clothes had quickly lost its novelty. But at least it had ensured that Banning was contained, should he suffer another episode. Especially at night, if the lindwurm venom failed to keep his dreams from becoming twisted echoes of his childhood.

The truth? He *was* becoming a liability. A danger to those around him. Losing control. Making mistakes. Mistakes which, on occasion, had been messy. And mess attracted unwelcome visitors. Visitors like O.O.T.I.S. But Banning would prove to his mentor that he was not just the sum of his failures. He would prove it to himself.

'Put them down there.' Banning nodded at a door on the far side of the room leading down to the basement.

It was the only other room in the house, aside from the lofted area where he slept, the bathroom, and the generous open-plan kitchen and living space in which they currently stood. But those were his spaces. Whatever the basement's original purpose had been, it wasn't storage. The drain in the middle of the concrete floor fuelled the darker theories of his imagination.

Hardly a guestroom, but it would do for now.

The incubus edged forward with the unconscious woman draped over his shoulder. He angled through the door in a way that didn't injure her. Banning followed after.

He removed his jacket and waistcoat, both fit for the bin. He tossed them onto the black leather sofa and sat. Dry lindwurm venom was impossible to remove from clothing. Not only did it permanently discolour fabric but it also left an odour that, while barely noticeable to humans, provoked a less than desirable response in certain species of cryptid. He would need to shower before his next engagement. Brushing at his shirt,

Banning sighed; it was also ruined. His clothing bill was becoming absurd.

He reached for the case on the glass-topped coffee table in front of him. It opened with a soft click, revealing an unused autoinjector and the glass cartridges he'd prefilled in the early hours of the morning.

Unease settled like a rock in the pit of his stomach. It had been easier to medicate as a child. He had choked back a handful of pills before bed and risen the next day—not necessarily refreshed but at least having slept through the night. And even on the rare occasions when his nightmares had cut through his chemically induced stupor and the whispers had become louder than the screams, their suffocating grip had always lessened upon waking.

But as an adult, something had changed. That fractured part of Banning, the piece that had detached the moment his world was razed to the ground, was no longer content to stay in the darkness. No longer satisfied to stalk the shadows of his sleep. Devoid of sentiment and reason, it took pleasure only in destruction.

In death.

It threatened to overwhelm him, to consume him, like the unnatural flames that had feasted upon his flesh and left him permanently scarred. He had lost control before. It would happen again. But worse than the dread of knowing it was the thought that, perhaps, deep down, the darkness was the real him.

The sound of footsteps pulled him from his thoughts. He snapped the case shut and pushed it back across the table.

Heimerich gave an almost imperceptible shudder. Obviously the basement had left a lasting impression on him. The incubus paused, taking in Banning's space properly for the first time. His gaze wandered over every item of furniture, every carefully selected statement piece, before resting on the glass tanks on the stepped, black shelving unit.

Banning grinned at him. 'Curious?'

He stood, walked over to one of the tanks and removed the lid, fishing around inside. Slowly, he brought his hand back out and showed the wriggling creature to the incubus.

Heimerich's nose wrinkled. 'A snake?'

'A lindwurm.' Banning uncurled just his finger and thumb so the sage-green reptile's two stunted front legs were visible. The lindwurm let out a warning hiss; the spines on its back rattled together as it snapped at the incubus. 'I'd have thought that you of all people would've recognised a lindwurm. Just how long have you been living in the mortal realm?'

Heimerich's features grew dark. 'Since I was a child.'

Undoubtedly, there was more to unpack there, but Banning had little interest in the demon's answer to his rhetorical question.

'I'm hoping to breed them,' Banning said. 'I have what I believe are three females and a male. Difficult to be sure though, but judging by the size, I'd say this one's the male. Smaller, you see. And the venom, while incredibly painful, is not lethal as from the females. The only guaranteed method of sexing them is to look at the flush of their underbelly scales under the light of the blood moon. And even then you have to get the timing spot on. Otherwise the females have a tendency to bite the males' heads off. But that's women for you, right?' *Like* I *would know.*

'Where did you get lindwurms?'

After easing the reptile back into its tank, Banning replaced the lid. 'I have my sources.'

When Banning didn't elaborate, the incubus frowned. His dark eyes fixed on the stain on Banning's shirt, then dropped to the case on the coffee table.

'Milk of the dragon.' Heimerich's tone was laced with disgust. 'You're a toxhead.'

Banning took an abrupt step forward, his teeth bared. 'How *dare* you presume to judge me? You, of all creatures. A parasite. Tell me, Heimerich, do you feed off your wife? Do you syphon her life force while she sleeps, just to prolong your wretched existence? Does she wake, wondering why she's so tired? So drained? Do you comfort her, knowing all the while that it's because of you?'

The incubus flinched. Any traces of revulsion were gone. Banning saw guilt. Shame.

'Let me make this clear,' Banning said to the creature. 'I'm not some brain-addled junkie. And you're not irreplaceable. Now go get the child and put her with her mother.'

Banning focused on his breathing, resisting the urge to lash out at the incubus. Heimerich rushed off to fetch the child from the car.

What was it about the toxhead implication that had got him so riled up? He'd received much worse insults. Had his authority challenged by far greater threats. He should have just laughed the comment off, but he'd let his temper get the better of him. Shown weakness. In front of a *demon*. Perhaps it was the insinuation that Banning had done this to himself. Or perhaps he knew that, before long, he was going to need something stronger than lindwurm venom.

It wasn't an addiction, it was a crutch. But was there really any difference?

Within minutes, Heimerich returned with the girl in his arms. Banning closed the main door to the safe house after him, the deadbolt sliding back into place.

'Put her in the same room as her mother. Oh, and take those too.' He gestured to a six-pack of bottled water on the marble-topped island that marked the kitchen boundary.

The incubus did as instructed, rewarding Banning with his obvious discomfort as he disappeared down the stairs once more. When he returned the colour had drained from his face.

'Make yourself comfortable, Heimerich. I'm going to get cleaned up.'

The incubus didn't move. 'Why keep them locked down there?'

'I'd have thought that was obvious.'

'No, I mean why aren't we taking them straight to Archibald Morgan?'

Banning paused. Was this curiosity or suspicion? 'Because Archibald Morgan is currently attending to more pressing matters.'

'For how long?'

'*Excuse* me?'

Heimerich held up his hands. 'There has to be somewhere more suitable to hold them, surely? That room...' He shuddered.

'It'll only be for a day. Two at the most.'

It was the only way. Taking them back to his mentor's manor before his return would ruin the surprise. He needed Archibald to know that he'd accomplished this on his own. That he was a valuable asset, worth the investment. There wasn't a chance in hell he'd let anyone take that from him. Including the incubus. He'd have to keep the demon under close scrutiny from this point on.

'But—'

Banning cut him off. 'But nothing. The woman and her child will remain here until Archibald returns. Oh, don't look so concerned. You'll be able to check on them again after our next engagement.'

'Next engagement?'

'In a rush, are we? It's not like you're paid by the hour. I told you, there's something else I need to take care of. Now sit.'

'Are you sure Archibald—'

'Ask me one more time whether or not these are Archibald Morgan's instructions and see what happens.' Banning ran his tongue over his teeth, glaring openly at the creature. This thing could be a problem. 'Let's make something clear, shall we? Archibald Morgan is like a father to me. I am his protégé. When you're talking to me you're as good as talking to him. Understand? Good. After all, who do you think taught me how to do this?'

He called upon his green magic, letting it flare across his knuckles, shaping it into a blade like before. Just long enough for the demon to blanch. 'Now, for the last time. Sit. Down.'

Heimerich perched on the edge of the sofa. His eyes locked on the glass tanks containing the lindwurms, but this time he didn't pass comment.

Feeling good, Banning headed for the bathroom to take a shower. On the way, he locked the door to the basement. As far as security went it was basic, but for the young girl and her mother, should they wake before his return, it would be adequate. He needed them. To get the dagger, to get the stone. Otherwise all his efforts would have been for nothing. He wouldn't disappoint his mentor again. He couldn't.

❧

Banning shut off the shower. There it was again. The sound of a door being rattled. He thought he'd imagined it the first time. He grabbed a towel, dried off quickly, and wrapped it around his waist.

He stepped out of the bathroom and caught the incubus in the act. 'What are you doing?'

Heimerich startled, jumping back from the door to the basement. 'Uh...'

'I wouldn't have pegged you for a peeping Tom. Not going to see much from there. You'd have to go downstairs to get a proper look.'

The incubus gaped at Banning's bare chest, his arms. Horror flickered across its face. 'No... I was just... you hit her over the head pretty hard.'

'She kneed me in the bollocks. It was below the belt. Quite literally. I can assure you my reaction was justified.'

Heimerich met Banning's eyes and immediately looked away. He knew the mess of scar tissue marring his body had repulsed the creature. Who could blame it? The disfigurement included three craters gouged out almost symmetrically either side of his collarbone, and ruined skin that ran from his chest to his navel, as well as the length of his arms, stopping in ragged lines around his knuckles. Ten years wasn't enough to numb the shock he felt each time he glimpsed his reflection in the mirror.

WEAK. The voice came unbidden, teasing the edges of his defences.

Banning froze.

No. He wasn't about to lose control. Not again.

The rustle of the lindwurms and the sound of his rapid breaths filled the space between them. Forcing a smile, Banning cleared his throat and gestured at his misshapen flesh. 'Like what you see? Does your wife know you like to ogle half-naked men when she's not around?'

Heimerich licked his lower lip, eyes still on his feet. 'No. She... uh... I...'

'I'm joking. Lighten up. Anyway, it's hardly the most impressive reveal we've had so far today, is it? Or do you need to be reminded?' He wriggled his fingers and sparks of green danced from their tips. The creature's mouth twitched nervously in response. 'Excellent. Now be a dear and go wait in the car with Oliver while I get dressed.'

Heimerich gave him a nod, glanced again at the basement door, and turned on his heel.

Banning watched him leave, throat tight. As soon as the door locked behind the creature, he staggered across the room and snatched the case containing the autoinjector off the coffee table. This shouldn't be happening. Not so soon after the last dosage.

WEAK.

He lurched back into the bathroom, blinking against the black spots in his vision, swallowing down his nausea. He could hear nothing above the pulsing noise in his ears.

Banning propped himself up against the sink, focussing on the feel of the marble beneath his skin. His fingers pressed into the edges of the autoinjector case.

Control. All that mattered was control. He just needed to slow his breathing. To focus.

Ten... nine... eight...

'You're okay.' He exhaled, lifting his head. A pair of blue eyes stared back at him through the condensation on the mirror. 'You're okay.'

His gaze tracked down to his chest almost of its own accord. The sight sickened him.

WEAK.

He could feel himself losing it. Feel the darkness seeping into his thoughts, penetrating his mind. Lunging for the case, Banning ripped the autoinjector free and held it against his thigh. *No.* No. He didn't need it. It was just a precaution. He could do this. He could pull himself back from the edge.

Seven... six... five...

He wanted to squeeze his eyes shut. To curl up in a ball on the floor. But he wouldn't allow it. He knew what would happen if he did. Knew that the pounding of his pulse echoing inside his skull would be replaced by something far worse. Replaced by the sounds of their anguished screams.

Four... three...

Chapter 11

'IT'S 2AM, GARRICK. IF we're caught, Mum and Dad will ground us. You know they don't like it when you sneak downstairs to practice your magic.' Banning gave his little brother a serious look. 'I'll show you once more, but then you have to promise that you'll go back to bed.'

Garrick treated him to a gap-toothed grin, shuffled back on his bottom an inch or two, and dragged his fingers through his dishevelled brown hair. 'I promise.'

Adjusting his pyjama sleeves, Banning stifled a yawn. He rubbed at his eyes and looked down at the thin white trail wafting up from the candle between them. At least Garrick had remembered the candle holder this time. Mum had been less than pleased the last time when she'd come downstairs to find wax fused to the carpet. 'I mean it. We've got school tomorrow.'

Banning waited until Garrick nodded, then closed his eyes and straightened his back. He gave his full attention to the rise and fall of his chest. To the sound of his breathing. Everything else was just a distraction.

He could feel the power flowing through his veins, pulsing in time with the steady rhythm of his heart.

Slowly, gently, he willed it up from his core and into his fingertips. Just a little. Just enough. His skin tingled.

Now that he was in the right state of mind, he could sense the energy infusing everything around him. The constant ebb and flow, like a living current. It seeped from the realm of fire and shadow, full of promise and limitless potential. He ignored it, just as their dad had taught him to do, instead seeking out the natural energy clinging to the tip of the candle's wick. Raising his hand, he fed his magic into it, coaxing the flame back into life.

Banning opened his eyes and grinned at Garrick's expression of awe. If he'd wanted to he could have done more, shaped the fire into something truly astounding. He released his hold on his magic, allowing the flame to gutter out; he didn't want to make his brother feel bad. Garrick struggled with even the simplest of exercises. For Banning, their gift came as naturally to him as breathing. Sure, he'd had his fair share of frustrations, but nothing compared to those of his brother. Maybe it was an age thing? Maybe he'd found it just as hard when he'd been seven?

'I find it easier when I close my eyes. You try,' Banning said.

Garrick licked his lips and did as instructed.

'Now, try and block out everything around you and focus on your power.'

Nothing happened.

'Concentrate,' Banning urged, his voice low. 'You should be able to *feel* the fire, like it's just another part of you.'

Garrick nodded, his face set in determination. The wick sparked fitfully.

Banning sat as still as possible, doing his best not to make a peep.

The blast of heat took him by surprise, but it was not nearly as impressive as the streaming jet of flame pouring up towards the ceiling. Banning gasped. Garrick's eyes snapped open and immediately the inferno abated, settling back into a contented flicker.

Banning gaped at the black stain above their heads then at his brother. The laugh bubbled up from his throat before he could stop it. He clamped his hand over his mouth, stifling a honk. The two boys giggled in hushed snorts, gasping and wiping the tears from their eyes, until the moment passed and they could both catch their breath.

'See, I knew you could do it.' Banning's smile wavered. The circles beneath Garrick's eyes were noticeably darker, his face ashen. 'You should really go to bed.'

'Okay.' Garrick stretched. He glanced at the ceiling again. 'Mum's going to be so mad when she sees that.'

'Don't worry, I'll get a chair and wipe it off. You go upstairs.'

'Thanks, Banning.' Untangling his legs, Garrick pushed himself to his feet. He was trembling visibly.

Banning winced. This was exactly why they weren't to practice their magic alone. The last time Garrick had pushed himself too far he'd passed out and landed badly, ending up with a black eye. Luckily that had been the worst of it. The first thing they'd been taught—the first thing their kind were taught, if Dad was to be believed—was to never, ever, drain themselves completely. It left them empty and exposed to realms beyond their own.

Garrick took a step forward and yelped, pulling his foot up sharply.

'What's the matter?'

'I stood on a stupid matchstick.' Teetering on one leg, he inspected his sole until it became too difficult to balance. He growled, frustration lending colour to his cheeks and tears to his eyes, and kicked out at the pieces of scorched wood, sending them scattering.

Banning rushed forward. 'Did you cut yourself?'

'No. I just—' His words were cut off by a sharp, high-pitched shriek.

Startled, Banning stood rooted to the spot. Garrick screamed again, flailing his leg. It was then that Banning saw the fire working its way up his brother's pyjama bottoms.

'Drop and roll.' Banning lunged at Garrick, knocking him to the ground. He beat desperately at the flames. 'Roll!'

But Garrick only thrashed in place, his screams a crescendo of panic.

'Mum, Dad... Help!' Banning continued to bat frantically at the scorched fabric. Thick curls of black smoke stung his eyes. 'Mum, Dad!'

Gritting his teeth against the blistering heat searing his palms, he chanced a glance at the door, willing them to come. The blaze was spreading fast. Rivers of liquid fire raced across the carpet, beginning from the candle on its side.

Banning shrank back, fear knotting in his gut. What if his parents didn't wake up? What if nobody came to help?

And that's when he realised: Garrick's screams had stopped.

'*Garrick.*' Banning grabbed his brother by the shoulders and shook him. His vision blurred; tears streaked down his cheeks. 'No, please...'

He heard a groan. So quiet he almost missed it.

'Mum! Da—'

An unseen force knocked Banning onto his back. He let out a painful grunt. Banning rolled over, cringing away from the flames that were now devouring the sofa. Confusion and fear vied for control as his mind tried to make sense of what just happened.

Garrick groaned again, louder this time. A wide circle of smouldering ash spread out around him, smoke coiling from its edges where the fire had been snuffed out. But, it was creeping back to his brother with hungry determination.

Banning crawled forward. The air crackled around him, quivering with an electric pressure that made his skin tingle and the hairs on his body stand on end. He knew what it was immediately.

'Garrick, no. Stop.' Mustering all his strength, Banning hauled his brother onto his back. 'Stop, Garrick, stop!'

Garrick's eyes rolled beneath the lids; his body twitched, but he didn't respond. The charred and peeling flesh where his pyjamas had burnt away was repairing itself. Dead tissue was sloughing off and being replaced by unblemished white skin.

Heart racing, Banning reached for his magic. It twisted from his grasp as rising panic obliterated his focus. The maelstrom of energy converging around his brother was dizzying. It called to Banning, inviting him to taste its power. To unleash his full potential. To be one with the realm of fire and shadow. He could be unstoppable. All he had to do was take it.

No.

He bit down on the inside of his cheek, drawing blood. The pain was enough to clear his head.

Heat pressed against him as the fire closed in. Smoke rolled across the ceiling in thick, undulating sheets. Banning whimpered, looking around wildly for an escape route, finding none. His body was unbearably hot now; the sweat had matted his hair to his forehead, dripping down his face in unpleasant, prickling beads.

The space behind him groaned, giving a bottomless judder that resonated bone-deep. Banning twisted round, wide-eyed, as reality itself tore apart. A dark chasm split the air, spewing great, dusty torrents that raked across his skin, engulfing him in a stench of rotten eggs. In a scrabble of limbs he jerked back, slick hands groping frantically at the shrivelled and blackened carpet, unable to look away.

Something moved through the putrid murk. Something big.

A calloused, grey hand shot out from the void, fingers splayed. It made a grab for Garrick's leg.

Banning threw up his arms, drawing energy from the flames around him, to raise a shield around his brother. Claws, met by sudden resistance, left a trail of white sparks as the creature's hand skittered across the shimmering force surrounding Garrick's unconscious form. The demon howled. It grasped and slashed at its prize again, to no avail.

Banning clenched his jaw against his waning strength. Even with the fire lending him its power, his defence wouldn't last long. If he could just drive the demon back even a fraction, he might be able to pull Garrick to safety and close the rift.

Banning willed the blaze towards the creature. Flame assaulted the demon's exposed limb in a deluge of red and gold. It withdrew sharply. The darkness that surrounded it was a churning miasma of shadow and ash, cast in a lambent glow.

Banning hooked his hands under his brother's arms and heaved him back.

The demon's voice rattled in the gloom, unintelligible clicks and hisses getting louder by the second. With a bestial snarl, it thrust its head through the breach, the fire ravaging it now a sickly shade of green. Its lower jaw was split apart, and thick strands of drool dribbled through countless rows of jagged teeth. It made another rasping sound, forked tongue flicking out, and fixed its gaze on Banning.

Terror seized him, locked in place by the crushing weight of its stare. He couldn't move. Couldn't think. Couldn't breathe.

The door to the living room burst inwards. Fed by the sudden rush of oxygen, the flames surged in a gluttonous frenzy, only to be driven back by a translucent arc, as his dad forced his way through the threshold.

'Banning, move!' His father's shouts were frantic, strained.

But it was too late.

Claws gouged into Banning's shoulders, piercing skin and muscle. He was wrenched off the ground and dragged towards the abyss. The demon cackled, its body convulsing, as liquid green flame rippled across its rough flesh.

Banning screamed, spasming in place where he hung, agony rendering his muscles useless. The heat was excruciating. It ripped down his arms and chest with such intensity, he thought he was being torn apart. He'd do anything to make it stop. He opened his mouth to beg, but all that came out were meaningless shrieks.

MINE.

The voice inside his head swamped his thoughts. He could feel its malice, its need for destruction, almost as if it were his own. It wouldn't be long before it took him over completely. Before it tore through the last shreds of his resistance. Their dad had warned them. Warned that there was always something lurking in the shadows, waiting for the chance to break through.

Garrick. This was all Garrick's fault. He had exhausted himself. He had drawn energy from the realm of fire and shadow. He had lured the demon into their home.

YES. KILL.

Rage flooded his veins, drowning out the pain. Numbing him to the torment. The relief was euphoric.

He glared down at his brother.

KILL.

It would be so easy. Garrick deserved to die. He'd brought it upon himself.

Banning nodded in agreement with the whispers, feeling the corners of his mouth curl upward. His brother *was* weak. How had he never noticed before?

Raising his arm, he drew on his power. It leapt from his core and ignited just below his skin, making his whole body tremble. Exhilarated, Banning reached for more. It had never been so easy, had never felt so right.

YES.

Magic blazed out from his palm. Identical in colour to the green flames still cascading down his body. He knew it was different. That it was wrong. His magic was blue.

And there was something else... a thought, so deeply ingrained that it was a part of his psyche. The more he focused, the more substantial it became, rising above the murmurs of the demon like a mantra.

Never drain yourself completely. Never leave yourself exposed.

He gasped, releasing the energy immediately, and stared down at his baby brother. *I was going to kill him.* A desperate sob burst from his lips.

The demon growled. It tightened its grip on his shoulders, claws stabbing deeper into his muscles. It lowered its head, scraping its coarse skin across Banning's cheek. He shrieked at the return of his pain, his vision tunnelling.

'Banning, listen to me,' his dad yelled. 'Look at me.'

He tried to lift his head, but he was too weak. Why was it suddenly so cold? Had the fire gone out?

'Don't use your magic. It's what it wants. Emma! Emma, get Garrick.'

'Mum...' The word felt clumsy in his mouth.

SHE DOESN'T LOVE YOU.

The voice was lying. Of course his mum loved him. Him and Garrick. She told them every day. Then why was she trying to save his brother and not him? Why had it taken her so long to get downstairs?

Flickers of green sparked across his fingers.

'Banning, no!'

He whipped his head up in time to see the glowing, blue circle of complex symbols careering towards him from his dad's outstretched palms. Pure magic.

It rolled over Banning harmlessly in a burst of crackles and sparks. The demon was not so lucky. Thick, angry welts bubbled and blistered wherever it was struck. With a deafening bellow that tore through the house, blowing out the windows in a shower of glass, it released its hold on Banning.

Banning hit the ground. The demon's voice still resounded in his brain; residual rage and hatred seeped through him like poison. He tried to push himself up, but ended up face planting on the floor, his arms numb and unresponsive.

Firm hands closed around his chest, dragging him backwards. Banning groaned, tilting his head to look up at his mum. She was grimacing. Ash smeared her skin. She looked pale and tears tracked down her face.

She hardly ever cried.

'I called you,' Banning whispered.

She didn't answer. Her breathing was heavy. Her eyes were wild and bulging.

Banning groaned. It hurt too much. Every slight movement sent a torturous jolt through him. His head lolled to the side. The fire from the candle still gorged on the edges of the room.

DOESN'T LOVE YOU.

'I *called* you,' Banning yelled at his mum, his anger unrestrained.

The flames shrivelled as he syphoned their energy, regenerating the skin and muscle of his minced shoulders. He twisted from his mum's grip, landing in an awkward heap before pushing to his feet. The agony of his arms and torso where the green flame had ravaged his skin still raged.

Inhaling, he willed the tissue to repair itself. Nothing happened. He stared down at his hands, blinking rapidly. The scars were still livid. Why wouldn't they heal?

HER FAULT.

He clutched his head. 'Make it stop!'

'Banning?' She reached for him.

KILL.

Giving her a sharp shove, he staggered back. 'Dad, I can't... the voice... I...'

'Emma, get Maida and get outside. Go. *Now*!' His dad's every syllable was strained, breathless.

Maida. Was his baby sister still upstairs? For the briefest moment, Banning thought his mum might argue. Her jaw clicked shut. She gave Banning one last pained look and turned for the hallway.

The *whoosh* of heat was the first thing that registered. Quickly followed by the flash of green. His mum hurtled through the air, her skull slamming into the doorframe. She crumpled into a heap.

Banning should've checked if she was okay. Should've helped her back to her feet. But he was already sprinting towards the creature, dodging flames of green and yellow. The throbbing pain of his scars was like a distant memory. Blood pounded in his ears. Red mist clouded his vision.

The demon had to die.

'*No.*' His dad whirled round, thrusting out an arm to stop him.

And in that one moment of distraction, the creature struck.

His dad jerked, eyes wide. A spray of crimson erupted from his open mouth. Claws jutted from his chest, caked in slippery chunks that slopped onto the carpet. His arm dropped to his side.

'Run...' His dad's warning was a gurgle.

'Dad. No... please. I'm sorry. Please, no...'

'Run...' No more than a wet rasp this time.

Sobbing, Banning fled. Between the smoke and his tears, he could barely see.

He half tripped, half stumbled over his mum, unable to right himself before crashing to the floor. He scrambled to his feet, noticing his brother for the first time. Garrick was out cold, and for a second Banning wondered if he was dead.

KILL. The voice pressed its way back into his thoughts.

His mum moaned. '... Garrick?'

DOESN'T LOVE YOU.

Didn't she recognise him?

Banning shook his head, trying to rid himself of the hateful whispers. Dropping to his knees, he brushed the matted hair from her face with trembling fingers. 'No, Mum. It's Banning. Get up. You have to get up.'

'Bann...'

'*Mum?*' There was no way he could lift her by himself. He needed help.

He grabbed the keys and fumbled the right one into the lock. He hauled the door open. Cold air rushed him.

Garrick stirred, whimpering softly.

KILL.

Banning gritted his teeth, seized his brother roughly by the arms, and dragged his unconscious body. His weakened muscles trembled beneath Garrick's weight, but between every breathless gasp and frustrated scream, he got them both outside.

Flames howled from the space where the living room window had been, spitting cinders and belching black smoke into the night. He stared, dumbstruck, as the fire stretched towards the second storey... towards his sister's bedroom.

'*Maida*!' Her name had barely left his mouth before he was running towards the house.

A flash of blue stopped him.

An ear-splitting boom followed.

A searing explosion of heat hit him.

Banning's world went black.

Chapter 12

'Looks like we beat uniform.' Sam pulled the Škoda Fabia up outside Meghan's house and killed the ignition.

'First thing I've been early for all week.'

Unbuckling himself, Nick leant forward to get a better look at the front of Meghan's house. Terraced. Small. With Charlie there as well, they must be living on top of one another. Guilt stabbed him in the chest. He clenched his teeth and exhaled.

'Yeah. I noticed,' Sam said. 'What's been up with you lately? I mean, you're not the most organised guy I know but you're not normally this bad.'

'I don't know,' Nick answered honestly, rubbing his neck and giving a tired sigh. 'It's like there's something buried inside my mind, desperate to get out. Every time I try to focus on it, it slips away...' He trailed off at how absurd it all sounded.

'Like you're losing your memories?'

Nick shook his head. 'That's just it. I can remember things, but it's like the memories are wrong. Like the details are off. The more I concentrate the more I get these headaches. It's messing up my sleep. Maybe it's just stress.'

Sam gave a lopsided grin. 'Or a brain tumour?'

Nick scoffed. 'Cheers for that.'

'What?' Sam's grin slipped from his face. 'Seriously though, maybe you need to go to a doctor. Get signed off for a week or two?'

'Don't you start. You're beginning to sound like Henry.'

'He might be onto something. Look, I don't mean to sound like a complete arsehole, but are you sure you're up to this?'

His words were like a slap to the face. Nick gaped at his colleague. Having someone—anyone—question his ability to do his job was bad. But coming from Sam, the man with a devil-may-care attitude and an inability to be serious about anything for more than five minutes, made it so much worse.

'Of course I'm up to this,' Nick spat, heat rising in his cheeks.

Sam held up his hands. 'You're dead on your feet. If you need to sit this one out, no one will think any less of you. You don't owe anyone anything. I'm just saying.'

'Well don't *just say*.'

'Jesus. Alright. Chill.'

'Chill?' He shook his head in disbelief. 'You saw the state of Charlie that night. Saw how beaten up he was. It was my fault. If I hadn't gotten him involved in that case...'

'Get over yourself, Nick.' The change in Sam's demeanour was instant. Gone was the concern, the caution.

'Excuse me?'

'You were doing your job, just like Charlie was. Enough of this wallowing, self-indulgent bullshit already. It's not you. You couldn't have known what was going to happen. Not unless you were a psychic. And I'm sure that if you had some magical ability to see into the future you wouldn't be sitting here with me right now.' Sam exhaled, his face softening. He placed a hand on Nick's shoulder. 'Look, it's not your fault. Really.'

Nick deflated. Without the adrenaline stoking the fires of his indignation, there was nothing left but the suffocating weight of exhaustion. He couldn't bring himself to meet Sam's eyes; instead he looked down at his hand, still gripping his shoulder. A simple gesture of reassurance, and from Sam of all people, but it was enough. He felt calmer.

Sam inched closer, increasing the pressure on his shoulder. His fingers felt surprisingly warm through the heavy layers of Nick's jacket and shirt. 'Seriously, Nick. It's not your fault Charlie got hurt.'

Maybe Sam was right. Maybe it wasn't his fault. How *could* he have known? But if it wasn't the guilt messing with his head, stopping him from sleeping, then what in the hell was wrong with him?

Sweat pricked his upper lip. Even without the engine running, the air inside the car felt too cloying. Sam was too close. It almost felt like he was radiating heat.

Nick shifted his weight and shook himself free.

Sam didn't seem put out. He said, 'Anyway, for a pensioner armed with a kitchen knife, I'd say Charlie held his own. Could've been a lot worse, given the circumstances.'

Kitchen knife.

Pain flared inside Nick's skull. A blazing wildfire of memories warped and twisted away from him. He clutched at his head and let out a low groan. He squeezed his eyes shut.

In the distance, he heard Sam calling his name.

'*Kitchen knife.*' Nick choked out the words, forcing them past his tight throat. But that wasn't it. He was missing something else. Something important. If only he could focus...

There. A single image. A dagger. Damascus steel etched with symbols, silver guard embellished with floral scroll filigree, marbled black handle inset with a red gemstone at the pommel. He knew that dagger. He'd seen it before...

Then, just like that, the image was gone. Sucked into the mire of his sleep-addled brain, lost beneath the muddied details of that night that had eluded him for the past three months.

Nick opened his eyes, his brain a throbbing mix of agony and confusion. Fumbling with the handle of the door, he got it open and all but fell out of the car.

The frigid winter air slashed at his exposed skin. He sucked the cold in; it raked down his lungs and made his eyes water. His breath became white vapour as he exhaled, and as he did, the residual fog inside his head began to lift. Emotions vied for control in him. Anger. Resentment. But mostly embarrassment. If Sam didn't think he was up to the task before, his little episode would have done nothing to assuage his doubts.

What's wrong with me?

The car bobbed lightly beside him as Sam climbed out. He closed the door with a soft click. 'You okay?'

Nick straightened. 'Yeah. Yeah, I'm alright. Migraine, I think.'

Sam's eyes widened. 'Your nose. It's bleeding.'

Nick rubbed at his nose; his fingers were smeared with red. 'Shit.'

'Maybe you really do have a brain tumour.'

Nick glared at him as he pulled out a tissue from his pocket and held it to his face. He'd half expected to see Sam's dopey grin, but was met instead by concern.

Steadying himself, Nick crouched and checked his reflection in the wing mirror. When the bleeding had stopped, he wiped the last splotches of blood from his face, pocketed the tissue, and stood.

'I'll go and assess the crime scene,' Sam said. 'You alright to go get the statement from the witness?' Before Nick could answer, he turned and walked towards the house.

Nick made another quick check for blood, then grabbed his notebook from inside the Fabia. There was nothing left to do but make his way to number nineteen and hope that he could get some answers.

He barely had the chance to knock before a woman with dark hair opened the door. Her gaze darted to the house next door then to him. She raised her thumb to her lips to chew on her nail, caught herself, then folded her arms across her chest.

Nick offered her a reassuring smile and held up his warrant card. 'Eleanor Bell?'

Eleanor nodded.

'I'm DC Nicholas Stacey. Thank you for waiting. Could you run me through what happened leading up to your call to the police?'

'Sure.' Eleanor exhaled a shaky breath, tracking his movements as he pulled a pen from his coat. 'I'd invite you in, but this isn't my house.'

'No, no. That's fine.' He hid his disappointment. Given what had just happened, he really could've done with a seat.

'Meghan was going to watch Poppy, my daughter, for me so that I could work. My sister's on her way to come get her now. She was meant to have a sleepover with Evie. They're friends from school. I went over to drop her off and saw that the door was ajar. I just assumed she'd heard my car and left it open for us, so I prepared to let myself in. That's when I saw all the broken glass and the... the blood. I called out but there was no answer. So I phoned the police.'

Blood? Lovett hadn't mentioned that. Nick scribbled notes and glanced up from his notebook. 'You didn't actually enter the property?'

'No. I mean... I did step inside, but I didn't go any farther once I saw the mess. Why? Do you think I should've gone in? Do you think... do you think they might still be inside?' Eleanor covered her mouth. 'Oh my God, I should have checked, shouldn't I? I just assumed that when they didn't answer... What if they're hurt?'

'Eleanor, you did the right thing. My colleague is inside now. Don't worry.'

She nodded, tension easing from her face.

'Did you notice anything else that was unusual? Anyone nearby? Any strange vehicles?'

'No, sorry. I live on the other side of town, so I wouldn't know which cars aren't normally here. I didn't notice anyone nearby, either, not that I can remember anyway. I wish I could be more help.'

'That's okay, you're doing great. Is there anyone you can think of that would want to harm Meghan or Evelyn?'

'You think someone...' Eleanor's breath hitched. She took a moment to collect herself, eyes brimming with unshed tears. She shook her head. 'No. No one.'

'Any recent altercations with anyone that Meghan might have mentioned?'

Eleanor blinked rapidly and averted her gaze. Her fingers worried at the delicate gold cross around her neck. 'No.'

She was lying.

Nick kept his expression neutral. 'Eleanor, anything you can tell me, anything at all, would be a massive help. Please.'

She met his eyes, lips pressing together, her internal conflict plain on her face.

A chilly breeze stirred between them. It needled under Nick's clothing and shuddered down his spine. He waited without breaking eye contact, as the bare hanging baskets swayed in his peripheral vision.

Finally, Eleanor broke the silence, 'Is this going to take much longer? Only I need to get to work. I know this is important. I do. It's just, I really need this job. I don't want to lose it. God, that makes me sound awful. It's just my boss. He can be... difficult.'

Nick underlined the words "difficult boss". 'Where is it you work?'

'Ron's Diner.'

The sound of footsteps, heavy and deliberate, caught his attention. He turned to see Sam waiting for him, face sombre.

'Thank you for your time, Eleanor.' With a nod, Nick returned his pen to his coat and made his way back to his colleague.

As the door to number nineteen closed firmly behind him, Nick braced himself for bad news from Sam.

'Forensics are on their way,' Sam said, his voice low. 'Judging by the amount of blood, someone got hurt. I think you'd better try Charlie again.'

Jesus.

Chapter 13

Charlie sat bolt upright and gasped. His mouth was dry, his throat raw. He blinked. Once. Twice. Slowly, his vision cleared, only to remind him of where he was. He forced his fingers to relax before they gouged holes into the padding of the examination table.

'Charlie. Thank Christ.'

Diane.

He glanced at her amber eyes, brimming with concern. He smiled, but dropped it when he remembered she was just another O.O.T.I.S agent. A liar. The relief on Diane's face turned into disappointment. She took a step back from the table.

Sachiko watched him.

His muscles ached. Every damned one. But it was nothing compared to the burning pressure in his arm where the creature had savaged him; it throbbed in time with his pulse, bringing waves of gut-churning nausea. Spots of blood seeped through the bandages where someone had dressed the wound.

Wait, was he still shirtless?

'What—' A coughing fit cut him off.

'Don't worry,' Sachiko said. 'It's just the after effects of the antivenom. By all rights you should be dead. If it weren't for your bond to the dagger...' He stared at her and Sachiko let the sentence die.

'Drink this, it'll help.' She offered him a plastic cup.

After a cursory check of the contents, Charlie accepted. The cool water invigorated his dry tongue, soothing the sandpapery chafe as he swallowed. Despite the queasiness, his stomach rumbled. An unwelcome reminder that he hadn't eaten since yesterday.

Ignoring the fact that all eyes were on him, he looked around the room. Kar'roc's Maw was back inside its casing, suspended in that otherworldly way that made his skin crawl. The mound of ash on the floor was gone. No traces of blood. No damage to the tiles. Nothing to indicate that the incident with the floating eel demon, or whatever the hell that thing was, had even happened. He looked down at his forearm.

Well, almost nothing.

'I'm afraid you're going to have a few more scars to add to your collection,' Sachiko said.

Diane cleared her throat pointedly.

Sachiko's eyebrows drew up. 'I'm sorry. I didn't mean...'

'Could someone please just get me my shirt?'

'Yes. Someone please do. He's making the rest of us look bad.' A deep voice resonated through the room, obliterating the awkward silence. It was a voice that Charlie recognised. A voice he hadn't heard in years, not since they'd worked together as DCs.

'Adeola.' Charlie swung his legs over the side and went to stand.

'No, no. Don't get up on my account. I heard you've had a rough morning.' Adeola Rousseau crossed the distance in quick, easy strides, a broad grin splitting his face. He shook Charlie's hand and gently squeezed the shoulder of his good arm.

'Christ, you haven't changed a bit,' Charlie said, accepting his shirt from Diane. He made an awkward, one-handed attempt to ease his bandaged limb through the sleeve.

'A few more greys and a bit more around the middle.' Adeola chuckled, giving his paunch a pat.

Charlie smiled, working his buttons clumsily. The pain in his arm was easing towards manageable, but he wasn't about to risk jostling it.

He paused in his efforts, frowning.

A memory, almost forgotten, teased at the edges of his thoughts. The night of Stephen's murder, when Charlie had been on his knees in the dirt next to his friend's mutilated corpse, he'd felt something calling to him. At that exact moment, he'd had the urge to pull the dagger in Stephen's chest free. After, he'd dismissed the sensation as bullshit, but Adeola had been there. He had grabbed his shoulder and given him a strange look. Charlie had dismissed it due to his grief.

But now, it made sense.

'How long have you worked for the Order?'

Adeola's smile faded. 'I know you don't like change, Charlie. You were never supposed to know about all of this.' He waved his hand at nothing in particular. 'About magic. Demons.'

'You haven't answered my question.'

Adeola met his eyes. 'Always. O.O.T.I.S is not confined to the UK. It's worldwide. Information, resources, everything is shared between branches so that we can work together to keep the world safe. My family and I moved to the UK from the Ivory Coast when I was a boy. When I was old enough, I was found a placement with the police force.'

'So you knew? About Kar'roc's Maw? About what it was when Stephen was murdered?' Charlie yanked the last button through the buttonhole, ripping it clean off the thread. He cursed as it skittered across the floor.

'No.' Adeola tilted his head, evidently deciding how best to phrase what he would say next. 'I could sense the power radiating off it. It wasn't until later, when the murders began and the dagger reappeared, that I became aware of what it truly was. When we went to exhume Stephen's body and found it missing, that's when we knew what we were dealing with.'

'You did *what?*' The words exploded from Charlie's mouth. He stood. The second he did, the black suit appeared in the doorway.

Adeola held up a hand, signalling for the man to remain where he was. 'We had to be sure.'

'So why didn't you stop him? If you knew that the demon was forcing Stephen to kill all those people, why didn't you stop him? Thirty-four years. Thirty-four fucking years, Adeola. I lost my marriage. My wife. My daughter. All because I was obsessing over Stephen's murder. Because I wanted to catch the people I thought were responsible. And now you're telling me that you knew it was him all along?' Charlie took a step forward. 'You did nothing about it. Nothing!'

The lights inside the casing for the dagger flickered as the symbols on the glass flared white. The black suit shifted where he stood, body tense. Adeola gave him a quick shake of his head. The man pursed his lips but otherwise didn't move.

'We tried,' Adeola said.

'You *tried?*'

'Yes,' Adeola's voice remained even. 'You have to remember, Charlie, the Boswells were scattered across the country, across the world, always on the move. There was no way to predict who the next target would be, or even find them before Stephen did. It's why we were always one step behind. When the killings stopped we lost Stephen completely. It was only by chance that Diane found him again, a few years later.'

'What!' Charlie took a step backwards. As he did, the back of his thighs hit the edge of the examination table.

Diane had found Stephen? *I'm an idiot.*

He turned to face her. 'All this time I thought you were just using me to satisfy your academic interest. To get closer to the dagger. But you were using me as bait.'

Diane winced. She dropped her gaze.

He willed her to argue. To shake her head and cut him down with a sharp comment about how he was being ridiculous. Granted, he'd have known it for a lie, but it might have softened the blow to his already bruised and battered ego. Stopped him feeling like a complete and utter mug.

Adeola's brow furrowed. 'After that Stephen was in the wind, until a few months ago. The rest you know.'

Charlie processed the information, clenching and unclenching his fists by his sides.

He relaxed his hands and blew out a steady breath. 'So what you're telling me is that you knew the demon was killing again and you let me, a normal man in his sixties, take it on alone? And now, I'm stuck with this thing—' he held up his left hand, showing Adeola the sigil, '—and being forced to undergo tests for hours on end. Because what? None of you can do your fucking jobs properly?'

Adeola's mouth pinched. 'What happened to you is most unfortunate.' He turned to Diane, eyes narrowed. She blanched, shrinking back from his glare.

'Unfortunate?' Charlie laughed. 'This is a joke. I was just attacked. In your headquarters. By a flying smoke eel. Piss-up and brewery spring to mind.'

'That's why I'm here. That *flying smoke eel*, as you put it, was a naeshin demon. I believe it may have been attracted to your link to the dagger.'

'No... When I held up the dagger it backed off. Anyway, it went for Sachiko, not me. I just got in the way.'

'I didn't say it was attracted to the dagger. I said it was attracted to your *link* to the dagger.'

'What does that mean?'

'The sigil on your hand binds you to the dagger's magic. Kar'roc's magic. You essentially have a direct link, albeit a weak one, to the demon realm. The naeshin may have sensed that connection and followed it. When it discovered you rather than a gateway back to its own realm it attacked. Naturally, it went for what it perceived to be the weaker of the two of you.'

Charlie's chest tightened. 'I attract demons now?' Was he putting Meghan and Evelyn in danger just by being near them?

'It's very unlikely,' Sachiko interjected. Adeola's brow furrowed. Oblivious to the silent warning, she continued. 'As demons go, species like the naeshin are primitive. All instinct and very little brain. They rely on rudimentary biological sensors to detect certain frequencies. To help them hunt, or to avoid danger. *If* the naeshin sensed your link to the dagger, it would only be because it was trapped inside the building with you. Every other magical artifact is warded to prevent it radiating magic, or in some cases, communicating with the outside world. Anywhere else, your sigil would be just a drop in the ocean of energies perceivable to the supernatural world. Indistinguishable to human, demon, or otherwise.'

Adeola cleared his throat. 'Be that as it may, I have concerns. We are still only theorising how you are being affected by the dagger. That's why I took the decision to assign Diane as your handler.'

So it's true.

'Thanks, but no thanks.'

'Charlie, please,' Adeola said. 'It makes sense. Diane has an intimate knowledge of Kar'roc's Maw. Of all of us here, she's the most qualified. After all, she was with you the night you became its master.' He shot another look at her. 'Who better to monitor your wellbeing?'

'Monitor my wellbeing?' Charlie scoffed. 'You mean babysit? I'm not a child, Adeola. I don't need to be watched over.'

Adeola heaved out a sigh, his expression sincere regret. 'I'm sorry, Charlie. I am. Usually in these sorts of scenarios we'd have altered your memories and you'd have gone about your life blissfully unaware that there was anything else in the world other than what you knew. But your connection to the dagger prevents us from doing that.'

'Altered my memories?'

'It's perfectly safe. Given the choice, wouldn't you go back to the way things were?'

Christ, had they all been given the same damn script? It was almost exactly what Diane had asked him earlier. And to think he'd believed she was being genuine. *Idiot.*

'Would I have been given the choice?'

The muscles in Adeola's jaw tensed. He met Charlie's gaze.

'That's what I thought,' Charlie said with a smirk. 'Thanks for the offer, but I'm sure Diane has better things to be doing. And, as I said, I don't need a babysitter.'

The light rustle of fabric caught Charlie's attention. The black suit had his fingers pressed against his earpiece. He strode over to Adeola and murmured something. Charlie caught the word 'incident'. Adeola's fleeting look in his direction wasn't missed either.

Rousseau nodded to the black suit, posture stiff. Wiping his expression clean, he returned to the conversation at hand. 'Diane is your handler and will remain as such for the foreseeable future. She'll explain what that means later. It's non-negotiable, I'm afraid. Anyway, it was lovely to see you again, Charlie.'

Charlie barked a humourless laugh. Tendrils of unease took root in his gut. 'I liked you better when you were just a DC.'

Adeola's mouth lifted into a sad smile. 'I was never *just* a DC.'

Without another word he exited the room with the black suit in tow. The steel door closed automatically behind them.

Silence pressed on him from all sides. Heavy. Suffocating.

Sachiko fidgeted in place, apparently at a loss for what to do or say.

Diane stood staring at the door like a rabbit caught in headlights. She turned to face him. 'I'm sorry, Charlie, this wasn't my choice. I'm sure the last thing you want right now is to spend any more time with me than you have to.'

Charlie didn't reply, not trusting himself to say another word. Not trusting *her*.

Diane released a breath, then left the room.

This day just gets better and better.

Chapter 14

THE NEXT FEW HOURS pressed down on Charlie's shoulders like a physical weight. Every step was a slog, hewing away at the fragments of his energy. He was spent. Emotionally and physically.

Despite the antivenom, he was still suffering the effects of the naeshin's bite. According to Sachiko—who'd stuck him with needles a few more times for good measure—he'd be sore for another day at least. He laboured one foot in front of the other behind the black suit. What he needed now was a shower and a shot of Lagavulin—though he'd settle for a comfortable chair and a coffee.

Diane walked beside him in silence. Whatever had transpired between her and Adeola was not clear, but it was obvious now that she'd inserted herself into the hunt for Stephen and ruffled a few feathers in the process. Clearly her agenda went beyond the dagger; he just needed to puzzle out why. Regardless of her motives, he couldn't help but feel offended that her designated punishment was to be assigned as his handler.

Well, they can take that idea and shove it.

Diane hadn't uttered more than half a dozen words to him since her return to the room. Would becoming his handler mean she'd need to relinquish her position at the library? That might explain why she was bent out of shape.

Charlie opened his mouth then closed it again, fiddling with the trench coat draped across his forearm. Why was it bothering him that the woman who'd lied to him, manipulated him was now giving him the silent treatment? Christ, he was too old for this bullshit.

A rich, silky laugh cut through the general din of activity and chatter. His head snapped up.

It couldn't be.

'Jasmin?'

Standing a way down the corridor, in animated conversation with someone, was Jasmin Khatri, his daughter's childhood friend and now partner. Her rich, brown hair that contrasted her sparkling blue eyes was pulled up into its characteristically tight ponytail. If ever he'd needed to see a friendly face, it was now.

'Jasmin.' He waved his hand at her, to get her attention.

The black suit stopped in place. 'Mr Haynes, please desist.'

'Charlie, don't.' Diane's tone was clipped, urgent.

'No, it's okay. I know her... Jasmin!' His voice echoed in the expanse, attracting more than a little interest.

'Mr Haynes,' the black suit said, 'that is enough.'

Ignoring him, Charlie lifted his hand higher.

'Charlie, stop!' Diane clamped her fingers around his arm.

He shrugged her off with a scowl.

'Jas—' His shout was cut short by a crushing pressure on his chest. The invisible force squeezed tighter, driving the air from his lungs. His eyes bulged as he stared at the black suit. His trench coat slipped from his grip, forgotten.

The man had his palms outstretched, glaring at him with such intensity, it was all Charlie could see amid his own choking gasps. The black suit gave him a pitiless smile, revealing teeth that looked a little too white. A little too sharp. His irises, dark just seconds ago, flooded with a blue so intense, Charlie's heart skipped a beat.

Those eyes...

His brain hurled him into the black despair of his memories. His nightmares.

Stephen stared back at him. His lips curled into a rictus snarl beneath his mutilated face. His preternaturally blue eyes blazed with impotent fury as Charlie grasped the hilt of the dagger buried inside Stephen's chest.

No. Inside Chekonost's chest.

Blood dribbled down Charlie's wrist as he uttered the words of the incantation. He could barely hold himself upright. The pain of his broken arm, his fractured ribs, screamed through him, adding their agonised screeches to the cacophony already inside his concussed skull. His strength gave way under the weight of Stephen's corpse. And then he was falling. Falling into the darkness. Falling into the void of excruciating grief. Falling...

The ear-splitting wail of an alarm yanked Charlie back to the present. Diane was screaming something at the black suit, but her words were swallowed up by the noise.

Charlie clenched his jaw and ground his teeth, battling against the rising fire in the pit of his stomach. In his tightened fist was the dagger.

The black suit gasped. Crimson light danced across the man's face, caused by refractions from the ruby in the blade's pommel. Brighter and brighter they became until his complexion all but bleached. The skin on his face rippled, flesh distorting to reveal unnaturally high cheek bones that drew the eye up to the sharp point of his ears. The man staggered back, like the strength had been sucked out of him.

Abruptly, the bonds compressing Charlie's chest receded. He sucked in air with a wheeze; it scraped down his throat.

'Woah!' Jasmin was between them in an instant, barging Diane out of the way in her haste. 'Hector, calm it down.'

Hector?

The black suit gestured wildly with his hand, signalling to someone Charlie couldn't see. The alarms stopped. Hector's eyes—dark once more—stayed on Charlie as his features morphed back into something more human.

'Charlie, we good?' Jasmin asked, her face tight with concern.

Charlie exhaled. 'Yeah. Sure. We're good.'

He stared at Hector. Both men's chests heaved.

'I can escort him the rest of the way.' Jasmin gripped Charlie's shoulder—a silent plea.

He lowered the dagger by his side. It whispered to him, a sonorous throb that quivered across his skin. He shuddered.

'That's in breach of protocol,' Hector said, enunciating his contempt.

'It's fine. I'll go with her.' Diane narrowed her amber eyes at the black suit. 'I'm his handler. I'll fill in the T4-80.'

'And the incident report?'

'Yes. *And* the incident report.'

Mollified, the black suit—*Hector*—glared at the dagger in Charlie's hand, then turned on his heel. 'The artifact needs to go back into containment,' he called over his shoulder.

Diane glared after him. After a few seconds, she shook her head, regained her composure and looked at Charlie. 'Look, I know this isn't ideal. I'll take the athame back to Sachiko. Then I just need to fill out some paperwork, make a few calls, and we can sit down and discuss everything properly. Is that agreeable?'

'Fine.' Charlie offered her the dagger's marbled hilt.

As she moved to take it from him, their fingers brushed. Their eyes met. A flush of warmth crept into his cheeks as he focused on the feel of her. Was she using her magic on him again? He glimpsed down at his left hand, but the sigil remained unresponsive.

As though she'd read his mind, Diane's eyes narrowed into slits. She plucked the dagger from him. Without another word, she stormed away.

'Making friends, I see?' Jasmin asked, nudging Charlie playfully in the ribs.

He winced, sucking in a breath.

'Shit, sorry.' She grimaced at the specks of blood on the sleeve of his shirt. 'What happened?'

'It's fine. Just attracted a bit of unwanted attention.'

She gave a nod, bent to retrieve his coat off the floor and passed it to him.

Charlie scanned the crowd, but Diane was gone, swallowed by the tide of bodies.

'Don't mind Hector,' Jasmin said. 'His kind are sticklers for the rules.'

'Oh, right. Hector... Wait, his kind?' His voice raised an octave. 'A demon?'

'What? No. Hector is a Dökkálfar. A dark elf.'

'An elf? Like Legolas?'

'Don't let him hear you say that.'

Charlie pinched the bridge of his nose. 'I don't want to know.'

'You asked.'

'Well, for someone who's supposedly a stickler for the rules, he seemed fairly happy to hand things over to Diane.'

'I'm not sure happy comes into it. She outranks him; he didn't have much of a choice.'

'She outranks him?' Diane... O.O.T.I.S...

This is wrong. This isn't my world. I don't belong here.

'So, what's with you and Diane?' Jasmin smiled at him. 'I saw the way you were looking at her. You *like* her.'

Charlie disregarded the question, instead focusing on the rhythm of his breathing. The impossibility of the last few months bellowed inside his skull, crowding out all rational thought. Why was it so damn hot?

'Jasmin, what are you doing here?' he asked, pushing the words out. Sweat beaded on his brow.

'The same thing as you, Charlie. Fighting the good fight. Hey, are you okay? You've gone pale.'

His vision tunnelled. He staggered back.

'Charlie?' Jasmin's voice was a distant hum.

She wrapped her arms around his torso and dragged him backwards. She sat him against the wall.

'Charlie?'

He blinked up at her as her face drifted back into focus. She was crouched in front of him, staring into his eyes.

'Sorry,' he murmured. He sucked in a breath.

'Honestly, Charlie,' Jasmin said, her smile at odds with the concern in her voice, 'one run in with a Dökkálfar and you go all giddy on me.'

'I haven't been sleeping well. Got a little lightheaded, that's all. I just need a bit of fresh air. Do me a favour, don't tell Meggy about this.'

Jasmin made a noise between a scoff and a laugh. 'Don't tell my girlfriend that her dad got a bit wobbly after seeing a dark elf? In a secret facility filled with more unknown species than the Amazon rainforest? Which he was only in because of his magical link to an ancient dagger, gifted to mankind by an archdemon? Yeah, I think I can manage that.' She looked him over again and frowned. 'Let me get someone to check you over.'

Charlie shook his head, waving off the suggestion. 'I'm fine.'

Using the wall for support, he pushed himself to his feet. Jasmin rose beside him. He was grateful that she didn't offer him a hand. 'I'm fine,' he repeated, noting her doubtful glance. 'Really.'

'Come on, let's go get you that fresh air.'

'A coffee wouldn't go amiss either.'

Jasmin smiled. 'Sure.' She gestured to the end of the corridor and let Charlie take the lead.

The sooner he got out of this hellhole the better. He just wanted to be back somewhere familiar. Somewhere comfortable. Somewhere away from elves, demons and witches.

Witches like Diane.

Chapter 15

BANNING STRAINED AGAINST THE seatbelt, bringing his mouth inches from Oliver's ear. 'Park next to the dented Mustang.' To his satisfaction the driver jumped, before recovering himself and giving a perfunctory nod.

Banning settled back against the leather, listening to the crunch of gravel beneath the tyres as the car pulled in and parked up. The outside of the building looked like an abandoned mechanic's garage, from the corrugated roof, propped up by structural steel beams to the wide open area beneath, which now served as parking. The actual interior—the former offices he supposed—took up roughly a quarter of the available space. A delightfully garish neon red sign above it read: Ron's Roadside Diner.

Making this his designated meeting point was reckless—he was a regular—but he needed to take care of things with Naomie once and for all. Two birds with one stone. He checked his watch, stomach knotting.

'I'm hungry,' he lied, unbuckling his seatbelt and turning to Heimerich. 'Are you hungry?'

The incubus stiffened, offering no more than a barely concealed look of disdain. Whether the creature was still salty about his forced transformation, or being coerced into abducting Charlie Haynes' family, Banning couldn't be sure. And, frankly, he didn't care. He'd made it plain that it would be in Heimerich's best interests to follow his instructions without complaint. Sulking about it was up to him.

Banning smirked. 'Excellent. This place does the most fantastic burgers. Patties as thick as your thumb, crisp bacon, and the cheese... oh my God, heaven in a bun.'

Oliver opened the car door. A gust of cold air rushed Banning, bringing with it the droning sound of passing traffic. As he climbed out, his shoes kicked up dirt that settled on the surface. He nodded his thanks to the driver.

The incubus had called him a monster. It was true. Something was broken inside him, something he couldn't rid himself of, no matter how hard he tried. He'd done terrible things. Horrific things. He knew what they all said about him. He'd heard the whispers. The dark and twisted rumours. Worse still, the sickening truths. And he wore them like armour, keeping everything and everyone out.

Until he'd let his guard down. Until Naomie.

Snatching a breath, Banning rolled his shoulders. Hearing Heimerich's footsteps close, he fixed his smile in place.

'Shall we?' Without waiting for a reply, Banning headed towards the diner, leaving the creature no choice but to follow.

The feeble chime of the bell above the door announced their presence. Normally, the smell of fried food would make him euphoric, but today it settled in the back of his throat like noxious fumes. Breathing through his mouth, he scanned his surroundings.

It was like stepping into fifties America, or so pop-culture had led him to believe. Black-and-white-checkerboard vinyl flooring was the stage for rows of padded, red leather booths and strategically placed tables. Props and memorabilia adorned every wall, surrounding the front section of a Corvette suspended above a working jukebox.

Sat alone in a corner booth, sucking on the straw of what appeared to be a strawberry milkshake, was Mundy Wilcoxson. He crammed a handful of fries into his mouth and gave Banning the briefest of nods. Returning the gesture, Banning crossed the diner with Heimerich in tow and slid into the seat beside Mundy. He motioned for the creature to sit opposite.

The beast of a man swallowed his food. 'Banning.'

'Mr Wilcoxson. Nice drink.'

Mundy stroked his thick, wiry black beard and gave a lazy shrug. 'It's a diner. Gotta have a strawberry malt if you go to a diner.' He relaxed back, rolling his neck with an audible crack and looked Heimerich up and down. 'Who's this? I didn't realise we were supposed to bring a date. Would explain why you're all suited and booted though.'

'This is Heimerich. He's helping me run a little errand.' Banning leant forward and said in a conspiratorial tone, 'He's an incubus.'

Mundy sat a little straighter. 'You don't say?'

'I thought that might get your attention.'

Focused on the creature, Mundy made a humming noise. 'And I thought your kind were supposed to be rare.'

Heimerich said nothing, yet the slight crease of his brow showed his curiosity.

Interesting.

Still, if there was anyone who would know the comings and goings of creatures such as Heimerich, it would be Mundy. Eight years in prison had not so much rehabilitated the man as given him a new direction in life. On the inside, anyone with half a brain knew there was money to be made in contraband. But Mundy hadn't used his ruthless ambition just to accumulate weapons or drugs; he'd used it to gather information. And he'd learnt a secret: the real money was in monsters.

Now, Mundy Wilcoxson was a big player in the black-market cryptid trade, smuggling creatures from myth, legend and nightmare across the veil to sell to the highest bidder. Against all odds, he'd managed to stay under the radar of the police and O.O.T.I.S since establishing himself in the game. That alone was worth the disgusting fee he demanded for his services.

Banning lowered his voice. 'So, when and where do I collect?'

'Yeah, I've been meaning to speak to you about that, kid.'

'Is that so?' Banning gave Mundy a hard look.

'Thing is, I lost two good men acquiring your latest asset.'

'Occupational hazard.'

'Good men are hard to come by.'

'We already agreed a price.'

Mundy lifted his thick shoulders in a shrug. 'Things change.'

'What do you see when you look at me, Mr Wilcoxson?'

'I see a prick in a suit.'

Banning's jaw ticked. 'I believe you see an easy target.'

'Nah, prick in a suit. Final answer.'

'We agreed a price. A very generous price. The logistics of your operation are none of my concern. Your men are none of my concern. We had an agreement.'

The sounds of the diner filled the space between them. The din of muffled conversations over the noise of food being prepared and staff seeing to their tables.

Mundy stroked his shaved head, then took a long sip of his drink. 'I've always wanted to know, kid, what's with the Krueger shit?'

The question caught Banning off guard. He frowned.

'The fucked up skin.' Mundy held up his own tattooed hands, showing Banning the backs, and wiggled his fingers.

'There was a fire.' He checked his watch again.

'Must have been a good few years ago, judging by those scars. You start it?'

'No,' Banning said flatly. 'I did not.'

Staring, Mundy ran his tongue over his teeth. Banning cursed himself for allowing distraction to dull the sharpness of his thoughts.

'Guess that means you don't like fire all that much.' With a flick of his wrist, Mundy produced a plain, brushed-silver lighter.

Banning forced a brittle smile, apt to shatter at any second.

In an exaggerated motion, Mundy flicked open the lid. He thumbed the spark wheel. A tongue of flame burst upward, lapping greedily at the air.

The urge to snatch the lighter from Mundy and launch it across the diner was immeasurable. It made Banning itch. He could feel his pulse thumping as the flame taunted him. He kept his gaze locked on Mundy, doing his best to control his breathing.

KILL. The suggestion seeped into his thoughts.

Not now. Not here. Not with Naomie due to arrive within minutes.

It took some effort to keep from reaching for the autoinjector in his suit jacket. He wouldn't reveal his weakness. Not to Mundy Wilcoxson. Not unless he had no other choice.

Ten, nine, eight...

'Sorry, you can't smoke in here.' A female voice cut across them.

Mundy clicked the lighter shut. He pocketed it and smiled at the blonde waitress. 'Sorry, sweetheart.'

Banning released a slow, steady breath and wiped his sweaty palms discreetly on his trousers.

'Banning.' The waitress stepped closer, tablet in hand. She fixed a loose strand of hair in place, giving him an eager smile. 'The usual?'

He grinned back at her and removed his jacket, using the momentary distraction to glimpse her name badge. 'Isla, you're looking beautiful as ever. The usual sounds great, thank you.'

Her smile broadened at the compliment. She stood watching him for a few seconds before seemingly realising there were other people at the table. 'One brisket burger, classic fries and a Coke it is.' She recorded the order and turned to Heimerich. 'And for you?'

'He'll have the same,' Banning said.

Heimerich cleared his throat. 'I don't eat animal products.'

'He'll have the same,' Banning repeated, inching his hand towards Isla as she tapped the order into the tablet. His fingers brushed her thigh, just below the hem of her blue gingham dress. She froze, a blush spreading across her cheeks, and met his gaze. Her skin was soft beneath his touch, warm. He worked his hand up slowly, deliberately, until a barely audible gasp slipped from her lips.

'Banning...' Her voice was a husky whisper. She closed her hand over his and removed it from her thigh. 'You'll get me fired.' Her attention snapped to the counter where the manager was talking to another member of staff. Bending low enough that her lips touched his ear, she whispered, 'I'm on break in ten minutes.'

He puffed out his chest, preening, giving her the expected response. He ignored the roil of complaint in his gut. Ten minutes. He checked his watch. *Cutting it close, but it should still work.*

Isla smoothed down her uniform and set off for the kitchen, her backwards glance at Banning filled with promise.

Mundy blew out a low whistle. 'Jesus, kid. You're gonna have to show me how you do that.'

Banning changed the subject. 'What happened to your car?'

'Hit a dog.' Mundy's wince was a delicious thing. That brash, burnt-orange Mustang was one of the few things the man seemed to care about. That and money.

'Looks near enough a write-off. Expensive. Must've been some dog.'

An unreadable expression flickered across Mundy's face.

'Back to the matter at hand,' Banning said. 'Where's the meet?'

'You gonna reimburse me for my men?'

Banning held Mundy's stare, unflinching. He'd had enough games. His nerves were raw. He willed energy up from his core. It would be so easy to squeeze the air from the man's lungs. To choke the last strangled breath from his insolent mouth, until his face purpled and his heart stuttered to a halt inside his chest.

Heimerich shifted opposite him. 'Don't. Please. It'll attract too much attention.'

Banning glared back. The incubus flinched. But the creature was right. He needed Mundy alive. For all that it rankled, he needed him.

For now.

Exhaling, Banning allowed his power to recede. *Reckless.* What good was he if he couldn't keep his wits about him? If he lost control? Again.

Mundy's eyes widened in realisation. He laughed, loud and unrestrained. 'Holy shit, kid. You were really considering it, weren't you? Maybe I underestimated you. Tell you what, you tell me how you got that pretty slip of a thing to agree to drop her panties for you and I'll honour the original price.' He nodded once at the kitchen from where Isla had just emerged, carrying a tray laden with food and drinks.

She sashayed from table to table. A drink here. A basket of chips there. Another waitress slowed to whisper something in her ear as she passed. They giggled, turning to give Banning an appraising glance. When she reached their booth, she set down their meals and gave Banning a wink. On any other occasion it would have set his pulse racing.

You knew the risks.

The mantra echoed through his head.

'I'll be out in five.' Tucking the empty tray under her arm, Isla waited for his nod, then set off towards a couple who was gesturing for the bill.

'Seriously, kid. I want to know.'

Mundy was starting to annoy him.

'It's the suit, Mr Wilcoxson. It's the suit.' He got up and grabbed his jacket. 'Stay here, I won't be long.'

Mundy smirked. 'That's nothing to brag about.'

Gritting his teeth, Banning ignored the comment and made his way to the exit, to Isla. A ripple of something that was neither excitement nor desire shuddered through him.

Chapter 16

From the outside, the O.O.T.I.S headquarters could easily be mistaken for some grand museum; a work of art in its own right. Vast didn't even begin to describe it. The building had to encompass at least five acres of land. The fact that it was largely ignored by the passersby was mind-boggling.

Charlie frowned up at the building, waiting for Jasmin. There must be some sort of cloaking magic involved there, but damned if he knew what, and damned if he wanted to find out.

Jasmin came to a stop beside him and offered him a plastic cup filled with black coffee.

'Sorry, there was a queue for the vending machine. You never did answer me about Diane.' Her breath fogged in the cold air.

Giving her a sideways glance, he accepted the drink. He took a sip. His nose wrinkled. The coffee was bitter. Ashy. 'A queue? For this? For an organisation that doesn't seem to be struggling for cash, the coffee's shit.'

'I know your tactics. Stop avoiding the question.'

The low thrum of his mobile vibrating spared Charlie from responding. He dug it out of his pocket, quirking a smile at her as he answered. 'Charles Haynes.'

'Jesus, Charlie. I've been calling you for the last two hours.' Nick. There was an edge to his voice that set the hairs on Charlie's arms on end.

'Nick, what's wrong?'

'It's Meghan and Evelyn, they're missing.'

Charlie staggered back. He crushed the cup, spilling scorching liquid over his hand. He dropped it with a hiss. 'What do you mean missing?'

'Evelyn was supposed to be having a sleepover with a school friend.'

'Poppy.'

'Yeah, Poppy. When Poppy and her mum Eleanor arrived, they found the door ajar. Eleanor let herself in and found smashed glass all over the hallway. She tried phoning Meghan, but didn't get an answer. Turns out Meghan's phone was still inside, along with her keys and bag. Car's still on the driveway. We've taken statements. Nobody saw or heard anything.'

'We're on our way.' Charlie hung up, thrusting the phone into his pocket. He dried his scalded hand against his coat and turned to Jasmin. 'Meggy and Evie are missing.'

Jasmin's eyes bulged, the colour draining from her face. She took a breath and nodded, feeling for the keys in her pocket. A silent understanding passed between them.

Not a word was uttered as Charlie sprinted after her to her car. His mind reeled. Scenario after scenario played out in his head. All the grisly details and all the horrors of a lifetime in the police force, casting a net to dredge up every grim and gut-wrenching outcome his imagination had to offer.

The engine roared into life and broke his concentration. He was in the car. Charlie didn't remember getting in. Jasmin made a sharp right, tyres screeching. His shoulder rammed against the central pillar. He ignored the flare of pain and buckled up.

'Why would anyone abduct my family? It doesn't make sense...' His voice trailed off. He stared down at the sigil marking his left hand.

No.

'Charlie?'

Clenching and unclenching his fists, Charlie fought for control. He needed a clear head. Connect the dots, just like any other case. Follow the facts.

Just follow the facts.

Someone was trying to get to him through his family. Someone who knew about his link to the dagger. Someone smart enough not to go after him directly. But nobody was supposed to know. Not about Kar'roc's Maw. Not about him. Not unless they had to. Which meant that either the Order had a rogue agent, or...

'O.O.T.I.S has a mole,' he croaked.

'Charlie, that's absurd.'

'Is it? Think about it. How many agents were there the night I got attacked?'

'Maybe two or three, excluding Diane.'

'Few enough that if one of them got it into their heads to make a move on the dagger, they'd be rooted out in no time. However, if they were to let the information slip, if there was interest from an outside party...'

Other than the slight twist of her mouth, Jasmin made no reply. Her silence spoke volumes.

'Adeola said my connection to the dagger prevented my memories from being altered,' Charlie prompted, hoping she'd agree. He needed to hear her say the words. Needed to know that he wasn't alone in his theory.

She nodded sharply, eyes fixed on the road, as she slowed for another corner. 'It's standard protocol that civilians have their memories altered after exposure to a supernatural event. It's a precaution, as much for their welfare as anyone else's.'

'So, it's safe to assume that nobody else knows about the dagger?'

'Yes. Only the agents that attended the scene when you fought the demon, and those on a need-to-know basis, should be aware of your link to Kar'roc's Maw.'

'Like you?'

'I'm going to pretend that you didn't just ask me that.'

'I—'

'Look, Charlie, you've always been like a dad to me. You, Megs, Evie, you're my family. I would *never* do anything that would put any of you in harm's way. I'm sorry if me not telling you that I work for O.O.T.I.S has put your nose out of joint, but I thought you'd appreciate some time to adjust to your new reality first. And yes, me knowing about the dagger is on a need-to-know basis. I was briefed after the fact. I don't know all the ins and outs of what happened but I know enough. I'm in a relationship with your daughter; it makes sense for me to know for fuck's sake. If your fragile ego can't cope with the fact there's more to me than you first thought, that's on you. Not me. That you'd even suggest I'd ever do anything to put you all in danger is a fucking insult.'

'I didn't mean… I know you would never do anything to jeopardise Meggy or Evie's safety. I was out of line. I'm sorry.'

Jasmin relaxed her grip on the steering wheel, the whites of her knuckles turning pale brown. After a few deep breaths, the tightness in her face eased. 'I know. It's okay. This is a shock for me too. It's not supposed to happen. Agents are vetted and then annually assessed. The higher the rank the more stringent the process. I'm not naive enough to say that it *couldn't* happen, but to risk everything, their careers, their freedom, by exposing the very secrets they've been sworn to keep?' She paused, every second unmasking her uncertainty. 'I should call it in.'

'Is that a good idea, given the circumstances?'

'It's not going to take them long to figure it out, Charlie. This is O.O.T.I.S we're talking about.' Jasmin pursed her lips. 'There'll be a file of all the agents who were in attendance the night you were attacked. If there really is someone leaking information, they'll be outed.

O.O.T.I.S is still the best chance we have of tracking down Megs and Evie.'

'You don't think Diane…?'

'It's very unlikely. Diane knows the dangers of Kar'roc's Maw more than most. I don't know how much you know about her past, and it's probably not my place to say, but the demon inside Stephen murdered her husband. In front of her.'

Charlie winced. 'Christ.'

No wonder Diane had been so keen to find out what he knew about the dagger when they'd first met. If anyone could understand not being able to let something go, it was him.

I've been an absolute dick.

He rubbed his ring finger absently. Not only had he completely blanked her since learning that she was involved with the Order—refusing to answer her calls or respond to her texts, like a stubborn teenager—but now he'd left her high and dry. As his handler, she was going to be in the shit once his departure became common knowledge.

He clenched his jaw.

There'd be time for apologies later. Right now, his family needed him. He couldn't afford to be distracted.

Chapter 17

BANNING THRUST HIS HIPS faster as Isla let out a throaty moan. She shifted her stance, adjusting her hands on the wall, strands of blonde hair spilling from her ponytail. He gripped her waist tighter, resisting the urge to look at his watch, and focused on the bricks at his eyeline.

The setting was hardly romantic. The walled-off employee car park behind the diner offered little in the way of aesthetics; it was either the dented, grey fire door to his right or the commercial wheelie bins to his left. But then, he'd never been one for romance.

'Don't stop, Banning,' she breathed.

It was almost a relief when he heard the familiar grinding sound of worn brake pads. Then a car door thudded shut.

Right on time.

'Banning?'

Naomie stood frozen in the folds of her thick winter coat, her lips parted in shock. The betrayal in her wide eyes cleaved his chest open. Tears spilled down her cheeks, leaving glistening trails down her perfect brown skin. He wanted nothing more than to brush them away.

Instead, he did up his fly in the few baffled seconds of silence it took for Isla to turn around.

'At least I know why you broke it off.' Naomie's voice was fierce.

Isla blinked up at him in confusion, her cheeks ruddy with a glow that had nothing to do with the biting air. She pulled her underwear back up. 'Banning? What's going on? I thought you said it was over between you two? Naomie, I swear, I thought it was over. I didn't say anything about it to you out of respect.'

'*Respect?*'

'Yes, I swear. I made the others promise not to say anything.'

'The *others*? God, does everyone know? How long has this been going on?' Naomie waved a hand. 'No, you know what? I don't care.'

'Naomie, I'm sorry,' Isla pleaded. 'I didn't want you to find out like this. It's only been a couple of weeks. Tell her, Banning.'

But Banning was still fixated on Naomie. He didn't trust himself to speak. Instead, he gave her a shrug, his face a mask of indifference. It was done. There would be no more phone calls. No more messages.

Whatever it was that he and Naomie had, it didn't belong to him. It belonged to the boy he was before he'd been changed. The man he could have been. But that future was gone, lost to the demon that stole everything from him. What had emerged from the blackened remains of his childhood was the scarred and wretched monster that stood before her now. He'd been foolish to think he could be anything else to her. Could offer her anything else. His recent episodes had proved that. Death was his gift and it was one he would not bestow upon her. Never her.

'You know what I've been through. You *know*! Jesus, you could have at least waited until the sheets were cold.' Naomie choked back a sob. 'You promised you wouldn't hurt me.'

No. I promised I would protect you. And I am.

He smirked.

'You're disgusting.' Naomie's face screwed up in a scowl, hands tight fists by her sides. Her arm twitched. Banning braced himself, but the strike never came. Violence was his native tongue, not hers.

She barged past them, yanked the door open in a squeal of rust and metal, and stormed inside.

He walked away, leaving Isla to stare after him.

Mundy's grinning mug greeted Banning as he lowered himself back into the booth beside him. He did his best to ignore the man, unwilling to give him the sordid details he so clearly sought. His food was cold, his appetite gone, but still he went through the motions of eating, forcing it down bite by stomach-churning bite.

Heimerich sat in silence, meal untouched. To say that he looked relieved by Banning's return was an exaggeration, but judging by the way he stiffened every time the trafficker so much as moved, it was obvious their time together had not been relished.

'So?' Mundy prompted.

'A gentleman doesn't kiss and tell.'

Mundy scoffed. 'A gentleman doesn't get his dick wet in the back of a car park in broad daylight.'

Banning wiped his mouth with a paper napkin and tossed it on the remains of his food. 'The location for tonight, please, Mr Wilcoxson.'

'Dockyard. The big slipway. You'll know the one, shit ton of windows in the roof. You can follow me up there if you want, see if anything else takes your fancy. Just make sure you're gone before the buyers arrive. Wouldn't want them thinking I'm running some kinda nursery.'

'Duly noted.'

Mundy squinted past Banning's shoulder, his mouth turning up in amusement. 'Looks like we might have a catfight on our hands, lads.'

It was at times like these that Banning swore his magic was a sixth sense. He knew what he would see before twisting in his seat.

In full view of every gawking customer, Naomie and Isla practically circled one another. Words were being exchanged. Heated words. And they were getting louder. Meals and conversations had been forgotten; all eyes were on the two young women. Even the heavyset manager looked entertained, making no effort to defuse the situation, that was until he noticed a few disapproving looks, hushed whispers, and more than one phone being pointed in their direction.

Amazing what the prospect of bad press could do.

Hoisting himself up from the counter, the man mumbled something to the pair and ushered them into the kitchen. But not before Naomie snarled a response and jabbed a finger at Banning.

Feeling the collective weight of the diners' attention on him, Banning turned back around. Mundy's infuriating grin was back.

'What?' Banning glared.

'You're porking both of them?'

'Pork is not a verb.'

A roar of laughter escaped the man's lips, drawing more stares. 'I knew it. You jammy son of a bitch.'

Heimerich cleared his throat, eyes flicking over the patrons before settling on Banning. 'We should leave.'

Mundy waved off the suggestion. 'What's the rush? The kid's clearly having a whale of a time.'

Ignoring him, the incubus continued. 'Shouldn't we go back and check that Charlie Haynes' daughter—'

A small metal plate with a receipt was slammed down on the table.

Banning arched an eyebrow at it, then looked up at the woman glaring down at him.

'Naomie,' he said, fixing his smile in place.

'You absolute prick,' she snarled.

Forcing a chuckle, Banning removed his wallet and placed a handful of notes on the plate. 'Can't forget the tip now, can I?' He gave her a wink and pulled out another, tossing it onto the pile.

Unadulterated loathing. There was no other way to describe her look. It radiated off her in waves. Penetrated into his core, boiling his insides, until he thought he might throw up every mouthful of food he'd forced down his throat.

Her nostrils flared, eyes glistening with hate. She snatched up the metal plate and stormed away. Chin up, shoulders back.

The trafficker chuckled. 'Looks like I'm buying myself a suit.'

Banning blinked. He wanted nothing more than to wipe the smirk off Mundy Wilcoxson's face permanently, but in the moment, he couldn't bring himself to so much as move. He was no stranger to pain, but this... this was new. It was like something had been ripped out of him, leaving him hollow. Broken.

No more phone calls. No more messages. No more Naomie.

Chapter 18

No amount of mental preparation was enough to stave off the heart-stopping dread of seeing a marked police car and a forensics van parked across his daughter's driveway. Charlie swallowed hard. The two uniformed officers sitting inside the car stirred when he and Jasmin approached, but settled back down after she held up her warrant card.

'Charlie. Jasmin.' Nick stepped away from the front door, face drawn. He looked paler than usual, dark circles stark beneath his light-blue eyes.

One look from his friend was all it took. A fist of ice struck Charlie's chest.

'Show me.'

Nick motioned for them to enter and gestured at the crime scene investigator crouched on the hallway tiles. 'Scenes of crime shouldn't be too much longer. They're just finishing up their final examination. Watch out for the glass.'

Cautiously, Charlie stepped across the threshold. At the sound of his footsteps the figure in white turned and stood, coveralls rustling lightly. Charlie's view opened and he saw shattered fragments of blue-and-gold crystal spread out across the floor. And something crimson in colour.

His breath hitched.

Blood.

He opened his mouth, but the words wouldn't come. He couldn't breathe.

Was it Meggy's blood or Evie's?

Sweat beaded on his forehead. He took a stiff step forward.

'Charlie.' Jasmin squeezed his shoulder. When he didn't respond, she increased the pressure, fingers clamping. 'Charlie.'

He tore his gaze from the crimson smears. Her eyes flicked to the sigil on his hand.

He made a fist. 'I'm okay.'

The female CS investigator watched the exchange, frowning behind transparent protective goggles. 'Detective, can I have a moment?' She directed the question to Jasmin.

With a fleeting glance at Nick, Jasmin gave a single nod then stepped back of the property, where she waited for the woman to join her.

Nick watched them disappear from view, his confusion clear. He returned his attention to Charlie.

It was obvious Nick had questions. In normal circumstances the detective would have passed comment, made a tongue-in-cheek remark to lighten the mood. But these weren't normal circumstances. Charlie was barely holding it together and his friend was treading on eggshells to compensate. Somehow the lack of banter made it worse. Made it real.

Finally, Nick broke the silence. 'Sam's just making a call.'

'Sam?'

'Bennett.'

'Ah. Right.'

'Maybe if you take a look around, you can see if anything's missing or out of place?'

'Sure.'

Careful not to disturb the debris, Charlie navigated around the shards of glass and entered the living room.

Nick followed.

'The smashed vases came from there,' Charlie said absently, pointing to the copper-framed side table, as he pieced together the scene. 'Evie's Switch is still here. So's her tablet. Not a robbery gone wrong.'

He was talking more to himself than to Nick, processing the room with clinical detachment. If he stopped, if he took even a second's pause, he knew he'd become a wreck. So he did what he always did, what his father had taught him to do as a young boy with his belt and his fists: buried his emotions.

'I know this is a really shitty situation, but is there anyone you can think of who would want to harm Meghan or Evelyn?' Nick asked. 'Meghan's ex-husband, maybe?'

Charlie's fingers on his right hand twitched towards the sigil on his left. He caught himself and forced his arms to his side. 'No. No one.'

'I'm sorry, Charlie. After everything you've been through recently, what with your house getting smashed up...' A strange expression flickered across Nick's face. His eyes glazed over, taking on a far-away look.

'Nick?'

The sound of Jasmin's knuckles gently rapping on the doorframe announced her presence. She joined them, took one glance at a despondent Nick and arched an eyebrow in question at Charlie.

He shrugged at her. 'Nick? Are you okay?'

Nick blinked. 'I... I uh... Sorry, Charlie, what were you saying?'

'I said no, there's no one I can think of.'

'Oh. Right.' Dragging a hand through his auburn hair, Nick blinked again. Unease furrowed his brow. Noticing Jasmin by the doorway, he cleared his throat. 'I think scenes of crime are done. I'm just going to check if there's anything else they need.'

'Sure. Thanks, Nick.' Charlie watched his friend leave. Nick was no stranger to pulling long shifts, but even so, Charlie had never seen him that dead beat before.

Charlie exhaled. He wasn't about to let the situation overwhelm him. He couldn't. Instead, he focused on Jasmin.

A mistake.

Every one of his emotions—the agonising concern, the crippling fear, the barely restrained anger—were echoed back in her look.

'What is it?' Charlie said, voice low.

'The blood is coagulated.'

'Meaning?'

'It's next to useless. We can't use it to track Meghan. Once clotted, the blood loses its potency and the spellwork won't take.'

'You can't even be sure that it's hers.'

'It's hers.'

A feeling of repulsion slithered through him. Of course O.O.T.I.S would know if it was Meghan's blood or not. They probably had DNA samples from every man and his dog on file.

His nose wrinkled.

Jasmin gave him a thoughtful look. 'But we could use yours.'

There was no disguising his wince as he caught on to her train of thought.

'Sachiko must have dozens of your blood samples in storage back at headquarters. I'll put in a call.' She reached for her mobile.

'It won't work.'

'Sure it will. As Meghan's father, the red cell antigens—'

'It *won't* work.'

The excitement on Jasmin's face dropped away. Her bewilderment shifted to frustration. Finally, the realisation set in.

She cursed. 'That bitch. Charlie I—'

He cut her off. 'It's fine.' The indiscretions of his ex-wife were not something he wanted to discuss. Not now. Not ever. 'I came to terms with it years ago. We have bigger problems right now. If we can't use the blood, is there a way to track using anything else?'

Jasmin gave a sharp shake of her head. 'If she had her phone on her, maybe. But even then, it would be a long shot. I don't think we're dealing with an amateur here. Whoever did this knew when and where to strike.'

'So we've got no leads. Nothing. Meggy and Evie could be...' He squeezed his eyes shut and pinched the bridge of his nose.

'No. If this really is about you, about the Maw, then they need Megs and Evie alive.'

He opened his eyes. 'There's a lot of blood, Jasmin. She's out there somewhere, hurt. And Evie, she must be petrified.'

And I feel utterly, fucking useless.

He'd seen cases like this before. Witnessed the first-hand anguish of parents who'd had loved ones go missing. Children. Only for their bodies to be found days or weeks later. And in his darkest moments, when even the whisky hadn't been enough to take the edge off, he'd imagined what it must be like for them. What it would be like for him. Until the dark thoughts had driven him to the harrowing edges of an abyss so bleak, it had been a struggle not to lose himself to it completely. But even the traumatic offerings of his fucked up mind couldn't compare to the terror and helplessness that threatened to annihilate him right now.

He staggered out of the room, forcing Jasmin to back out of his way.

He needed air.

It was too hot. Every breath came faster than the last. Every tattoo beat of his heart an explosion in his skull. He couldn't make out what Jasmin was saying to him. He didn't care. He had to get outside. Get out before he suffocated.

Glass crunched beneath his shoes. Something slick gave way beneath him. He pitched forward, landing on the tiles with a grunt.

'*Jesus*, Charlie!'

Wheezing, he pushed himself to his knees, one hand braced against the wall for support. He gulped down a painful breath, then another, allowing the ache of his ribs to ground him.

'Charlie, are you okay? You scared me.' Jasmin crouched beside him. Her eyes took in every inch of him, no doubt checking for injuries.

The glass dug into his shins and he exhaled. 'I'm fine.' With an effort, he moved to push himself up. There was a gleam on the wall at his eye line, so faint, he almost missed it. 'What's that?'

Jasmin leant in, squinting at the iridescent streaks. She trailed her fingers over the markings.

'Shadowburn. I've seen this before. I think we have a lead,' she whispered.

'Shadowburn?'

She startled, snatching her hand back. Her lips pressed into a thin line. For a moment he thought she wasn't going to answer, but then she set her jaw and looked him square in the eyes.

'It's an organic chemical residue.'

'Residue? From what?'

Jasmin rubbed her fingers together. 'A very particular species of demon.'

Charlie suppressed a shudder.

'These markings are the result of a sudden and unexpected transformation, sort of like a defence mechanism. Similar in a way to the alarm pheromones that wasps release when attacked, but visible. Usually, these kinds of demon leave no trace of their presence. None. Revealing themselves in daylight goes against their nature. They're stealth hunters, able to conceal themselves in shadow. To walk the veil between realms.'

'So what happened to cause it?'

'My guess? Someone hurt it.'

'Meghan fought back?'

Jasmin paused a moment. 'It's possible. But generally speaking, humans don't pose much of a threat to demons.'

'How does this help us?'

'Because this isn't how they hunt. They don't abduct people. It means that whatever demon was here is working for someone, that it's familiar with our realm. Has connections. Contacts. And I know someone who can help us.'

Hope bloomed in Charlie's chest. But it was fragile, already beginning to wither beneath the weight of his doubt. 'That CS investigator, she's an agent, right? That's what that little pow-wow was about earlier?' Jasmin's nod came as no surprise. 'Wouldn't she have called this in already? For all we know, someone could have already tipped off the abductors. If they suspect anyone is on to them...'

'These creatures are rare. Without knowing what to look for, it's extremely unlikely that anyone here would recognise the residue—assuming they even saw it in the first place. You only noticed it because it was right in front of your face. The only way O.O.T.I.S is going to know is if I call it in.'

He waited, leaving an unspoken question hanging.

'Look,' she said, answering it. 'I think you're right. There's no way this is all some unfortunate coincidence. I have a contact, but she won't talk to O.O.T.I.S. This has to be done under the radar.'

'Fine. Count me in. But won't the Order be able to track us?'

'You? No. Me? Under normal circumstances, yes. But as long as I stay close to you, we'll be fine.'

He didn't understand. 'Close to me?'

She pointed to his hand. To the sigil. 'Why do you think they assigned you a handler? Your connection to the dagger creates some sort of magical dead zone around you. They can't track you. It's why they've been watching the house. Tailing you wherever you go. Just keeping tabs on you isn't enough anymore.'

'Oh.'

'Charlie, if we do this, there could be serious consequences. O.O.T.I.S is going to be pissed.'

Charlie gave her a level look. 'I'd burn O.O.T.I.S to the ground if it meant getting my family back.'

She gave him a smile that was all teeth. 'That's all I needed to hear.'

Chapter 19

'AND YOU SAY THAT Meghan and Evelyn eat at this diner regularly?'

Nick pulled his gaze from his notebook to look at the woman sitting across from him. Mrs Williams, a colleague of Meghan's. She fidgeted in the chair, worrying at the rose-gold band on her thumb. The gesture reminded him of how Charlie always rubbed at his ring finger when he got anxious. Nick pressed his lips together and looked down at his scrawled handwriting.

'Yeah, that's right,' Mrs Williams said. 'She's got a friend that works there. Eleanor... something.'

'Eleanor Bell?' Eleanor hadn't mentioned that Meghan and Evelyn were regulars when he'd taken her statement earlier. It could be something. He had the address of the diner somewhere in his notes... He'd pull it out later.

'Yeah, I think so. She's always talking about the place. Evie loves it. To be honest, I think Meghan goes there mainly to support Eleanor. Food's supposed to be good, if you like slabs of fried meat.'

'I don't.'

'No?'

'I'm vegan.' Nick heard Sam's scoff. He glanced up to see the grinning detective roll his eyes. *Dick.*

'Oh. They do vegan stuff there too,' Mrs Williams said. 'That's what Meghan and Evie get nowadays. But yeah, I think they went there on Thursday. Apparently she got into a bit of a spat with the manager over something she heard him saying to one of the waitresses. The guy who runs the place is a real piece of work.'

Nick checked his notes from his interview with Eleanor. He'd underlined the words "difficult boss". Her reasons for lying to him earlier had just become crystal clear. 'Did she say how bad this spat was?'

Mrs William's eyebrows shot up. 'Oh. No. I don't think it was anything bad enough for him to... From what she was saying he was just being a bit pervy, y'know? He makes them wear these skimpy little retro uniforms. All the front of house staff are female, mostly young, all pretty. I think she just gave him a piece of her mind, that's all. She's very strong-willed. Doesn't mind ruffling a few feathers. You should hear her at work.'

Takes after Charlie.

Mrs Williams added. 'God, I hope her and Evie are okay. Do you... do you think you'll find them?'

'We're doing our absolute best. Thank you for your time, Mrs Williams.' Nick stood.

'You're welcome.' She followed suit, escorting him and Sam into the hallway. Giving Nick one last sad smile, she opened the front door and held it in place. 'Let me know if there's anything else I can do to help.'

'We will.'

The door thunked closed. They walked back to the car.

'You just can't help it, can you?' Sam's mouth quirked up as he unlocked the car and reached for the handle.

'Help what?'

'Telling everyone that you're a vegan.'

'She asked,' Nick said indignantly, getting inside the Fabia and fastening his seatbelt.

Sam slipped into the driver's seat, the car bobbing lightly. 'I think you'll find she didn't. It's like you're recruiting.'

'Whatever.' Rolling his eyes, Nick continued. 'It looks like we've got a stop to make.'

'Excellent. I could go for a burger right about now. Oh, don't look at me like that. I'm never going to join your almond-milking cult. Anyway, I'm helping to save the planet.'

'*Excuse* me?'

'Cows. Creepy buggers. That dead-eyed stare? Doesn't fool me for a second. You know they're up to something. Given half the chance, they'd turn on us.'

'You're not serious?'

'I've read about it. Farmers trampled to death, dog walkers attacked...'

'I don't believe you.'

'It's true. And not just farmers—'

'No, I mean I don't believe that you can read.'

'Funny. Just don't come crying to me when we're overrun by the killer bastards.'

Nick sighed. 'Remind me again why it is I keep working with you?'

'I'm a loveable rogue, that's why.'

'I'm not sure that's how I'd describe you.'

'No?'

'No.' Nick tapped his lip. 'How can I put this politely? You're a strange little man.'

'I've been called strange before, but nobody's ever accused me of being little. In fact—'

Nick held his hand up. 'You're too much, you know that?'

'That's what she said.'

'*Jesus*. Can you just drive?'

Chuckling, Sam started the engine and pulled away.

'So this sleep problem you've been having,' Sam said, flicking up the indicator and making a right, 'you say it started around the time we were on that Caravan Cannibal copycat case?'

Nick frowned. He couldn't remember telling Sam that's when it had started, but then his head was a bit foggy of late. 'Uh... yeah, about then. But it's been worse these past couple of weeks.'

'Stress maybe? Charlie was banged up pretty bad. It's lucky he had the foresight to grab that kitchen knife or he'd have been a goner before we got there.'

'Yeah,' Nick said numbly.

Kitchen knife. That's what he'd written in the reports, although thinking back on it now, that didn't feel right. Charlie's old case files had mentioned a dagger. A creeping sense of déjà vu unsettled his thoughts. He could have sworn...

Nick froze.

Images exploded in his mind. They twisted and flickered, revealing a glimpse of detail, only for it to morph into something else. The pressure inside his skull was unbearable. Gripped by vertigo, he choked out a breath.

'Pull over,' he gasped, fingers jabbing at the buckle of his seatbelt.

Sam brought the car to an abrupt halt, just in time for Nick to throw the door open and vomit across the kerb.

'Jesus, Nick, are you alright? Here.' Sam handed him a bottle of water.

Nick reached out for it, hand shaking, fingers clumsy. He yanked off the lid, took a swig, swished water around his mouth and spat it out.

'Want me to drive you home?' Sam said.

Taking another mouthful, Nick swallowed and shook his head.

'You sure?'

'Just do me a favour, would you?' Nick pulled the car door closed and buckled up. 'Stop talking about it. There's something... I don't know. I just... can we not?'

Sam nodded, his frown deepening as he regarded Nick with obvious concern. 'Here, let's try something. A little breathing exercise.'

'Seriously?'

'Hey, there's more to me than just my good looks, you know. I have depth. Right, now shut your eyes.'

Nick gave him a confused look. 'Huh?'

'Shut your eyes.'

'I swear to God, if you tell me to open my mouth...'

Sam chuckled. 'Right, now open—'

Nick jerked back, snapping his eyes open.

'I'm kidding. *God*, you're so highly strung. Shut your eyes.'

With one last warning scowl, Nick obliged.

'Hold out your hands, palms facing up. Just do it. I'm not going to pull any funny shit.'

The light pressure of Sam pressing down on his hands was oddly reassuring. Warmth radiated from the man's skin, seeping into Nick's flesh. Until that exact moment, he hadn't realised just how cold he was. A sense of calm wrapped around him like a blanket, enveloping him so completely, all the stress and the anxiety became little more than a distant murmur.

'Now, tell me again what you remember about the night we arrived at Charlie's house.' Sam's tone was soothing.

'I said I didn't want to talk about it.'

'Just humour me.' Sam increased the pressure on Nick's palms.

It was as if all the tension was pouring out of him. The knots in his muscles loosened. The dull ache inside his head ebbed away

'Charlie texted me,' Nick answered mechanically. 'We arrived with uniform. The front door had been kicked in. There was broken glass and warped metal from the staircase panels strewn across the hallway. Ciara

Torres and her daughter Addison were there, terrified but unharmed. I went upstairs. Uniform followed, you stayed with Ciara and Addison. The bathroom wall was damaged. Brick fragments and dust everywhere.'

'And Charlie?'

'Charlie was hurt.' The memories came to the fore. Clearer than they'd been in weeks. Shaping so perfectly, it felt like he was watching them play out in front of him. 'A woman... Diane I think her name was, pulled the body of the serial killer off him and helped him to sit up.'

'The Caravan Cannibal?'

'No, a copycat. He was in his late thirties. Just some sicko trying to recreate the murders. I helped Charlie to get up. Get downstairs. Waited with him until the ambulance arrived.'

'You said Diane pulled the body of the serial killer off Charlie. He was already dead when you got upstairs?'

'Yes. Fatal stab wound to the chest. From the kitchen knife Charlie had brought upstairs for protection.'

Sam removed his hands from Nick's. Nick opened his eyes. The pain in his head was completely gone. He felt relaxed, rejuvenated almost.

'What was that?' he asked, staring down at his palms. 'Reiki or something?'

Sam laughed, not unkindly. 'Sure, something like that. How are you feeling? Not going to puke again if I start driving, are you? I mean, that sort of thing's acceptable after a night out on the lash, but while we're on the clock? Just seems like a waste.'

'I feel... I feel great, actually. Wait, you didn't lace that water with something, did you?'

'Like I'd want to roofie you. Let's get to this diner. You're probably hungry after that.' Sam motioned at the kerb. 'Mrs Williams said they serve grass burgers.' He started the car.

Nick let his comment slide. When was the last time he'd felt this refreshed?

Whatever Sam had done it had worked.

Chapter 20

CHARLIE LIFTED HIS SHOE. Plastic shards from the hypodermic needle he'd just stepped on dusted the pavement. *Lovely*.

He cast a sidelong glance at Jasmin. She caught his expression and cocked her head in confusion.

Rather than explain, he cleaned his shoe on the ground and looked up at the grimy, beige-clad, high-rise block of flats. They looked like stacked shipping containers with windows.

Dismal.

He'd always hated this area. Burglaries, assaults, stabbings were rife, and it only went downhill from there. No wonder it ranked in the top ten most dangerous neighbourhoods in the county.

His stomach knotted. This was where Jasmin grew up?

'What?' she said, catching him glancing at her again.

Her blue gaze slid from his face to his hands.

Squeeze, release. Squeeze, release. Squeeze, release.

'Charlie, just get it off your chest already.'

'Why didn't you tell me?'

She gave him a blank look. 'Tell you?'

He made a wide sweeping arc with his arm. 'Christ, Jasmin. This place is notorious. Do you know how many serious crimes happen round here?' He shook his head at the old mattress and remains of a bed that had been fly-tipped alongside smashed beer bottles, lager cans and more used needles. 'I'd have let you stay with me if I'd known.'

'I know you would have, Charlie. I know. But I was sixteen when my parents kicked me out. I wanted my independence. I didn't want to have to rely on anyone else ever again. And anyway, staying with you would have been too awkward.' His forehead creased and she smiled. 'What with me having a massive crush on your daughter and everything.'

Charlie squeezed the bridge of his nose. 'I wish you'd have said something. Just thinking about you living here as a teenager...' He grimaced. 'Sixteen? You wouldn't have been eligible for tenancy until you were eighteen. How...'

The thought was lost when a dull ache spread out from the sigil on his hand.

He stared up at the block of flats. Sat behind the dingy white guard rail of a second floor balcony, smiling serenely down at them, was a woman in her late eighties. The chair in which she sat occupied most of the available space. Her hands moved in a steady rhythm; it took Charlie a few moments to realise that she was knitting. She placed the knitting on her lap and adjusted the intricate knot at the front of her headscarf.

'Jasmin, child. What a pleasant surprise,' the woman called down.

'How long has she been sitting there?' Charlie muttered, rubbing at his hand and trying to place the subtle accent.

'Auntie, I'm sorry it's been so long.'

Auntie? It was clearly nothing more than a term of endearment, because there was no resemblance whatsoever. And from what Jasmin had told him about her family, he was confident that this woman—whoever she might be—was no relation by blood or marriage. Still, the genuine warmth on both their faces made it plain that they shared a bond, despite Jasmin having never mentioned an "auntie" before.

First O.O.T.I.S, now this. What else didn't he know about her? He turned to her, the question plain on his face. She shook her head, gesturing instead for them to move nearer to the balcony.

When they were close enough to hold a conversation without broadcasting to the other residents, they stopped.

'Aren't you going to introduce me to this handsome young man?' The woman's smile broadened, carving furrows into the already creased skin around her milky-white eyes.

'She's blind?' Charlie kept his voice low.

'Come now, don't be so hard on yourself.' The woman's hearty chuckle echoed around them. 'Come on up, child. And bring your friend.'

Charlie scowled. 'Nothing wrong with her hearing.'

Jasmin snorted in amusement at his reaction and walked towards the doors.

The inside of the building was nothing like he'd anticipated given its surroundings. For one thing, the graffiti and overwhelming smell of urine was missing. And there was no litter anywhere on the ground. Not a shred. Charlie racked his brain, trying to remember whether he'd ever set foot inside this particular block before, and came up blank.

He followed Jasmin up the winding flights of stairs to the second floor. She paused and frowned back at him over her shoulder, like she was second-guessing their visit here. He gave her what he hoped was a reassuring smile. She let out a breath, walked up to one of the doors and rapped her knuckles on it.

The corridor was quiet. Eerily so. No muffled arguments behind closed doors. No barking dogs. Not even the sound of children playing.

A chill fingered its way down Charlie's spine.

The door to the flat opened in a waft of woodsmoke and lavender. The woman from the balcony—Auntie, stood in the opening, a wide grin on her face. She was shorter than he expected, but in no way frail. And there was a youthful energy about her that made Charlie question his original assessment of her age.

'Come in. Come in. You can't stand there all day.'

Stepping aside so Jasmin could take the lead, Charlie entered the flat and closed the door behind him. The overwhelming scent of incense hit the back of his throat. He stifled a cough. Light flickered from countless candles, some no more than stubs, wax ribboning down their misshapen sticks. It was a wonder the place hadn't burnt down.

Every available surface was crammed with jars and bottles containing Christ only knew. Dried flowers? Herbs maybe? He couldn't be sure. And then there were the other things, some of which were highly flammable: wooden statues, obscure carvings, ornate masks and even animal skulls. What wouldn't fit on the straining tables, cabinets and sideboards had been mounted on the walls so that wherever he looked, something stared back at him.

But that wasn't the worst of it. Countless crystals hung from small hooks that pricked the ceiling. How it hadn't collapsed from the added weight was beyond him. It was like standing beneath some immense, kitsch chandelier. Death by skewering hadn't entered his mind until now.

His heart pounded. Charlie pulled his arms in tight against his sides, squeezing his hands into fists.

'Jasmin, child.' Auntie adjusted her shawl and spread her arms. Jasmin beamed, rushing forward to fill them.

Feeling like an interloper intruding on a private moment, Charlie dropped his gaze to his feet.

'Aren't you going to introduce me?' She released Jasmin from the embrace.

'Auntie, this is Charlie. Charlie Haynes.'

Charlie stepped forward and extended a hand without thinking. An immediate flush warmed his cheeks when he realised what he'd done. Before he could pull his hand back, Auntie batted it away with a tsk, grabbed him by the arm and pulled him down into a tight hug.

'I... uh...' he spluttered. Jasmin almost choked on her laughter. He was still floundering when Auntie let him straighten again.

'Sandalwood and vetiver? Handsome *and* you smell nice.'

Charlie cleared his throat and glared at Jasmin as her laughter subsided. He looked at Auntie and studied the milky whites of her cataracts.

As if sensing his thoughts, she tapped a finger on her temple lightly. 'There is more to sight than just seeing. Now, make yourselves at home. There's tea in the pot. Take a seat, my dear,' Auntie said pleasantly, gesturing to what he assumed must be a chair buried beneath a mound of blankets and throws.

His OCD kicked in and Charlie gave Jasmin a horrified look. She shrugged and settled into a similar looking heap.

'Thank you,' Charlie managed, struggling against the unwanted thoughts triggered by the mess. 'I think I'll stand if it's all the same.'

'Suit yourself.' Auntie waddled towards the kitchen.

Charlie looked up at the crystals above him. Some spun in lazy circles, no doubt caused by the breeze they'd created by opening and closing the door. The light danced over them, through them, casting rainbows that put him in mind of the ruby set in the hilt of Kar'roc's Maw. With a grimace, he pushed the thought aside and focused instead on the crystal nearest to him.

It was blue, cut in the shape of an ornate tear drop, its facets toying with the light, it seemed to throb and pulse. He watched the blues ebb and flow, like ripples of water captured in time. It held his attention until everything else seemed to fade away. Even his anxiety about the encroaching decor became a distant memory.

A sharp pain between his thumb and forefinger yanked him back into the moment. He staggered a little, his stomach clenching, as if he'd plunged from a great height. He sucked in a breath, attempting to get his bearings back.

Through milky eyes, Auntie watched him thoughtfully from the doorway of the kitchen. She dropped her gaze to his hand and he found himself wondering, not for the first time, whether she could really see.

She chuckled. 'Soul stones. Beautiful but dangerous. Try not to stare. Don't worry, thanks to your connection to the realm of fire and shadow, your soul is safe—from the stones at least.'

'Realm of fire and shadow?'

'The demon realm.'

Christ, he hated all this supernatural bullshit. 'Wait... how did you know?'

Tsking, the old woman disappeared back into the kitchen. 'I told you, young man,' she called out, her voice muffled, 'there's more to sight than seeing.'

He glanced down at the sigil and frowned.

Auntie returned moments later with a mug in each hand. She passed one to Jasmin who accepted it with a smile, and immediately took a sip. She offered the other to Charlie. Feeling uneasy, he tore his eyes from the mug to the rest of the room. 'No, thank you. I'm okay.'

'Are you sure about that?'

It was a loaded question. Rather than bite he simply said, 'I'm not thirsty, but thank you.'

Auntie shrugged and eased herself down into a chair with a groan. She looked across at Jasmin. 'So, what brings you here, child?'

Jasmin exhaled and lowered her mug, her posture stiff. 'I need to speak to Rhea.'

'I see. After all these years?' There was tightness to Auntie's words.

Charlie watched the exchange, trying to discern what had been left unspoken.

'My partner Meghan and her little girl were kidnapped from their home sometime this morning. There were almost invisible markings on the wall. Shadowburn. I've seen it once before. When I was with Rhea. The night we were attacked. I just... *we* just need to speak to her. See if she knows anything.'

Auntie sucked her teeth. 'And how does Charlie fit in with all of this?'

'Meghan's my daughter,' he answered.

For the second time, the woman's sightless eyes found the sigil. She nodded and turned her attention back to Jasmin. 'Rhea is not the girl you remember.'

'I wouldn't know,' Jasmin said bitterly. 'You've seen her then?'

'Not for nearly twenty years. Not since the night she brought you to my door.'

Jasmin frowned. 'Then how would you know she's not the girl I remember?'

Auntie sighed, her shoulders sagging. 'Knowledge is a heavy burden; once borne, you will forever feel its weight. Are you sure this is what you want?'

Jasmin glanced up at Charlie. For the first time since he'd known her she looked uncertain.

'Do you want me to leave?' he asked her.

'No. Please stay. I'm just... you might... I don't want you to start looking at me differently.'

Charlie crossed the room and crouched in front of her. 'Jasmin, you're like a daughter to me. There's nothing that could ever change that. Nothing.'

The look of doubt on her face wrenched at his heart. He straightened. Jasmin had always been an open book. At least that's what he'd thought. But finding out that she worked for the Order, and now that she was hiding something big enough she thought it could change his opinion of her? It was starting to knot his stomach.

Jasmin squared her shoulders and nodded at Auntie. 'Tell me.'

Chapter 21

Auntie began, 'Rhea was a troubled girl, as you know. Always getting tangled up in the wrong crowds. That night she came to me with you in her arms, she was terrified. Battered and bloody... How she managed to carry you up those stairs to my door I've no clue. Maybe she still had the strength to walk the shadows, maybe it was the adrenaline. I can't say for sure. But you, there was barely a scratch on you, yet I knew that whatever had happened, you'd got the worst of it.

'Barely seventeen, not even an adult, and your soul was fractured, your life force a thin and wavering thread. Something had ripped you apart from the inside. You wouldn't have lasted the night, and even if by the grace of the good God you had seen morning, your body would have been no more than a prison. Alive but not living.'

Charlie shifted his weight; a floorboard creaked beneath him. Auntie gave him a withering glance and took a sip from her mug, before continuing.

'Rhea begged me to save you. But a broken soul is no easy fix. And I would know.' She pointed a knotty finger to the crystals hanging from the ceiling. 'The way your soul had been shredded... it was in tatters, pieces missing. Those pieces needed to be restored. But as you know, child, I couldn't just put a complete new soul in your body and be done with it. No, no. That soul would have taken over, and what would be the point in saving you just for you to become someone else? I had to take splinters from several souls and bind them to you. Make you whole again. Fiddly. *Very* fiddly. Too much of one and it would threaten to dominate, not enough and the working would unravel over time.'

'Hold on,' Charlie interrupted. 'Are you saying that Jasmin has the souls of other people inside her?'

Auntie sucked her teeth. 'Is that so hard to believe? You have a direct connection to the demon realm. If you do not learn to strengthen your own soul that link will eventually eat away at your mind piece by piece, until you are little more than a puppet to the demon that marked you.'

'*What?*' Charlie choked. He gaped at the sigil on his hand, feeling sick.

Sighing, Auntie shuffled farther back into her chair. 'What did you expect to happen when you made a deal with a demon?'

'A deal? I didn't make any deal. I just used the Maw—'

She straightened with shock; tea sloshed over the rim of her mug. 'Maw? Kar'roc's Maw?'

'Yes.' The sick feeling in his stomach intensified.

Auntie let out a low hiss. 'Then it's true. The Brimstone Chorus has begun.'

'Brimstone what?'

'Each realm—our realm, the demon realm, all of them—exists within its own pocket of time and space. Each pocket has its own song—'

'*Song?*'

The wrinkles around her mouth became more pronounced. She continued with an impatient breath. 'Frequencies, vibrations—whatever you want to call it. The veil between realms, it acts as a buffer, protecting one world from the next. It waxes and wanes, and occasionally things slip through. Sometimes, things are lured through. Demons have been trying to breach the human realm since the birth of mankind. It's said that should the veil ever fall they will succeed, and that the Brimstone Chorus will herald the end of days. Kar'roc's Maw was designed to do exactly that. To rend the veil apart. And *you* have made a pact with the archdemon who created it.'

Charlie gulped. 'A pact? I didn't... I—'

Auntie fanned her hands. 'Calm yourself. All is not lost.'

'Calm myself?' How in the hell was he supposed to do that? If what she was saying was true...

No. It couldn't be. She was winding him up, trying to get a rise out of him. Having a laugh at his expense. Either that or she wasn't all there. Just one look at her flat told him all he needed to know. And the stuff she was saying about souls? Christ, she honestly seemed to believe it.

Dismissing him with a wave of her hand, Auntie returned her attention to Jasmin. 'As I was saying, I took pieces of several souls and bound them to you. You know this of course. But what I didn't tell you, at Rhea's request, was the price it cost her. There's always a price, child. I'm the keeper of the souls, of wayward spirits without a body that are unable to pass on.'

Well, that answered Charlie's question. She had a screw loose.

He shook his head. 'Wayward spirits?'

Auntie tutted. 'If you feel the need to interrupt my story one more time, you can go wait in the corridor.'

He frowned, but remained silent.

'Wayward spirits,' she repeated, jabbing a finger into her thigh to emphasise each word. 'It happens. A miscast spell. A summoning ritual gone wrong. There are endless possibilities for why a soul might become displaced. And it's up to people like me—soul keepers—to make sure those souls get back to their bodies. Or, if that's no longer a possibility, ensure they don't try and take another. A soul needs a body as much as a body needs a soul. A body without a soul can become a vessel for beings beyond our realm, those which cannot manifest on our plane without a physical form. A soul without a body will, in time, become a malevolent force in its own right. But—' she held up a finger when Charlie opened his mouth, '—everything comes at a cost. Where was I? Ah, yes... Rhea. The working required a trade.'

Jasmin gasped, the colour draining from her face. 'You took Rhea's soul?'

'Not all of it, child. Just enough to repair those I used to save your life and to replenish the energy I exhausted in the working. Plus a little extra for emergencies.'

'Emergencies?'

'A soul isn't the same as life force. It doesn't repair itself over time. Yes, it may learn to adapt without the missing pieces, but once broken, it will never be what it once was. Rhea's soul is diminished. She gave away the best parts of herself to give you a second chance. But I kept a little extra back as a contingency, should the need ever arise, should Rhea become so lost that she became a threat. I needed a sure way to find her.'

Charlie saw Jasmin blink away tears shimmering in her eyes. Her face carried a cocktail of emotions he knew all too well: sadness, guilt, anger. All mixed together with a dash of self-loathing. Jasmin and this Rhea girl must have been close.

Auntie pushed up from the chair and crossed the room to where Jasmin was sitting. 'Here, let me take your mug. As much as I enjoy your visits, I think it's time for you to get going.'

Jasmin didn't respond.

Charlie pried the mug gently from her grasp and passed it to Auntie, who frowned at the young woman sympathetically before bustling off to the kitchen. Charlie placed his hand on Jasmin's shoulder and gave it a soft squeeze.

'Come on, Meggy and Evie are relying on us.'

Jasmin's head snapped up, her eyes sharp. She gave him a nod and rose to her feet.

Auntie returned seconds later and tugged on a green crystal attached to the ceiling. The clear thread holding it snapped with a ping.

She offered it to Jasmin. 'It will lead you to Rhea.'

Accepting it solemnly, Jasmin allowed herself to be swept up in a final hug.

'Be careful, child.'

'I will.' She looked at the gleaming, green crystal in her palm and sniffed.

Charlie got to the door first and opened it, holding it in place. He'd had about all he could stomach of this. Jasmin brushed past him, still fixated on the soul stone.

'Young man?' Auntie said.

He stopped and turned, curiosity getting the better of him.

'Learn how to strengthen your soul. And by the good God, don't do anything to make your link to the realm of fire and shadow any stronger than it already is. Time is not on our side. Try not to make things worse.'

'Sure. I'll try.' *Worse? How could I possibly make things any worse?*

Just before the door closed, she said, 'Things can always get worse.'

He shuddered.

It wasn't until they were halfway down the flight of stairs that his unease began to dissipate.

'So, we've got part of a soul in a crystal. What's next?'

'Next we find Rhea.' Jasmin's lips curled into a snarl. 'Then we beat seven bells out of the sorry bastards that took Megs and Evie.'

Chapter 22

THE DYING LIGHT OF the afternoon sun stained the sky as Sam drove them to their next destination. Nick rolled the stiffness from his shoulders and took another look at his notes. The day so far had been utterly fruitless. With every hour that passed, he felt the knot of anxiety in his stomach tighten. What had happened to Meghan and Evelyn? Nobody had seen them. Nobody knew where they were. He couldn't even begin to understand what Charlie must be going through.

He glanced at the satnav on the dashboard as it instructed Sam to turn right, and sighed. The leads were drying up. Hopefully they'd unearth something at the diner. It was a long shot, but all they needed was a lucky break. They should've split the tasks between them. Divide and conquer; that's how it was usually done. Maybe they'd even have something by now. But Sam had insisted he remain by Nick's side, given that Nick had already suffered a bloody nose and emptied his stomach over the pavement. Perhaps Sam was right to be cautious, but that didn't stop frustration from nurturing the seeds of his resentment.

Gravel crunched under the tyres as Sam pulled into the car park. He cut the engine.

Glancing up at the neon sign, Nick climbed out of the car. The smell of meat and grease wafted towards him. It made his stomach turn. He tightened his grip on his notebook and set his jaw.

'Let's have a quick word with the manager,' Nick said, already striding towards the diner.

He pressed open the door, the heat hitting him like a wall, and stepped inside followed closely by Sam.

A waitress with long black hair—Naomie, according to her name badge—came to greet them. She could have passed for a model. Her skin was flawless, her face symmetrical, with even features and dark, sharp eyes. They were the same height, he realised, which only made her short dress seem all the shorter. It barely concealed her modesty.

Nick's mouth pinched. Why were these girls being forced to wear such ridiculous and demeaning uniforms?

'Table for two?' She gave them her best smile. Despite the flash of brilliant white teeth, he recognised the weariness behind it.

Sam's face lit up.

'No, thank you,' Nick said. 'We're here to speak with the manager.' He held up his warrant card, ignoring his colleague's obvious disappointment.

Naomi nodded. 'Sure, I'll take you to him. This way... uh...' She squinted at his card. 'Detectives.'

Nick noted her lack of surprise. If the skimpy uniforms hadn't already coloured his opinion of the diner's manager, then Naomie's complete acceptance of their being here to question the man had.

Everywhere he looked the walls were crammed with cheap and tacky memorabilia. A desperate attempt to recreate a sense of nostalgic fun for a client base not old enough to care.

'Ron?' Naomie stopped behind a man who was leaning across the counter separating the dining area from the kitchen. He was barking orders at a young lad in chef's whites. 'There are a couple of detectives here to see you.'

Ron turned, droplets of sweat glistening on his pink scalp. His jowls wobbled slightly as he looked Sam up and down, then Nick.

'How can I help you?' Ron said, dismissing Naomie with a look.

Nick produced a photo and handed it to the man. 'I was wondering whether you might remember a young girl and her mother eating here last Thursday? Both Caucasian, dark hair, green eyes. Mother in her late thirties, around five six in height. Daughter eight years old, around four three. Meghan and Evelyn Bowden-Haynes.'

Ron held the photo in his sausage-like fingers. He brought it closer to his face, squinting at it through beady eyes. 'Sorry. Don't look familiar. Do you know how many people eat here in a day? Let alone a week? I can ask some of the girls, but I doubt they'd remember.'

Nick continued. 'We have reason to believe that you and Meghan may have had a disagreement.'

'Disagreement?' He took another look at the photo, then narrowed his eyes at Nick. 'Wait. Am I being accused of something here?'

'Nobody is being accused of anything. I'm just asking a few questions.'

'People try it on. Take the piss. They'll say anything to blag a discount or a free meal. Sometimes things get a bit heated. I can't be expected to remember the face of every Tom, Dick and Harry who tries to get one over on me. Maybe I did have words with her, how am I supposed to know? I don't recognise her, or her daughter.'

'They eat here regularly.'

Ron wiped his forehead with the back of his hand and grunted. 'Loads of people eat here regularly. Don't mean we're on a first name basis. Believe it or not, I'm not here every day. I've got a life. Anyway, I don't work front of house. I didn't spend years building this place up from the ground just so I could wait tables.'

Nick believed him. The man had all the people skills of a steaming pile of manure, but he didn't seem to be hiding anything. There had been no look of recognition on his face when he'd eyeballed the photo. No subtle shift in body language depicting unease. Nothing.

Nick nodded to the CCTV camera in the corner of the room. 'Could we get the footage off of that?'

Ron scoffed. 'That's a dud. I only put them up to help prevent sticky fingers. And to make sure the customers behave themselves. Like I said, I can show this photo around to some of the girls, but we get quite a high turnover round here, so...' He let the sentence tail off and gave Nick an apathetic shrug.

'Thanks for your time,' Nick said.

Another dead end. What was he going to tell Charlie?

'Yeah. Sure.' Turning his back on them, Ron jabbed a finger at the nearest member of kitchen staff. 'I'm not paying you to stand there and gawk. I swear to God, if that food comes back, it's coming out of your wages.'

The two detectives made a beeline towards the exit.

'Class act,' Sam muttered.

'Tell me about it.'

Nick pulled the door open, the bell above him chiming by way of a goodbye.

'No Eleanor Bell,' Sam added.

'No,' Nick agreed. 'But if she was working here this morning, it's possible her shift is over.'

Sam made a *hmm* of acknowledgement. 'Still think we should've grabbed a bite to eat.' He gave the diner a forlorn backwards glance as they headed for the car.

Nick sniffed. Even outside, the smell of fryer fat clung to his clothes. He longed for a hot shower and a strong cup of tea.

'Detectives?'

They turned as one. It was the waitress who had greeted them.

'Naomie?'

She licked her lips nervously. 'I uh... I heard you say the name Haynes?'

Nick took a step forward. 'Bowden-Haynes. That's right.'

'Like Charlie Haynes?'

Nick's jaw dropped.

'Yes,' Sam answered, shooting him a frown. 'Do you know Charlie?'

'No. I just overheard someone talking to my ex earlier... Well, no, he wasn't even that. Just a sort of fling... I guess.' She scowled, her breath fogging in the cool air as she spoke. A breeze caught her hair, whipping it across her face. She shivered and wrapped her arms around herself. 'Anyway, the man that was talking, I heard him say the name Charlie Haynes. I don't know if that helps at all?'

'Yes.' Nick regained composure and fumbled a pen from his pocket. He opened his notebook. 'Yes it does. Your ex, can you give me his name? His contact details?'

Naomie winced. 'I deleted his number from my phone. All of the messages too. Sorry, if I'd known... His name's Banning. Banning Lawrence.'

Nick jotted it down. When Naomie went quiet, he looked up from his spidery handwriting.

She chewed on her lower lip, and stared down at her shoe as she scuffed it against the gravel. 'I should have known.' Her words were a whisper. She shook her head and straightened. 'I should have known, y'know? All the signs were there. He said the right things. Told me everything I wanted to hear. Made me feel like I was the centre of his universe. But he never once introduced me to any of his friends. Never told me anything about his family. I don't even know where he lives. Every time I brought it up he just said he preferred my place, that I wouldn't like his housemates. He joked that they were all venomous reptiles. I'm such a fucking idiot.' She looked up at Nick suddenly, eyes wide, as if worried she might have offended him.

Nick gave her a half-smile. 'It's fine. Go on.'

'I caught him with one of the other waitresses. Back there, in the employee car park earlier today. He just stared at me, like he couldn't care less. Do you know he even came back in afterwards? To finish his meal. The arsehole.' She balled her fists by her side, jaw clenched.

Nick allowed her the time to calm herself. She was strong. Not a tear in sight, just anger—understandably—and embarrassment.

Naomie exhaled slowly. 'Anyway, he was with these two men. One of them mentioned the name Charlie Haynes, said something about going back to check on his daughter.'

Nick's heart skipped a beat. This was it. This was the break in the case they needed.

'Could you describe Banning and these men for me? Any distinguishing features?'

'Yeah, of course. Banning's white. About five feet eleven, maybe six feet. Brown hair. Blue eyes. In his twenties. Usually wears a black suit. He's got these scars on his hands and arms, burns or something. I think they might be on his body too, I don't know. He always kept his shirt on.' Her eyes widened. 'Sorry, I didn't mean for that to come out.'

'No, that's fine. Don't worry about it, really,' Nick reassured.

'The other two were also white, in their forties maybe? I... I didn't really take a good look at the one who was talking, but he had dark hair. The other one looked like he should be in a biker gang or something. Skinhead, tattoos, thick black beard, real gym freak.' She paused and rubbed briskly at her arms. 'Is it okay if I go back inside now? I'm freezing and Ron will only get the arse if I take much longer.'

'Sure. Go ahead. Thank you, Naomie.'

Her nod was lost in the brace of her shoulders against the cold. She jogged back towards the warmth of the diner.

Squinting against the waning light, Nick stared down at his notes. It wasn't much to go on, but at least it was something.

Sam shifted beside him, gravel rasping beneath his weight.

Naomie turned. 'I almost forgot.' Her voice carried across the car park, only slightly muffled by the hum of traffic. 'The big guy, the one with the tattoos, I saw his car when he left. Really stood out. A big orange Mustang with a huge dent in the bonnet. Hope that helps.' Without waiting for a reply, she ducked inside.

'Holy shit.' Nick rummaged in his pockets. His fingers trembled as he pulled out the crumpled scrap of paper he'd written on that morning with the description of the car that had hit Lily.

This wasn't just a lead, it was a game changer.

Chapter 23

THE UNEASE ON THE incubus' face was delectable. The creature had absolutely no idea what he was about to witness. He was in for a real treat.

Banning sniffed the air. With the industrial buildings acting as a windbreaker only, they didn't prevent the odour rolling off the River Medway from reaching them. Or the glacial chill that came with dusk in January.

He pulled his jacket tighter, resisting the urge to use his magic. There was no telling what fail-safes Mundy had implemented; the last thing he needed was to become target practice for a ragtag crew of trigger-happy mercenaries. Perhaps if Oliver hadn't lost the Mustang at that last set of lights it wouldn't be an issue, but the driver was Archibald Morgan's man through and through. Archibald had made it clear that he wouldn't tolerate any action that may draw unwanted attention, even for something as trivial as running a red.

When they'd first parked up, Banning had had his reservations about the location. Situated not far from a main road, it seemed an unlikely venue for a trade.

Reckless even.

But now, with the slipway in front of him and the immense, disused smithery and ropery at his back, he could appreciate the brilliance of choosing this spot. They were completely cut off from view. Walled off by brickwork and steel. And should any hapless passers-by stumble upon them, the loading and unloading of crates would appear entirely appropriate for the setting. As long as they didn't look *too* hard.

And if they did? Well, that was Mr Wilcoxson's problem, not his.

In the last few metres to the slipway, the gaps between the structures closed and the water became lost to sight. Banning looked up.

Mundy had been right about the windows. There had to be hundreds of them, judging by what he could see from this angle alone—leaded plain-glass squares that dominated the vast, sloping timber roof. The lower part of the slipway was all horizontal, whitewashed wooden panels—a recent addition by the looks of it—broken only by structural steel beams every twelve feet or so. It was easy to imagine that the area was once used to construct warships. The utter size of the place was astounding.

Banning approached the two men in yellow high-vis jackets stationed at the cavernous entrance to the building. There were no doors, but he felt an almost subtle vibration in the air. The resistance ghosted across his skin, setting the hairs on the back of his neck on end.

He peered between the men, unfazed by their tense shift in posture, to the set of heavy-duty security gates that gaped open to allow access to the forklift trucks. Nothing to attract unwanted attention. Nothing out of the ordinary.

Banning knew better.

He took another step forward.

The man on the left blocked his path.

'I'm here to see Mr Wilcoxson,' Banning barked at him. The trafficker couldn't have been more than five minutes ahead of them.

The weak-jawed man sneered at him and thumbed his nose, bringing Banning's attention to the scar that ran across its bridge. Evidently, he figured himself to be the muscle.

Masking his irritation, Banning tried again. 'I'm here to see Mundy.'

'Says he's here to see the boss.'

'Yeah, I ain't deaf.' The other man, the older of the two, grunted. He stood ramrod straight, feet shoulder width apart, arms behind his back.

Banning stiffened. He moved to the side only for the man to obstruct him again. This time, he pressed his fingers into Banning's chest. Banning exhaled through his nose and looked at the offending hand, then met the man's eyes, unblinking.

Uncertainty flickered across the thug's Neanderthal-looking brow. He let his arm drop.

'Touch me again, and I promise you it will be the last thing you'll ever do,' Banning warned.

'Just let 'em through, Clint,' the second sentry said. 'You've had your fun.'

Clint muttered under his breath and stepped out of the way, glaring at Banning and Heimerich as they passed through the protective barrier.

The smell inside the barrier struck Banning like a fist to the face. An animal reek that was as much bodily waste as it was fear. It brought tears to his eyes. The true extent of Mundy's operation was now clear.

A few of the men bustling inside paused to look up at their sudden entrance, with curiosity rather than alarm. Apparently, a few of them recognised Banning, and looked none too pleased at his arrival. They returned to their tasks, moving large crates and hauling empty cages into neat rows. Two of them were carefully unloading a toorkboar into one of the barred enclosures.

Curiosity piqued, Banning stopped to watch.

It was similar in appearance to the wild boars he'd seen at the wildlife parks his grandmother had taken him and his brother to as children. Although, the resemblance ended there. Two sets of formidable tusks protruded from either side of its upper jaw. A row of thick, yellow spikes ran the length of its spine. The creature writhed and bucked, red eyes rolling back into its head, mouth frothing with each frantic squeal. Blood matted the coarse bristle where the loop of cable, attached to the end of a long, metal rod, bit into its thick hide.

Banning turned to Heimerich. The light from the building highlighted how the incubus' face had blanched. Banning saw the twitch of his jaw, the sudden rise of his eyebrows and the widening of his dark eyes.

'You're trafficking cryptids.' Heimerich's voice was a whisper, all but lost amid the flurry of activity.

'Technically, no. Mr Wilcoxson is trafficking cryptids. I'm just here to collect.' Banning clapped the creature on the shoulder. Heimerich didn't react, gaze locked on the scene in front of him. 'Come on. You'll want to see what I'm buying.'

Looking sick, the incubus followed him farther inside the slipway.

'Kid, what took you so long?' Mundy strolled towards them. He skirted around a wet stain on the concrete, as likely to be blood as it was excrement, and grinned. 'Thought you weren't gonna show for a minute there.'

'I wouldn't miss this for the world, Mr Wilcoxson.'

'Wish you wouldn't call me that, kid. Makes me feel old.' Mundy eyed Heimerich. 'What's with him?'

'I think he's just a bit overwhelmed.'

The trafficker shrugged. 'First time's always an eye-opener. You should see what I've got on the mezzanine.' He pointed to the wooden flooring above his head.

'Oh, I've got a feeling it's not his first time in a place like this. Is it, Heimerich?' Banning looked at the incubus.

The creature said nothing, still fixated on the toorkboar that was secured inside its enclosure and ramming the bars with its tusks. Each blow produced a shower of white sparks. The runes etched into the frame of the cage flared in time with the beast's frustration.

With a fleeting frown at Heimerich, Mundy returned his attention to Banning. 'We've got it in a crate out the back.'

Excitement bloomed in Banning's chest. For the first time that day, his grin was genuine. 'Lead the way.'

Mundy turned and headed for the other side of the vast building.

'Oi. Be careful with that,' he snarled at a man grappling with a bird-like creature. 'It's worth more than your fucking life.'

The man mumbled an apology that exploded into a scream when claws raked down his arm, splitting his skin open in a spray of crimson. He wrestled the giant bird into the cage with a curse. Its black wings beat in a frenzy of feathers and dust as it keened. Its wail created a response of snarls, clicks and grunts from the caged cryptids around it.

Mundy tsked as they continued on. 'Amateur.'

Another blood-curdling shriek, followed by a gunshot stopped them in their tracks.

Banning turned. The feathered cryptid had escaped its cage. It twitched on the ground, one of its wings twisted unnaturally beneath it. Blood seeped from the gaping cavity in its chest. It made one final rasping noise, then stilled.

The veins on Mundy's temples bulged, the tendons in his neck standing out like thick cords. His face had turned a dangerous shade of red. He rounded on the man with the gun in his hand.

'You fucking pillock. I already had a buyer lined up for that one. Where the fuck am I supposed to get something to replace it at such short notice?'

Mundy punched the man in the face. The man reeled back, losing his balance. He landed hard on the ground. The gun flew from his hand with the force of the impact. Mundy stood over him, mouth set in a snarl. He lifted his foot and brought his heel down on the man's nose. Again. And again. Until there was nothing left but the squelching, meaty mess of pulp.

The trafficker glared down at the bloodied flesh and gore, his chest heaving with exertion. He took a breath, stepped back, and wiped the soggy chunks of man clinging to his shoe against the concrete.

Heimerich gagged.

Banning rolled his eyes.

'Clean this up. Now!' Mundy roared at another. 'And let this be a fucking lesson to the rest of you. Don't damage the merchandise.' He turned back to Banning and inclined his head in the direction they'd been heading. 'Apologies about that, kid. Shall we?'

Banning's mouth quirked up. 'After you. Shame about your clothes.'

Glancing down at the dark stains, Mundy cursed, 'Bollocks.'

Stepping out of the slipway was quite literally a breath of fresh air. The rotting seaweed smell of the river was easy compared to the animal stench that still clung to the inside of Banning's nostrils. And even that was forgotten the moment he saw the reinforced metal crate waiting for him beneath the artificial glow of the floodlights.

The crate had to be six feet tall. Additional panels had been bolted to the side. Despite that, the steel was warped in places where its occupant had tested the strength of its prison. Even at this distance, Banning could feel the power radiating off the runes that marked every inch of the container. He knew these creatures were strong, but seeing the crate, seeing the damage the creature had inflicted upon it in spite of the spellwork, it gave Banning a new appreciation for just *how* strong they were.

He beamed. *Finally.*

'Here it is,' Mundy said, stopping by the crate's side and thumping his fist against it.

Banning readied himself, waiting for the creature to react. When he heard nothing but silence, he couldn't help but feel disappointed.

'Open it,' he instructed.

'I'm not sure you want us to do that, kid,' Mundy said. 'It took an awful lot of effort getting it contained in the first place.'

'I said open it.'

Mundy waved over two of the men smoking just outside the slipway's side door. 'Grab the catch poles and open the crate.'

The two men exchanged a nervous glance. One of them flicked his cigarette onto the dirt and ground it out with his boot. 'You sure, boss?'

'Kid wants to inspect his merchandise.'

The second man took another drag of his cigarette, crushed the butt against the wooden panel behind him, and blew the smoke out the side of his mouth, giving a shrug that was a little stiff. He marched towards the back of one of the Ford Rangers and grabbed two thick poles out of the cargo bed. With a nod, he tossed one of the poles to the other man. It was only when the metal caught the light that Banning saw the wards that marked it.

Precautions. Good.

Both men headed for the crate. There was a moment's hesitation, then as one, they positioned the hooked end of their poles into two notches on the crate door. Each man pulled until there was a firm *clunk* and waited for the go-ahead.

Mundy pressed his lips together and turned to Banning. 'It's going to be an absolute ball ache to get that thing back in there again.'

Banning didn't care.

'If it gets loose, I'm billing you for the trouble...' Mundy commanded his two men. 'Open it.'

Chapter 24

THE DOOR TO THE crate slammed into the ground.

Mundy's men braced.

Heimerich's breath caught.

Banning's adrenaline spiked.

This was it. The moment he'd been waiting for. *The moment I get my life back.*

Blinding white light blazed along the length of the grappling poles. Banning blinked away the imprint of the runes on his sight and watched as the creature took a measured step forward.

Beneath thick black fur, its claws flexed and gave a penetrating screech as they scraped on the crate door. But that was not what held Banning's attention. It was the beast's white head. A marvel of evolution, so stark in contrast to its dark pelt, it could easily be mistaken for exposed skull. Only a trained eye would be able to distinguish the contour of muscle, the ridge of tendons beneath the taut flesh, but that close, it would be the last thing they ever saw.

'Delightful.' Banning moved forward.

The slits of the creature's nostrils flared, inhaling his scent. It blinked, its eyelids folding back languidly over molten halos. Banning wasn't fooled. There was intelligence there. Alert. Calculating. It was watching him. Tracking his every movement. Gauging the distance between them.

The slight flex of its claws was the only warning before the creature pounced, but it was warning enough.

Banning threw up a shield, drawing energy from the earth around him. Green light flared bright as the demon ploughed into it, dragging Mundy's two men along for the ride.

Banning grunted, the impact knocking him back a good few inches. The beast snapped its jaws at him, thick strands of drool flying from its mouth. The barrier held, but did little to mask the foetid stench of the creature's breath or the musky smell of its fur. Flashes of light sparked from the collar around its neck, the wards doing little to subdue it. What would it be capable of if they weren't there at all?

Realising that it was getting nowhere, the creature stopped its assault, lowering its head to stare at Banning through the translucent shield. The breath from its nostrils swirled in thin white wisps. Mundy's men rose to their feet, looking pale.

With a taunting smirk, Banning let the shield drop.

The beast lunged. Before its teeth could get a purchase around his neck, Banning jabbed his fist into its jaw. His green blade of energy sprang into life. The creature roared, making a deafening explosion of sound that sent shockwaves across Banning's body. It reeled back, and the sudden change in direction wrenched Mundy's men violently from their feet once more.

Sweat trickled down Banning's face. He stood, chest heaving, his eyes locked on the beast, as it pushed itself back up. A wide circle of glistening frost spread out from his feet.

The beast turned its head to regard him. A low growl rumbled through its chest. Molten hatred glowed from the hollows of its skull-like head, but it did not attack.

Banning adjusted his stance. Frozen mud cracked away from his shoes. He waited. Ignoring the pounding of his heart. Ignoring the grunted curses of Mundy and his lackeys, who were hurriedly scrambling to their feet for the second time. Ignoring everything but the minute movements of the creature in front of him. He kept his gaze locked on its stare, challenging it to make the next move. His breath fogged with each slow exhale.

Finally, it blinked and lowered its head in submission.

Banning grinned. 'Thank you, Mr Wilcoxson. You can put the hellip back in the crate now.'

After a few seconds of stunned silence, Mundy scoffed, 'You're kidding?'

'I'm more than satisfied, thank you.'

The muscle beneath Mundy's eye twitched. The men either side of the hellip stared, their slack-jawed disbelief rapidly giving way to open aggression.

All eyes were on Banning. It was an error on their part.

Banning merely watched as the hellip whipped its head to the side. Alerted by the sudden motion, the man on the other end of one catch pole turned. With the rigid pole creating distance between them, there was no way for the creature to launch an obvious attack against him. Still, the man's eyes widened in alarm. The hellip stretched its jaws open, causing the man to tighten his grip on the metal rod and take a cautious step back.

Mundy's warning shout came too late.

Clear fluid shot from the creature's throat in dual streams, striking the man in the face. He collapsed to the ground, clawing at his own eyes, writhing in the dirt.

In one swift lunge, the hellip clamped its jaws on the man's chest, cutting his tortured screams short. Clothing and skin ripped as the hellip jerked its head back, creating a spray of red. Down the creature went again, boring deeper into the gaping chest wound it had created.

Bone splintered. Muscle tore. Blood gushed freely.

The creature lifted its dripping jaws and devoured what was either an organ or a hunk of muscle in two wet bites. Within seconds, the man's corpse was reduced to a hollowed out mess of savaged tissue and jutting bone. The hellip raised its head and darted its long, black tongue out, licking the blood and clumps clean from its white, skull-like face.

Heimerich retched.

'Evolution,' Banning mused. 'That's why it doesn't have fur around its head. Similar to a vulture in a way.'

Nobody seemed to be listening. The hellip was only half secured.

'For fuck's sake. Good for nothing wards. What the fuck protection am I paying for?' Mundy darted behind the creature and snatched up the pole still attached by the hook to its collar. 'Carmichael. Carmichael! Don't just stand there, help me get this thing back in the crate.'

Between them, Mundy and Carmichael managed to reverse the hellip into the crate and seal the door. With its stomach full, it put up little resistance. Mundy glared at Banning. The trafficker was coated in the dead man's innards. They had saturated his clothing. Thick, fibrous globules dripped from his face, making him look like he'd just stepped off the set of some cheesy slasher movie.

Banning smirked. 'You've got a little something on you.'

Mundy snarled. 'You think this is a fucking joke, kid? Look at the state of me. I'm covered in guts.'

'Hold that thought.' Banning raised one finger and pulled his vibrating mobile out of his pocket.

'Are you fucking serious?' Mundy roared, spittle flying from his mouth.

Banning turned his back, unlocking his phone as it continued to vibrate in his hand.

No.

The motion sensors had been tripped inside the safe house. Ignoring Mundy's torrent of creative curses, Banning pulled up the feed from the cameras. The child and her mother were out of the basement. How was that possible? He'd locked the door himself.

He narrowed his eyes at Heimerich.

Banning weighed his options. He wasn't about to leave the demon to his own devices, but he wanted eyes on the hellip. Security that the trafficker wouldn't make any rash decisions in his absence, especially given his current mood.

He returned his attention back to his mobile as he made up his mind. There was no way Mundy would let the incubus leave his sight, and should Heimerich try anything... well, the world would be a better place with one less demon in it.

'I need to go and take care of something,' he said to the incubus. 'Help Mr Wilcoxson with the clean up.'

'Where are you going?' Mundy spat. He was in front of Banning now, jabbing a finger into his chest. 'This ain't some fucking storage service. You buy the goods. You take them. You leave.'

Banning batted his finger away, wrinkling his nose at the smear of the dead man's blood now on his hand. 'You're a man down. Heimerich can assist you while I'm gone. I won't be long. We'll be out of your hair before your other guests arrive.'

The sound of Mundy grinding his teeth filled the space between them.

Mundy considered the incubus. 'Fine.' Thrusting a hand into his trouser pocket, he produced a slim leather pouch and the same brushed silver lighter from earlier. Without breaking eye contact with Banning, he selected a cigarette and sparked up, the jittering flame illuminating his blood-spattered face. 'But this is the last time, kid. You've cost me enough already.'

Banning gave a tight nod in response, his eyes tracking the lighter nervously until the trafficker pocketed it.

With an exhale, he glanced at his phone once more and headed back to the car, where Oliver was waiting. He couldn't risk losing the girl or her mother. Couldn't risk disappointing his mentor yet again. No. He was going to prove his worth once and for all.

Chapter 25

'Wait, you're telling me that this big mystery tattooed guy—the one Naomie saw Banning talking to—is the same bloke who hit your dog with his car this morning?'

Nick nodded at Sam as they climbed the flight of stairs to the detective's office. The last thing he wanted to do was show Sam just how out of breath he was. It would only set him to worry again.

'What are the odds of that?' Sam mused. 'And you got his reg details?'

Nick gave another nod.

Sam paused in his climb. 'Fuck me, Nick. You look like you're about to keel over. I thought you said you were feeling better?'

'I am. It's just... stairs.' Nick gave up the pretence and sucked in a deep, wheezing breath. The truth was he was running on fumes. Worse still, the throbbing pain behind his eyes had returned with a vengeance.

He needed to lie down. To sleep. His shift should have ended nearly two hours ago and his exhaustion was becoming as much physical as it was mental.

But exhausted or not, he needed to see this through.

He had to. For Meghan and Evelyn. For Charlie. And as much as it might make him a selfish arsehole, for himself.

Pushing open the door to the office, Sam gestured for Nick to go ahead of him. 'There you go, old man.'

Nick glared. 'We're the same age.'

'Then how come only one of us is going senile?'

'What?'

Sam's eyes flicked to Nick's empty hands.

My notebook.

Nick groaned a curse. 'You let me get all the way up here before you thought to say anything?'

'The exercise is good for you. Helps maintain bone density.'

'We're the same age!'

Sam chuckled. 'Give me the reg details for that car. I'll run it through a PNC check while you go grab your notebook.'

Feeling defeated, Nick rummaged in his pocket for the scrap of paper, and handed it to Sam. 'You're an absolute arse, you know that?'

'Yeah. I know.' With a lopsided grin, Sam ducked through the door, leaving Nick with nothing else to do but trudge back down the stairs.

⁂

Five minutes later, Nick tossed his notebook on the desk and sat down heavily in his chair. The squeaking noise earned him a few curious glances from those on the late shift, and a flat look from Lovett. It came as no surprise that she was still on duty. They'd all stopped questioning her presence, the light-hearted remarks about her living there having worn thin after the first few months. Nick held up a hand in apology.

'Anything?' he asked Sam.

'Maybe. Pulled up the registered keeper. This your guy?' Sam wheeled to the side so that Nick could get a better look at the monitor.

Nick leant in. His heart rate increased. From the screen, Mundy Wilcoxson stared back at him. His beard was a little shorter and the streaks of grey a little less pronounced, but it was clearly the man he'd seen that morning.

'That's him.'

'Not sure I'd want to meet him in a dark alley.' Sam whistled low as he scanned the list of prior convictions. 'That's quite a record. And you had an argument with him in the middle of the road?'

'Yeah. On hindsight, probably not the smartest move.'

'I'm surprised he didn't just lay you out.'

'I think he might have, if it wasn't for Lily.' Something nagged at the back of Nick's mind. Something he couldn't quite place. He squinted at the image of Mundy.

'Lily?' Sam asked.

'My Rottweiler.'

'You named your Rottweiler *Lily*?'

Nick pursed his lips. 'Henry named her. Brought her back from Spreewald as a birthday present.'

'Spreewald, as in Germany?'

'Yeah, his parents have a farmhouse in the middle of the forest there. Anyway, I think she must've spooked Mundy because he jumped back in his car and drove off.'

'Lucky for you. Seems like a nasty piece of work. Let's go pay him a visit, see if he knows anything about this Banning Lawrence. Speaking of...' Sam clicked the mouse, bringing up another browser window. 'I found an article about him.'

'Really?'

'Mmm. From ten years ago. Nothing much. He saved his kid brother from a house fire. Mother, father, younger sister, all died in the blaze. Says here they think it was started by a lit candle.'

'Jesus. Naomie was right about the scars then. Is there anything else?'

'No. Nothing. You don't suppose Naomie just wants to land him in the shit? I mean, she had to be pretty pissed about catching him in the act with another waitress.'

'Except I never mentioned Charlie by name,' Nick said. 'Not to her or Ron.'

With another click, Sam closed the article. 'Mundy Wilcoxson it is.'

'Wait.' Nick suddenly knew what was bothering him. The photo, the convictions... 'How did you access this without a date of birth?'

After a moment's pause, Sam shrugged. 'Insurance.'

Nick shook his head. 'It took me five minutes to get my notebook. Tops. There's no way you did your little search for Banning and spoke to the insurance company in that time.'

Sam shrugged and smiled. 'What can I say, I'm efficient.'

'I'm not buying it, Sam.'

His smile faded. 'Jesus. I wouldn't have pegged you as the paranoid type. Seriously, I think the lack of sleep is beginning to affect your judgement.'

Nick bit his tongue and folded his arms across his chest. Sam's eyes darted from Lovett to Nick in an almost subconscious gesture.

Sam added, 'Do you want to check out this address or what?'

'Of course I do.' He pushed his suspicions to the back of his mind. He needed to stay focused.

Whatever Sam was hiding, he could figure it out later.

Chapter 26

THE EMERALD-GREEN CRYSTAL PRACTICALLY hummed with energy, sending out quivering vibrations like static electricity. With a frown, Charlie watched it sway in time with the motion of the car, where it hung off the rear-view mirror. The sigil on his hand began to itch.

He cleared his throat. 'Can you feel that?'

Jasmin nodded, eyes fixed on the road ahead. 'It means we're getting close.'

She'd remained painfully quiet during their journey. He recognised the struggle on her face, the familiar pain that came from ripping open an old wound you thought had long since healed. He'd worn that look enough times over the years, after his marriage with Debbie had collapsed.

'You and this Rhea, the two of you were close?'

She flinched. 'Once. When my parents kicked me out, I had nowhere to go. Literally nowhere. My cousin Nishaa would occasionally let me spend the night on her sofa. That's where I told Megs I was living, but I couldn't stay there for more than a day or two at a time. She didn't want the family finding out that she was helping me. I don't blame her. That's just the way things were. The way *they* were.'

Jasmin forced the bitterness from her tone. 'Anyway, I had this friend from school. She lived with her older sister in one of the flats in the block we were at earlier. They let me stay with them. Her sister didn't really care what we got up to, as long as we didn't make too much noise or mess. I got an evening job in the kebab shop round the corner, to try and pay my way. Plus I needed money for myself, to buy clothes and things. One night we had a bit of trouble with this group of lads hanging around outside. They'd gone by the time I'd finished my shift, so it was no big deal. I took a shortcut, didn't want our food to get cold.'

Charlie cringed as he guessed where this was headed.

'They came out of nowhere. I tried to ignore them, to run, but they caught up. One of them knocked the food out of my hands while the others laughed. Another grabbed me, started dragging me somewhere. I screamed for help. Screamed at the top of my lungs, until I got a fist to the gut. And there was Rhea. She beat the absolute shit out of them. I mean, I'd never seen anything like it. One minute they were all booze-fuelled testosterone, then the next they were tearing up the pavement. She helped me back to my feet, bought me some more food to take back to the flat. We started spending time together, until it became more than just friendship. She was my first...' She paused, giving Charlie a horrified look, like she'd just remembered who she was talking to.

He waved his hand for her to continue. 'What went wrong?'

'She was a bad influence. I knew that. But you don't care at that age, do you? It adds to the thrill. If I'd known then what I do now, I'd have seen the signs. She always had money, bought me little gifts. So I thought nothing of the fact that she had a mobile. That she had several mobiles. Never questioned it. I was so wrapped up in us. In her. She made me feel safe and wanted. And I was so desperate to feel wanted.'

Jasmin swallowed, refusing to meet Charlie's eye.

'Then one night, I'm walking back to the flat and I hear arguing. I mean, it's a dodgy area, so I don't think too much of it, just keep my head down. But then I hear Rhea's voice. I go investigate and see these rough looking people surrounding her. She laughs and one of them punches her in the face. Knocks her to the ground. Before I know it I'm there, shrieking for them to stop. As soon as she sees me everything about her changes. She's no longer this self-assured, cocky hard-arse. It's like... she's scared. One of them grabs me and she gets really angry. He tells her to back off, and when she doesn't, he pulls a knife on me.

'Then she just transforms into this thing. I don't know how to describe it. Like a living shadow, darker than night. I remember just standing there, staring as these black tendrils exploded out from her. They left gleaming trails wherever they touched. Next thing I know I'm on my back with this prick straddling my chest. I can't move. Can't breathe. Can't scream. He wasn't human,

I know that now. I guess I passed out there and then, because when I woke up, I was in Auntie's flat. Rhea was gone. No goodbye. No note. No anything. Just gone.'

Charlie blinked. *Christ*. And he thought his childhood had been a shit show.

Jasmin continued. 'This will be the first time I've seen her since then. But if what Auntie says is true, we need to keep our guard up. She was tough as nails back then. I dread to think what she's like now.'

'What was she?'

Jasmin hesitated. 'A succubus.'

Charlie's eyes widened. What in the hell was he supposed to say to that? Questions formed in his mind but died on his tongue. He turned to look out of the passenger window, thumbing his ring finger.

'A succubus,' he said, finally.

'Yes.'

'The demons that seduce people in their sleep? That kind of succubus?'

'It wasn't like that,' she said defensively. 'That's a misconception. Succubi and incubi are dream eaters. They feed off their victims while they sleep, drain their life force. It's not fatal, in fact most people wouldn't even notice, and those that do would just chalk it up to exhaustion. There's no sex involved. Not usually.'

'Okay...'

'It's *not* a sex thing, I swear.'

'I said okay.' He really didn't want to be talking about this anymore.

A car drove past on the opposite side of the road, the headlights bathing them in a transient glow.

Charlie's phone vibrated. Giving the crystal one more suspicious glance, he pulled his mobile from his pocket. *Another* missed call from Diane.

No doubt she'd be livid when she eventually caught up with him, but that was a problem for his future self. He wanted to trust her. But what did he really know about her?

Sweet Fanny Adams, that's what. Revelations about her husband's death aside, there was every possibility she could be the mole leaking information about his link to the dagger. To assist in his family's abduction. And if not her, then who?

He could rule Nick out for one. He'd known the man for years. Although, he'd known Jasmin since she was a girl, worked alongside her in the same station, and would never have suspected she worked for the Order if he hadn't seen it with his own eyes.

His jaw clenched. It could be any one of the officers who'd attended the scene the night he'd bound Chekonost back inside the dagger. Anyone of them could be working for the Order. But hell, why stop there? It could be anyone within O.O.T.I.S who had access to information about him.

He swore under his breath.

'Holy crap,' Jasmin said, staring at his phone.

He cocked his head at her. 'What?'

'Your phone. It's archaic. I thought you had a smartphone?'

'Archaic? I'll have you know that it's got built-in FM radio, thank you very much. And a camera.' He huffed in mock indignation. 'This is an old one I still had in the drawer. Battery isn't great, but it'll do for now. There's a lot to be said for a phone you can answer just by pressing a button. None of this swiping rubbish. My other one got smashed when Stephen... when my front door landed on top of me.'

Or maybe it was when I got launched across my hallway like a ragdoll.

He put the mobile away and ran his hand down his jaw. It was bad enough his dreams unearthed every last horrifying detail of that night; he didn't need to relive it when he was awake too.

'Do you know what?' Jasmin said. 'It really doesn't surprise me that you've got a drawer full of your old handsets. I bet they're categorised by make and model. No... by size...' She nudged him lightly with her elbow.

The shuddering pulse coming from the crystal intensified.

They fell into silence as Jasmin drove. The hum of the tyres made a soft droning sound inside the car.

Charlie sighed, adjusting his seatbelt and turning towards Jasmin. 'You know there's a distinct possibility that Rhea could be the one who took Meggy and Evie.'

'I know.'

The rest was left unspoken between them.

Jasmin pulled the car over and killed the engine. 'I think we're here.'

Chapter 27

"HERE", AS IT TURNED out, was the car park behind a Grade II listed factory, which, if Charlie's memory served him correctly, had once been used to manufacture vehicles. An architectural marvel in its day, the building now stood abandoned. A five-storey shell of exposed concrete, red brick and glass. Commercial sheds all closed to business for the evening flanked its left, the wide arches of a railway bridge its right. With nothing but the ambient glow of the distant streetlights, it was exactly the sort of place you might find yourself permanently relieved of your belongings.

'Seems about right,' Charlie muttered to nobody.

Following Jasmin's lead, he climbed out of the car and gently nudged the door shut. The rushing river at their backs and the murmur of far-off traffic would only do so much to conceal the sound of their arrival. Charlie watched as Jasmin pressed the crystal into her pocket.

He gritted his teeth. *What are we walking into?*

Jasmin made her way to one of the bricked-up bridge arches and flattened her back against it. She turned to give him a nod.

He picked his way towards her, careful not to step on anything that would make noise, and craned his neck to see what had caught her attention.

A blonde-haired woman in her early forties was perched on the bonnet of a white BMW 3 Series, her posture relaxed. The way she observed the men in front of her both equally and casually told Charlie all he needed to know. She was braced for trouble.

So this is the infamous Rhea?

He wasn't sure what he'd been expecting. Some kind of red-skinned, horned she-devil with wings and a forked tail perhaps? He'd been way off the mark. If he hadn't been told that she was a demon he'd be none the wiser.

Rhea was all hard lines and confidence. The top of her hair was pulled into a messy bun that showed off an aggressive undercut, and exposed several ear piercings. Black tattoos snaked down her neck, to disappear beneath the collar of a wraparound coat that looked neither waterproof nor warm. Charlie resisted the urge to pull his own trench coat tighter. Whatever this little get-together was, she evidently didn't expect it to last long.

The four—no, make that five men laughed and postured, but despite all their bravado, there was a brittle tension in the air.

Five to one. Not good odds.

'Let's do this then shall we, ladies?' Rhea pushed off the bonnet and took a step forward.

The laughter stopped. Two of the men scowled at her. Two grinned. The final one showed no emotion, a pair of sharp eyes tracking her every move. He was the one to watch.

With a smirk, Rhea sauntered around to the back of the car and opened the boot. The men followed. One of them let out a low whistle that carried across the car park.

Charlie shuffled to the side, craning his neck to get a glimpse of what was in the back of the white Bimmer. Jasmin's hand clamped down on his shoulder. She shook her head. Charlie arched an eyebrow at her, but moved back into the shadows, trusting her instincts. A heartbeat later, old sharp eyes was staring directly at the space where he'd just been standing.

Charlie's stomach knotted. *What the hell?*

He waited until the man gave up and returned his attention back to the contents of the boot before he inched forward again. A howling breeze whipped across the river, catching his trench coat and giving it a series of sharp snaps that were all too loud.

Charlie sucked in a breath and shuffled back.

Old sharp eyes' head jerked up. He sniffed the air, his face contorting into a sneer. 'We've got company.'

He had barely inclined his head to where Charlie and Jasmin were standing before the other four men began sprinting in their direction.

Jasmin grimaced. 'There goes the element of surprise.' She stepped into the open.

'What are you doing?' Charlie hissed. 'Shouldn't we be running?'

'No point. They'd catch us.'

'What do we do now?'

'Fight, I guess.'

'Fight? Jasmin, this is suicide.'

'I'll try and hold them off. You make a break for the car. Get out of here.'

If she thought for one moment that he was going to leave her in the lurch, she had another think coming.

He sucked in a breath and stood beside her, exhaling slowly in a futile attempt to slow his pounding heart.

She gave him a nod. 'Just do me a favour, would you?' She flicked her gaze to his balled fist. 'Try to stay calm.'

Charlie said nothing as the men closed the distance between them. Rhea and old sharp eyes brought up the rear.

The nearest goon, apparently deciding he was in no immediate danger, visibly relaxed. 'What's this then? Out for a late night stroll with your Dad are you, love?' he drawled.

Rhea's dark eyes bulged with recognition. She schooled her expression in an instant, but not before old sharp eyes had noticed.

'You know these people?' It wasn't a question but an accusation.

'No, I—' Rhea's words were cut short as old sharp eyes made a gesture with his hand and she pitched violently through the air. She struck the arch with a sickening thud, sending exploding mortar and brick dust scattering across the concrete.

Jasmin gasped.

Charlie felt his throat tighten.

Rhea pushed up to her knees, unhurt, her face set in a snarl.

It was an abrupt reminder that, despite appearances, she was a demon. A shudder rippled down Charlie's spine.

Old sharp eyes stalked towards the fallen succubus. Everything about him promised violence. 'Who are they, O.O.T.I.S?' He must have noticed Charlie's flinch, because his mouth twitched upward in satisfaction. 'This bitch set us up, boys. Kill her. Kill all of them. I'll start loading the merchandise.'

Shit.

Jasmin lunged forward in a blur, throwing a punch that connected with old sharp eyes' nose. He staggered back, eyes squeezed shut, hands clasping his face. Using his temporary blindness as a distraction, Jasmin drove her elbow into the stomach of a second man.

Charlie struck out at the brute in front of him, knuckles connecting with his face. The man's head snapped to the side, but otherwise he didn't move.

Double shit.

The thug turned his glare on Charlie, lips curling back over his teeth in a low growl. He cracked his neck and wagged a finger. 'Uh-uh-uh. That wasn't very nice now, was it?' Light glinted off something clutched in his other hand.

Charlie twisted just in time to avoid the knife. But a second strike caught his arm. His skin blazed as the blade sliced through his coat and split his flesh open. Yelping, he cradled his arm to his chest, blood seeping between his fingers, and backtracked away from the bridge.

The darkness cast by the barren shell of the forsaken factory pressed him on all sides until the weight made his lungs feel heavy. Blood pounded in his ears. Cold sweat trickled down his spine. What he wouldn't give for his shotgun right now.

How in the hell was he supposed to fight this thug? He had no weapons. No plan. No backup. If they died here, who would save his daughter? His granddaughter? *No.*

He squared his shoulders and stopped in place, raising his fists and taking a wider stance to lower his centre of gravity. The fabric of his coat stuck to his hot and wet injury where the knife had slashed him. His arm muscle trembled. He was fucked, pure and simple, but he had to try.

The goon drew nearer, toying with him. His footsteps echoed unnaturally, rebounding off brick and concrete to create an eerie rhythm that was jarring against the sound of Charlie's rapid breaths.

Charlie braced.

A shadow of dark tendrils detonated behind the thug, coiling around his body. His mouth contorted in a silent scream. Black fronds twisted down his throat, forcing the air from his lungs in strangled chokes.

The sight was giving Charlie vertigo. Turning his face away sharply, he staggered back. It was like staring into a void; the shadows were so dark, they sucked the detail out of everything, flattening reality into nothingness.

And then the shadow was gone.

The thug lay motionless on the ground, a death mask of sheer terror on his face.

'Charlie?' Jasmin's voice cut through as he tried to process what had just happened. He was distantly aware that it wasn't the first time she'd called his name. Christ, how long had he been standing there?

He tore his gaze from the corpse to see her staring at him with concern.

'Charlie, your arm.'

She'd barely taken a step before the writhing mass of darkness appeared out of nowhere and surged towards her.

'Jasmin, watch out!'

Chapter 28

BANNING TENSED. THERE WAS nothing he could do to stifle the birr of the deadbolt retracting. No way to conceal his entry into the safe house from the girl and her mother. The last thing he wanted was another knee to the bollocks. Just the thought of it made him feel nauseous.

In one swift movement he pushed the door open.

The woman was waiting for him, her green eyes narrowed to slits. He knew that look intimately; fear masquerading as anger. He saw it reflected back every time he glanced in a mirror. She pulled her daughter behind her, shielding the girl.

Banning inched inside.

The woman charged forward with a primal roar. She whipped her arm up revealing the vase she had clutched in her fist.

Poetic.

She threw it at him. With a casual upward flick of his wrist, Banning was immediately surrounded by a shimmering wall of energy. The vase shattered against it harmlessly.

The child screamed.

'What are you?' Hysteria gave the woman's words a shrill edge.

Banning slipped fully inside, pulling the door closed behind him. They backed away, their chances of escape destroyed. Much like his vase.

He frowned, surveying the state of the room. Trashed didn't even begin to describe it.

They'd pulled the place apart, desperate to find an escape route. Anything that could be used as a makeshift battering ram or crowbar had been tested to its limits. There were scuffs across the windows where they'd been struck repeatedly.

A futile effort—the glass was bulletproof and layered with polycarbonate.

Ugly craters had been gouged out of the walls, exposing the acoustic membrane underneath. Soundproof though the house might be, Banning was suddenly appreciative of the additional layers of spellwork that hid it from the outside world.

Everything was ruined. Everything he'd spent months of his life decorating, furnishing, arranging. Everything.

He drew in a breath, silently counting down from ten before he snapped his gaze to the raven-haired little girl still screaming in the midst of all the mess.

'Quiet! *Sit* down.' Banning pointed to the sofa, covered in plaster and debris. 'Both of you.'

The ear-piercing shrieks stopped, but neither hostage moved a muscle.

'I promise I won't hurt you.' Banning addressed the girl softer now, pointing slowly at her mother. 'But I *will* hurt her. So. Just. Sit. Down.'

For a moment the girl looked as if she might refuse, her trembling jaw jutting out defiantly. Something in his expression must have changed her mind because her shoulders sagged. She perched on the edge of the sofa with her mother, clinging to the woman's hand and watching him with wide, pale-green eyes.

'How did you get out of the room?' he asked, speaking with a calm he did not feel.

The mother glared at him. The girl swiped at the tears running down her cheeks and sniffed.

'How did you get out of the room?' Banning repeated, frustration eating away at his composure. 'I'm going to ask you one last time then I'm going to get annoyed. *How* did you get out of the room?'

Silence followed.

'Fair enough.' With his hand, Banning made a quick cutting motion through the air.

The woman's eyes rolled back in her head. She crumpled to one side, the cushioned leather absorbing the weight of her unconscious body.

The child shrieked again; the sound penetrated Banning's skull like a rusty knife had been jabbed in there.

'What have you done to my mum?'

'Remember what I said. I wouldn't hurt *you*...' He let the sentence hang.

Fresh tears welled in the child's eyes as she stared down at her mother. She drew in a shaky breath. 'It w-wasn't locked.'

'*What?*'

'The door, it wasn't locked.'

'Impossible. I locked it myself.'

'It wasn't. I swear.' The child's voice broke, tears spilling down her cheeks. 'Is my mum... is she dead?' When Banning didn't answer, she hugged herself and started to weep.

Banning crossed the room to the basement door and inspected it from both sides. It didn't appear to be tampered with in any way. His brow creased. The child's crying was starting to grate on him. It had been years since he'd heard sobs like that and they stirred up memories he'd spent a lifetime trying to forget. Memories of his brother. Memories of his parents, his sister. Memories of the demon.

He shook them away.

'Stop!' he said. The girl's blubbing only got louder. He softened his tone, 'She's not dead. Just stop crying.'

'W-why are you doing this to us?' The girl's words were stuttered, coming out between short, sharp breaths.

Banning ground his teeth and focused on the state of the room. How had they managed to make such a mess in such a short space of time? He would have been impressed if their destruction wasn't so infuriating. Some of the things he'd collected were one-offs. Irreplaceable.

The lid on one of the lindwurm tanks was askew. His heart thundered and he rushed over to it. Empty. He hissed through his teeth and looked around for the missing male.

'What do—'

'*Shh*. Quiet.' Banning strained to listen. Without the male, all chances of establishing a breeding pair were done for. He had no idea what the captive lifespan of a female lindwurm was; it was hardly a topic that came up in casual conversation. And, somehow, he didn't think Mr Wilcoxson would be open to the idea of securing him another specimen anytime soon. If he lost his venom supply...

No. The male had to be in here somewhere. He just needed to find it.

Exhaling, he forced his body to relax and extended his senses. Concentration was key. He blocked out the sounds of the sniffling girl, letting his power become an extension of himself.

There.

The lindwurm was under the sofa, its needle-like claws skittering across the grey oak flooring, as it scurried forward on its front legs while dragging the rest of its body behind.

'Why—'

'For the love of God, shut up!'

The girl's eyes widened. She shifted positions, her socks brushing against the floor. The lindwurm hissed, its spines unfolding. It fanned them in a cautioning display of anger. Oblivious, the girl kicked her feet back nervously, still fixated on Banning.

The creature lunged for her ankle.

Banning thrust out his hand, whipping a blast of energy across the room. It struck the lindwurm, sending it backwards along the floor, until it struck the wall with a sharp crack.

His stomach dropped. He hurried across the room and scooped up the creature, confirming what he already knew.

No. No. No.

Bile crept up into his throat. Banning swallowed it back and squeezed his eyes shut against the black spots dancing across his vision.

Ten, nine, eight... It was no good, he couldn't breathe.

WEAK.

The voice trickled into his panic, threatening to burst the banks of his self-control. *No.* He couldn't let it take over. He couldn't give himself to the dark rivers of poison running through his mind. He needed the girl and her mother alive.

His clammy hand reached for the autoinjector.

Seven, six, five...

He inhaled, holding the breath until his lungs began to burn and his anxiety plateaued, then released it. He wouldn't be a slave to his fear. Slowly, he took his fingers out of his pocket. Inhale. Exhale.

You still have the hellip.

His heart rate slowed. He opened his eyes.

The girl gaped at the lindwurm, then at him.

'W-why did you kill it?' she whispered.

'Why? Because it was about to bite you. Just one bite from a male lindwurm for a child of your size would be excruciating. Not fatal, but as the venom worked its way through your bloodstream, you'd feel like your veins were boiling. You'd be in agony.'

What little colour remained in the girl's face drained away. She gulped and turned her pitiful gaze back to her mother.

Banning placed the lifeless lindwurm back inside its tank. He'd deal with it and the rest of the mess later. Right now, he had more pressing problems.

'You... you saved me?' the girl said.

'*What?*' Banning spun round to look at her. Hope flickered across her face. 'I didn't save you. I just stopped you from getting hurt. There's a difference.' He tsked at her look of confusion and crossed the room to stand in front of her. 'Let me make this clear. We're going to get into a car now. I'm going to carry your mother. You're going to do exactly what I say if you want her to stay alive. Do you understand?'

The hope in her eyes faded. She nodded.

'If you try to run, if you scream, if you so much as look at another person before we get to the car, I will hurt her. And it will be your fault. *Your* fault. Is that clear?'

She nodded again.

'Good.' Banning stooped to lift the unconscious woman. He struggled with her dead weight. Heimerich had made it look a lot easier earlier.

Banning shifted her into a manageable position and walked awkwardly towards the door. He turned and nodded at the child. 'Open the door and go ahead of me.'

The child choked back a sob but did as she was asked.

He headed through and let the door lock behind him. He ushered the girl towards the car where Oliver was waiting for them, rear passenger door already open.

'In,' Banning said.

The girl obeyed. He placed her mother carefully on the back seat next to her and slammed the door. Taking a deep breath, Banning smoothed his hair and exhaled.

There was nothing for it, he was going to have to take them to the slipway and keep an eye on them. It wasn't like there weren't cages to spare there.

Chapter 29

JASMIN'S EYES WIDENED AT Charlie's warning to watch out. She spun round.

The rolling shadows coalesced into the form of Rhea. A very naked Rhea.

'Rhea?' Jasmin ventured.

Charlie held his breath. This was it. The moment they discovered just how much shit they were really in.

'Jasmin!'

Rhea's squeal caught Charlie off guard. He stared dumbly as the woman flung herself at Jasmin, wrapping her in a tight hug.

What was happening? Was this some kind of trick? A tactic to get them to lower their defences?

He scanned the car park for trouble. The men who'd attacked them were very much dead, their twisted bodies sprawled across the concrete. The sight should have turned his stomach, but instead he felt a twinge of satisfaction. It made him uncomfortable. Was that really how he felt, or was he being manipulated by his connection to the dagger? Either way, it wasn't right.

The two women broke apart. Tears glistened on Rhea's cheeks.

Noticing the sheen in Jasmin's eyes, he scowled. Was she really buying into this bullshit?

'Jasmin,' Rhea said. 'My God, it's good to see you. You haven't changed a bit.' She gave her an appraising glance. 'Not a bit.'

Charlie coughed, making Jasmin jump. *Yep, I'm still here.*

Stepping up beside her, he shrugged out of his trench coat and offered it to Rhea. She took it, grimacing at the blood-soaked ripped sleeve, and put it on. After tying the belt in a firm knot around her waist, she sized him up, then turned back to Jasmin with a grin.

'What're you doing here? How did you find me?'

'Auntie,' Jasmin said. Her fingers twitched next to the pocket containing the soul stone.

Whether the gesture had been unintentional or she'd simply changed her mind about revealing it to Rhea, Charlie couldn't be sure. Either way he was glad she kept it hidden.

Something about the succubus felt off. After all these years, after sacrificing a part of her soul to save Jasmin, she just greets her with open arms? Without an ounce of suspicion or bitterness? It didn't add up.

Rhea rolled her eyes, her smile never slipping. 'I should've known.'

'I need to speak to you about something,' Jasmin said.

'Oh?'

'My girlfriend and her daughter were abducted this morning. There were markings on the wall.' She scanned the surrounding area, as if seeking evidence to back up her claims. She continued. 'They were the same markings I saw on the ground near the flat the night I got hurt. The night you left.'

Years of pain, years of resentment sounded like they were neatly packaged in those four little words.

Charlie rubbed his ring finger, regretting that he was no longer a smoker.

Rhea's mouth pressed into a hard line. 'You're not suggesting that *I* took her?'

'*What?* No. Of course not. Rhea, I need your help. I know your kind are rare…'

'My kind? What would you know about my kind, or did Auntie fill you in on that too?'

Jasmin fanned her hands. 'That doesn't matter. Look, I know you're a succubus. I know that the markings I saw were shadowburn. I also know—'

Rhea stared at her. 'Hang on… so you *are* working for O.O.T.I.S?'

'That's not important. What *is* important is that I know there aren't many succubi in our realm—'

Rhea folded her arms and barked a laugh. 'And you thought what? That we all get together? Have a catch-up over a nice cup of tea and a slice of cake?'

'Ree, please.'

Charlie exhaled, his breath fogging. They were getting nowhere. Wasting time. He squeezed and released his fists rhythmically, in a desperate attempt to calm his nerves. He was close to being pushed from the familiar grips of anxiety into a full-blown panic attack.

Blood continued to trickle from the gash on his arm, dripping down his knuckles. All he wanted was his daughter and granddaughter back. For all he knew they could be seriously hurt. What if Jasmin was wrong? What if whoever took Meggy and Evie didn't need them alive? His breathing became rapid and a cold sweat pricked at his palms. A dull, throbbing ache radiated across his hand.

'Charlie?' Jasmin's voice pulled him back from the brink. 'Charlie, you're okay. Just breathe. Breathe.' A crease appeared between her eyebrows as her eyes lowered from his face to his clenched fist.

'What's his deal?' Rhea asked, giving him a look he didn't appreciate.

'Nothing, he's fine.'

Rhea's brow wrinkled. 'Me and O.O.T.I.S, let's just say we don't see eye to eye...' She sighed, apparently making up her mind. 'There's a guy. Real nasty piece of work. Got all kinds of contacts. Imports cryptids through the veil.' Jasmin shot her a look. 'Don't look at me like that. Anyway, I've heard he's got a succubus on the payroll. I can take you to him if you like? Won't be cheap, mind—he doesn't give anything away for free—but if anyone knows anything, you can bet your bottom dollar it's him.'

Jasmin smiled. 'That would be great, thank you.'

'So, what, O.O.T.I.S is so short on staff that they only send two agents out now?'

Charlie scoffed.

'We're not exactly here on official business,' Jasmin replied, giving him a warning look to say nothing.

Rhea lifted one brow. 'They don't know you're here?'

'I didn't want them to find out about Auntie.'

Rhea considered that, then gave Jasmin a nod. 'I can respect that. Off the radar. First things first, we need to get the old-timer patched up. If he loses anymore blood I think he might black out.' She avoided looking at his arm as she trailed her fingers down the curve of one of her ears, where the earrings were now missing. Her mouth turned down at the edges.

'I'm not going to a hospital,' Charlie snapped.

'Nobody said anything about a hospital,' said Rhea. 'My place isn't too far from here, we'll go there. A couple of stitches—'

Charlie barked, 'I'm fine. Let's just go meet your guy.'

'In case you hadn't noticed, I'm not exactly dressed for the occasion.' Rhea flapped the ruined trench coat. 'And anyway, I'm going to go out on a limb here and say that neither of you has a spare twenty grand on you?'

Jasmin spluttered. 'Twenty grand?'

'I told you, information don't come cheap.'

Christ. Where in hell were they going to get that kind of money at this short notice?

Rhea smiled. 'Lighten up, you two. You look like someone just pissed in your coffee. I know where we can get the money.'

'Convenient,' Charlie muttered.

Jasmin shot him a warning glance. 'We're running out of options.'

His jaw made a clicking noise, but he held his tongue. She was right.

Rhea beamed. 'Excellent. We have a plan. This is going to be fun.'

Chapter 30

CHARLIE TOOK A STEP back, putting distance between him and the entrance to Rhea's flat. How could anyone live like this? It was a mess.

No, that was being too kind. It was a squalid hellhole. He'd seen drug dens that were more appealing. And that was *really* saying something.

His anxiety kicked in as he eyed the mattress in the middle of the discoloured grey carpet, bedding strewn across it, clothes piled in an unkempt heap beside pillows that had seen better days. The only actual piece of furniture he could see was a battered garden chair, its frame flaking with rust. Next to it, a small wooden crate—complete with dirty plate and a half-eaten piece of toast—served as a makeshift table.

Charlie let his eyes drift as he balled his fists. Half a dozen mugs with mouldering contents had been abandoned on various surfaces, some on the floor. Everywhere he looked, he was met with discarded food containers, crisp wrappers, and some things he couldn't even begin to identify.

Squeeze, release. Squeeze, release. Squeeze, release.

He stared down at his shoes and, realising he was standing on a large, black, damp patch on the shared hallway carpet, took a half-step forward.

'Charlie? Are you okay, do you need to step outside?'

His attention snapped to Jasmin. He shook his head, fixating on her face.

Inhale. Exhale. Repeat.

'I'm okay,' he said, offering her a wan smile.

'What's wrong with him?' Rhea's voice made them both start. She shook her head in confusion and scooped an armful of clothes up off the floor, then tossed them into the kitchen area. 'Seriously, is he sick or something? I don't want him puking outside my front door.'

'He's not sick. He just has an issue with... uh, clutter.'

'You sure he's not going to puke?'

'I'm fine. It's manageable,' Charlie said, his voice tight.

'Fair enough.' Rhea collected up a few of the plates and continued to redistribute the mess around the room. 'So, you coming in or what?'

Charlie forced his feet forward, keeping his arms tight against his body as he negotiated past the doorframe. Jasmin closed the door behind him, exposing him to the full, musty stench of mildew and the sour tang of curdled milk.

'Want something to drink?' Rhea asked.

'Christ, no,' Charlie blurted. Jasmin nudged him with her elbow. 'I mean no thank you.'

Rhea put the stack of plates on the counter. 'I can fix you something to eat if you're hungry?' There was a sardonic twist to her mouth.

'No, really. Don't trouble yourself,' Charlie said.

'You sure?'

She was definitely enjoying this. 'No. Thank you.'

'Jas?' Rhea asked her.

Jasmin shook her head. 'I have to admit, Rhea, this isn't the sort of place I pictured you living.'

'No? And what exactly did you picture? Some cottage in the countryside with little, white picket fences and a garden full of roses? Or maybe a nice townhouse by the seaside where I could take a stroll along a pebble beach and paddle in the surf?' She slammed a mug down next to the stack of plates. Brown liquid sloshed over the rim, splattering her skin. Sucking her teeth, she snatched up a tea towel and dried her hand.

Her anger caught Charlie's attention. He exchanged a glance with Jasmin.

'Look, Ree, I'm sorry. I didn't mean anything by it,' Jasmin said softly, the concern in her voice genuine. 'It's just nothing like what you used to talk about having when we were younger.'

Rhea dragged her fingers through her hair, pulling the bun loose, and slipped the hairband on her wrist. Her features softened. 'What did you expect, Jas? Nothing turned out like I wanted it to. I lost you. I lost my home. I lost myself. The world isn't what I thought it was going to be. But you grow up. You move on. That's just the way it is. Especially for people like me.'

Jasmin stepped forward leaving Charlie to stand alone—an observer to a clearly private conversation. 'It doesn't have to be that way, Ree.'

'No?' Rhea scoffed. 'Wake up. Sometimes things just don't work out. Sometimes the good guys don't win. Sometimes if you want to take on crooks you just have to become...' She waved her hand in the air, searching for the right word.

'Better?' Jasmin ventured.

Rhea sighed. 'Worse. The world is full of monsters. The only way to survive is to be a worse monster than the ones around you.'

'That's not true.'

'Who are you trying to convince—me or you? At some point you'll see it too.'

The two women stared at each other, locked in silence.

A small brown shape scurried across the floor from behind the crate. Charlie jumped back, his shoulders colliding against the door. '*Christ.*'

Jasmin whipped round to face him, scanning for the threat. Not seeing any immediate danger, she relaxed her stance and gave him a questioning look.

He cleared his throat, feeling his cheeks flush. 'A mouse.'

Rhea rolled her eyes. 'Case in point. He'd get eaten alive out there.' Giving Charlie a shake of her head, she crossed the room, grabbed a small towel and tossed it to Jasmin. 'For his arm. He's bleeding on my carpet.'

'No.' It was almost a growl. 'Not a chance that thing's touching my skin.'

'It's clean.' Rhea grinned. 'More or less.'

'Jesus, Charlie.' Jasmin let the towel drop to the floor and held up her hands. 'At least let me see how bad it is.'

Reluctantly, he offered out his arm. She unbuttoned the cuff and rolled up his sleeve. He jerked, wincing as the material grazed his tender flesh. It was a struggle not to pull away completely.

She inspected the wound then frowned at the spots of dried blood on his shirt where the naeshin had sunk its teeth into his other arm, and met his gaze. 'Doesn't look like there's any real damage. You're lucky.'

'Yeah, I feel lucky.'

'Rhea was right. We're going to have to stitch it.'

He cast a glance around Rhea's flat, his heart rate increasing. 'No, it's fine.'

'It's really not,' Jasmin insisted, pulling his arm closer to her.

'I said it's fine.'

'You say that a lot, y'know. "I'm fine", "It's fine". I nearly believed you the first time,' Rhea said. She rifled behind a stack of mangled magazines, completely unperturbed when half the pile toppled to the floor.

Charlie frowned. 'It'll heal.' He looked at Rhea then back to Jasmin, and lowered his voice. 'I heal fast. I don't need stitches.'

Rhea slammed a medical bag down on the crate beside them, making them both jump. 'You're getting stitched, gramps. As much as your blood is adding to the aesthetic, the sight of it turns my stomach.'

'You're joking, right?'

Jasmin unzipped the bag, pulled out a suture kit and turned it over in her hands. 'She's not. She's always been squeamish around blood.' She placed the kit down and continued to root through the bag until she found a packet of latex surgical gloves and a bottle of sterile saline. 'Let's get the wound cleaned up a bit, if nothing else.'

He nodded.

Rhea, squeamish? Not a chance.

He recalled the image of the dead man she'd left at his feet, his face contorted in a silent scream of agony and fear. Rhea was dangerous. A monster. A demon. But she'd saved Jasmin's life. And sacrificed a part of herself in the process, if Auntie was to be believed. So, not always a monster.

He gritted his teeth and rubbed idly at the sigil. Is that what had happened to Stephen? His old friend's sense of right and wrong had always been the backbone of his personality. If having a demon possess his body could corrupt him so completely, what did that mean for Charlie as its master?

A sudden, sharp pain in his arm forced the thought from his mind. 'Ow!'

'Don't be such a baby,' Jasmin chided.

'I said I didn't need stitches.' He glowered at the curved needle penetrating his skin.

Jasmin rolled her eyes. 'For the love of God, Charlie, you can be such a child at times. It's just a needle. You've been through far worse. I saw the state of you when you were in hospital, so don't give me this crap.' Using the tweezer-like forceps as a temporary grip, she adjusted her hold on the needle driver.

He growled but stayed put.

'One—' he hissed as she fed the needle through his flesh, '—that was a life or death situation. Two, if I get sepsis from you doing this inside this hovel, it's on you.' He cast his gaze around the flat again and pulled a face at the collection of hair and dust on the skirting board.

'Rude.' Rhea smirked when he flinched, but when she dropped her gaze to his wound, she paled and turned away.

He felt a brief surge of satisfaction before a sharp pain jolted through his arm like livewire. Cursing, he glared at the needle driver to see Jasmin loop the suture around it and, in one deft movement, clamp the thread jutting from his skin, laying the knot.

'*Seriously?* Can't you just finish it all in one go?'

'I'm not a doctor, Charlie. Individual stitches are easier.'

This was absurd. He didn't need stitches. He needed to find his family. It had been hours and they still hadn't heard from whoever had abducted Meggy and Evie. If this really was about the dagger, shouldn't someone have made contact already? Demanding an exchange? A ransom? Anything?

Christ. Where were they? Where was his daughter? His granddaughter? Were they okay? Had they been hurt?

His heart thrashed inside his chest.

What if they were being tortured? What if someone was trying to extract the information that neither of them had?

His fingers curled into fists. His breathing got faster.

What if they're already dead?

The skin between his thumb and forefinger started to burn.

Jasmin slapped him across the face, snapping his head to the side. Pain flared in his cheek. He blinked at her in disbelief. 'You *slapped* me?'

'You need to calm down. Take a breath. If you don't we're fucked, Charlie. Remember what happened earlier, at headquarters?' She lowered her voice to a whisper, the needle forgotten in her hand. 'If you summon the dagger now, we've lost our only advantage. The kidnappers can just kill you and take it. Then what?' Her lips pinched. 'Isn't repressing your emotions what you do best?'

Ouch.

Jasmin jabbed the needle into his arm.

He jerked back. 'Ow. *Shit.*'

Rhea was watching them in quiet speculation. Her gaze flicked to his hand and the sigil before she turned away, busying herself with more clutter.

Charlie narrowed his eyes. Jasmin was right. The dagger was what they wanted. He couldn't risk losing it.

'There, all done.' Jasmin tied off the last suture and cut the thread. She gently dabbed at the remaining blood with a piece of gauze, then wrapped Charlie's arm in a bandage.

'I knew it was here.' Rhea flipped a second crate onto its side, revealing a square of carpet that was at least three shades lighter than its surroundings. She crouched and dug her fingers under, peeling it back. After a moment or two of fiddling, she removed a segment of floorboard and produced a small black safe.

Jasmin gaped. 'You keep your money under a crate?'

'It's not like anyone's going to find it.' She looked pointedly at Charlie. 'I mean, the place is a dive.'

Charlie smiled. *Smart. Disgusting, but smart.*

Rhea opened the safe and pulled out wads of fifty-pound notes. She started counting them out in a pile, licking the tip of her thumb when they stuck together.

Charlie grimaced. 'That's not hygienic.'

'What? It's not the worst thing I've had in my mouth.'

'I don't want to know.'

Jasmin leant forward, staring at the cash. 'Is it enough?'

'No.' Rhea reached into the safe again and pulled out a bundle of waxed paper packets bound by elastic bands. The stamp of a silhouetted black dragon was just visible in the gap between her fingers. 'But I know where we can get the rest.'

'Is that *heroin*?' Charlie hissed.

Rhea chuckled for a moment then her laughter died. 'Oh, you're serious? No. This is far more valuable than heroin. It's Dragon Scale.'

'Dragon scales?'

'Not dragon *scales*. Dragon Scale. Dragons don't exist. It's lindwurm venom. Powdered lindwurm venom to be exact.' When it became apparent Charlie was none the wiser, she rolled her eyes. 'A type of demon toxin.'

Charlie rubbed at his jaw and turned away. 'Now I *really* don't want to know.'

Chapter 31

'ARE YOU SURE THIS is it?' Nick peered out of the passenger window. Whatever he'd been expecting, it certainly wasn't a perfectly manicured front lawn adorned with whimsical gnome ornaments. Their smiling faces stared back at him under the anaemic orange glow of the streetlights. His nose wrinkled.

Sam brought the car to a stop. He pulled the key out of the ignition and frowned at the garden, clearly sharing Nick's thoughts. 'It's the right address. There, look.'

Partially obscured from the road behind a wall of conifers, its colour faded beneath the night sky, was a dented, burnt-orange Mustang.

'How do you want to play this?' Sam asked.

Nick licked his lips. 'You'll have to do the talking. Things might get heated if he sees me and puts two-and-two together after this morning.'

'Sure, no problem. If I'm not back in ten minutes, assume I've been eaten by a garden gnome.' Sam flashed his trademark smile and unbuckled his seatbelt.

'I'll give you five.'

Sam climbed out of the car, walked briskly to the house and tried the bell.

The Fabia was buffeted by the strong wind that whipped up dried leaves and dust across the bonnet. Nick felt immensely grateful for the residual warmth from the heaters.

Sam pressed the bell again and took a step back.

The front door opened. Nick ducked low in his seat.

Mundy Wilcoxson stepped into view, a towel wrapped around his waist, revealing more tattoos. Sam held up his warrant card. The man squinted at it, gestured for Sam to enter and, with a quick scan of the outside, closed the door after them.

Nick chewed on the inside of his cheek. His gut was telling him that this was a mistake. But Sam was a big boy and could take care of himself. He glanced at his watch and shifted in the seat.

Nope, screw it. This was a stupid idea. He couldn't leave Sam alone with Mundy. The man had a list of convictions longer than the Post Office queue on pension day.

Nick clambered out of the car and jogged up the driveway. Goose bumps pricked his flesh, caused by something other than the chill in the air. What had they been thinking doing this alone? They should have arranged for uniform to go with them.

Just calm down, no point in getting worked up over nothing.

He approached the door, lifted his hand to knock and hesitated. A loud grunt sound followed by a muffled thud froze the blood in his veins. *Shit.* Before his brain could catch up, he yanked the handle down and shoved the door open.

His breath caught.

Sam was sprawled on the tiles, blood seeping from a nasty gash on the side of his head. But he was breathing. Mundy was standing over him, back to Nick, holding what looked like an abstract, bronze sculpture.

'Mundy Wilcoxson,' Nick said, surprising himself with how steady his voice sounded. 'I'm arresting you for the offence of assaulting an officer. You do not have to say anything, but it may harm your defence if you do not mention, when questioned, something which you later rely on in court. Anything you do say may be taken and given as evidence.'

Mundy let the sculpture drop and turned to face Nick. The recognition on his face was immediate.

'Well, well, well.' He sneered and took a single step forward. 'Ain't this a happy coincidence?'

'Stay where you are!'

'Or what, pretty boy? Where's your backup? You've fucked up.'

Nick's blood pulsed in his ears. He kept his eyes locked on Mundy.

The man gestured behind him; the movement made Nick's every muscle tense. 'Take a look around, you ain't in Kansas anymore.'

That's when Nick noticed them. Cages. There had to be at least half a dozen he could see. At least two of them contained small animals of some kind.

A wolfish grin spread across Mundy's face. 'That's right. Recognise them? Your little O.O.T.I.S buddy sure as hell did.'

O.O.T.I.S? A flurry of motion inside one of the cages drew Nick's focus. Whatever was behind the bars, he couldn't identify it. Using the distraction as an opportunity, Mundy inched forward.

'Don't move,' Nick barked.

Mundy took another step.

'I said, don't move!'

The sound of metal clattering startled Nick. Whatever was in the cage was launching itself against the bars in a frenzy of rasping grunts and snorts. His eyes widened. In those few seconds, he completely forgot about the man standing in front of him.

And that was his mistake.

Mundy pointed a gun at his face.

Where the hell did that come from?

'Didn't think this one through, did you?' Mundy drawled. 'I think you're forgetting I remember where you live. Got any family?'

Those three words hit Nick like a fist. *Henry.*

'That's what I thought.' Mundy tilted the gun to taunt him, exposing strange symbols stamped across its length as he did. 'So, here's what's gonna happen. You're gonna tell me why you and your little mate here are snooping around. You're gonna tell me who else knows you're here. You're gonna tell me everything I want to know. Every last fucking detail.' He nodded at the wedding band on Nick's finger. 'Or I'm gonna go to your home and put a bullet in the head of your missus. What do you think about that?'

Nick held his hands up. 'No one knows we're here. I swear to God, it's just me and Sam.'

'That's good news. For me, I mean. Not for you or him. You're both completely fucked.' With an amused grunt, Mundy lowered the gun and squeezed the trigger.

'No!'

There was no ear-splitting pop. No muzzle flash. Nothing decades of watching tacky action films had trained him to expect. The back of Sam Bennett's head simply exploded out. Bone fragments and brain matter rained down around his body, hitting the floor in soft, wet splats.

Nick's legs turned to jelly. He staggered back, barely able to keep himself upright, eyes still locked on Sam's corpse. *No.* This couldn't be happening. This couldn't be real.

Slowly, mechanically, he lifted his head to look at Mundy.

The man was doused in Sam's blood. It had sprayed up his body leaving droplets of red to stain the towel around his waist, drip down his exposed skin and mist in his beard. Without so much as a blink, Mundy grinned and showed Nick the weapon. The residual white glow of the markings etched into the gun faded back to black.

'Wouldn't want to spook the neighbours. Cost me a pretty penny to have this weapon customised.' He tilted his head to look at Sam, directing Nick's attention back to the exposed shards of white as well as the bloodied mush seeping from the shattered hollow of Sam's skull. 'But as you can see, it was worth it.'

Nick gulped. There were no words. The man was insane.

This was it. He was going to die here.

'Now, let me ask you again, why are you here?' Mundy said.

'I... I...'

'Tick tock, pretty boy.'

'We... we were following up a lead on a missing persons case.'

'Bullshit.'

'It's true!'

Mundy tutted in part disappointment, part irritation. 'Let's try something a little bit easier, shall we? Now, where does a dozy prick like you get a dog like the one I hit?'

Nick stammered, struggling to keep up. He felt lightheaded, unable to catch his breath. 'I don't... I don't... what?'

'The dog. Where did you get the fucking dog?'

'S-she was a gift. A birthday present. Fr-from my... my—'

Nick heard footsteps before a shape appeared in his peripheral vision. Someone else was in the house. He started to turn, his body still leaden, his mind still numb. Something hard slammed against the back of his head with a deafening crack. Pain was the last thing that registered before Nick hit the floor.

Chapter 32

CHARLIE IGNORED THE DULL throbbing in his arm as he walked. He glanced over his shoulder. Christ, he couldn't believe that *this* was the plan. Collect drug money—and from a public playing field no less. It made his skin crawl.

Rhea was bad news. He could feel it in his bones. Why was she helping them? What was her endgame? There was no way she was doing this out of the kindness of her heart. Guilt over Jasmin maybe? No. He wasn't buying it. There had to be something in it for her, something he was missing.

He frowned at the small parade of shops they passed. The windows that weren't boarded over with plywood had been pitted with rock-sized dents, spidery cracks spreading out from their centre. Fragments of glass littered the edges of the pavement, glistening beneath creeping fingers of frost.

'And I thought the part of town you grew up in was rough,' he murmured at Jasmin's back.

She didn't answer.

The wasting glow of the streetlights made grasping shadows of every nook and cranny. Ravenous.

Desperate. He could feel eyes on him wherever he looked. It was like someone—or something—was lying in wait, biding their time until he let down his guard. Even if there hadn't been a dull ache spreading from the sigil, he had experience enough to know what danger felt like. Other than the three of them, there wasn't a soul in sight.

He curled his hands into fists. Resisting the urge to stuff them into the pockets of his ruined trench coat, he cleared his throat. 'And this is where we'll find your friends, is it, Rhea?'

Rhea looked back at him, adjusting the strap of the duffle bag containing spare clothes and ill-gotten cash slung over her shoulder. 'I'm not sure *friends* is the right word. Acquaintances maybe. But yeah, this is where we'll find them.' With a shrug, she faced the front, but not before she glanced at Jasmin.

Charlie scowled with suspicion. At first, he'd accepted these fleeting looks as the sentimental interest of an old flame, but now, in the darkness, they felt more predatory than nostalgic. There was no way Jasmin hadn't noticed. Maybe she had and didn't mind.

'This way.' Rhea nodded at a darkened alley feeding down the side of a small pharmacy.

Of course it is.

The yellow light coming from the flat directly overhead offered little illumination. If they were to get attacked right there and then, Charlie knew the curtains wouldn't even twitch. He exhaled a plume of white breath, shook his head and followed.

They emerged from the alley into a playing field next to a small car park. The car park looked disused, if the warped frame of a burnt-out Ford Fiesta and two heavily vandalised charity donation bins were anything to go by.

'Upstanding citizens are they, these acquaintances?' Charlie asked.

Rhea barked out a laugh. 'You're funny, Charlie. I like that about you.'

That didn't make him feel any better.

Jasmin fell back to walk by his side. 'It's okay, we can trust her.'

Charlie stopped dead in his tracks. 'Are you joking?' He barely lowered his voice, not caring if Rhea heard him. 'What happened to keeping our guard up? You're letting your emotions cloud your judgement. She's a demon. A criminal. Auntie explicitly warned you about her. All that stuff with the souls... or have you forgotten?'

The change in her expression was instant.

Jasmin's face screwed up, her eyes ablaze, as she took a step closer to him. 'How could I ever forget? You've got *no* idea what I went through. None. I understand you're scared, Charlie. I understand you're angry. I am too. I love Meghan. I've loved her with every part of my fractured soul since I was old enough to understand what love was. I would never do anything to put her in harm's way. Her or Evie. *Never.*'

He flicked his attention to Rhea. 'I don't trust her.'

'You don't trust anyone.'

'I trust *you*, Jasmin.' He softened his tone. 'I trust you.'

She took a breath. 'Then trust me now.'

A droplet of icy rain struck Charlie's face.

He turned up the collar of his trench coat. 'Fine.'

Jasmin nodded. 'Come on.'

A few metres ahead of them Rhea waited, picking at the chipped varnish on her nails. She glanced up when they joined her, her expression neutral.

The rain started in earnest, falling in piercing sheets and saturating everything around it in seconds.

'This is just great,' Charlie grumped.

'What's the matter, gramps? Afraid you might catch pneumonia?' Rhea spread out her arms and threw her head back, opening her mouth wide.

Well, that certainly helped to clarify things. She was clearly insane.

Charlie gave Jasmin a questioning look. She shrugged back, a smile lifting the corners of her mouth.

'Can we just get to where we're going?' he said.

Blinking the water from her eyes, Rhea turned her attention to Jasmin. 'Do you remember when we used to go for walks in the rain?'

Charlie made a disapproving sound.

Rhea pouted and narrowed her eyes at him. 'Do me a favour, Jasmin, next time you come and see me, don't bring the fun police.' She walked away without waiting for a response.

There wouldn't be a 'next time'. The only reason they were here was to find his family. And Jasmin was not interested in rekindling what they'd had. But it wasn't his place to say. Jasmin wasn't a child. She could speak for herself.

Instead, Charlie pulled his trench coat closed, grimacing at the feel of the wet fabric on his skin, and followed. His face was so numb, every droplet of rain felt like a shard of glass stabbing his flesh. Rhea might only have been trying to get a rise out of him with the pneumonia comment, but it might not be far from the truth.

Wet mud sucked at his shoes as he crossed the field. Away from the lampposts the darkness was formidable, pressing in around them, choking out the light. Even so, he could just about make out three figures moving in the distance. He trudged forward, doing his best not to stumble on the slick and shifting earth.

The figures drew closer, male, the sound of their voices, dampened by the downpour growing louder with every step. The men watched them approach, their faces obscured by the shadows of their hoods.

'Nice weather for ducks, innit?' the man on the left drawled.

Rhea stopped, raising a hand for Charlie and Jasmin to do the same. Although she kept her posture relaxed, Charlie could see the slight stiffness in her movements and the hint of tension in her jaw as she donned a smile.

The man—no, not a man, he couldn't have been more than nineteen—took an eager step forward. 'You bring the stuff?'

'Sure.' Rhea dropped the bag and reached into her jacket.

'Whoa. Nah, nah, nah.' The teen was in front of her in a second. He clamped his hand around her wrist.

Charlie stiffened. This wasn't right. The hierarchy here seemed off.

Rhea smirked at the young man. 'Problem?'

'Unbutton slowly and I'll get it out.'

'Now there's an offer I can't refuse.'

The teenager snorted. 'Don't get cute with me. I know you're a doughnut bumper.' It didn't stop him from staring at her chest though as she deftly worked the buttons.

Rhea unfastened the last one and held her jacket open. The teen rifled through her pockets and pulled out the stack of waxed sachets. After a quick once-over of the goods, he tossed the stack to one of the others—a lad with barely enough patchy stubble to warrant shaving and an illegible tattoo scrawled in stylised script above his eyebrow—who stashed it immediately.

Letting the jacket fall closed, Rhea held out a hand. 'Money.'

'Change of plans.' The teenager shrugged. 'See, I've moved up in the world.'

'Is that right?' Rhea's reply was clipped.

'Ain't room for both of us here.' The two lads beside him snickered.

Rhea smiled. 'That's funny, I was thinking exactly the same thing.'

The teenager's brow furrowed, just as the sigil on Charlie's hand began to pulse.

Shit.

Chapter 33

THE SPACE WHERE RHEA stood burst apart in a surge of rolling shadow. Fronds, darker than pitch, twisted and thrashed around her. She was no longer human. Eyes the colour of hot coals smouldered within a featureless face. Thin, pulsing, red veins laced across the hard lines of her obsidian body.

Charlie staggered back, shock making a captive of his senses.

The three lads fanned out, triangulating their position around the succubus.

'That s'posed to impress me? You've shown me yours, now let me show you mine.'

The lead teen, the one who'd been doing the talking, grinned. He cracked his neck, eyes never leaving Rhea. The skin on his face rippled, like something was trying to squirm its way out of his skull. A hollow laugh released from his throat as protrusions of grey erupted over his body, shredding flesh. What was left standing in his place was a creature carved from rock.

The thing launched itself at Rhea, driving its fist into the spot where she'd been standing just seconds before.

The ground quaked, and the force of it rode up through Charlie's legs and into his chest.

Disorientated, Charlie blinked. One of the teenagers was directly in front of him. His heart lurched. Was this kid another one of those *things*?

The youth struck out at him. There was just enough time to throw his arms up against the incoming fist and deflect the punch. His sutures burst apart, muscles screaming from the strength of the strike.

The teen came at him again, driving Charlie back. He couldn't get a shot in. Blow after blow rained down on him. He slipped in the sludge, his calves burning, as he fought to stay upright. The ache of the naeshin bite had returned to harry him. The sigil on his hand flared. A low snarl escaped his mouth.

Charlie blocked purely on instinct, the rain blurring his vision. He twisted into the teen's feint, taking the full force of the fist to his ribs. Then, he was on the ground, pain radiating through his side. He rolled away from the source of impact, scrambling in the slippery mud to push back to his feet.

Jasmin was suddenly on top of the youth. Lambent-blue silhouettes trailed behind her, looking like echoes in time, as she pummelled him with punches of her own. No, not behind her, *around* her. Each silhouette had a distinct form, some male, some female. Every strike, every slight adjustment of her body was carried out in perfect unison with at least one of the figures.

It was like they were fighting for her. *Through* her.

Charlie gasped at the sight. As he did, one of the glowing outlines turned to look at him.

He recoiled, his feet losing purchase on the slick ground. He landed with a hard thud, the wet mud doing little to absorb the impact. Sucking in a painful breath, Charlie pushed to his knees.

Jasmin grabbed the neck of the teenager's hoodie. She hoisted him up and brought him close until his face was inches from her own. She snarled something at him under her breath. He mumbled a response.

Her face contorted into a sneer. She headbutted him, making a cracking sound that twisted Charlie's gut. The teen's body went slack. She let him drop. The blue figures behind her merged, absorbing back into Jasmin as if they'd never been there at all. She stood and stepped away from the boy.

Charlie saw the shallow rise and fall of the lad's chest. The relief he felt was palpable. Seeing Jasmin like that, the unrestrained violence, it was troubling. Hell, it was downright terrifying—shadowy, blue figures aside.

All three attackers were down. The one that had transformed into... whatever that had been, was prone on the ground, naked and human, and covered in a mix of blood and sludge. There was a deathly pallor to his skin.

A human Rhea jerked a wad of fifties free from the coat of the tattooed teen who'd pocketed her stash. 'Got the money.'

For the second time she was stark naked. It took Charlie a heartbeat to register, as he struggled to compartmentalise everything he'd just witnessed. He averted his eyes and focused instead on Jasmin.

Rhea gave an amused snort as she squelched through the mud.

'What was that?' he asked Jasmin.

She pointed at the thing that had attacked Rhea. 'That?'

'No, I saw people... coming out of you. Like they were pulling the strings and you were just a puppet.'

Jasmin scraped back the hair plastered to her face and considered her next words. 'Do you remember what Auntie said in the flat about using pieces of other souls to bind mine back together?'

'Yes?'

'That was them. Auntie didn't just choose them at random. She selected warriors. The strongest. The wisest. She chose pieces of souls from those she thought would be able to protect me. Guide me. They're a part of me now, so are their skills. Their strengths. Their memories...' She trailed off with a far-away look, blinking the rain from her eyes. 'I can't really explain it. When I let them take a measure of control, it's like everything they had in life flows through me. Speed, reflexes, intuition. I get it all.'

'So what you're telling me is that all those times we sparred at the gym, you were pulling your punches?'

She laughed quietly, some of the tension easing from her face. Charlie smiled at her, welcoming the familiar distraction—something else to focus on.

'Maybe a little,' she conceded.

'Right, it's okay,' Rhea announced. 'You can look now, gramps.'

He turned to see Rhea's spare outfit was already sodden with rain. She crouched over the lad Jasmin had laid out and started rummaging through his clothes. He groaned, but otherwise didn't move—still out for the count.

Seeing the kid was still a kid turned Charlie's stomach. He hadn't transformed. He wasn't some demon. Some monster. For all Charlie knew, he'd just got caught up with the wrong crowd and was now lying in the mud, getting his pockets turned out.

'Bonus.' Rhea said, as she waved another wad of notes. She waggled it at them before tossing it in her bag and zipping it shut. 'Let me just deal with him first and we can go meet my contact.'

'Deal with?' A feeling of revulsion crept up and settled in Charlie's throat. He blinked through the rain, eyes seeking out the third kid with the bad ink job—the one Rhea had fought. The twisted angle of the lad's neck told him all he needed to know.

'We can't leave him alive.' She placed her hands either side of the second youth's head.

Charlie lurched forward at Rhea and the unconscious teen. '*No!* He's just a kid.'

'He's not *just a kid*. And if he talks? If he sends more of his mates to come after us? What then? You need to decide, Charlie boy, if his life is worth more to you than Jasmin's girlfriend and her kid?'

Her words hit him like a blow to the gut. He shrank back.

Rhea moved with inhuman speed, snapping the second boy's neck.

'No!' Charlie's shout came a second too late. There was nothing he could have done to save the kid. What chance did an ex-detective have against a demon?

What chance did he have of saving Meggy and Evie?

'They would have killed us,' Jasmin said softly.

'You didn't even try to stop her.' Jasmin flinched. Charlie got no gratification from her fleeting acknowledgement that she'd done nothing to save the dead teen.

Rhea flashed him a grin. 'If it makes you feel any better, he wasn't human. Not entirely anyway.'

Charlie's jaw clicked.

The humour slipped from her face. 'I told you, if you want to survive in a world full of monsters, you have to become something worse.' She stepped over the corpse and spat rainwater from her mouth. 'Shall we get a move on?'

Charlie squeezed his fists tight, nails biting into his flesh. Not trusting himself to speak, he fell in behind the two women.

Jasmin increased her pace to come level with Rhea. 'Where are we headed?'

'Dockyard.'

'And this contact of yours, he's going to be okay with us just dropping in?'

'For twenty grand? Yeah, I'd say so. I've given him the heads up. He knows to expect us.'

'Are you seriously okay with this, Jasmin?' Charlie blurted out.

Both women turned to look at him.

'She just murdered three people. Right in front of us. And you don't seem the least bit bothered. Is this what they teach you at O.O.T.I.S?'

Rhea cocked her head, regarding him with interest. She only broke her gaze when Jasmin stepped towards him.

'Charlie, I—'

'They were kids, Jasmin. Christ, the one who went for me couldn't have been more than sixteen.'

'He was going to kill you, Charlie.'

'You don't know that.'

'Jesus Christ.' Rhea held up her arms. 'Wake up, gramps. You'd be dead right now if it wasn't for us. Why are you even here anyway? It's clear you don't work for O.O.T.I.S.'

Charlie shut his mouth. He glared at her.

Rhea stalked forward. 'Answer me. What's Jasmin's girlfriend got to do with you?'

'Rhea, don't,' Jasmin warned.

'Fine. This is how you want to play it?' Rhea squared up to Charlie. 'Do you even know what I am? I'm a succubus. A dream eater. I can literally pull the memories out of your head. Whatever's in your subconscious, all those forgotten thoughts, hidden feelings? I can pluck them out one by one. I can drain the life force from you in a matter of seconds. Now normally I'd just take a little. You'd feel a bit lethargic, like you've got a hangover, nothing you couldn't sleep off in a couple of days. But I'm done playing games and you're starting to piss me off. You either tell me what's really going on here or I'll get the answers myself.'

The sigil throbbed, intensifying in response to the adrenaline flooding his body. This woman was vile. A killer.

But they needed her.

'She's my daughter. Jasmin's partner is my daughter. They took her and my granddaughter.'

'Why?'

'I have something they want. That's all you need to know.' He closed his fist, covering the raised scarring on his hand. Her eyes tracked the movement through the rain and the darkness.

"Stealth hunters", that's what Jasmin had called Rhea's kind.

He lifted his chin at her, resisting the urge to back away. 'Satisfied?'

Rhea nodded, adjusting her grip on the duffle bag. 'Wasn't so hard now, was it?' She faced the front and trudged forward.

Charlie swallowed.

Call him paranoid, but there was a weight to the look she'd just given him, like his value had suddenly increased.

Chapter 34

BANNING CHECKED HIS WATCH, grinding his teeth.

This was unacceptable. He'd been waiting inside the slipway for over an hour now. He'd left the incubus with Mundy as a double deterrent, to stop both demon and trafficker from getting any bright ideas while he was otherwise indisposed. He just hadn't expected the pair to steal off into the night together.

Questioning Mundy's men had proved next to useless. The ones able to communicate beyond grunts were unwilling to share the trafficker's whereabouts. It was more likely they didn't know. Either way, it was beyond irritating.

More than once he'd considered just taking the hellip and leaving Heimerich to fend for himself. But Archibald Morgan appeared to have a vested interest in the incubus, so letting him fall foul of Mundy and his men wasn't an option. It was also possible he'd need Mr Wilcoxson in the future. That meant staying on the trafficker's good side and playing nice.

For now.

Biting back a curse, Banning resumed his pacing. The animal stench he'd grown accustomed to; it was the constant noise that was getting to him. If it wasn't the yammering howls, grunts and snarls, it was the raucous laughter of Mundy's goons. Or the quiet sobs of the girl in the cage beside him.

They were by far the worst. The pitiful, stilted huffs. The incessant wet sniffles. It reminded him of how his brother had wept in the weeks after they'd lost their parents and sister. How Garrick had nestled into their grandmother's arms and bawled, until his eyes were red and his throat was raw, as if he'd bore no blame.

How Banning had hated him then. Hated him with everything he had. And yet, even now, he knew that if he had to repeat that night over again, he would still drag Garrick from the flames. Love and hate, his grandmother had said, were two sides of the same coin.

Lost in thought, he traced the bulge of the pouch in his jacket pocket. Catching himself, he blinked, and levelled his gaze at the crying girl, huddled on the floor beside her insentient mother. She blinked up at him then quickly looked away, shuffling closer to the unconscious woman.

'Was the waitress not enough? You bringing your own fun now?'

Banning turned sharply when he heard Mundy's voice. He stepped away from the cage, keeping his expression neutral. The incubus was notably absent.

Mundy sauntered towards him, wearing a slim-fit, grey-check waistcoat and matching suit trousers. The top few buttons of his white shirt were open, his sleeves pushed up to his elbows, exposing even more of his tattoos and a bloodied bandage on his right arm. He hooked his thumbs in his pockets, grinning. 'Not too shabby, eh?'

Banning forced a smile. 'Nice suit. Out to impress?'

Mundy looked past Banning. His grin disappeared. 'Christ, kid. That's a child.'

'Yes. Thank you, Mr Wilcoxson. Observant as ever.'

The trafficker didn't react to the jibe, still frowning at the girl who swiped her tears with the cuff of her sleeve. Apparently he had some morals after all.

He met Banning's gaze. 'Follow me, I've gotta little surprise for you.'

Before Banning could take a step, Mundy hooked his finger and thumb in his mouth and whistled. His goons appeared with a speed not matching their bulk—two of them with guns at the ready. Was the trafficker seriously about to double-cross him?

Banning froze, drawing energy up from his core. It prickled along his skin, ready, waiting.

'Unlock the cage. They're coming with us,' Mundy instructed, pointing at the girl and her mother.

The first goon obliged, sliding the door back in a rasp of metal until it clattered to an abrupt stop. He thrust a hand out at the child in a clumsy grab attempt. She scrambled back, kicking out wildly. He caught her ankle on the second lunge and dragged her towards him. She thrashed, fighting to escape his grasp, but her attempts were futile. With a firm yank, he had her out and on the ground. The goon closed his thick fingers around her upper arm, hauling her roughly to her feet, while the second scurried in to retrieve her mother.

'*No*, don't touch her!' The girl's shriek was raw with terror. She clawed at her captor's hand, digging her nails into his skin. His grunt of amusement was cut short when she twisted sharply and sunk her teeth into his arm.

'You little bitch.' The goon wound his fingers into her raven hair and wrenched her head back, revealing crescent-shape bite marks welling with blood. He raised his hand to strike her across the face.

And then stopped.

Straining in place, his face reddening with exertion, he stared in bewilderment at his frozen limb.

'Under no circumstances is the child to be harmed.' Banning's voice cut through the man's confusion. He directed the question at Mundy. 'Understood?'

The trafficker shrugged, but his gaze lingered on Banning's outstretched arm a fraction too long for him to believe his indifference.

'Good.' Releasing the goon by lowering his hand, Banning turned to the girl. 'Remember our little conversation earlier?'

She nodded, paling, and shot a backwards glance at her mother who was now in the arms of the second goon.

'Excellent. Right then, Mr Wilcoxson, you mentioned a surprise?'

Mundy turned to lead the way. Banning nodded at the bandage around the trafficker's arm.

'Trouble?'

'Yeah, you could say that.' Mundy grinned at Banning, gingerly prodding at the wound. 'All will be explained, kid. All will be explained.'

The trafficker directed them back through the winding maze of cages and crates. Fragments of chaff and stalk floated like dust motes beneath the artificial lights hanging from the wooden rafters. When the angle allowed, Banning could just about see several men liberally distributing straw across the concrete to create a makeshift path. No doubt for the luxury of the buyers arriving later. It did not, however, extend to the area of the slipway on which they now found themselves, in a place where unsightly truths would shatter the illusion created for the rich and super rich. Despite his misgivings about the man, Banning had to admit that Mundy knew what he was about when it came to his business. Logistics aside, the planning involved in such a large-scale operation was mind-bending.

Barriers had been erected where necessary, preventing certain species from catching sight of each other. They sniffed the air, their agitation all too obvious inside the confines of their cramped enclosures.

After rounding a corner, past a particularly fractious gulon hissing its malcontent, Mundy turned and spread his arms out in a flourish. 'Ta-dah.'

Banning opened his mouth and closed it again. After the build-up, the contents of this particular cage were somewhat of a let-down. 'A man and a dog? I don't know what you've heard about me, Mr Wilcoxson, but my preferences don't fall that way.'

Mundy chuckled, opening the neighbouring cage and gesturing for the woman to be placed inside. 'I've seen what you like, kid, big fucking tits.'

Banning tutted. 'Language, Mr Wilcoxson.'

'Oops. Sorry, sweetheart.' Mundy grimaced at the girl. 'Big fucking *boobs*.' He arched an eyebrow at Banning and smirked.

Banning snapped his fingers, making the child flinch, and pointed at the cage. 'In.'

She eyed it warily, chewing on her lower lip, then ducked inside and sat next to her mother. A strangled gasp escaped her lips. She choked back a sob, eyes on the unconscious auburn-haired man in the adjoining cage. It almost looked like she recognised him.

Banning cocked his head. *Curiouser and curiouser.*

A low growl froze him in place. The Rottweiler had its face pressed up against the bars, teeth bared, ears pinned back.

'Thing needs a muzzle,' Banning remarked.

'Muzzle?' Mundy scoffed. 'Do you know how hard it was just getting the collar on that thing? Heimerich can vouch for that.' He motioned briefly with his hand.

Banning followed the movement. Heimerich stood off to one side, staring at nothing in particular. 'Are you trying to tell me that the intrepid Mundy Wilcoxson was nearly bested by a *Rottweiler*?'

'That ain't no Rottweiler, kid. That's a hellhound.'

'Right.'

Mundy tutted. 'Fine, a hybrid then. Still, solves my little problem from earlier.'

The memory of Mundy stomping on his lackey's face came to Banning's mind. 'And this is of interest to me how?'

'Because the owner of *said* hellhound, this ginger prick here—' he thumbed at the man in question,'—is a detective.'

Banning narrowed his eyes. His patience had worn thin hours ago, now it was threadbare.

'And he's got your name written down in his rozzer notebook.'

Now *that* got his full attention. '*What?*'

'Heimerich, chuck us the notebook.'

Heimerich turned mechanically. In the incubus' hands was a black, A4 notebook. He increased his grip, like he might refuse. Then he licked his lips and tossed it through the air. Mundy caught it one-handed and waved it at Banning triumphantly.

'Show me,' Banning said.

'So it *is* of interest then, eh?' Mundy held it out to him with a taunting smirk.

'Yes. Show me.' It was an effort not to snatch the thing from the trafficker's hands. Banning flicked through the pages, almost ripping them in his haste, until he got to the last scrawled entry.

He dug his fingers into the cover, warping it. *No.* The thorns of betrayal snagged his lungs, slashing as they twisted through his chest, making each breath more agonising than the last. *Naomie.*

'You know what they say, kid, don't shit where you eat.'
You knew the risks.

It was what he'd wanted, for her to hate him, for her to never lay eyes on him again. It was the only way he could keep her safe. The only way he wouldn't be a threat. What he hadn't been prepared for was how much it hurt in return.

Banning smoothed his features. He wouldn't show weakness in front of men like Mundy Wilcoxson. 'And how is it you happened upon said detective?'

'Turned up on my doorstep with a mate. But I weren't really in the mood for visitors, if you know what I mean.' He shrugged and tugged at the collar of his shirt, the smirk not leaving his bearded face. 'Was about to off this one too, but then old Heimerich here near enough brained the geezer. You should've seen him hit the ground.'

'Is that so?' He arched an eyebrow at the incubus, noticing that the creature had undergone another change of outfit.

Heimerich answered by way of a dark look.

'Still,' Banning continued. 'I find it hard to believe that an ordinary mortal would be in possession of a hellhound. Hybrid or otherwise.'

'I had the same thought, so Heimerich was kind enough to take a peek inside his head. Turns out the prick is absolutely clueless. Was given the thing as a birthday present by his true love. Ain't that sweet? My guess? It bonded with him as a pup. And being a house pet, it's never had cause to transform. Didn't appreciate being hit by my car though, I can tell you that much for free. Just watch.'

Mundy snatched a crowbar from the top of a wooden crate, stepped forward and pushed it between the bars, aiming for the auburn-haired detective. Before it came anywhere close to making contact, the Rottweiler surged forward, snarling and barking in a fit of rage. Sneering, Mundy shoved the crowbar all the way into the cage and prodded the man.

A howl erupted from the dog; the runes scored into the metal collar around its throat sparked fits of white light. Even the markings etched into the constructs of the cage were ablaze with preventative magic.

Silence descended, suppressing every snort, whine, click, grunt and squark. The absence of sound pressed into every crack and every crevice, smothering everything it touched.

'See? Won't let anyone near the fucker. Damn near tried to rip my arm off when we collared it.' Mundy nodded at his bandaged arm, and pulled the crowbar out of the cage. 'Even for a hybrid the thing's fucking lethal. Good job Heimerich was here. Seems to have a way with cryptids. Managed to get in and out of the rozzer's gaff without getting a scratch on him. Twice, in fact. Had to walk the shadows, mind—cheating if you ask me. Once for the hellhound. Once for a change of clothes. Weren't about to have his bare arse touching my leather seats. Surprised he managed to find something that fit. He's gotta have at least six inches on that ginger pillock.'

For the first time in a long time, Banning was speechless.

A deep, throaty growl rumbled from the Rottweiler. It stalked away from the front of the cage and lay beside the detective.

Stroking his jaw, Banning regarded the incubus. 'It seems our Heimerich is full of surprises today.'

Mundy chuckled. 'You're telling me. Could be I'll have a few jobs lined up for him in the future.'

'Is that so?'

Banning rocked back on his heels. As he did, he watched the dog's reaction. Its eyes tracked his every movement. In two quick strides Banning was in front of the cage. The creature snarled but didn't move.

The warning was clear, but that was all it was. *Interesting.*

Slowly, Banning hunkered down beside the bars and slipped his hand through, towards the detective.

The Rottweiler erupted in a fit of rage. It launched itself at the bars, strings of drool flying from its muzzle, as it snapped at Banning's fingers. He wrenched his arm back, adrenaline spiking.

'Christ, kid. That's a good way to lose a hand,' Mundy said.

Banning took two steps back, keeping his eyes on the dog. 'Heimerich?' The incubus jerked at the sound of his name. 'Since you appear to have such a way with the creature, be a dear and get me the detective's ID.'

Every muscle in Heimerich's body was stiff as he approached the cage and crouched beside it. He fed his hand through the bars and cautiously unzipped the man's jacket, revealing a lanyard around the detective's neck. In one quick motion, he snatched the warrant card free and tossed it to Banning. The Rottweiler huffed and returned to the unconscious man's side.

Mundy let out a low appreciative whistle. 'He's got skill.'

'He certainly has.' Banning peered down at the plastic card. Detective Constable Nicholas Stacey. 'As enlightening as this has all been, I think it's about time we settle up and I get out of your hair, wouldn't you agree, Mr Wilcoxson?' With a flick of his wrist, he tossed the warrant card back between the bars.

He'd seen everything he needed to.

Chapter 35

Nick's eyelids fluttered open. He groaned. Every heartbeat sent a pulse of agony through the back of his skull. Gingerly, he touched the swollen lump there and hissed. His fingers came away clean, that was something at least. He squeezed his eyes shut and inhaled too deeply. The stench of ammonia and animal waste hit the back of his throat, causing him to turn his head and retch.

He let out a groan. *Jesus, where am I?*

Something wet and cold prodded him in the face, accompanied by a series of huffs and snorts.

'Lily?' He pried his eyes open again, just as a rough pink tongue trailed over his cheek and nose.

Sitting up, Nick tried to push Lily away. What was going on?

'Nick?' It was a woman's voice.

He turned. The movement filled his vision with spots, dizziness washing over him like a wave. After a few deep breaths, the sensation passed.

Nick blinked and saw in an adjoining cage, huddled together, backs pressed against the bars, were Charlie's daughter and granddaughter.

'Meghan? Evelyn? Thank Christ you're okay.'

'Don't move,' Meghan said. 'I think you might have a concussion.'

That would definitely explain my symptoms. He sucked in another breath, pushing past the feeling of lightheadedness and shuffled the rest of the way around.

'Where's Bennett?' He gasped suddenly, as his brain caught up with his mouth. Images of Sam in a pool of his own blood, his skull blown apart, entered Nick's mind.

The words wouldn't come. He sucked in a sharp breath, blinking back tears.

Meghan shook her head. 'There's nobody else. Just us.'

Nick regained some composure. 'How long have I been out?'

'I... I'm not sure. I only came around a little while ago. Evie said you were already in the cage when they moved us.' Her voice cracked.

'What happened? How did you two even get here?'

Meghan looked at him, eyes filled with unshed tears. 'We were at home, waiting for Evie's friend Poppy to come over. I heard a noise and just assumed they'd arrived early. When I went downstairs there were these men in the hallway. One of them was holding Evie in his arms.' She pulled her daughter in tighter against her body. 'He looked familiar, but I couldn't place him. The other one hit me over the head. We woke up in a house, in a basement. We managed to get upstairs, but we were trapped. Then he came back, the one who hit me. I tried to fight, but there's something not right about him. It was like... Oh God, I'm going to sound crazy... It was like he used magic to stop me. The last thing I remember was him asking us questions. Then I woke up inside this cage.' She flicked her eyes at something outside the bars. 'With those.'

Nick followed her gaze, taking in his surroundings properly.

'Holy shit!' He flinched back, despite the protest in his throbbing head. Everywhere he looked there were cages. Rows and rows of the things stacked to the rafters and filled with... creatures. Except they weren't like any animals he'd ever seen. It was as though someone had taken several species, hacked them apart and put them back together again without bothering with the instructions.

That explains the reek. He gagged and swallowed down bile.

What the hell was this place? Some black market for genetic experiments?

And the noise. How had he not noticed before? It was deafening.

'Jesus.' Nick pushed himself carefully to all fours and crawled towards the cage door. He gripped a bar in each hand and shook. He pulled with all his strength, yanking on the metal, in the desperate hope that it would give.

'It won't work,' Meghan murmured. 'We've tried.'

She was on the edge; he could see it in her face. She was holding it together for her daughter.

Nick squinted up at one of the cages opposite, just as whatever was inside hurled itself at the bars. Each clattering strike caused strange symbols to flare white around its enclosure. They reminded him of the crystal rune stones Henry had insisted on leaving around the house.

He went cold. *Henry.*

What was it Mundy had asked him—got any family? If he'd got Lily, did he have Henry too? He could be hurt, or worse.

Panic twisted his gut, gouged at his heart, clawed up his throat. It almost ripped him apart as he wheezed through his strangled breath.

'I have to get us out of here... Lily!'

He pulled the dog closer and examined the metal collar on her. She buried her muzzle into his chest, almost knocking him over with excitement. His trembling fingers met cold, hard metal; it tingled beneath his touch, unfamiliar and threatening. There was no catch. No obvious release. Instinct warned him against trying to prise it apart. Instead, he worked it upward against the grain of Lily's fur, exposing her original collar underneath. After a few fumbled attempts Nick jerked it free and, pink leather quivering in his hands, inserted the metal prong on the buckle into the keyhole of the cage door.

A jolt of electricity shot up his arm, flinging him backwards. He landed hard.

Evelyn huffed out a sob.

Nick pushed himself up, blinking the spots from his eyes, regretting every action that had led to this moment. He cradled his arm, muscles spasming, and gritted his teeth. There *had* to be a way to get out of this. He tasted blood and forced himself to calm down.

He didn't know what he noticed first, the looming shadow or the footsteps, before someone approached the cage. Lily's tail thumped against the floor. Nick craned his head back and looked up.

His eyes widened in shock. It couldn't be.

'Henry?'

Chapter 36

'WHAT ARE YOU DOING here?' Nick blurted, his sluggish brain trying to process what was happening through the throbbing pain in his arm.

Henry squatted beside the cage, his face contorted with concern.

'Henry?' Nick repeated. 'Are you okay? Are you hurt?'

It wasn't until Meghan shuffled back with Evie that Nick's mind caught up. 'You... escaped?' Uncertainty caused his voice to waver. God, he needed it to be true.

Meghan narrowed her eyes at Henry. 'Nick, this is one of the men who took us.'

No. She was wrong. It couldn't have been Henry. His husband wouldn't be involved in something like this. He *couldn't* be.

So why wasn't he denying it? And why couldn't Nick swallow past the lump in his throat?

Evie pressed into Meghan's chest, her sobs muffled.

As he looked at his husband, Henry winced and shrank in on himself. And in that moment, with that one unconscious admission of guilt, everything Nick knew about the man he loved was thrown into question.

No. This isn't right. This can't be right.

He doubled over and spewed what was left in his stomach on the floor of the cage. After a few dry heaves, he drew in a shuddering breath. Tears stung his eyes.

'Nick, listen to me,' Henry said.

Nick shook his head, exhaled.

'Listen...'

'No.'

'Nicholas, please. I'm going to try and get you out of here.' Henry glanced over his shoulder then shuffled closer. 'Please, you have to trust me.'

'Trust you?' Nick scoffed.

Henry visibly recoiled. 'Please, there isn't much time. I'll explain everything later. I just need you to close your eyes.'

'No.'

'Okay, Nick. Just... just try not to scream. Any of you.' He glanced at Meghan.

Try not to scream, why? The thought was wiped from Nick's mind when Henry became engulfed by an explosion of shadow. Dark fronds whipped the air, unfurling to reveal a black figure at their core.

All around Nick, creatures hurled themselves at the bars of their enclosures, creating a clatter of metal, and emitting their fear and aggression in a clamour of screeches and bellows.

It barely registered because of what Nick saw before him...

His mouth fell open. Those eyes. He'd seen them staring back from the depths of his nightmares, when he'd been on the precipice of waking. Red like the smoky afterglow that follows a raging blaze.

The thing before Nick moved closer. It stretched out an arm, reaching through the gap in the bars. Almost hesitantly, it extended out its black, claw-like fingers in invitation.

Nick shrank back, his heart rabbiting inside his chest. This couldn't be happening. He was hallucinating. Sleep deprivation had finally caught up with him. Either that or his mind had snapped.

It happened. His job was demanding, sometimes traumatic. Burnout, anxiety, depression—seldom talked about but rife within the force. And what with all the budget cuts... he wouldn't be the first to suffer a mental breakdown.

'Take my hand,' the voice grated, like stone against stone. But it was clearly Henry's. And it was familiar enough to pull Nick out of his spiral. '*Please*, Nick. I don't know how long we have before he comes back.'

A dozen questions formed on Nick's tongue. He swallowed them and reached for the hand.

'Nick, no! What are you doing?' Meghan was frantic.

Nick closed his fingers around Henry's hand.

Hot air rushed forward to meet him, thick with the stench of sulphur. The world around him started spinning, creating a heady mix of vertigo and weightlessness. Before he realised, Nick was staggering to his feet on the other side of the cage, his white-knuckled fingers still gripping Henry's.

Meghan and Evelyn stared at him in disbelief. Lily huffed out an excitable bark, her tail thrashing the air as she bounced around inside the cage. Henry shushed her and beckoned her forward. She bounded towards the bars, tongue lolling. His obsidian fingers curled into the scruff of her neck and, in a writhing burst of shadow, she appeared beside him.

'How are you doing that?' Nick stared into the featureless face of his husband.

'When I become my true self, I can cross the space between this realm and the next—the veil. We call it walking the shadows. Think of it like stepping through a door. As long as I keep a foot in each realm I can take you with me, but only for short distances. The veil is dangerous. Moving more than a few feet and we'd be noticed.'

'That doesn't... I don't...' Nick trailed off.

Henry turned to Meghan and reached out his hand. She gaped back at it, unmoving.

'I know you don't trust me—'Henry started.

'You *kidnapped* us,' Meghan snarled.

'I know. Believe me, if there was any other way...' He shook his head and pitch-black tendrils twisted in the air around him. 'Banning is dangerous, but he's just the errand boy.'

'Errand boy?' Meghan shook her head. 'I don't understand any of this.'

'Please,' Henry said. 'This is your only chance. If Banning comes back and sees us trying to escape...' He didn't need to finish.

Meghan squeezed Evelyn tighter.

'*Please.*'

Her worried gaze met Nick's. He gave her a nod, hoping that it came across as confident. Hoping he was making the right decision.

'Okay... Come on, Evie. We'll go together.'

'Mum, I don't trust that monster.'

Nick sensed Henry flinch beside him.

'Neither do I,' said Meghan, 'but I trust Nick.'

Evelyn pursed her lips. 'Okay.'

Together they crawled towards Henry's outstretched hand and into the billowing shadows. Lily gave another bark as they stumbled free, the sound swallowed up by the din of the other creatures around them.

'Stay low. Follow me.' Henry bent, making himself smaller. He was already tall, but now, swathed in living darkness, he seemed to fill all the available space. 'There's a main road on the other side of the dockyard. Once we're out of the slipway we'll head there.'

Nick gestured for Meghan and Evelyn to go ahead of him.

Between the revelations about Henry and the blow to the head, he could barely focus. Still, he put one foot in front of the other, crouching past cages and crates, as they worked their way through the building. They stayed in what little shadow there was, aided by Henry's ability to draw them deeper into the nooks and crannies that were forgotten by the light.

Every now and again, Henry signalled for them to stop or retrace their steps. Because of it, Nick didn't notice the men with guns at first, roaming between colossal beams of wood and steel, indifferent to their odd surroundings. He'd even caught sight of one or two of them stationed on the mezzanine floor above. It sobered him to know that without Henry, they wouldn't have got more than a hundred yards.

When at last they reached an exit, Nick froze. There was no way they were getting out. Men stood either side of the doorway, each with a rifle held against their chest, finger close to the trigger.

'What do we do now?' Nick whispered, hearing the mild hysteria in his voice. Meghan eyed the men with concern and pulled Evelyn behind her, clearly sharing his thoughts.

'Wait here. I'll deal with the men.' Henry turned to Nick, placing a black hand on Lily's head. 'When I give the signal, run as fast as you can towards the door. Don't look back. Don't stop.'

'What about—'

Before he could ask, Henry was gone.

Chapter 37

NICK SQUINTED, DESPERATELY SEEKING any sign of Henry.

Nothing.

No swell of shadow. No rush of imploding air. Where was he?

And then Nick saw it. The rising swirl of black, rolling up like fog from the slash of darkness just beneath the wooden door. It inched upward in slow, lazy curls, wrapping unnoticed around the men's ankles. There was no warning. The men dropped as one, their bodies hitting the ground. Nick heard Meghan's gasp, Evelyn's startled yelp, and knew that everything he was seeing was *really* happening.

The wooden door swung open. Henry stood on the other side, all but lost to the backdrop of the night. The glow of his smouldering eyes and the molten veins threading his body were the only indication he was there at all.

Not one of them needed prompting. They ran as fast as their legs would carry them, hurtling through the door without care or hesitation.

Nick stumbled, his eyes struggling to adjust to the darkness after the glare inside the building. Someone grasped his shoulder, stopping him before he pitched forward onto the ground. He turned to see Henry looking down at him. Part of him wanted to wrench his arm away. Instead he gave a sharp nod of thanks and continued forward. Each footstep sent spasms of pain through his skull.

'Which way?' The hostility in Meghan's voice was unmistakable.

'I... I'm not sure,' Henry admitted.

'Fantastic.'

'Just give me a second to get my bearings.' Henry slowed, taking in their surroundings. 'This way.'

They tramped in silence, the sound of Lily's panting rising above the distant hum of traffic. They were cut off from the main road, looming industrial buildings closing them in like a maze. Nick shuddered, feeling the biting chill in the air all the more now that sweat clung to his skin. He spotted the river. They were still inside the dockyard. Not great.

Once they breached the perimeter of the buildings they would be exposed to open stretches of concrete, dirt, and the odd patch of winter-bare grass between them and their escape. They would either have to take their chances in the open or try and navigate through the warren of abandoned steel and brickwork they'd just escaped from.

What they needed was help. A lot of it. Breathing heavily, Nick searched his pockets for his phone. *Of course they took it.*

He couldn't hold his tongue any longer. 'Henry, what in the *hell* is going on? Who were those people? What do they want with Meghan and Evelyn? What was that place? What were those things? Why did you turn into... into smoke?' Every thought, every half-formed question burst from his mouth. But he kept moving. Henry kept looking over his shoulder and that told him time was not on their side.

'Those people are cryptid traffickers. And they're dangerous. Really dangerous. Those cryptids? Demons mostly. Every single one of them smuggled through the veil to be sold to the highest bidder. The majority of the creatures are juveniles. Easier to manage. To control. It's what happened to me.'

'To you? But your parents—'

'They're not my parents. My *real* parents were slaughtered. By humans. Traffickers like those men. I was taken to an underground black market, but something went wrong. I'm not sure what. The next thing I knew, the place was on fire. People were screaming. Dying. Some of us escaped, the lucky ones. We tried to help the others, but not everyone got out. There was smoke everywhere. The fire destroyed everything. I ran. Too weak to take my true form. Too weak to walk the shadows. I kept running until my feet bled. Then somehow I found myself alone. Lost. So I just walked. For hours. Maybe even days. That's when they found me—the German couple. I don't know if they knew what I was or not, I honestly can't remember much of my first few weeks with them. But they took me in and gave me a home.'

'Jesus.' Nick swallowed. It was too much to process. Cryptids? Demons? But there was no denying the truth. One glance at his husband was enough to tell him that. 'What would traffickers want with Meghan and Evelyn?'

'Not the traffickers. Banning. He wants the dagger. He wants Kar'roc's Maw.'

'Kar'roc's Maw? What's that?'

Henry smiled ruefully. 'You can't remember. The Order concealed your memories.'

'The Order? Henry, I don't understand a word you're saying.'

'That night at Charlie's house, it wasn't a copycat murderer. It was the real Caravan Cannibal. A demon. You saw it. More importantly you saw what banished it. A dagger with a red gemstone in the hilt. Banning wants that dagger, but only its master can summon it.'

'Its master?'

'Charlie.'

Meghan missed a step. 'Charlie? As in my dad? That Charlie?'

'Yes, *that* Charlie.' The bitterness in Henry's tone was all too familiar. 'He took custody of the dagger when he performed the binding ritual—'

Nick collapsed and hit the concrete. He clutched his head. The pressure inside his skull was too much. He couldn't catch his breath.

Images flickered and flashed behind his eyes, flooding his brain with such intensity, it felt like his skull might explode. They buckled and warped, spiralling out of reach only to surge back again, never quite the same. He saw Charlie enclosed by a translucent circle. Then Charlie not enclosed by a translucent circle. It was like his brain couldn't decide between two realities, and it was tearing him apart from the inside. Someone was shouting at him, but the words were no more than white noise.

Just when Nick thought he might die, the pain ebbed enough that he could fill his lungs.

He sucked in ragged breaths through gritted teeth, tears streaming from his eyes. A breeze cutting across the ground offered him momentary relief, its icy fingers cooling his sweat-drenched brow.

He inhaled deeper now, vaguely aware of Lily's low whimpering. A strange, tingling sensation radiated out from his temples. He peeled his eyes open to see Henry—still enveloped by winding shadows—knelt on the ground beside him, his hands pressed firmly but gently on either side of Nick's head.

'I remember,' Nick rasped. 'I remember everything.'

'You need to get up.' Henry's relief was replaced by urgency. 'We need to go now.' He helped Nick to his feet and tried unsuccessfully to shoo Lily away as she butted her large head against Nick's legs.

'What happened?' Nick asked, leaning on Henry for support. Meghan and Evelyn were visibly shaken. He offered them a weak smile, letting them know he was okay, but he could tell from their expressions that they weren't convinced.

'I unlocked your memories. Removed the spellwork.'

'Henry, I don't... understand?'

'Makes two of us, pretty boy.'

Nick's head snapped up. He saw Mundy Wilcoxson fiddling with his mobile, flanked by half a dozen men who were pointing guns at them.

Henry took a step forward, putting himself between them and Nick.

Mundy slid the phone back in his pocket, swapping it for a handgun. He wagged a finger at Henry. 'Don't get any bright ideas. Care to explain what the fuck you're doing? Please don't tell me the kid was right about you.'

A guttural growl rumbled behind them, so loud the ground quivered beneath their feet. All heads turned.

'I think it's safe to say that I was on the money, Mr Wilcoxson.'

A man stepped out of the shadows with something in tow. Nick's gaze was fixed on the creature by his side.

The thing looked like a shaggy, black bear. But where the fur on its head should have been was only exposed skull. The slits of the beast's nostrils quivered.

Henry's shout cut through the stunned silence. 'Run!'

Chapter 38

'Come now, Heimerich... or should I call you Henry? There's no need for dramatics.' Banning chuckled without humour.

The hellip stalked next to him, Banning gripping the chain attached to the collar on its neck. As the creature shifted its weight, he felt the links flex between his fingers. Energy shuddered through the wards that had been worked into the metal.

'I have to say, I'm impressed. You're good, I'll give you that. You're very good. I mean, I was second-guessing myself when you unlocked the door at the safe house and let the girl and her mother escape. And when Mundy told me that you near enough brained our dear detective here, well, that was believable. Not entirely in keeping with what I've seen of your spineless character, but still believable. Obviously, you finding clothes that fit at the detective's house was a bit of a giveaway. There's no way they could have been his.' He inclined his head at the detective constable. 'But what *really* let you down was that.'

He pointed languidly at the girl's glowering mother, allowed it to drift over the child before coming to a stop on the Rottweiler.

The dog took a single step towards him, lips peeled back as it let out a warning snarl.

Banning smirked. 'Why didn't it react when you got close to its owner? Why, when it nearly took my hand off for trying to touch him, it didn't flinch when you unzipped his coat just inches from its face? You misled me, Heimerich.' He tilted his head, focused on the incubus. 'You do not, in fact, have a wife. You have a husband. And he's standing right there.'

'Henry, how does he know your name?' The detective's face wrinkled in confusion, then came the moment of clarity. 'This is who you've been working for?'

Vindication.

'Exquisite.' Banning laughed. 'Oh, Heimerich, you're worth your weight in gold. You really are.'

The incubus shook his head. For the first time Banning saw more than seething resentment and anger in the demon's glowing-red eyes. He saw fear.

'You actually care for him, don't you? Haven't you ever heard the old adage "don't mix business with pleasure"?' A demon capable of love? It was like something out of a teen romance novel. Not waiting for an answer, Banning regarded the detective. 'It seems that I'm not the only one that *Henry* has been misleading.'

The detective snarled. 'What's that supposed to mean?'

Heimerich took a half-step forward before evidently remembering the guns and stopping. 'Nick, don't listen to him.'

'You're the job, Detective Stacey. You see, dear Heimerich has been providing us with information. Information that you have locked up inside here.' He tapped his temple. 'Information that had been deliberately altered to stop you from remembering the truth.'

'You're lying!'

'Am I? Then let me ask you this. Had any trouble sleeping recently? Find yourself losing time? Experiencing headaches?' The shift in the detective's body language was slight, a small drop of the shoulders, a blink that was a second too long. 'No doubt it's been happening on and off for years. To be blunt, I'm surprised you're not dead. The mind is delicate. Unravelling someone else's spellwork is a dangerous thing, but leaving it in place while attempting to access what's underneath?' He blew out an exaggerated breath.

'Henry, what's he talking about?'

The incubus flinched at the sound of his name, but made no reply.

'Don't worry, Detective, the two of you will have plenty of time to hash this out. And now, I'm going to have to insist that you and your friends come back with us.'

The detective stepped forward, dog by his side. 'Like fuck we will.'

'I fail to see you have much choice in the matter.'

The hellip stretched its skeletal jaws in a wide yawn, its long black tongue flicking across its teeth. Apparently that was threat enough. The Rottweiler surged forward, claws skittering across the ground.

Mundy's men opened fire and Banning hissed, 'Stop. Idiots! The girl.'

Bullets bit into the canine's flesh, but still it came. It wasn't until one ricocheted off the concrete, striking the creature's collar and obliterating the wards in a glaring flash of white, that Banning threw up a shield.

The creature's transformation was spectacular. Muscle warped and deformed. Bone shifted and buckled. Its undulating hide stretched to accommodate its increasing bulk, pulled so tightly over its solid frame, every ridge of its spine stood to attention. It still had the shape of a canine, the general feel of a dog, but its proportions were no longer to scale.

It opened its jaws to reveal teeth that were more suited to the prehistoric era. The taut skin around its muzzle stretched and tore before knitting together again. The effect was a constant ripple of flesh that was as mesmerising as it was disgusting. The hellhound padded forward, exaggerated claws scoring the ground. Its eyes blazed with incandescent rage.

With a flick of his wrist, Banning directed his magic through the chain, releasing the lock on the hellip's restraints. Metal clanked on the concrete. The cryptid charged.

In unison, the beasts reared up on their hind legs, colliding in a frenzy of teeth and claws. Bodies thrashed and writhed, a blur of brute force and savagery. The hellip swiped, slashing deep, bloody gashes in the hellhound's flesh, and thrust its head towards the wound. Before the hellip's teeth could make purchase the hellhound twisted. The momentum of its body drove them barrelling into the side of a small building. Brick detonated in a cloud of dust, exposing the building's devastated interior.

The child screamed as a hunk of flying debris shattered on the ground beside her. She stumbled into her mother's arms. Dust and mortar coated them both as they scurried back.

Sparks erupted in stuttering showers from inside warped metal housing. Wires, ripped from their casings, buzzed and hissed—electricity still powering them despite the damage. Banning flinched, his fingers twitching close to his jacket pocket. It didn't take long before the creatures hurtled back into the open.

Bullets rattled across the dockyard in sharp, deafening bursts.

'*Stop* shooting.' Banning lunged for the nearest man, grabbing a hold of his gun and attempted to wrestle it free. Everything was going to absolute shit. If the girl or her mother got hurt, got killed...

No. He wouldn't let Mundy's goons ruin everything.

Someone grabbed his shoulder, yanking him backwards. He spun round, barely keeping upright and glared at the scarred face of his assailant. He immediately recognised the weak jaw of the

Neanderthal thug in the high-vis jacket who'd tested his patience earlier that day. Clint.

Banning opened himself up to the natural energy around them. The temperature dropped suddenly and frost spread out in a wide, glistening circle beneath their feet.

'What the—' The goon folded with a grunt when Banning's fist connected with his gut.

'I promised you that if you touched me again it would be the last thing you ever did.' Banning's breath misted. He stole from the man's life force, letting the energy flow through his body. It would be so easy to take it all. To fill to the brim with raw, intoxicating energy. But he wanted to enjoy this. To savour the moment.

'Wh... what?' The thug yelped when Banning hauled him upright. He tried to take a step back, but was too weak to fight in Banning's grip.

'A promise is a promise.' His fists knotted tighter the fabric of the man's clothes. Releasing one hand, he summoned his magic. The ethereal blade burst from his knuckles, casting a green glow across the sickly pallor of the thug's dumbfounded face.

'No. *No!*'

His pleas fell on deaf ears. In one easy strike, Banning thrust the blade into the man's chest. There was something almost intimate in how his power coursed through the other man's heart, allowing Banning to experience every rapid beat. The organ ruptured, muscular tissue obliterated with such force that Banning could actually hear the crack of the sternum. He let the corpse drop.

Still heady with exhilaration, he didn't notice the billowing mass of shadow hurtling towards him.

Chapter 39

IT HAD BEEN A long time since Charlie had been to the dockyard. As a child, Meghan had shown about as much interest in boats as she had in his other leisurely pursuits. After half an hour of her sulking he'd thrown in the towel, abandoning the idea as a lost cause. That had been their first and last visit.

A gust of wind rattled through the corrugated metal sheets covering the dilapidated building to their left.

He shivered. The chill, bone-deep, penetrated his damp clothes. Every inch of him felt stiff. Numb. He rubbed his hands together briskly and glared at the back of Rhea's head. The duffle bag draped across her shoulder bobbed in time with her steps, containing wads of cash and sachets of Dragon Scale. He winced as he replayed the image of her snapping that kid's neck. How had it come to this? He was out of his depth.

Suck it up, Charlie. Meggy and Evie need you. He'd get them back. Whatever it took.

Charlie adjusted the sleeve of his ruined trench coat as he walked. 'Is there anything we need to know about your contact?' His arm had stopped bleeding—the sutures ripped out after their most recent skirmish—but the injury still throbbed. No doubt Sachiko would have something to say about it the next time he saw her, assuming O.O.T.I.S and Diane didn't have his guts for garters first. His phone had rung pretty much on the hour every hour.

Diane was persistent, he'd give her that.

Rhea smirked. 'Other than the fact that he's a complete arsehole and a criminal?'

Charlie opened his mouth, but a sharp look from Jasmin shut it.

'Just let me do the talking and you'll be fine,' she added.

Raised voices echoed in the distance.

Charlie frowned. 'What's happening?'

'Whatever it is, it doesn't sound good. Look.' Jasmin pointed at a huge industrial building, its sweeping wooden roof covered in evenly spaced windows. Unlike the other buildings around them, it appeared to be in good repair. Half a dozen or so men poured from its entrance, headed away from them at a sprint. The guns in their hands confirmed they were more than dock workers.

'Should we follow them?' he spoke quietly.

Rhea snorted. 'You want to go *towards* the men with guns? It's probably just some creature that got loose. Stick to the plan.'

Charlie watched until the last of the men had disappeared from sight. He'd learnt to trust his gut a lifetime ago, and right now it was telling him something was off. 'I don't like it.'

'You came to me. You asked me for help. Want to back out now? Fine. That's on you.' Rhea turned to walk away.

Jasmin stepped forward. 'No, that's not what he meant. Is it, Charlie?'

He didn't answer, having caught sight of the interior of the building. Cages. More than he could count. Rows upon rows of them and not one empty that he could see. It took him a second more to realise what was bothering him about the set up. There was no sound. Not a peep. With that many animals crammed together, he'd expect to hear a racket.

Magic. A chill ran down his spine.

Outnumbered. Outgunned. And that was before all the hocus-pocus crap. If shit went sideways, their odds of surviving didn't look good.

Charlie clenched his fists and blew out a breath. 'So the plan is we just waltz up and ask your guy nicely if he knows anything about the creature that took my family, in exchange for a bag full of drug money—all while trying not to get ourselves killed?'

Rhea gave an amused smile. 'Near enough.'

'And he's not just going to shoot us?'

She jiggled the duffle bag. 'Not if he wants to get paid.'

'What about *after* he's been paid?'

'You're such a cynic, gramps, anyone ever told you that?'

'It's come up.'

'I know this guy—'

Charlie interrupted. 'This *complete arsehole?*'

Rhea rolled her eyes. 'Yes, he's an arsehole. But I've had dealings with him before. As long as you don't do anything stupid it'll all be good. Anyway, he'll want you gone before the buyers show up, so we'd better hurry.'

Charlie hesitated. 'I still don't like it. What's in the cages?'

'Cryptids. I told you he imports them. Lindwurms, gulon, toorkboar. The usual. I heard he even got his hands on a sigbin once.'

He wrinkled his nose. He didn't need to understand everything to read between the lines. 'A black-market, cryptid trafficking ring.'

Rhea shrugged.

His brow furrowed. *Lindwurms?*

The sound of a gunshot obliterated his train of thought.

'It's fine,' Rhea said. 'Like I said, probably just something got out of its cage.' She gave them no time to argue, striding towards the slipway and the man in a high-vis jacket standing guard outside.

Charlie shot Jasmin an exasperated look. They followed Rhea.

The guard watched their approach with a reserved expression. Charlie noted his stance—arms behind his back, feet parted. Ex-military without a doubt.

'Here to see Mundy,' Rhea said, stopping a few metres away from him and pulling the duffle bag from her shoulder.

He eyed it briefly. 'He's stepped out.'

'We'll wait inside.'

'No. You won't.'

'Look, I respect you're just doing your job, but don't be a dick. We got caught out in the rain, we're bloody freezing. It's got to be three degrees out here. You wouldn't want this old-timer ending up in intensive care, would you?' She thumbed at Charlie. 'Anyway, he's expecting us.'

'Sorry. No one in or out until the boss is back.'

'That's bullshit.'

The guard's posture shifted. He let his arms fall to his sides.

Jasmin cleared her throat. 'Uh, Rhea—'

'I *said* he's expecting us.' Rhea dropped the bag and took two steps forward.

'And *I* said no one's coming in until he's back.' The guard nudged the side of his jacket open, revealing the gun holstered at his hip.

She threw up her arms in defeat. 'Fine.'

The tension in the man's shoulders lifted, but he kept his hand where it was.

Rhea bent to retrieve the bag, giving Charlie and Jasmin a wink.

Charlie's eyes widened.

Seeing his reaction, the guard closed his fingers around the gun. Rhea whirled round as a single coil of shadow shot from her raised palm to curl around his wrist. She yanked. The guard dropped the gun; it clattered on the concrete floor.

Charlie dived for the weapon, snatching it up. Adjusting his stance, he aimed it at the guard. 'Move and I'll blast your head off.'

For a second he really meant it. Revulsion churned his gut. What was he becoming?

The man's shock slowly shifted to doubt, although his gaze kept flicking between Charlie's face and the gun. 'Pull that trigger and this place will be swarming with people in seconds.'

'Find me something to tie him up with,' Charlie growled.

The rush of air imploding behind him made every muscle in his body tense.

Rhea stalked towards the guard, tendrils of pitch devouring the light from the building.

The man's eyebrows arched, not in alarm or astonishment but confusion. 'You! What the hell are you doing? Just wait until I—' The darkness took him before he could finish.

Charlie lowered the gun. Had the man recognised her? Or was he just familiar with demons? What was it Rhea had said about there being a succubus on the payroll?

The guard, deathly white, toppled to the floor. He struck it with a thud.

'What now?' Charlie asked, turning away from another of Rhea's victims.

'Now, we go inside,' Rhea's altered voice rasped inside his head.

'So much for not doing anything stupid,' Jasmin muttered. She gave Charlie's shoulder a squeeze as she passed, stepping over the guard without a second glance.

He squared his shoulders, the gun heavy in his hand. He'd come this far. What choice did he have but to follow?

A high-pitched scream, chased by the *dut dut dut* of an automatic weapon, resounded in the distance. Charlie went rigid. He'd recognise his granddaughter's shrill cry anywhere.

'Evie... We need to get over there. Now.'

Before he could set off in a run, Rhea grabbed the front of his trench coat. Her obsidian claws shredded through the material, scoring his flesh.

'I can shadow-walk us there,' she said. 'All of us. But not if you're holding the gun. Give it to me.'

Heartbeat thrashing in his ears, Charlie pressed the pistol into her hand. He stared at a spot beyond Rhea's churning shadows, already fearing the worst.

Darkness smothered him so completely he lost all sense of himself. The world around him lurched. His stomach dropped.

And then it was over. He staggered back, barely aware of Jasmin beside him, and tried to blink his eyes into focus.

Rhea released her grip and stepped away. The retreat of her darkness exposed him to moonlight and the glow of artificial lighting. The faint scent of sulphur lingered in his nostrils.

'Evie! Meghan!'

'Dad?' Hearing his daughter's voice struck him with such relief, his knees almost buckled.

Something hard pressed into the small of Charlie's back. He froze and his blood turned to ice. He should have seen it coming. Should have known.

Always trust your gut.

He raised his hands slowly in the air.

'Atta boy, no sudden moves,' Rhea said, jabbing him with the gun.

Chapter 40

Charlie's anger reached boiling point. He was so close, damn it. His girls were just there.

Intense pain stabbed his skin at the site of the sigil. He blinked and focused on the chaos unfolding around them. Men, armed with semi-automatic rifles, tore past him amid bellows of confusion and panic. Not because of their sudden entrance, but because of the two nightmarish creatures locked in a savage clash, decimating all life in their path.

'Dad!'

'*Meggy.*' He took a half-step forward. Rhea jabbed the gun harder into his back.

'Don't be a hero,' she drawled.

'Hiding behind a gun?' he snapped. 'I thought you were supposed to be a big bad demon.'

'I'm not an idiot. When push comes to shove, there's not much faster than a bullet.'

Beside him, Jasmin tore her gaze from the bedlam. Seeing Charlie's upstretched arms, her expression morphed from shock to anger, then she too raised her arms.

'Good girl,' Rhea said. 'Now, do everything I tell you and I won't have to kill him.'

'How could you do this?' Jasmin spat. 'I trusted you.'

'I know you did, Jas. You always were naive. I did warn you. To survive in a world full of monsters you have to become a monster. I've had to survive out here a long time. I'm not the girl you used to know. She died saving your life that night.'

Charlie growled; his muscles trembled with impotent fury. He was utterly helpless. He'd brought this on himself. What in the hell had he been thinking trying to go it alone? He'd barely survived in the battle against Chekonost, and that had been one on one.

Rhea was right, he was a cynic. Maybe if he'd let Diane help him, maybe if he'd set aside his misgivings about the Order and his fear of the unknown, his family would be safe right now.

Christ, what if he'd sentenced them all to death?

He began to shake; his vision tunnelled.

Jasmin turned her head towards him just a fraction. 'Charlie, you need to calm down. The worst thing you can do right now is lose it. Breathe.'

The sigil on his hand throbbed, pulsing in time with the rapid beat of his heart.

'Charlie,' Jasmin repeated. 'If you don't get it together, there will be no reason for them to keep Megs and Evie alive. You need to calm down. For them.'

He snapped out of it. She was right.

Charlie inhaled until his ribs strained, then released the breath. Yes, he might have fucked up, but damn it if he would do anything else to put his girls at risk—Jasmin included.

'Enough!' a male voice roared.

Before Charlie could identify its owner, green light exploded outwards. He shielded his eyes against it.

Rhea was watching the display. He used her distraction to ram his elbow backwards into her chest. The impact sent a jolt through his arm; it felt like he'd struck solid marble. Jaw clenched, Charlie shook off the pain, and sprinted forward.

An invisible force struck him, stopping him mid-lean into a squall that whipped at his coat and blasted him with grit.

The wind died down, releasing him.

A young man in a dishevelled three-piece suit stood with his arms outstretched, face set in a grimace, chest heaving. At his feet, writhing in obvious agony and clutching at their side, was a man without a shred of clothing on. Sweat glistened on the injured man's body, despite the extra layer of frost spread out around them.

It was neither the nude nor the ice that held the young man's attention. His focus was on the grotesque beasts that had been tearing into each other just moments before. Now, they were suspended in the air inches from the ground, a couple of dark silhouettes encased in translucent spheres.

'Detective, I suggest you control your pet, or I *will* kill your husband.'

'No, please!'

Charlie recognised that voice. Nick? That meant...

Charlie took another look at the naked man. *Henry?* What in the hell was going on? And did he say *pet?* No way one of those trapped beasts was Nick's Rottweiler.

'Mr Wilcoxson, if you would be so kind...' The young man's voice quivered, his use of magic clearly taking a toll.

'Whatever you say, Banning.' The response was dripping with sarcasm. Even so, the man tossed a metal collar at Nick's feet with a clatter. Nick bent to pick it up, hands trembling.

'Now, I'm going to release the animal,' Banning said. 'If it so much as growls in my direction I will end him. Do you understand?'

Nick nodded.

'Good. Now call it.'

'Lily.' Nick took a breath. 'Lily, here girl.'

The raw emotion on Nick's face twisted Charlie's gut. Meggy, Evie, now Henry. How many other people's lives would be ruined because of his connection to that cursed dagger? Because of him?

The sphere of energy around Lily shattered. She landed with a thud, the muscles in her legs bunching as she braced for impact.

'Lily, come, girl.'

The beast lowered her head and took a menacing step towards Banning, a low snarl rumbling from her chest. Banning arched a single dark eyebrow and made a fist. He showed it to Henry in reply to the threat. Green sparks danced across his knuckles.

'Lily, come here. Here girl.' Nick's voice broke. 'Lily, now!'

Ears flattened, Lily gave the man one last defiant glare. A ripple ran down the protruding ridges of her spine. She twisted round to face Nick.

'Come on, that's it,' he coaxed.

When the beast trotted over to Nick, his relief was unmistakable. No sooner had he put the collar on her than her body began to shudder, flesh spasming, skin shrivelling, until Charlie saw an ordinary black-and-tan Rottweiler.

The collar clicked shut.

Charlie's stomach dropped. Whatever advantage they may have had was now gone. They were surrounded, more armed goons having appeared during that display. And with Rhea only a few feet behind him, there was nothing he could do to change a thing.

Freezing, terrified and utterly defeated, his shoulders slumped. He was numb, physically and emotionally. He'd let them down. Meghan, Evie, Jasmin, Nick, Henry. All of them. Squeezing his eyes shut for a moment, he exhaled.

The bear-like creature had also been released. It thrashed violently against the restraints being placed upon it. Every hostile roar, every menacing growl reverberated across the open space between the buildings, shuddering up through the concrete and into Charlie's legs. For a second, he thought his thigh muscles were twitching in time with the tremors.

Wait. That's not right.

Slowly, he inched his hand inside his pocket and closed his fingers around his vibrating mobile. He checked the screen and his heart gave a feverish jerk. *Diane.*

Archaic or not, there was something to be said for a phone with physical buttons.

He jabbed his thumb against what he hoped was the answer button, and said a silent prayer to whatever God might be listening. If he could get a message to Diane, let her know where they were without raising suspicion, they might just have a chance.

Sensing a presence behind him, he removed his hand as inconspicuously as possible and raised his arms. Shadows twisted and coiled in his peripheral vision.

Rhea nudged him with the gun, the metal digging into his spine once again.

'So this was your plan all along? Lead us to the dockyard then sell us out to the highest bidder?' he accused Rhea. 'Put us up for auction alongside all those creatures?' There was no telling what was about to happen but he needed to give Diane as much information as he could. He hoped it would be enough.

'Highest bidder? Auction? Pretty full of yourself, aren't you? Nah, I was just bringing you to see the boss.'

'Boss? So *you're* the succubus on the payroll?'

The gun's muzzle bobbed against his back. Charlie assumed Rhea had just shrugged.

'It's not like I didn't spell it out for you. Where d'you think the Dragon Scale comes from? Don't get many lindwurm this side of the veil, that's for sure. I should thank you, by the way, for your help earlier. Those little shits needed taking out. Plus now I've got a cool twenty grand to play with.'

Charlie growled. 'I knew it. You set us up. Couldn't handle the competition, is that it? A few teenagers try and muscle in on your turf so you kill them. For what—to send a message?'

'My *turf*? You really are all kinds of old.' Rhea scoffed. 'They were cutting the product, gramps. Skimming off the top. That's bad for business. And you saw the way they went after me... Jumped-up little pricks. Anyway, what do you care? I held up my end of the bargain. Not only did I bring you here but I solved your little mystery for you, too. See, turns out those markings you found, the shadowburn, they weren't made by another succubus. They were made by an incubus. An incubus who just so happened to show up on the boss' doorstep earlier today. And once I told Mundy that you were looking for just such a creature, I have to say, he became very interested in meeting you.'

Incubus? A dream eater. He turned his gaze to Henry, who was being dragged to his feet by two men. It all made sense. O.O.T.I.S *did* have a mole. Only Nick had absolutely no idea he'd divulged anything.

Charlie's shoulders sagged.

'As fun as it's been catching up, I've got shit to do. Start walking.' Rhea added, 'Hey, at least you found your daughter and granddaughter, right?'

Unsure if it was a threat, Charlie did as she ordered.

'Sorry, gramps, nothing personal.'

'Feels pretty damn personal from where I'm standing.'

'You're a good guy. You are. Charging in here on your white horse, ready to put your life on the line for your family. To save the day. It's admirable, but it's also stupid. Do y'know why?'

He didn't answer.

Rhea continued. 'Because this is real life and in real life, people get old, they get weak, they die. Good people get hurt. Get killed. And bad people? They just get on with their day. I warned you, Charlie, you're just a man. No powers. Nothing. You'll never win against the likes of them. Just give it up. Tell him whatever it is he wants to know. He might go easy on you.'

She nudged him with the gun again. He picked up the pace until he was back by Jasmin's side.

'Oh, one more thing...' Rhea slipped her free hand into Jasmin's pocket almost sensually, and removed her mobile. 'I'll be taking this.' She waggled it in the air then crushed it. Glass and plastic shattered. She launched the remains of the device. It burst apart on the concrete, not quite disintegrating but not far off.

Rhea reached for Charlie's mobile next.

Shit. Once she saw his phone screen it would be game over.

'Don't touch me.' Charlie twisted away from her. 'I'll get it, damn it.'

She jabbed metal into his flesh, hard enough to bruise. 'No. You won't.'

The sound of his coat being shredded was like a death sentence had been whispered in his ears. There was nothing he could do. No way for him to end the call before she saw it.

Rhea plucked the phone from his trench coat.

This was it. He was fucked.

Chapter 41

'Huh,' the succubus said, unimpressed. 'Dead. Not surprised, given an ancient piece of shit like this.'

She dropped the phone to the ground; it hit it with a crack. Apparently it wasn't worth the effort of throwing.

Banning took in the new arrivals with interest. Shadow curled around the succubus where she stood. She was almost identical to Heimerich in his true state, smaller perhaps, but otherwise he'd struggle to tell them apart.

What was it that Mundy had said about Heimerich? *And I thought your kind were supposed to be rare.*

He should have paid more attention to the trafficker at the diner. Maybe if he hadn't been so distracted by his thoughts of Naomie he'd have picked up on it.

It added up. The she-demon would give Mundy and his men free rein in the veil, or at the very least, could point them in the direction of a gatekeeper. What didn't make sense was why she was holding two people at gunpoint.

He glanced over his shoulder, to where Heimerich, in human form, was being hauled along by two of Mundy's thugs. He looked barely able to support his own weight.

That was going to be an issue. Banning had half a mind to kill the incubus here and now, but it wasn't his place to make decisions on behalf of his mentor. Still... he had the child and her mother. And the hellip—paid for in full.

And now that detective had been exposed to the truth about his husband, he really had no further use for the incubus. Leaving him with the trafficker was not an option, Heimerich knew too much. About Kar'roc's Maw, about Archibald Morgan. No, the incubus had to die.

A loud *whump* followed by a flash of orange, coming from the crumbling brick shell of the electrical control room, made him flinch.

'Oi you.' Mundy's voice thundered. He set off in a jog towards a dumbstruck looking man not much older than Banning himself. 'Yeah you, you dozy twat. Get that thing fixed before it sets the whole dockyard alight.' He waved his arms at the partially demolished building, where curls of black smoke were drifting from the wiring.

Whatever the man said in response was lost when the wind changed direction. Mundy's look became a shade darker. He jabbed a finger into the man's chest, forcing him to take a step back.

'Do I look like I give a fuck you're not an electrician? Get it fixed. You see those barrels?' He gestured to an exposed gap in the wooden panelling where dented metal drums, faded with age and blistered with rust, sat in haphazard piles between disused machinery. 'Yeah?

Well the chemicals inside those barrels are flammable. Extremely flammable. I've got buyers turning up within the next few hours and they ain't coming for a fucking barbeque. Get it sorted. Now.'

Banning swallowed and fingered the autoinjector in his pocket. He walked away, keeping his eyes fixed ahead.

'I don't care, just do it.' Mundy's rants faded with the distance.

By the time the trafficker made a reappearance Banning was back inside the slipway proper. He'd almost forgotten the stench—if anything it seemed to have gotten stronger. And the noise was making the sharp, stabbing pain behind his eyes worse. He squeezed them shut and rubbed at his temples, leaning against the bars of an empty cage. All he had to do was wait for the hellip to be placed back in its crate and he could get as far away from this hellhole as humanly possible.

The sound of footsteps pulled him from his thoughts and opened his eyes.

Mundy grunted. 'You and me need to have a little chat.'

Straightening his jacket, Banning gave the trafficker a sideways glance. 'Is that so?'

'I make it a point of pride to stay outta any business that ain't *my* business. But now, not only do I have the rozzers showing up on my front doorstep looking for you but I've got these fuckers looking for *him*.' He thumbed at the incubus. 'Being that you've landed me in the shit—and I'm not even counting the men you lost me—I want to know who it is you're working for. And

I want to know what this geezer's got that's worth you kidnapping his daughter and granddaughter over.'

Banning stiffened, staring at the pensioner being herded away by the succubus.

So this was Charlie Haynes? Master of the legendary Kar'roc's Maw? He didn't look like much. In fact, he looked like he was about to drop from exhaustion. Bloody, bruised and, for some reason, wet. This was some mistake, surely?

Extending his senses out to the man, Banning tried to get a sense of the energy around him. The reaction was immediate. Charlie Haynes balled his left hand into a fist and turned to glare at him. That was until the succubus prodded him with the gun.

What a fortuitous turn of events.

Rubbing at his jaw, Banning smiled. All the unfortunate incidents, frustrations, and disappointments he'd caused Archibald Morgan over the years, they would all soon be forgotten. The moment he delivered Charlie Haynes to his mentor, Banning would finally prove himself capable. Worthy. No more menial tasks. No more demeaning errands. Everything was falling into place.

Mundy caught his expression and nodded. 'Yeah, I ain't just a pretty face. The old timer's got something. Something worth having. And I want to know what. Come on, kid, enlighten me.'

'I don't think so.'

'Look, this ain't the time for a dick measuring contest. I get it, you got balls. But I want to know what kind of shit you've gotten me into, and I want to know right fucking now.'

'No.'

Mundy sucked his teeth. 'Last chance.'

'The *rozzers*, as you so eloquently put it, turned up on your doorstep because they had *your* registration details. I read the detective's notes. As for these two *fuckers*, it would seem that they were brought here by the succubus at your behest.'

Mundy didn't move. He ground his teeth. 'You really are a piece of work, kid.' The trafficker exhaled and shook his head. He pulled the leather pouch containing his silver lighter from his pocket. Placing a cigarette between his lips, he brought the lighter to his mouth, and thumbed the flint wheel.

Banning went rigid. Felt his insides go cold.

Muffled shouts erupted outside the building. Mundy turned, cigarette forgotten. 'That fucking control room. I told that dozy—'

The sound of the blast that came was deafening.

The side of the building collapsed in an eruption of flame and smoke.

There was no time to react. No time to shield himself.

Banning hurtled through the air as heat rolled over him in a blistering attack. He hit the ground awkwardly. His head slammed into the concrete. Stars exploded across his vision.

He heard screams. Frantic, agonised, desperate. Were they his?

His world went black.

Chapter 42

Nick forced his eyes open to see a haze of dust and smoke. He spluttered a cough, fragments of debris scattering from his hair and clothes, and pushed himself up to sitting. A good section of the slipway's side panelling had been destroyed, its steel beams buckled and warped where they'd taken the brunt of the explosion. Curtains of flame dripped from the floor of the mezzanine where the wood had been set alight; fat globules of fire rained down to the concrete below. Above, gaping holes in the roof belched columns of black smoke into the sky.

All around Nick, blackened cages lay twisted and deformed, the charred occupants smouldering inside. Those that were still alive had been driven into a frenzy, hurling themselves against the bars in fits of shrieks and grunts. Something small ran past him. He flinched back, pain jarring him.

'Nick?'

'Henry?' Nick called back, his voice muffled by the ringing in his ears.

Henry was slumped against a crate that had somehow escaped any real damage; his body was coated in a thick layer of grime. He was grimacing and pressing his hand to his side.

Nick crawled towards him as quickly as his deadened limbs would allow. 'Henry, you're hurt.' Gently, he tried to prise his husband's hand away from the injury, but Henry only hissed and shook his head.

'There's nothing you can do. I'll be fine. I just need a minute.'

'Let me see, I can help.'

'There's nothing to see. It's internal.' He blew out a breath, batting Nick's hand away weakly.

Internal? Nick's stomach dropped.

'Seriously, Nick. It's fine. I'm already healing. Once I catch my breath I'll be okay.'

Too exhausted to argue, he decided to change the subject. 'Henry, where's everyone else?'

'I... I don't know...'

'Meghan? Evelyn?' Nick shouted. 'Charlie? Jasmin?' *Jesus*, even Lily was gone. He thought he heard a noise. 'I'm going to see if I can find anyone.'

He pushed himself to his feet with a groan and took a few unsteady steps in the direction of the noise.

'No, Nick, it's not safe,' Henry pleaded. 'You need to get out of here.'

'Not without the others.' With a lurch forward, he cupped his hands to his mouth. 'Charlie? Jasmin? Meg—'

'Nick, I'm here.' The voice was female. And close.

'Jasmin?' He squinted, looking for anything vaguely human through the churning haze.

'Watch out!' Jasmin crashed into him, knocking him back.

A wooden beam smashed into the floor where he'd just been, missing him by inches. He stared at it, unable to move.

Jasmin was screaming. A giant piece of wood had splintered off the beam and speared her calf, pinning her in place.

He unfroze. *'Jesus.* Jasmin, don't move.'

A low growling sound reverberated around them. Nick's eyes widened. Stalking towards them was the creature that Banning Lawrence had released against Lily. It paused to flex its toes, its claws scraping the ground, and lowered its skull-like head.

'Holy fuck!'

The thing leapt, clamping its jaws around the beam with a crack of rupturing wood. The muscles in its hind legs bunched. It hauled its prize back. Jasmin bellowed, clawing for purchase in the filth, as she and the beam were dragged across the ground. Nick and Henry grabbed her arms, heaving her forward. Her screams ripped through Nick's skull, but her terror and agony spurred him on. Another pull snapped off the piece of the wood that was skewering Jasmin's leg.

The creature snarled, releasing the beam with a violent jerk of its head.

'Henry, do something,' Nick shouted.

Thrusting out his arm caused Henry pain. He let out a cry. Shadow whipped up and out from his palm, striking the creature between the eyes. It jerked its head back with a startled yelp. Nick held his breath, waiting. The thing glared at Henry, shook out its shaggy black fur and turned, to give chase to something unseen in the distance.

The sound of gunfire echoed somewhere inside the building, muffled by the din around them. Nick shuddered. How the hell was he supposed to get Jasmin out of here? The woman, practically the same height as him, was all muscle. Even if he wasn't half concussed, Nick wasn't sure he'd manage it, and Henry didn't look in any fit shape to help.

Jasmin writhed as Nick tried to hook his hands under her armpits. She cried out and shook her head. 'I can't... you need to snap it off.'

'What?'

'The wood... I won't be able to walk.'

Nick looked down at the injury to see she was right. The piece of timber was large enough that it would obstruct her ability to move. '*Shit.*'

'Just do it, Nick!'

He swallowed hard and hunkered down. He gripped the shard with his right hand while his other braced against her calf, and yanked. Jasmin cried out, her body going rigid. He repositioned himself, his left hand now slick with her blood, and gave another firm tug.

Jasmin roared. The wood snapped.

Nick threw the remnants to the ground, wiping his palm down his trousers. A jagged stump still protruded from her flesh but at least now she'd be able to limp out of here with his support. He hoped.

After a few shallow gasps of air, Jasmin gritted her teeth. 'Help me up.'

Nick locked his arm around her waist. He frowned down at her leg. 'Think you'll be able to walk?'

She nodded. They took a step together, the weight of her body bearing down on him as she hobbled forward.

Henry was already on his feet, staring at the fire where it raged with renewed vigour. He was no longer clutching his side, but every movement made him wince. 'I need to find Banning.'

'Are you joking? You can't go back in there, it's suicide. You're hurt.'

'You don't understand—'

'No, Henry. I don't understand.'

Henry stopped walking. 'I really fucked up. I'm so sorry. I never meant for any of this to happen. I got in too deep. I did my best to try and keep you safe. It's why I got you Lily, so that she could protect you if anything... happened to me.'

'Happened to you? Henry, what are you talking about?'

A series of sharp, brittle popping noises halted the conversation. The roof windows exploded and rained glass down, stirring up clouds of dust and sprays of ember where they struck below. The mezzanine floor creaked above them, wood snapping and cracking ominously.

'You need to get out of here, while you still can,' Henry said. 'I love you, Nick.'

Nick opened his mouth to argue, but before he could reply, Henry erupted into shadow and disappeared.

'Henry?' Nick's heart stuttered.

'Nick,' Jasmin said. 'We need to find the others.'

Nick looked down at her leg and shook his head. 'I need to get you out first. You can't even stand by yourself.' He knew it was the right call, but it did little to ease the dread crushing his chest.

They picked their way through the slipway, headed for the outside. Past the charred corpses of animals and men. When at last they reached the exit, they were hit by a rush of frigid night air. Jasmin was clearly in a lot of pain. Every step brought a grunt, and sweat was matting her hair to her face, but she filled her lungs and struggled on. They weren't out of the woods yet.

'What in the hell is going on, Jasmin?' Nick asked. 'Where did you and Charlie come from?'

'We were set up.'

'Set up?' He glanced over his shoulder, to make certain that nothing had followed them out of the burning building.

'Earlier... at Meghan's h-house. We f-found markings on the wall.' Jasmin took another step, sucking in a sharp breath. 'No one was supposed to know about Charlie, or the dagger. We thought the Order h-had a mole.'

'The Order? Henry mentioned the Order.'

A grimacing Jasmin waved for Nick to stop. She wiped her brow, leaving streaks in the dirt and grime. Her muscles shuddered beneath his grip. After blowing out a breath, she clenched her teeth and signalled to Nick that she was ready to start walking again.

'Think, urgh, think of them as a s-sort of s-supernatural police force. Charlie and I decided to go it alone. *Ah...*'

'Do you need to stop?'

'No. No, k-keep going.' Jasmin grunted. 'I knew s-someone like Henry, with the same abilities, thought she might be able to h-help us identify who left the markings. But she sold us out, brought us here.'

'Banning said that my memories had been altered. That was the Order?'

'Yes. It's p-protocol.'

'And that Henry had been providing him with the information. Is that true?'

'I'm guessing so.'

'And you work for them? The Order?'

Jasmin nodded.

'Charlie too?'

'No. He knew nothing about any of this until the Caravan Cannibal c-case a few months ago.'

When I started having trouble sleeping. Stopped being able to function.

'That's why Henry was digging around inside my head? Because I was there that night? Because I saw something I wasn't supposed to?'

She nodded again.

'I guess that explains why he didn't want me having anything to do with Charlie,' he muttered.

A scream ripped through the slipway behind them before cutting off abruptly. It sounded male. Nick shuddered.

'What's going to happen to him? To Henry?'

Jasmin turned to look at him. 'I'm not sure. Life imprisonment w-within O.O.T.I.S. Maybe less if he co-operates, tells them... tells them everything he knows about w-who he's been working for.' She gestured for him to stop. 'H-here is good.'

Nick helped to ease her onto the concrete as gently as possible. The farthest part of the building was engulfed entirely, smoke and ash rising up above the flame in great raging torrents. A glut of fire burst from the smog, followed by a low, juddering creak, as a huge section of the roof collapsed. Needles of glass, glowing steel and smouldering wood scattered across the ground. He was thankful that Jasmin had made it as far as she had, otherwise they'd have been caught in the barrage of debris.

Jasmin drew in a breath, her eyes wide. 'No... Meghan! Evelyn!'

Without a thought, Nick charged back towards the blazing slipway.

Chapter 43

WEAK.

'No!' Banning screamed, his eyes snapping open. He darted his gaze around the space. Thick black smoke billowed from the flames, consuming everything around him.

How long have I been lying here?

His throat tightened. His palms became clammy. Tongues of red and yellow hell flicked out, tasting his fear.

He fumbled for the autoinjector, his fingers clumsy in his haste. Gone.

No.

He twisted and clambered frantically to his knees. Fingers tearing at straw and filth, he crawled across the concrete. It had to be here. It had to be.

The fire was getting closer, its suffocating heat squeezing the air from his lungs. Embers seared his face, singed his hair. He batted at them, every desperate breath he took filling his nostrils with the stench of his scorching skin.

Dark spots filled his vision.

YOU'RE WEAK.

No.

He bit the inside of his cheek until his mouth filled with blood. The pain smoothed the raw edges of his panic. He was back in the moment. Back in the now.

'Looking for this?' The incubus stood over him, red eyes burning within the mass of shadow. Clutched in its talons was his autoinjector.

Banning swallowed the blood and the chunk of his cheek. Hysteria bubbled from his throat, releasing a spray of crimson droplets. His laugh was too high.

'Something funny, Banning?'

'Give it to me.' He lurched to his feet and made a drunken swipe at the injector. The creature stepped back, taunting him. Banning stopped. 'What do you want?'

'I want you to suffer. I thought about killing you. I'm sure you'd deserve it. But then that would make me like you. And I'm nothing like you. I've never hurt anyone intentionally. Never even come close. There's something wrong with you, Banning. It's like a poison festering in your core is rotting you from the inside out. *You* are the worst kind of monster, the kind that hides behind a faultless smile and the perfect words, while everything around you crumbles. I might be a monster on the outside, but you... you're a monster on the inside.'

KILL.

Ten, nine, eight...

'You have no idea what will happen if I don't take it...' Banning said between gritted teeth; the scars on his arms and chest prickled uncomfortably. It had nothing to do with the heat. 'Give it to me. Now... before it's too late.'

Breathe.

Heimerich surged towards him. Darkness flowed around him, swallowing the light, as he became one with the smoke and ash. 'You exposed me! Now Nick knows what I am. It's only a matter of time before the Order finds out. I'll have no choice but to run. You took everything from me. Everything! I had a life. I was happy.'

'Monsters don't deserve happiness.' Banning wiped the blood dribbling from his mouth on the back of his hand. His every muscle was trembling. Sweat trickled down his spine. 'Give it to me.'

Seven, six, five...

'Fuck you, Banning.' Heimerich lunged at him.

Banning pivoted a second too slow. Claws raked down his chest, splitting open material and flesh in one swipe. He grunted.

Pain wouldn't stop him. He'd felt worse.

Heimerich's face was inches from his own. 'I'm not going to kill you, but I hope you die here.'

And then Banning felt the impact. Heard the crack of the autoinjector.

The incubus stepped back, brushing shards of plastic and glass from its palm.

Banning gaped down at his chest. At the stain of lindwurm venom mingling with the blood seeping into his shirt.

A fist of ice punched him in the gut. He staggered back, making a strangled noise. 'What have you done?'

Red eyes, smouldering with unchecked hatred, stared at him. Shadow rolled inwards, imploding with a pop, as Heimerich disappeared and air rushed in to fill the empty space.

Breathe. Just breathe.

There was nothing more he could do.

KILL.

The voice raged inside his head, pervading his thoughts with such loathing, there was room for little else. The demon was so much stronger than before, its hold on him all but absolute.

Banning had wondered over the years what would have happened if the demon had possessed him completely. If Banning had depleted his store of energy as his brother had his own. That's what the demon had been seeking that night—an empty vessel. A body without the will or means to resist. Instead it had to settle for him, someone who it could never quite overwhelm. Never quite seize full control.

Yet it had left something of itself behind in Banning. An echo of its presence. A dark poison that lingered ever present, just beneath the surface. He'd tried so hard to fight it. But something had changed in recent months. The lindwurm venom had been losing its effect. A single dose had been enough to keep the voice at bay for weeks, but now, his nightly injections were not enough. He was a danger to everyone around him. A ticking time bomb.

Something shiny caught his eye. He held his breath, daring to hope, and edged forward.

There.

Hidden beneath the straw where the incubus had been was a cartridge. A single, glorious cartridge. He dropped to his knees and snatched at it. The glass was still intact. But the autoinjector was gone.

Four, three, two...

He growled in frustration, battling the urge to hurl the cartridge away. There must be something else he could do.

Concentrate.

Ingesting it would be useless. Maybe he could douse the lacerations on his chest? Yes, that could work. He could use the natural flow of energy within his body to help guide the venom into his system.

With slick and trembling fingers he removed the cap. The needling irritation running down his arms and chest was now an incessant burn. He exhaled and blinked through the sweat blurring his vision, ignoring the turmoil and the harrying flames around him.

Come on, come on.

A blur of motion came a second before the sound of a high-pitched squeal. And then Banning was flat on his back. Excruciating pain radiated up into his shoulder.

He cried out and thrashed his limbs, in an effort to land a blow on his attacker. Then he saw it. The toorkboar.

It came at him again, gouging him with its tusks, trampling him with its hooves. The cartridge in

Banning's clenched fist cracked; glass stabbed his palm as the precious venom leaked down his wrist. The creature became frantic, nostrils flaring, eyes rolling, as the smell of the toxin sent it into overdrive. It slammed its head against him with enough force to shatter bone. Banning screamed in raw agony.

Mouth frothing, tusks blood-soaked and caked with chunks of his shredded flesh, the beast swung its head again.

ONE.

Rage consumed Banning, annihilating the last of his crumbling resolve. Without the lindwurm venom, there was nothing he could do to stop the demon. No way to fight. It owned him now, drowning his thoughts until there was nothing left but toxic hatred.

YES.

Banning grinned.

He felt alive. Free. Of fear. Of guilt. Nothing now but the desire to destroy. To kill.

He closed both hands around each of the toorkboar's tusks and rose to his feet, hauling it off the ground. The beast struggled against his grip, its body convulsing with panic. Banning laughed.

It was a laugh that was not entirely his own. A laugh that silenced even the shrill, drawn-out shrieks of the terrified animal.

YES, KILL.

With a sharp yank, he split the creature in two. Its innards spilled out, hitting the ground in wet, meaty plops. Blood sprayed on his face, his clothing, his shoes. Wet and warm, and with that familiar metallic scent.

Discarding what remained of the cryptid, Banning licked the red droplets from the edges of his mouth and rolled his neck.

DAGGER.

Yes. He needed the dagger.

Energy eddied around him, offering him sweet relief from the pain of his battered body. The dark power was a part of him. His birthright. And he would deny himself no longer. Going against everything he'd been taught to do, Banning drank it in, giving himself freely to the realm of fire and shadow. Exhilaration surged through him. His muscles trembled from the intensity, making the hairs on the back of his neck stand on end.

With a shudder, his wounds began to knit closed. The splintered fragments of his ribs realigned themselves; the bone set with odd quivering pops. His body remade itself, until all that remained were the scars gifted to him by the demon the night he'd been reborn.

He squelched through offal. Cinders rained down around him, flame leaping from beam to beam picking through the carcass of the building, leaving nothing but skeletal steel in its wake. Yet Banning scarcely felt the heat, his thoughts too consumed by bloodlust and the overwhelming need for carnage. Distantly, a part of him was screaming to be heard, but whatever the voice was trying to tell him was muted by the thundering power surging through his veins.

THE CHILD.

Of course. The *child*. All he needed was to find the child and Charlie Haynes would bring the dagger to him. And as luck would have it, he could just make out her muffled whimpers in the raging fire.

Whimpers and fire. That's what had destroyed him all those years ago.

Whimpers and fire. That's what had *made* him all those years ago.

Chapter 44

THE RINGING IN HIS ears was the first thing Charlie noticed.

He opened his eyes to bright and blinding light. His entire body throbbed.

Groaning, he rolled over onto his hands and knees. He stayed like that for a moment—breath ragged, throat raw—then staggered to his feet, grasping at the bars of the nearest cage for support.

He was still alive. Just about. He blinked at his hands covered in ash. Blood wept from his thumbnail that was hanging on by a thread. He yanked it off with a wince.

Slowly, mechanically, he pushed away from the bars that were blackened and warped. There was something dead inside. An animal with bone protruding through its scorched and mangled pelt. He shook his head, dismissing it, and surveyed his surroundings.

Carnage. Absolute carnage.

Everywhere he looked there were creatures. Some were running through the rippling window of heat where the panelling on the building had been blown apart, making a desperate bid for freedom. Some were staggering around, disorientated. Some were on the ground and wouldn't be getting up again.

'Meghan? Evie?' he bellowed, his shout drowned out by the blood pumping in his ears. 'Meghan? Ev—' Dust hit the back of his throat; he choked out a cough. Charlie staggered forward.

There was a creak above him. Followed by a snapping sound.

He looked up to see the glowing beam give a shudder before it cracked and hurtled towards the ground. Charlie launched himself to the side, shielding his face. Wood struck concrete in an eruption of ash and ember. A wave of heat hit him, enveloping his body in a grimy cloud of smoke. With a curse, he slapped out the sparks singeing his clothes and scorching his skin. It wouldn't be long before the entire structure collapsed.

'Meghan, Evie, if you can hear me shout.'

He listened, waiting.

Nothing.

Christ, where were they? Where were his girls?

Something clamped down on his arm. He jumped and spun round. Eyes like molten rock stared back at him.

'It's me.' Henry's voice sounded as disembodied and grating as Rhea's.

'You've got some nerve.' Charlie balled his fists by his sides. It was all he could do not to take a swing at the incubus.

'I'm sorry—'

'*Sorry?* You abducted my daughter, my granddaughter! They could be dead for all I know.' He squared his shoulders, taking a step towards Henry. Visceral rage quivered through his body, throbbed in his veins. The sigil flared, but was a distant sting compared to his desire to throttle the creature before him.

'Charlie, you need to calm down.' The shadows around Henry rolled.

'Don't you *dare* tell me to calm down.'

'I know I can never make things right. I never meant for any of this to happen. I was scared.' The rolling shadow receded with a dull snap, leaving Henry naked and hunched over, clutching at his side. He was panting, his face ashen. 'Hit me, if it makes you feel better. I know you want to. I deserve it.'

Charlie curled his lips back. He raised one fist. Then he let his arm drop with a frustrated growl. 'If I hit you, I won't be able to stop. Christ, Henry, you could have said no. You could have lied. You could have done anything, but you chose to give up my family.'

'I'm a coward. I was so afraid. So afraid of what they might do to Nick. Of what Banning might do. He's dangerous. He would have known if I'd lied. And if not him then Archi—'

'We don't have time for this. I need to find Meghan and Evelyn before this place comes crashing down around us.'

'Charlie Haynes.' He heard the voice as clear as day, but something about it sounded off.

'It's Banning. I thought the toorkboar would have finished him off... shit.' Henry winced. 'You need to go, Charlie. You need to get out of here now.'

'I'm not going anywhere until I find my girls.'

Banning taunted, 'Charlie Haynes, I have someone here that *really* wants to see you.'

A scream followed. Piercing and terrified, and all too familiar.

'Evie!' Charlie sprinted forward, vaulting over the burning beam. The flames caught the cuff of his trousers, scorching the fabric and charring his skin. He ground his teeth against the pain, and continued on.

Even without Banning's voice to guide him, he knew he was headed in the right direction. And when his flesh prickled with pain from the sigil, there was no doubt in his mind that he was where he needed to be.

Using his momentum to barge through a blockade of empty cages, he staggered to a halt. Just beyond some shattered crates and the remains of an old lifeboat stood the young man in the three-piece suit.

And in his grip was a sobbing Evie.

HE COMES.

Banning didn't need to see Charlie Haynes to know he was nearby. Even without the demon tipping him off, he could feel the man's connection to the realm of fire and shadow. He then saw the vortex of energy spiralling around him.

Curious, Banning reached out with his power, gently prodding and probing the vortex. Pain like a lightning strike ripped through his body. He flinched back.

THE BOND PROTECTS HIM.

Banning recoiled, pulling the child back with him as his muscles spasmed from the shock. The girl's sobs reached a crescendo as she tried to wrench herself from his grasp. He hated the sound of wailing; it grated like nails on a blackboard. Reminded him too much of his brother, Garrick. This was all Garrick's fault.

KILL.

His grip tightened on the child.

She shrieked.

'You promised you wouldn't hurt me,' she squealed, tears tracking lines through the ash on her cheeks.

He flinched as her words briefly penetrated the roiling murk of toxic sludge polluting his mind. He *had* promised the child he wouldn't hurt her.

DAGGER. The demon's command obliterated the thought.

He trailed his gaze to the child's mother, still unresponsive, despite the bedlam. She wasn't dead. He could feel her body's natural energy, from the subtle shift of how it flowed with each beat of her heart, with each rise and fall of her lungs, with each slight twitch. He'd found her like that. Shielding her daughter. What mother wouldn't do everything in her power to protect her child? His mother had died trying to protect him.

PROTECTING GARRICK.

Banning growled. It was true.

It was Garrick she'd tried to save. Not him.

It was Garrick his father had told her to save. Not him.

Garrick had played with fire and yet Banning had been the one to get burnt. Well, now the whole world could burn.

A blaze of green erupted across the scar tissue on his chest and fed down his arms. Insatiable tongues of flame lapped at the air.

The child screamed a feral sound, raw with fear. She writhed and squirmed in his grip, beating at his arms, clawing at his skin, desperate to escape the sudden and intense heat of his magic. But Banning couldn't feel the green burn. He couldn't feel anything except hatred and desire. He wanted the Maw. *Needed* it.

With Kar'roc's Maw he could rend this world apart. Awaken a new age of demons. The Brimstone Chorus had already begun; there was no stopping it. And he would be its harbinger, its catalyst—the spark needed to obliterate the veil once and for all. Humanity would fall and Banning would bathe in the blood and torment of all those who refused their fate. It was time to take his place as a God over men.

DAGGER.

Yes. If Charlie Haynes would not surrender the dagger voluntarily, he would just have to provide an incentive.

He dragged the mewling child in front of him and extended her arm out. She screamed, lashing out with her other fist in a futile effort to stop him.

Haynes gasped. 'Please, no... No!'

Banning smiled.

A single strike was all it took for the girl's arm to break. He took pleasure in hearing the nauseating *crack* it made.

Chapter 45

Evelyn's scream rang in Charlie's ears. And he'd stood there and let it happen.

White-hot rage ignited in his chest. Exploded from his throat in a roar.

This had to end. Now.

Kar'roc's Maw responded instantly, and in a second, he felt the smooth marble of its hilt pressing against his palm. The familiar rhythmic pulse the dagger emitted quivered through his skin. He squeezed his fist tight then was struck from behind. The impact knocked the dagger from his grasp. Charlie twisted and fell awkwardly, hitting his ribcage on the concrete. With a grunt, he rolled onto his back.

Henry was on top of him in a flash, pinning him down.

'Charlie, no!'

'Get off me.' Fuelled by adrenaline, Charlie bucked and twisted, but With Henry's full weight on his chest, he only managed to squirm an inch or two.

'It's what Banning wants. The dagger. Please, I don't want to hurt you.'

'Get the *fuck* off me.'

'You'll kill us all. This isn't just about Evelyn and Meghan. Every man, woman and child on this planet will die. I can't let you do this. I'm sorry.' Henry drew back, fist raised, the muscles in his torso bunching as he did.

Before he could land the punch Charlie reared up, locking his arms around Henry's chest and pulling the man down on top of him. In the time it took for Henry to gasp, Charlie had already manoeuvred himself into a better position.

He exploded upward and pivoted his hips, forcing Henry to rotate until their positions were switched. Charlie delivered two swift punches to Henry's face before untangling himself and lurching back to his feet.

Where was the damned dagger?

Two steps. That was all he'd managed before someone dragged him back by his shoulders. He cried out as anger and frustration took the last of his reason. He spun round. Henry was gone, replaced by the writhing mass of darkness that marked him for what he truly was. A demon. A monster.

'I'm sorry, Charlie. I really am,' the incubus said.

He ploughed his shadowy form into Charlie's upper body, hurtling him back. Charlie smashed into empty cages. The force of the hit juddered through his bones with such intensity, he worried something had broken. Metal had warped beneath him. Bars, bent and snapped, shredded his clothes and carved deep gashes into his already bruised flesh. Charlie groaned.

Through the gap in the wreckage, he saw Henry racing towards Banning.

He tried to pull himself free of the twisted metal, but yelped. A wave of agony rode up through his thigh, turning his vision white. *Shit.* He was stuck. Impaled on jagged steel.

Evelyn shrieked.

The sound turned Charlie's bowels to water. He swallowed hard. With his anxiety in overdrive he could barely breathe. Every stilted gasp filled his lungs with smoke and dust. He coughed as pain lanced through him. A wide, red stain was spreading through his trousers where the bar poked through.

He glanced around, desperate for help. Desperate for someone. Anyone.

He was on his own.

Gritting his teeth, he hauled himself up and off the metal. Muscle and flesh tore free from the spike, wet with blood and shreds of what he hoped was his trousers.

Charlie hobbled forward. He hadn't stood a chance against Banning before, but now he was fucked. Every hitched step was excruciating. But hurt or not, he needed to help his girls. And if he had to die trying, then so be it.

Ironic that a gammy leg would be what got him killed when it was what had saved him the last time he'd squared off against a monster.

He'd been lucky to survive against Stephen. Despite the speed and his strength, and his ability to heal himself, Stephen had been a slave to the demon. And the demon a slave to the dagger. But Banning? He had no idea what he was. A witch? A demon?

A distant *whump* sound as another part of the slipway's roof collapsed set off a chain reaction. The sudden influx of air riled the fire into a frenzy. Glass shattered in a series of stuttered pops, steel screamed, and debris fell in glowing red droplets.

Charlie flinched back, but his leg buckled with the abrupt movement. He flailed his arms and landed on his backside, biting back a yell. The throb in his leg was like a thousand needles piercing all the way down to the bone. Blood gushed from the wound. It couldn't be his femoral artery; he'd have lost consciousness by now. But he did feel lightheaded. That was to be expected with blood loss, right?

He shook his head, trying to clear his thoughts.

A red gleam caught his eye. The dagger. He stretched out his arm and grasped for it, but his sweat-slicked fingers couldn't hold on.

Focus. He took a breath and exhaled, then shuffled closer, dragging bloody streaks behind him. His vision blurred with the effort. This time his fingers closed around the guard, the filigree scroll lending him grip. He snatched it to his chest. The crimson gemstone pulsed light across its facets in a hypnotic way.

He lifted his head; the movement caused his stomach to roil.

'Banning...' His voice was little more than a rasp.

From his position Charlie could see Meghan, collapsed on the floor. A fist of ice clenched his gut, dulling the pain in his leg. He couldn't tell if she was breathing.

He flicked his gaze to Evie. She was kneeling by Banning's feet, her broken arm clutched to her chest, her face screwed up and a deathly shade of white. Henry's efforts to fight Banning were in vain. Every lash of shadow was immediately deflected by a blaze of green.

He needed to do something. Fast.

Banning's eyes locked onto Charlie's, then trailed down to the dagger. He cocked his head, mouth curling into a smile, and gave Charlie a wink. An actual fucking wink. Then, he took a step forward, green flame rippling across his body.

Henry took the opportunity to strike, the glowing magma threads on his obsidian body obscured by his thrashing whips of darkness. He launched himself at Banning, talons raking at him in lethal swipes. But his strikes skipped over some invisible barrier, trailing off in green sparks and completely ineffective. Banning's grin never faltered as he said something to Evie, then he seized her roughly by the arm and yanked her to her feet. Her wail was cut short by shadow rolling upward and enveloping the three of them.

'Evie!' Charlie clawed at the ground, trying to push himself to his feet. His muscles trembled, and he collapsed.

Charlie screamed. All his fear. All his desperation. All his helplessness. It ripped out of him in that one agonised howl.

Rhea's words entered his mind. *If you want to survive in a world full of monsters, you have to become something worse.*

With a huff, Charlie clamped the Damascus steel blade between his teeth and pressed his palms against his thigh until they came away slick. He dragged his bloodied hands across the concrete. Again and again he repeated this until he had completed the crude circle. With a quick wipe of his hands on his trench coat, Charlie removed the dagger from his mouth, careful not to touch the red stone set into its pommel.

He squeezed his eyes shut and visualised the text written on the pages of *Ritualistic Sacrifice in Ancient Magical Practices.* The same pages he'd failed to return to Diane. Pages that he'd pored over every night for the last three months.

'With Solomon's Seal I summon thee. With Solomon's Seal I compel thee. With Solomon's Seal I bind thee to this mortal vessel.'

He plunged the dagger into the wound on his thigh. He screeched from the pain.

'Chekonost I have dominion over thee. Thou art my servant until the end of days. Serve me. I command you!'

Electricity shot through him, so hard it silenced his scream. The pain was blinding. Like nothing he'd ever felt before. It ripped through every nerve ending and every fibre, pulling him apart from the inside out. His skull was on fire. If he could have cried out for death, he would have. Charlie collapsed to the side, desperate to catch a breath to ease the burn in his lungs.

Everything hurt. And then... it didn't.

He ripped the dagger from his leg and tossed it to the ground. He felt... strong.

Charlie glanced at Banning. The shadow surrounding him had receded; whatever Henry had attempted had clearly been unsuccessful.

Tension bloomed inside Charlie's head. A disquieting pressure that sent a shiver down his spine. And then that also stopped.

YOU. Chekonost spoke inside his mind, radiating hatred.

Save my daughter, my granddaughter.

He could feel the demon's emotions. Scorn. Defiance. And a hint of wry amusement.

TECHNICALLY THEY AREN'T—

I command you to save Meghan and Evelyn. Now.

WOULDN'T HURT YOU TO SAY PLEASE.

The demon invaded his muscles, taking control of his body. Before he could react, Charlie was on his feet, running towards Evie.

In a single, fluid movement, the demon wrapped Charlie's arm around Evie while striking out at Banning's solar plexus with the other. Time seemed to slow. Charlie watched the young man's eyes widen in surprise as his fist connected with him. And then Banning was stumbling backwards.

Banning recovered almost immediately. His livid gaze fixed on Charlie, a look that promised nothing but pain. Green light erupted on his fist, an extension of the eerie fire currently licking his body. He took a menacing step forward.

Chekonost reacted with a low growl that came from the back of Charlie's throat.

WE SHOULD RUN.

Evie whimpered against Charlie's chest, her body trembling. He pulled her tighter.

A dark shadow entered his peripheral vision. Henry hit Banning side on, pitching him over. The two wrestled in the smouldering charcoal remnants of the mezzanine, ash and ember scattering as they traded blows.

WE SHOULD RUN. NOW.

Not without Meghan.

But there was no way he'd be able to carry both Evie and Meggy.

He shifted his granddaughter in his arms, assessing the damage to her arm, to see if she was in any fit state to run. A shard of bone was jutting out of her skin. A compound fracture. His gut twisted.

Heal her.

I CANNOT.

Heal her! I command you.

I CANNOT HEAL HER. IT IS BEYOND MY CAPABILITIES.

Even as the words resounded inside his head he knew they were true. A sob bubbled up from Charlie's throat. He wanted to scream.

He repositioned his grip on Evie, desperate not to jostle her. She yelped in pain anyway; the sound wrenched at his heart.

BUT I CAN HEAL YOU.

Charlie felt his wounds tingle as they began to knit together. His muscles twitched as gashes in his skin closed.

No.

NO? He could sense the demon's confusion.

Just the wound on my thigh. Nothing else.

'Charlie? Charlie... *Christ*, you're alive,' Nick's voice filtered through the smoke behind him.

His eyes widened when he saw Evelyn, then he looked at her arm. He drew in a sharp breath. *'Jesus!'*

'Nick, I need you to get her out of here. She needs an ambulance.'

Nick nodded.

Charlie handed Evie to Nick, flinching at the sound of her tortured whimpers.

'She'll be okay,' Nick said with a nod.

'Go. *Go!*'

But Nick didn't move. His expression went slack and his face lost all remaining colour.

'Henry!'

Chapter 46

Charlie turned to see Henry strike the steel girder. The impact sent another shower of debris and orange sparks scattering down from the remains of the blazing roof. Henry folded forward and landed in a heavy heap, his shadow bursting apart to reveal pale flesh. The indent his body had left in the metal had exposed Banning's true strength. It was a wonder Henry had survived, incubus or not.

I TOLD YOU, WE SHOULD RUN.

Wait. Where *was* Banning?

Nick shuffled with Evie in his arms, eyes wide with concern.

'Nick, go. I'll get Henry. Please just get Evie out of here.'

A startled Nick tore his gaze from his husband and glanced down at Evie. Without another word, he turned and ran through the thick clouds of smoke spewing out from the side of the slipway.

Charlie sprinted to Meghan's side, where he dropped to his knees and checked for a pulse. All his pent-up anger released in one huge sob of relief.

'Meggy? Meggy, can you hear me?' Louder this time he said, 'Meggy?'

SHE IS UNCONSCIOUS, NOT DEAF.

Ignoring the demon, Charlie eased his daughter into a seated position and locked his arms around her, preparing to pull her to standing. A flare of green light stopped him in his tracks.

'*Banning*,' Charlie growled, like the name was a curse on his lips. He stiffened, torn between getting Meghan to safety and wreaking bloody havoc on the boy who had dared to harm his family. But his daughter needed him. And he'd given his word to Nick about getting Henry.

Banning had found the dagger; for all the good it would do him now. Without the demon's essence inside it, it was little more than an ornate knife. Maybe the fire would take him and the Maw both, send them back to the flaming depths of hell where they belonged.

Charlie got ready to lift Meghan a second time when Banning, clutching Kar'roc's Maw, threw his arms wide.

What in the hell is he doing?

A circle of green light illuminated the ground around the boy, bleeding outward and forming a complex pattern of concentric rings intersected by geometric shapes. Interspersed throughout were blazing symbols. Symbols that Charlie recognised from the pages he'd studied every day since becoming the Maw's master. Symbols that were etched into the blade itself.

NO. NO! I WILL NOT BE IMPRISONED IN THAT WRETCHED DAGGER AGAIN.

Chekonost's roar resounded through Charlie's head. He released his grip on Meghan and covered his ears. It did nothing to stop the noise.

WE MUST STOP HIM.

Charlie sprang to his feet and ran. Faster than should have been possible. Harder than he'd ever run in his life. He could feel his muscles strain, but they didn't burn like they usually did. He supposed the demon was to thank for that.

He sped towards Banning, his eyes on the dagger.

Charlie ploughed into an invisible force. The impact knocked him flat on his back; it rattled his teeth and jolted his spine. With a groan, he rolled over onto his knees.

BARRIER.

No shit.

Banning didn't even glance in his direction, his face turned upward. The circle pulsed around him, air blasting from its perimeter, creating an eddying storm of dust and debris that harried the smoke and fire.

Charlie shielded his eyes and blinked away the imprint of the patterns and symbols on his vision. His stomach lurched suddenly, like he was in freefall. He gasped when the sensation grew stronger by the second.

'Charlie?' Someone said.

He saw a dark shape in the vortex behind Banning. A low rumble followed.

'Charlie?'

This time he recognised the voice. *'Diane?'*

A feeling of contempt rolled through him, sudden and unexpected, rising above the sickening somersaults of his insides.

THE WITCH.

'Charlie, we need to get you out of here.' The air whipped Diane's blonde hair across her face. He saw her amber eyes, wide with concern. She checked him over, then touched his arm and the bloody slash on his trench coat.

Questions waded through the sludge of his demon-infested mind. When had she arrived? How much had she seen? Did she know? That he was now playing host to the monster that had killed Stephen? The demon who'd slaughtered her husband?

I DID NOT KILL STEPHEN. HER HUSBAND THOUGH...

Images flickered behind his eyes. Memories that were not his own seared into his brain. He heard a penetrating laugh, full of loathing and spite. He saw a much younger Diane staring back at him, ashen and trembling. His hands were covered in the bloody entrails—still slippery and warm—of the man writhing on the floor.

'No...' Charlie yanked his arm from Diane's grasp.

He couldn't look at her, even knowing that she'd misinterpreted his reaction. The second-hand guilt, the revulsion, the shock—it was all too much. In those borrowed recollections, he had smelt the copper tang of blood. He had felt the weight of another man's guts in his hands.

Charlie pointed to his daughter. 'Meghan and Henry need help. Please.' He thought Diane might argue. Might try her magic to change his mind. Instead she nodded, her wounded expression turning hard, and hurried over to Meghan.

Another deep reverberation juddered through the ground. If he hadn't known better he'd have mistaken it for a growl, but it was the death rattle of an old and gutted building on the brink of collapse.

A dark shape moved past him. And then another. It should have occurred to him that Diane wouldn't have been alone.

Several black suits spread out around Banning, arms outstretched, mouths working in silent chants. The green circle around the young man faltered, the sigils stuttered. Banning's expression became darker. His eyes blazed with fury. But there was sweat on his forehead and a slight tilt to his mouth that hinted at exhaustion. He rolled his neck, widened his stance. The symbols flared brighter.

Charlie grunted as his stomach rolls increased. What had started as an amusement ride drop was now a full-scale assault. It felt like he was being ripped apart from the inside. He opened his mouth to scream but all that came out was a strangled rasp.

The black suits doubled their efforts. The brightness of the circle wavered again. Then one by one the sigils guttered out, until the circle was nothing more than a fading afterglow. Banning bellowed his frustration. He swept his hand in a wide arc. The air shimmered, bristling with an almost static discharge that prickled Charlie's skin. Some of the black suits managed to deflect whatever magic Banning had projected their way; others dropped like stones, dead before they hit the ground.

Charlie pitched to the side out of the way of the magic. Relief shuddered through him, but it was short lived. The demon's thoughts exploded in a cluster bomb, creating panic.

RUN.

Banning met Charlie's gaze; there was not a shred of humanity in those cold blue eyes. A smirk twisted his mouth. He directed his attention on Diane who was crouched over Meghan and oblivious to the looming threat.

Fresh anger surged through Charlie. He rode it like a wave. Let it pull him to his feet. He tore towards Banning, feeling the demon lend him its strength, work his muscles, push his body to the brink. The river of green flame ran down Banning's arm to pool in his palm. It formed a spectral fireball. Charlie winced.

I'm not going to make it.

The smoke cloud behind Banning burst apart. A malformed creature charged forward, the taut skin around its muzzle peeled back in a snarl. Charlie recognised the vague canine shape from earlier. Lily.

Banning threw his arms up, wielding the pommel of the dagger like a weapon. Lily's teeth clamped on his fist, around Kar'roc's Maw. She thrashed her oversized head, once, twice, severing his hand from his wrist in a geyser of blood. Her jaw worked the hand in two bites. One of Banning's fingers fell from her mouth as she swallowed the remainder.

THAT THING REALLY SHOULD BE ON A LEAD.

Banning screamed, the green fire covering his torso snuffing out. He cradled the stump, face contorted in pain. Spurts of crimson blood saturated his clothing and dripped down his exposed flesh. He staggered.

UH OH.

Wait, what?

Everything happened at once. The temperature in the air plummeted. The inferno around them shrank back as flame was replaced by a spreading layer of frost. Charlie's limbs became lead and the energy drained from his body. What remained of the roof above them shuddered and creaked and, with a final roar of fractured steel and wood, it collapsed.

He threw his arms up and prayed for a quick death.

The concrete beneath his feet trembled with repeated thuds. Each impact sent a quiver up through his legs. The thuds sounded oddly muted, distant almost. Charlie opened his eyes to see a black suit in front of him, moving their fingers in complex patterns.

Hector.

The dark elf had enclosed them within a dome of pulsing blue shapes and symbols. Everything outside of it was black. It took a moment for Charlie to realise that he and Hector had been encased by the rubble of the building.

'Christ,' Charlie murmured.

Hector looked over his shoulder with a grimace then turned his attention back to the shield.

Something final above them shifted, sending a burst of crackles and sparks across the dome's exterior.

'I think that's the last of it.' Hector thrust out his palms and the magic surrounding them detonated outward.

Charlie gaped at what was left of the slipway, hardly a wall left standing. Great mounds of ash sat among the tortured remains of warped steel; black residue sifted off in flurries where the breeze caught it. Not everything had burnt. There were still a few timber beams and sections of the mezzanine amid the blackened wood. Not to mention the remains of several, misshapen metal cages.

'Meghan?' Charlie raced over to his daughter. The ruins shifting beneath his feet forced him to clamber on his hands and knees in sections. More than once he was met with a heat so startling, by the time he reached Meggy, his palms were a blistered and weeping mess.

'She's alive.' Diane sounded exhausted.

'Thank you.' Charlie swallowed down the lump in his throat and knelt by his daughter's side. He brushed her cheek and blinked back tears.

Diane was watching him.

He cleared his throat. 'The smoke.'

TRAGIC.

She smiled but it slipped away when she noticed his thigh. 'You're hurt.'

Charlie followed her gaze to his mended leg, his heart rate increasing. *Shit.*

'Oh, no, I'm fine.'

AND YET I GOT NO THANKS.

'I landed on one of those creatures when the building exploded.' The lie tasted bitter. He swallowed it anyway. 'Must've torn my trousers at the same time.'

Before he could think of anything else to say, the sounds of scratching came from beneath the shifting debris. Lily's head popped out from under a crumbling heap. Looking like a Rottweiler again, she pulled herself free, claws scrabbling on the unsteady surface, and lolloped towards Charlie, pink tongue flopping to the side.

Coming to a stop beside him, she shook herself clean and sat, looking up at him with wide, brown eyes.

'Lily.'

Beating her tail at the sound of her name, she nudged his hand, giving the sigil a cursory sniff.

INTERESTING. THE HELLHOUND LIKES YOU.

Feeling numb, Charlie gave Lily a pat on the head. His hand came away sticky. He grimaced and wiped it on his trousers. Blood. He'd been so transfixed on Meghan and Lily that Banning had slipped his mind completely.

Was he dead? Buried beneath the remains of the slipway? Had he escaped? There was no trace of him, and being a witch, Charlie guessed it wasn't beyond the realms of possibility that he had survived.

HE IS NOT A WITCH. HE IS SOMETHING ELSE. SOMETHING STRONGER. SOMETHING BETTER. Chekonost considered his own words before reaching a conclusion. HE WOULD HAVE MADE A GOOD HOST. Charlie felt the demon's regret.

He shook his head in disgust. *He's a psychopath. A murderer. He abducted my family!*

DON'T RUB IT IN.

Don't speak to me.

Charlie walked to where he'd last seen Banning. He frowned down, remembering the nauseating image of Lily chomping on Banning's severed hand. There was no way he could have gotten away, not with a haemorrhaging wound like that.

As he stared out into the night, it dawned on Charlie that his vision was perfect. The sky was thick with angry, grey clouds, broken only by the occasional slit of moonlight that dappled the concrete below. Not enough light for an ordinary person to see clearly. Yet, he could make out details that would have eluded him, even in his prime. It was like a veil had been lifted from his eyes. Overwhelming, disorientating and wonderful.

Until he remembered the cost.

His shoulders sagged.

THAT IS JUST RUDE.

I said don't speak to me. You've served your purpose. Once I put you back in the dagger that's it, we're done.

The demon scoffed. IN CASE YOU DID NOT NOTICE, THE MAW IS CURRENTLY INACCESSIBLE.

Charlie glanced down at Lily. She was still staring up at him. Her tail gave a lazy thump to acknowledge his attention.

So, I wait until she's passed it. He suppressed a shudder at the thought.

Hollow laughter echoed in his mind.

Charlie thought back to his conversation with Sachiko that morning... Lily was a hellhound... A flicker of hope sparked in his chest. Before the thought had formed fully, he felt another wave of amusement roll through him.

SHE IS A HYBRID. HER TRUE NATURE MUDDIED WITH THAT OF A COMMON MUTT. THE DAGGER WOULD HAVE BEEN DESTROYED IMMEDIATELY IF HER LINEAGE WAS PURE, BUT IT IS NOT. SHE WILL NOT PASS IT. IT WILL REMAIN INSIDE HER INDEFINITELY, UNLESS IT IS FORCIBLY REMOVED.

Charlie stumbled back a step as the words hit home. Lily nuzzled at his fingers, her nose wet and cold against his skin. He would have wiped them clean immediately, but his arms were like lead.

I'm stuck with you, demon.

I AM NOT THRILLED BY THE PROSPECT, EITHER. YOU ARE OLD. YOUR MIND IS BROKEN. BUT, I SUPPOSE, AT LEAST YOU ARE NOT CRIPPLED.

My mind is not broken.

It scoffed again. IT IS LIKE YOU HAVE ERECTED MENTAL BARRIERS. EVERYTHING THAT SHOULD BE OPENLY ACCESSIBLE HAS BEEN LOCKED DOWN. THE GREY MATTER IN YOUR BRAIN—

Enough.

YOU SHOULD BE PLEASED. YOU ARE APPARENTLY LESS SUSCEPTIBLE TO—

I said enough.

THERE IS STILL A WAY WE COULD BE FREE OF ONE ANOTHER.

Charlie perked up. *I'm listening.*

IF WE CAN LOCATE A GATEKEEPER, IT MAY STILL BE POSSIBLE TO TRANSPORT MY ESSENCE BACK THROUGH THE VEIL AND INTO MY BODY. YOU WILL BE LEFT TO YOUR PITIFUL EXISTENCE.

A gatekeeper?

YES. I— The demon's reply was cut off by a blood-curdling scream.

Chapter 47

'Henry!' Nick fought against the black suit as he dragged him back from the slipway.

'Sir, please. It's not safe.'

'My husband is still in there!'

'Sir—'

Nick brought his elbow up to meet the man's jaw. It made a sharp crack. The man staggered back, hands flying to his face.

Nick hared off towards the building. The building that had just collapsed under its own weight. The building that was belching out choking black smoke and rippling heat, and scattering smouldering red chunks across the concrete.

Henry could already be dead. Banning had tossed him like a rag doll. And the way he'd hit that beam?

No. Henry had to be alive. Charlie too.

Ignoring the tight cramp in his side, Nick pushed himself harder. His calves were burning, but he couldn't stop.

He spotted movement in the wreckage, so slight, he almost dismissed it.

Debris flew upward, blisters of motion bursting one after the other. A flash of blue followed, then Nick saw Charlie standing behind another man in a black suit, his slate-grey, wool trench coat flapping around his legs.

Nick raised his arm, about to call out, when Charlie darted off into the ruins of the slipway. He scanned the mess of wood and ash, his gaze finally coming to rest on Henry.

His husband was propped up against the warped remains of a cracked steel girder, very much alive and talking to someone Nick didn't recognise.

He released a breath of relief.

Slowing to a stop, Nick folded forward and grasped his thighs, allowing himself a shaky laugh. He wiped the sweat from his brow, attempting to catch his breath.

The sound of pounding footsteps made him turn.

'Move!' the woman warned as a dark shape reared up behind her.

There wasn't time to move. There wasn't time to react. The woman ploughed into him, sending him sprawling.

Nick pushed himself up and lifted his head. Just feet from where he lay, Banning's creature had pinned the woman to the ground. The spine-chilling cry that ripped from her throat should have triggered a response in Nick. But it wasn't until something warm and wet splashed on his cheek that he was able to process the scene.

He scrambled back, fighting his rising terror. The beast pulled its jaws free from the woman's abdomen, bringing with it thick, purple-grey cords of dripping intestine. Its white skull glistening with dark stains looked almost black beneath the floodlights.

Nick gagged. When the creature plunged into the woman a second time, he scrambled to his feet and bolted. He didn't dare look back.

The deep growl that followed chilled him to the core. But the scrape of claws against concrete… that's what turned his blood to ice.

'Nick, keep running!' Charlie's shouts echoed in the space ahead of him.

The creature was getting closer. Its rasping breath was getting louder.

His legs were like jelly. He wasn't going to make it.

Nick's foot caught on something hard. He lost his balance and pitched forward. He slammed against the ground and squeezed his eyes shut, waiting for the creature to finish him off.

This was it.

He heard the sound of rushing air behind him.

Nick pushed up to see Henry wrestling the monster back, his shadow coiling around its limbs, shrouding it in a darkness so black the sight made him dizzy. Lily appeared a moment later, vaulting over him at full tilt to plough into the creature.

The creature reared, using its bulk to break free from Henry's tendrils. In one savage move it swiped where Lily had been a second before. It growled in frustration, lowering its head to mount a charge.

'Nick, come on.' Charlie grabbed his arm, hauling him forward with more strength than he thought possible.

'What about Henry...' Nick murmured.

'He'll be fine. You won't.'

But Nick saw Henry was flagging. He swerved a second too late and the creature's teeth scored his obsidian skin, emitting a high-pitched screech as it did.

Henry straightened, took a single step then crumpled to the ground.

'Henry... No!' Pulling out of Charlie's grip, Nick raced towards his husband, pain gone, fear gone. Pure adrenaline fuelled him. He dropped next to him, scraping his knees against the concrete.

Lily yelped when the beast sank its teeth into her thigh. She recoiled, but the flesh was already knitting back together. The creature stretched its jaws wide. Lily twisted at the exact moment Charlie knocked Nick backwards, out of the way. Two jets of clear fluid struck the spot where he'd just been, splattering both Henry and Charlie.

Their screams froze Nick to the spot.

Lily howled, snapped her jaws and lunged again.

Nick stood, paralysed by the sight of the two men writhing on the ground. When Henry became human again, Nick knew that his husband was in serious trouble. He reached out a hand.

He was distantly aware of the dark shape of the creatures as they fought. Of the animal roar. And then he pitched backwards, caught beneath Lily's weight as she rolled head over tail. His neck whipped back. His skull smashed against something hard.

Everything went black.

‘Nick? Can you hear me? Nicholas?’

Nick sat up, ears ringing, vision blurred. He inhaled and out; the beat of his heart kept time with the throbbing in his head.

‘Nicholas? Do you know where you are?’

He felt dizzy. Nauseous.

‘Get off me, you stupid fucks.’

Blinking, Nick searched for the gravelly voice. A tattooed man with a shaved head and a thick, wiry beard was being restrained by two men in black suits. He looked familiar. Mundy Wilcoxson.

It all came flooding back.

Nick got to his feet and shoved past the woman trying to ask him questions.

‘Henry?’ He lurched forward. ‘Henry?’

The creature that had been attacking them lay dead, surrounded by more people in black suits. A pool of what looked like blood spread out from its body, the shaggy black fur around its throat matted and glistening wet in the artificial light.

‘Henry?’

He spotted him on the ground.

Nick stumbled towards him, ignoring the calls of the woman following. Why wasn't Henry answering him? Why wasn't he moving?

‘Henry? *Henry?*’ In a second he was on his knees, his hands on Henry's face, in his hair. Frantic, desperate for any sign of life. Any moment now, Henry's eyelids would flutter open and he would gasp a breath.

Any moment.

Nick trailed his gaze over Henry's body, and settled on his chest covered in gashes, livid bruises, dirt and ash, but saw nothing obviously fatal. No limbs missing. Nothing twisted at the wrong angle. No sign of anything wrong, other than the fact that he was unconscious.

Except there was no rise and fall of his chest.

Nick choked out a sob. He looked up to see a man standing over his husband. There was a slight twitch to his mouth, a pitiful look in his eyes. It told him more than words ever could.

'No, no. It's not... I can't... He's not...' A fist of grief punched him in the chest. It squeezed his heart, harder and harder, until he couldn't bear it anymore. Nick collapsed on Henry, tears dripping from his eyes.

Charlie was by his side in an instant. He draped an arm around Nick's shoulder while he bawled his eyes out.

He couldn't be sure how long he'd been there, clinging to his husband, but when the tears ran dry and were replaced by numbness, he finally allowed Charlie to coax him gently to his knees. He gazed up at his friend and found an expression not so much sympathetic as understanding.

Nick got to his feet, waving off Charlie's offer of help.

'What...' He cleared his throat. 'What happened to him?'

'Venom,' Charlie said simply. 'I'm sorry, Nick.'

'From Banning's creature?'

Charlie nodded.

'But... it got you too. I saw it. It got you too... and you're fine.'

Charlie rubbed at his jaw and lowered his gaze before answering. 'It did. But this morning I was attacked by a naeshin demon. Apparently the antivenom's still in my system. They think it gave me a sort of cross protection.'

Nick shuddered out a breath. Henry had never liked Charlie. Maybe he'd been right. If it wasn't for Charlie and the dagger he'd still be alive.

He dismissed the thought with shame.

No. This wasn't Charlie's fault. If anything, it was his. He'd involved Charlie in the Caravan Cannibal case; he'd pointed out the dagger to him. None of this would have happened if it wasn't for *him*.

A low growl followed by barking caught his attention. Two agents—apparently from the Order—were manhandling Lily into a crate.

'Lily!' Nick sprinted towards them, Charlie at his side. 'What the hell do you think you're doing? That's *my* dog. Get her out of there. Right now.'

The two agents exchanged a glance then looked past Nick's shoulder. He heard footsteps first, then a deep voice.

'I'm afraid we can't do that, Nicholas.'

Nick turned to see a dark-skinned man in his mid-sixties. Charlie was frowning, but didn't seem overly surprised by his arrival.

'That's my fucking dog,' Nick objected.

'That's no dog. That's a hellhound hybrid. It's dangerous. In the interests of public safety I'm going to have to insist it comes with us.'

'She is a *she* not an *it*. And I don't give a fuck whether you insist or not. She's *my* dog.' Nick squared up to the man. All around him people in black suits adjusted their stance, as if preparing to intervene. The man waved them down.

'Give him a break, Adeola,' Charlie said. 'He's just lost his husband. Let him keep the damn dog.' He lowered his voice. 'She's all he's got left.'

'I'm afraid that won't be possible. A hellhound, even a hybrid, is too unpredictable. By its very nature it is a threat. We can't risk that it... *she* might transform when provoked. What if she hurt someone? What if she killed them? We can't allow it. I'm sorry, Nick. We'll keep her at O.O.T.I.S headquarters. Rest assured, she'll be safe.'

Nick opened his mouth to speak, but Charlie cut in. 'That's bullshit. Nick's had that dog for years. He wasn't even aware of what she was until today. If she was able to control her transformations for this long, even as a puppy, I doubt she's as much of a threat as you're making her out to be.'

'No, Charlie. You have no idea what she's capable of. My job is to protect humanity. We can't have a hellhound loose among the general populous.' Seeing that his argument was falling on deaf ears, Adeola frowned. 'What if someone took her? What if someone wanted to use her as a weapon? We've already had a security breach.' His look was pointed. 'The threat will be contained.' He turned to Nick, his expression softening. 'We can erase her from your memories. You won't miss her. You won't remember you ever had her. Or if you prefer, we could replace her with a normal Rottweiler.'

It wouldn't be Lily. 'No! There's no way I'm agreeing to this.'

'You really don't have a choice, Detective Stacey.' With a nod, Adeola indicated for the men to load Lily. She dug her paws in, hackles raised, as she shook her head from side to side. Another agent appeared to help with the efforts.

'No!' Nick lunged forward but someone pulled him back. Lily stared at him through the bars, her large brown eyes full of fear and confusion, her tail tucked between her legs. He felt the sting of fresh tears as they manoeuvred the crate onto the back of the vehicle and closed the doors.

Charlie turned to Adeola. 'You heartless bastard.' There was venom in his voice that Nick hadn't heard before.

'It's for the best,' Adeola said. He gave Nick a sympathetic glance and walked away. Charlie followed after, his curses fading with the distance.

Nick curled in on himself. There was a void inside him, leaving him broken and incomplete.

'Detective Stacey? Nicholas?'

He lifted his gaze from his shoes.

A woman strode over to him. 'My name's Veronica. I'm here to check you over. If you'd like to come this way?'

She led him towards the back of a van. He sat on the edge; the van dipped beneath his weight. He was vaguely aware of someone else in the back with him, but he didn't care enough to look. Charlie appeared shortly after, his mouth a thin line. He clasped Nick's shoulder.

Nick understood. They were going to alter his memories again.

Veronica gently pressed her fingers against his temples. He flinched, but met her eyes. 'Please don't make me forget my husband,' he said weakly.

She gave him a small nod.

Pain detonated through his skull, feeling like a thousand red-hot needles stabbing him—searing his brain. His body convulsed, his muscles cramped. After what felt like an eternity, he peeled his eyes open. He heard Charlie calling his name in alarm.

'W-what happened?' Nick said.

Veronica was gaping at him, her mouth a perfect O. She snapped out of it and frowned at the man in the van. 'I can't place the spellwork.'

'What?' The man stepped forward, the van bobbing with the motion.

'It... I... Something's altered his brain. Changed the pathways. His memories can't be reworked.'

'That's impossible. Let me try.'

Nick opened his mouth to object, but his mind was too foggy to speak. Light pressure was applied to his temples before he blacked out.

When he regained consciousness, Charlie had the man from the back of the van pinned on the floor.

Nick pushed himself back up gingerly. He could still remember. Lily. Henry. Everything.

The man that Charlie had immobilised turned his head. Nick recoiled with a gasp. The man was no man at all but a creature with sharp teeth and a misshapen jaw.

'Charlie, watch out! That thing, it's not human.'

Charlie's brow furrowed in confusion. He looked down at the creature, still restrained beneath his grip, then back at Nick.

'Can't you see it?' Nick's voice rose an octave.

Charlie shook his head, bewilderment giving way to concern.

The thing gaped at him. 'You can see through my glamour?'

Suddenly, all eyes were on Nick.

Chapter 48

Banning peeled his eyes open and groaned. Every inch of him ached. He snatched a breath, regretting it at once when the muscles in his chest cramped. The grinding throb behind his temples was making him nauseous. He tried to lift his fingers to the sides of his head.

He screamed when he saw the stump of his right wrist.

Banning doubled over and emptied the contents of his stomach on the grey oak flooring. With a whimper, he collapsed into the black leather sofa and swallowed acrid saliva. He went to wipe his mouth, but swiped with the missing appendage. He let out a wail.

Gradually, the details came back to him. The fog of his mind receded to expose the fragments bit by bit. It had happened again. He'd lost himself. He'd allowed the demon to take possession of his senses. What had he done? How many people had he killed this time?

God, that little girl. He'd promised her he wouldn't hurt her.

Banning pitched forward, bringing up more bile. The sound of her arm snapping, the memory of the bone stabbing through her flesh—it would stay with him for years to come.

Where had it all gone wrong?

Heimerich.

He growled. The incubus had smashed his autoinjector. Robbed him of control. Turned him into a monster.

Banning examined the stump. The skin was smooth. Completely healed over without a trace of scarring. If it wasn't for the flaking stains of red, one might even assume he'd been born that way.

Shaking his head, he slumped back against the seat and closed his eyes.

He'd lost his hand.

He'd lost the hellip.

He'd lost the dagger.

'Fuck.'

'My sentiments exactly.'

Banning jerked at the sound of the voice.

Archibald Morgan was leaning against the marble-topped kitchen island, lips pressed together, giving him a parental look of disappointment. He eyed the stump and let out a frustrated sigh.

'H-how did I get here?' Banning asked, failing to keep his voice level.

'How indeed.' His mentor pushed off from the island and stood in front of him. 'I've always had a soft spot for children without a family. A lasting consequence of my own childhood I've no doubt. Especially when that child exhibits qualities that set them apart from the others. You could be a great man, Banning. Yet you consistently choose to take the path to iniquity. I am, in part, to blame. I saw it in you even then, but I also saw your potential. We are each responsible for our choices, and your misgivings are an extension of my choice to mentor you. If it were not for the promise I made to a friend a long, long time ago, I would have already terminated my tutelage.

'Your task was simple. Remain out of trouble until my return. I thought that given such a small window of time, you would curb your natural inclination to contravene even the most basic of instructions. Clearly I was wrong. And now I have had to cut my own plans short just to straighten out your mess. Perhaps I expect too much of you. You are, after all, still a child, relatively speaking. I was an impertinent youth once.'

A wistful expression touched Archibald's face, then disappeared.

He continued. 'Do you know for how many centuries I have avoided the Order? In all my years, I only once became known to them under this name, and yet with a single transgression, you threaten to expose me. For over two centuries, my plans have been set in motion, and I will not have them compromised. Not even by you. Not when I am so close. Now the incubus is dead, the stone is inaccessible, and you have revealed my hand. Any advantage I may have had in securing Kar'roc's Maw is now lost to me. Thanks to you.'

Banning flinched.

'And yet, I feel I owe you an apology. I have been remiss in my duties towards you. I should have known that, given the weakening of the veil, your...

affliction would have become more difficult to manage. It occurs to me that had I not lost sight of my other responsibilities, this unfortunate turn of events could have been avoided. Things will only get worse for you, Banning. With the Brimstone Chorus already set in motion, you will not be able to stave off the darkness indefinitely. No venom exists that is strong enough. Not even that of the hellip. My success is your only hope. Fortunately for you, the fragment of stone embedded in Kar'roc's Maw is only one of three still to elude me.'

Banning's hope fell. It had taken his mentor a lifetime—several lifetimes to locate the other pieces of Solomon's stone. How long would it take to find the remaining two?

'Do not fret, there is an alternative solution.'

'A solution?' Banning shuffled forward.

'Yes, but it comes at a cost.'

'Anything.' There was no hesitation. None. 'Whatever the cost, I'll pay it.'

Archibald's face darkened. He stared through Banning, a distant look in his eyes. 'A word of caution—and trust me it will serve you well—never accept anything blindly. There are costs that no one should have to pay. *Ever*. Trust me.'

'Wha—' Banning cleared his throat. 'What's the cost?'

'There is a spell—some may even call it a curse—that will keep the toxins polluting your mind at bay.' He held up a warning finger when Banning sucked in a breath. 'However, the spell is powered by its bearer, a poison in itself. It will take decades off your life. The more you use your gifts the stronger you become, so it will too. As the veil degrades the spell will channel more of your energy, to prevent the demon's residual essence from becoming dominant. And should I fail, should the veil fall completely... well, I think you grasp the concept.'

Decades off his life? His kind lived centuries. Archibald Morgan himself was over two-hundred years old. It hardly seemed a cost at all. But there was something about the expression on his mentor's face that made him hesitate.

'How long will I have?'

'Impossible to speculate. At best, if you never utilise your powers, if you never put yourself in a position of physical or emotional stress, you may have the life span of a mortal. But given your proclivity for making a nuisance of yourself and the current decline of the veil, I'd wager another ten years.'

'*Ten* years?'

His mentor nodded.

'But it could be less?'

'Yes.'

Ten years. If that. He might not even make it to thirty. But it would be ten years without the fear of losing control. Ten years without the constant threat of becoming a homicidal monster. No more sleepless nights, terrorised by nightmares of his past actions, all because he'd miscalculated his dosage of lindwurm venom.

No more lindwurms. No more cryptids.

'I'll do it. Please.'

'You are certain? This is not a decision to be taken lightly. Once in place it cannot be undone.'

'I'm sure, sir.'

'Very well.'

Stepping around the puddle of vomit, Archibald placed his hands on Banning's shoulders. He didn't need to feel the subtle vibration in the air or the slight drop in temperature to know his mentor was using magic. It pulsed through his body, working in harmony with his natural energy. A prickling sensation warmed his chest, an odd feeling but not unpleasant.

'Should you wish to change your mind, this is your last opportunity.'

'No. I want this. Do it.'

Archibald's grip intensified. Banning saw something like sympathy in the furrow of his brow. Archibald gave a small nod and the tingling in Banning's chest increased.

The gentle warmth became an uncomfortable burn. The uncomfortable burn became an unbearable torture.

Banning cried out, fighting against the desire to wrench free. The energy inside him felt all wrong. Like a riptide pulling at his core too fast. Sweat plastered his clothes to his body, matted his hair to his scalp.

His skin was on fire. The brush of his shirt against his chest was excruciating. He yanked it away with his left hand, buttons ripping free, in a desperate bid to stop the pain.

And then it was over.

'It is done.' Archibald dropped his hands and took a step back.

Banning rasped out a breath. He was suddenly freezing, his muscles trembling so violently he couldn't speak.

He glanced down at his chest where his ruined shirt gaped open. Emblazoned across his skin just beneath his clavicle and extending almost nipple to nipple, was a circle. It was similar to the summoning circles he'd seen in his studies, but the patterning was different, the symbols unfamiliar. He trailed a finger across the glaringly white mark. It stood raised against his flesh, above the existing scar tissue.

Adjusting his suit jacket, Archibald headed for the door. He gripped the handle as he turned and said, 'You will return to Cornwall, to your brother, and await the arrival of my daughter.'

'Mary...' Banning whispered the name. He shuddered.

His mentor smiled without warmth. 'Indeed. I will send a car for you in the morning.' He scanned the chaos of the safe house one last time. 'Be ready and waiting at 6am.'

And with that, Archibald Morgan left.

Banning chewed on his lower lip. He was going home. Back to Cornwall. Back to Garrick.

He could already feel the remaining years of his life slip away.

Chapter 49

Sachiko placed the tablet down with a dull metallic thud and drummed her nails gently on the burnished silver worktop. She paused, made a pensive humming noise, and faced Charlie.

He frowned at her. 'What?'

'Your bloodwork. Based on the half-life of the antivenom we gave you, I'd have expected more antibodies. Especially given that you were then exposed to hellip venom.'

'It's been three days since the naeshin attacked me; that's got to be long enough for everything to return to normal.'

'We specifically developed the antivenom to have a longer half-life to prevent complications such as coagulopathy.'

He gave her a blank look.

'Bottom line, you should have more antibodies. It's almost as if the antivenom didn't bind to the toxin's enzymes at all. It's like your body eradicated the venom by itself.'

'Oh.' He brushed at a nonexistent crease on his trousers. 'You did say that my connection to the dagger had its benefits. Maybe this is another one of them?'

'Maybe.' The way Sachiko was sucking on her lower lip told him she was unconvinced. 'We've yet to establish how your bond will be affected now that Kar'roc's Maw has been... contained.'

Not for the first time, her dark eyes drifted to the empty cabinet in the centre of the room.

He followed her gaze. Part of him longed for the dagger to still be suspended there, hovering under the glow of the LED lighting. He rubbed his thumb over his ring finger. 'What will you do now?'

She gave him a smile. 'Oh, don't worry about me. It's not as if Kar'roc's Maw is the only artifact here that needs to be investigated.' There was a touch of emotion in her eyes. Sadness? Disappointment maybe?

She caught him staring and arched an eyebrow. 'What?'

'You don't seem happy about it being gone.'

She hummed then stepped up beside the chair he sat in. 'We'd only just brushed the surface with the Maw. Had only just begun to unravel its mysteries. And now we'll probably never know.'

'Surely that's not true? Lily will pass it at some stage?'

I HAVE ALREADY TOLD YOU, SHE WILL NOT.

Sachiko smiled again. 'Unfortunately not. Her physiology is not like that of a normal dog. The dagger doesn't show up on X-rays in her canine form. But we were able to get other images that show the ethereal shadow.'

'The *what*?'

'Hmm, how best to explain it.' Sachiko considered her words, tapping her finger on her lip.

SHE THINKS YOU ARE AN IDIOT. YOU SHOULD RIP OUT HER THROAT AND EAT HER EYEBALLS.

Charlie flinched.

'It's a bit like a magical aura. There but not. Lily's true form is a manifestation of energy from the veil between the demon realm and here. When she ingested the dagger, she did so in that bubble of magic. So the dagger is here but it's also not. Just like she's a hellhound but also a dog. Does that make sense?'

Charlie's brow furrowed. 'I think so.'

YOU HAVE NO IDEA WHAT SHE JUST SAID. SHE WAS CORRECT IN HER ASSUMPTION, YOU ARE AN IDIOT. I OWE HER AN APOLOGY.

Quiet.

'How about we test your eyes again?' Sachiko suggested. 'It will be interesting to see whether or not anything else has changed.'

'Sure.' Charlie swivelled the chair around and started to read the top line of letters aloud.

'Hang on a sec.' Sachiko jogged over to the eye chart, pulled off the card and replaced it. 'Sorry, just want to make sure. Some people memorise these things after a while.'

NOW SHE QUESTIONS YOUR INTEGRITY.

She'd be right to, wouldn't she? I'm lying to her about having a demon stuck inside my head.

When Sachiko watched him curiously, Charlie focused on the eye chart. He could see every row of letters perfectly, even the last.

'If you don't mind, start with the smallest line you can see.'

'Sure.' He made a quick count of the lines just to be sure she wasn't trying to have him over, then counted four up from the bottom and read the letters aloud.

Sachiko nodded. 'Twenty-twenty. Just like before. Other than your bloodwork nothing much appears to have changed. Your blood pressure *is* slightly more elevated than usual, but I suppose given what you've been through recently, that's to be expected. Do you have a pen I could borrow?'

'Erm... there might be one in my coat.' He pointed to the brown waxed jacket hanging on the stand. It wasn't nearly as comfortable as his slate-grey trench coat had been, but at least it was warm and waterproof. 'Top pocket. Are you telling me that in a place like this they don't provide you with pens?'

She smiled at that. 'They do, but you wouldn't believe how quickly they go missing.' After some brief resistance from the button on the pocket, she brandished the pen triumphantly and went to jot something down. 'How are your daughter and granddaughter getting on, by the way?'

'They're still a bit rattled. They don't remember anything about what *really* happened, obviously.' A touch of bitterness crept into his tone as he remembered Nick in the van. 'They think someone broke into the house but got scared off when Eleanor arrived with Poppy. Evie thinks she tripped and fractured her arm when they ran upstairs to hide.' He shook his head at how farcical it sounded. 'Meghan's got one of those home-security-system guys coming over, to give her a quote. Of the two of them, it's affected her the most. Evie's just pleased she got to have a blue cast. Her arm was healed to an extent; she won't have a scar or any tissue damage. What I don't understand is why the person who healed her left the fracture at all...' He let the question hang in the air.

'Minds are tricky things,' Sachiko said. 'The memories aren't removed—that would be too damaging. They're just layered over with suggestions. The brain can only process so much; anything traumatic or anything that doesn't fit in with reality will often be suppressed, but I'm sure you're aware that's not always healthy. So, instead of doing more damage, we merely provide a palatable alternative. With children it's harder. Their minds are still forming, still creating new connections and pathways. There's more potential for damage than with an adult mind. We only change what we absolutely have to. So Evie's narrative retained the break.'

'I see.'

'How about you? How are you doing with all of this?'

'Me? I'm fine.' She gave him one of her looks. 'Okay, no, I'm not fine. But I took up the offer of medication this time, so at least I'm not getting anymore nightmares.'

There was a knock at the door. Diane entered, holding a coffee carrier with three cups.

'How's it going?' Diane asked.

'We're pretty much done here,' Sachiko said. 'He's all yours. Do with him as you wish.'

A hint of colour crept into Diane's cheeks. She avoided Charlie's gaze, passing one of the cups to Sachiko, who accepted it with a delighted grin.

'I can go?' Charlie asked. At Sachiko's nod, he got out of the chair and grabbed his jacket. He draped it over his forearm just as Diane pulled the door open.

'Oh, Charles...' Sachiko said.

He turned to see the pen she'd borrowed hurtling towards him. The muscles in his arm twitched in response, but he didn't try to catch it. The pen hit him in the chest then dropped to the floor. He picked it up and raised an eyebrow at Sachiko.

'Sorry. Just testing a theory.'

SHE KNOWS. KILL HER.

'Right. Well, I'll see you in a week or so, I suppose.'

Letting the door swing shut behind him, he nodded to the black suit waiting to escort him back through the headquarters. He pocketed the pen.

'What was that about?' he asked Diane, trying to sound as genuine as he could.

'Honestly? I've absolutely no idea. Sachiko can be... unpredictable at times.'

'Fair enough. Is one of those for me?' He nodded to the carrier hopefully.

'Yes, don't worry. I bought it from the shop across the road. Cappuccino, that's what you drink isn't it?' She handed him one.

'It is. I'm impressed.' He removed the lid, took a sip and let out a satisfied sigh.

'I remembered it's what you ordered last time.' The flush returned to Diane's cheeks, deeper than before. He liked the way it looked on her.

URGH. WHAT IS THE OBSESSION WITH THIS FEMALE?

He glanced away, taking another sip of coffee.

Diane fiddled with the edge of the cardboard carrier. 'How's Nick?'

'He's not great. Losing his husband and finding out that their relationship was engineered from the start? Well, he's not coping. And whatever Henry did when he unlocked Nick's memories apparently altered the part of his brain that processes images. So, on top of everything else, he now sees monsters wherever he goes. Sees straight through their glamours. Like on Grimm.'

'Grimm?'

'It's... never mind. He's checked himself into Alnus House.'

'The mental health treatment hospital?'

Charlie nodded and swallowed another mouthful of coffee.

'Probably for the best. This can all be a lot to process at first, as you're aware, and that's without losing a spouse.' Sadness touched her eyes. Charlie tried not to flinch.

He said, 'I tried to see him, but he's refusing visitors. I'll try again in a few days. I promised him I'd drop in on Lily from time to time. I think she's just as scared and confused as he is.'

'Give him time. He'll reach out when he's ready.'

'Look, Diane, I want to thank you. You saved my daughter. If it wasn't for you turning up when you did, I'm not sure what would've happened. I'm sorry I gave you such a hard time.'

FIRST STEPHEN, NOW YOU. I CANNOT SEE THE APPEAL. YOU SHOULD PURSUE A YOUNGER MATE. THIS ONE IS PAST HER PRIME.

Charlie blinked, taking another sip of cappuccino.

First Stephen?

HE ALSO DESIRED THE WITCH. I SUPPOSE IT WILL GIVE THE TWO OF YOU SOMETHING TO TALK ABOUT.

Diane glanced up at him, her loose, golden-blonde curls brushing the tops of her shoulders. 'I'm just glad you finally decided to answer one of my calls.' She paused, taking a breath then blowing it out. 'Charlie, I hope you don't think this is out of line but we never did get to finish our first date. I was wondering whether I could take you out for dinner?'

AND IF CONVERSATION WAINS, YOU CAN ALWAYS BRING UP THE TIME I RIPPED OUT HER HUSBAND'S INSIDES.

Charlie choked. He covered his mouth, so not to spit his drink all over Diane.

Her face dropped. 'I understand. I'm sorry. I think I misinterpreted the signals.'

'No. No, I'm sorry. It just took me by surprise, that's all.' There's no way he could go on a date with Diane, not while playing host to the demon responsible for murdering her husband. 'I'd love to go to dinner with you. I really would. It's just not the right time for me. A lot's happened. I just need a little space.' He cringed inwardly at how weak that sounded.

'Of course.' Diane waved her hand, as if trying to dispel her embarrassment. 'I completely understand.'

AWKWARD.

Charlie made a show of checking his watch. 'I should really get going. I promised Meghan I'd be back by lunch.'

'Of course. I'll escort you out.' With a nod she dismissed the black suit, who, to his credit, hadn't reacted to the painful exchange.

He couldn't tell if he'd disappointed Diane or offended her. Probably both. But it was for the best. Until Chekonost was out of his head, he couldn't trust his reactions around her.

'Lead the way.' He offered her a wan smile. She probably thought he was an absolute arsehole.

YOU *ARE* AN ABSOLUTE ARSEHOLE. I VERY MUCH DISLIKE YOU.

Wincing, Charlie fell in behind Diane and let her lead him back through O.O.T.I.S headquarters. Feeling like a complete coward, he couldn't think of a single thing to say as they walked. By the time they neared the exit his drink was as cold as the atmosphere.

A sudden rising excitement radiated through him.

What?

CAN YOU NOT FEEL IT?

Feel what?

Charlie scanned the cavernous entrance hall, his curiosity getting the better of him. An instant later the sigil pulsed, the dull throb spreading out across his hand. The sea of bodies parted as half a dozen black suits marched through. At their centre—wrists bound by some seriously heavy-duty looking, warded handcuffs—was a young, blond man no more than nineteen. His bright green eyes locked onto Charlie's.

A GATEKEEPER.

Epilogue

'THANK YOU, CHARLIE. I really appreciate you coming with me.'

'Don't mention it.' Charlie smiled, pausing on the flight of stairs, as he waited for Jasmin to catch her breath. He glanced around the stairwell. After everything he'd been through, the run-down block of flats didn't seem nearly as foreboding as it had the last time they'd been there. 'How's the leg?'

'A little stiff. But all things considered, I got off lightly.'

'Remind me again why it is they couldn't just heal you?' Charlie already knew the answer, but he felt Jasmin could do with the distraction.

She blew out a breath, gripping the handrail for support. 'The Order doesn't have the resources to heal every agent who gets injured in the field. They patch you up and send you on your way.'

'They hardly seem strapped for cash.'

'It's not a question of money. Most of the employees are human. And those that aren't don't necessarily have the skill sets required to become a medic. Trust me, some of those guys you wouldn't want near you with a wooden spoon, let alone a scalpel.'

Jasmin took another step and screwed up her face in pain.

'Are you sure you should be weight-bearing on it?'

She scowled at him.

He held up his hands. 'Fine. I've got nowhere I need to be right now.'

'Funny.'

'Seriously though, Jasmin, couldn't someone else have done this for you?'

She put her hand in her pocket where Charlie could see the outline of the soul stone. 'No. I owe Auntie everything. If she doesn't want O.O.T.I.S to find out about her, I have to respect that. It's just... it's the only way I can think to protect her.'

'She doesn't strike me as a woman who needs protecting.'

'You're probably right. Even so, I think I should be the one who returns it. I don't want it, that's for sure.' Her shoulders slumped.

'It's not your fault, you know that don't you?' Charlie descended the steps to stand by her side.

'It is. I stay awake sometimes thinking about that night, even after all these years. I shouldn't have even been there, Charlie. I went looking for trouble. Put myself in that position. If I'd just gone home, just kept my head down instead of sticking my nose in, then things wouldn't have gone to shit. I wouldn't have gotten hurt, and Rhea wouldn't have needed to save me.'

'Jasmin, stop.' He gripped her hand, looking into her eyes. 'You can't go down this road. It's not your fault

Rhea went bad. She chose to give a part of herself to save you. It was a choice. *Her* choice. And so was everything that happened afterwards. She chose to get in bed with the likes of Mundy Wilcoxson. She chose to sell us out. Life is made up of choices, some good, some bad, some unimaginable, but they are *our* choices to make. So please, don't blame yourself.'

Jasmin sniffed, blinking rapidly. 'That's quite insightful, you know.'

'I have my moments.'

A laugh bubbled from Jasmin's lips. It warmed his heart to hear it.

'You certainly do.'

I THINK I MIGHT VOMIT.

Charlie jerked his hand from Jasmin's. She gave him a questioning look.

'Cramp,' he offered weakly. 'Let's get upstairs, shall we? It's a bit chilly down here. Wouldn't want to catch pneumonia.'

She gave him a stoic nod.

They climbed to the second floor without speaking. Jasmin's occasional grunts and laboured breathing were the only sounds rising above their echoing footsteps.

The smell of woodsmoke and lavender hit them before they'd reached Auntie's flat. With one final check to make sure Jasmin was okay, Charlie rapped his knuckles on the door.

No answer.

Charlie knocked again. 'You think she's gone out?'

'Maybe. Try the handle.'

He did. The door swung open.

Jasmin gasped.

The flat was empty. No furniture. No appliances. Nothing. If it hadn't been for the countless pinpricks peppering the ceiling, where the crystals had once hung, he'd have thought they were in the wrong flat.

As Jasmin hobbled off to investigate the other rooms, Charlie remained where he was. He scuffed his shoe on a dried bit of wax on the floorboards. Flecks of white flaked off and stuck to the sole.

'She's gone.' Jasmin sighed. They'd both known it. 'She left a note.'

'A note? I thought she was blind?'

Jasmin rolled her eyes. 'She has friends, Charlie. I'm not the only one she took care of.'

A mocking chuckle pervaded his mind, filling him with a sense of unease. He suppressed a shiver. 'What does it say?'

'I don't know. It's addressed to you.'

'Me?'

Limping towards him, Jasmin held out the envelope. He took it, frowning as he read his name scrawled across the front. There was something small and hard inside. He prodded at it, the paper wrinkling beneath his finger.

'Aren't you going to open it?'

He tore the envelope open and slid the note out. As he scanned the words, his stomach clenched.

Jasmin coughed to get his attention. He rolled his eyes and read aloud.

'Charlie, if you're reading this you will already know that I'm gone. I must prepare. Things are far worse than I feared. Humanity sits on the edge of a precipice and I will do everything in my power to tip the odds in our favour. Remember what I said. Learn to strengthen your soul. You're a good man, and by the grace of the good God, I pray that it will be enough. I enclose a gift. When the time comes, you'll know what to do with it.' He tipped the item into his hand and held it up for Jasmin to see; it was a plain, polished black ring with a small, round diamond set into its centre. He shook his head and continued. 'P.S. Tell Jasmin that I'm proud of the woman she's become.'

A range of emotions flickered across Jasmin's face.

'On the edge of a precipice,' Charlie mused. 'That doesn't sound good.'

She didn't respond.

Charlie squinted at the ring suspiciously, trying to decide whether or not he should place any stock in Auntie's words.

'I'm not much of a jewellery wearer.' He put it on his right ring finger. When it wouldn't go beyond his knuckle, he swapped it to his little finger. 'I look like a pimp.'

Jasmin's snort of amusement broke the tension. 'Hardly.'

He moved to take it off. She placed her hand lightly on his, stopping him.

'I'd leave it on. If Auntie thinks you'll need it, then you'll probably need it.'

'I haven't worn a ring since Debbie. Won't it look a bit odd for me to start wearing one now?'

'I'll say I bought it for you.'

'As punishment for what?'

She tsked. 'It's not *that* bad.'

He tugged gently on the ring. It wouldn't budge. 'What the—?' He tugged harder and a dull throb radiated from the sigil.

MAGIC.

Typical.

'You know what, I think I'll just wear it.' He'd deal with it later; now wasn't the time to let himself get flustered.

Jasmin gave him a knowing smile. 'Stuck?'

'Yep.'

'I'm sure she has good reason.'

'Right. So, what are you going to do about the soul stone?'

'I don't know.' She pulled the emerald-green crystal from her pocket. 'I can't take it back to headquarters; there'd be too many questions. Part of me wants to track Rhea down again...' The muscles in her jaw worked. She closed her fist around the stone. Charlie worried it might shatter in her grasp, but then she exhaled and loosened her grip. 'Is there any chance you could take it?'

'Why?'

'Just until I decide what to do.' She gave him her best smile. 'Please?'

Charlie sighed and held out his hand. The second the soul stone touched his flesh, a lightning-strike of white flashed from the ring on his finger, enclosing the crystal with a sharp crack. The soul stone shattered in his palm.

He jerked back. 'Gah!'

Jasmin laughed raucously.

Charlie glared at her and rubbed at his hand. 'Nope. That's it, I'm leaving.'

She shuffled after him, still laughing. He stalked out of the flat and down the corridor.

Laughter echoed in his head.

Shut up.

WHY? IT WAS AMUSING. YOU CRIED OUT LIKE A STARTLED CHILD.

Clenching and unclenching his fists rhythmically, Charlie huffed out a breath. He glanced down at the ring. It was all too much. First the dagger, then the demon, now this. What next?

DO YOU NOT KNOW? ARE YOU SO OBLIVIOUS?

Chekonost's strident voice resounded through his mind, gouging into every crevice, giving Charlie no escape from its loathing.

THE FALL OF MANKIND.

Thank You

Readers are the most powerful and effective tool when it comes to independent authors such as myself. So firstly, I would like to thank you for taking the time to read my book. Secondly, if you enjoyed it, I would be very grateful if you could leave a review (just a few words would do) on whichever platform you prefer.

Don't forget!
If you haven't already, you can get your **FREE** Brimstone Chorus starter story at elizabethjbrown.com

Acknowledgements

My heartfelt thanks:

As always, to my husband and son, for enabling me to fulfil my dreams.

To the friends and family who still agreed to read my early and unedited drafts, even after the last time.

To my amazing cover artist Ben Baldwin and my eagle-eyed editor Kate Gallagher, whose talents have made this book the best possible version of itself.

To Mundy Wilcoxson, who, despite knowing exactly what I intended to do with it, agreed to let me use his name for one of my characters.

Finally, to my Advance Readers, for all your time and effort. I appreciate it more than you know.

Author Note

Please note that I am a British author and use UK English spelling and grammar throughout my books.

About the Author

Elizabeth was born in Kent, England. This probably explains her obsession with tea and cake. She currently writes the Brimstone Chorus series, dark fantasy featuring demons, witches and a whole host of things that go bump in the night.

For more information about Elizabeth J. Brown and her books, please visit elizabethjbrown.com

Readers' group:
www.facebook.com/groups/1361685394266696
Facebook: @ElizabethJBrownAuthor
Twitter: @EJBrownAuthor
Instagram: @elizabethjbrownauthor

Books by Elizabeth J. Brown

THE BRIMSTONE CHORUS SERIES

The Foundling - FREE download
(elizabethjbrown.com)
The Laughing Policeman
The Fractured Few